DAVID TALLERMAN

Crown Thief

FROM THE TALES OF EASIE DAMASCO

ANGRY
ROBOT

ANGRY ROBOT
A member of the Osprey Group

Lace Market House,
54-56 High Pavement,
Nottingham,
NG1 1HW, UK

44-02 23rd Street, Suite 219,
Long Island City,
NY 11101
USA

www.angryrobotbooks.com
Easie does it…

An Angry Robot paperback original 2012.

ISBN 978-0-85766-250-7
eBook ISBN 978-0-85766-251-4

Printed in the United States of America

9 8 7 6 5 4 3 2 1

To Ruth Aoife Ewan

For when you're a little older

With endless thanks to Mum and Dad

CHAPTER ONE

"Things are looking up for Easie Damasco."

"Hrm?" Saltlick stared down at me questioningly. That, at least, was how I interpreted the expression smeared across the giant's lumpish features. In truth, it could have been anything between mild annoyance and indigestion.

"My luck is on the turn," I explained. "Yours too. Take my word for it."

Saltlick's face broke into a grin, and he nodded enthusiastically.

Ahead, the small militia we travelled with – half amateur soldiers gathered from around the Castoval, half guardsmen from nearby Altapasaeda – chose that moment to break into song. Or rather, *songs*, for the minute the Castovalians struck up a bawdy tavern ballad, the Altapasaedans countered with a clamorous northern marching chant.

It was an amiable enough competition. Here were men who'd helped defeat the despotic Moaradrid, foiled his plans for the Castoval, and now were heading home as heroes; those all seemed good enough reasons for high spirits.

I shared the soldiers' cheerfulness, if not their musical inclinations. My belly was full, so was my purse, and no one was trying to kill me. Together, those facts made for a vast improvement on my recent circumstances. Saltlick, too, trudged along with a slight but steady smile. While it took a lot to disturb his natural contentment, for once even he had his reasons to be happy. Moaradrid's plot to enslave his people had ended conclusively with the warlord's death. Now it was only a matter of uniting his tribe and returning home, and I'd seen enough of the giants' idyllic mountain enclave to appreciate how appealing that prospect must be.

Only Alvantes and Marina Estrada, riding just ahead of us, were exempt from the general good cheer. Alvantes had hardly spoken since we'd set out yesterday. I'd noticed time and again how Estrada watched him, obviously wanting to penetrate his gloom but not quite daring. She'd pressed her horse closer to his on a dozen occasions, only to fall back when he failed to so much as notice her presence.

Now, however, she seemed finally to have steeled herself. Encouraging her mount to a trot, Estrada pulled a little ahead of Alvantes. "They don't mean to be callous," she said softly. "They haven't forgotten the friends they've buried."

Alvantes reined in sharply, almost forcing the entire procession to a halt. "You think I don't know that? It isn't a soldier's way to wail and weep over death." Then, plaintively, "Marina… I'm sorry. That was inexcusable."

"No, it wasn't. But I wish you could talk to me. Is it…" She finished the sentence with her eyes, which lingered for a moment on Alvantes's bandaged wrist, now resting uselessly across his horse's neck. The hand that should have been there was buried behind us, amidst the grave plots of his fallen guardsmen – one more notch on Moaradrid's sword.

"It hurts constantly," he admitted. "It itches, too, which is almost worse. But no, it's not that either."

"Then what?"

"Honestly… Marina, if I knew, I'd tell you. I suppose I can't help wondering what my life means now. Am I still guard-captain of Altapasaeda? Can I rebuild the guard, with so many of them gone? Will the King even allow it after we failed to protect the Prince?"

Estrada reached to touch his arm, let her fingers hang there for a moment. "Maybe you're expecting too much of yourself. You've been through a lot, Lunto."

"Maybe if I'd expected more of myself," he said, "it wouldn't have come to this. Maybe if I'd done my job I wouldn't need to go and tell the King his son has been murdered."

"And if you hadn't intervened, Moaradrid might have murdered the King himself by now. You saved the Crown."

Alvantes started at that, as though she'd struck an unexpected nerve.

"You did everything you could," Estrada went on, apparently not noticing. "Even the King has to understand that. As for the rest… just give it time, will you? Let yourself heal."

"Of course. Thank you, Marina." Alvantes made an effort to sound like he meant it. If it didn't fool me, it certainly wouldn't fool Estrada. Nevertheless, she let her mount fall back, leaving him to his despondency.

Poor, stubborn Alvantes. Of all of us, save perhaps Saltlick, he'd suffered most from Moaradrid's brief, bloody visit to the Castoval. Now the man was too damn noble to realise he'd won. I didn't know whether I felt more like slapping him or giving him a manly hug.

If I attempted either, he'd undoubtedly break my arm, so I settled for the third option of trying my best to ignore him. My plan to travel on with him to notify the King of his son's death was already beginning to seem absurd. Why subject myself to Alvantes's dismal company when my world was so full of options? With most of its leadership dead in the battle against Moaradrid, the Castoval would be in chaos for months. I doubted anyone would be too concerned with my past indiscretions. For the first time since I'd learned to walk upright, I had a clean slate.

"No more being told what to do for either of us," I said, picking up my conversation with Saltlick where I'd left it. "Especially not you. You can rescue your friends and go home the conquering hero." I glanced once more at Alvantes and Estrada. "Women go crazy for heroes. You can find yourself a pretty giantess and settle down. There *are* pretty giantesses, right?"

Saltlick nodded bashfully.

"Hey, don't look like that! You should have more confidence." I studied his features for some compliment-worthy trait. The general impression was of a knobbly, milk-white turnip. The best I could say was that it was basically proportional, and I wasn't convinced that would do much to bolster his self-esteem. "You have a good heart," I finished weakly. "Women like that too."

It was enough to bring back his smile, at any rate.

My stock of compliments exhausted, I finished with an amiable pat to Saltlick's wrist – the only part of his arm I could comfortably reach – and returned my attention to the rambunctious troops. The Irregulars had moved onto a song I knew, "The Farmer's Other Donkey," while the Altapasaedans were countering with another deafening march. Singing over each other at the tops of their voices, all but blocking the road, they were quite a spectacle.

The thought reminded me of something that had troubled me vaguely since we'd started back towards Altapasaeda. This was the less commonly used route to the south-eastern Castoval, relegated to a back road by the grand stone bridge known as the Sabre that the Altapasaedans had constructed. Even taking that fact into account, I'd have expected more traffic than we'd seen. Not a soul had passed us. No one had stopped to gawp at the column of armed men blocking the road from verge to verge.

Even for a back road, that was curious. More, I couldn't deny that it made me a touch uneasy. With Moaradrid dead and his surviving troops scattered, shouldn't everything be returning to normal?

A black-edged cloud drifted over the sun. I cursed beneath my breath.

"Things *were* looking up for Easie Damasco," I muttered.

At that moment, the road crested a low rise, and for the first time our objective revealed herself: Altapasaeda, greatest and only city of the Castoval, lay across the northward horizon like a drunken hussy sprawled on her divan.

Altapasaeda, grandiose marvel of needlessly baroque architecture and frivolous design. In theory, it was the one real intrusion of court-controlled Pasaeda into the Castoval, the bastion of our Ans Pasaedan oppressors from beyond the northern border. However, under Panchetto, there'd never been much in the way of oppression. The Prince had held little interest in anything that wasn't edible or quaffable, and had mostly concentrated on ensuring his life remained a never-ending party – at least until Moaradrid ended both party and life. In the meantime, his spell on the throne had cost his subjects little besides the infrequently levied taxes that funded his indulgences.

All told, I could imagine worse obituaries than *He was a hopeless oppressor, but he could certainly put away the truffle-stuffed grouse.*

"This way," barked Alvantes. He'd ridden some distance in front, past the head of the column. "Left at the junction."

I struggled to remember what lay to our left. I vaguely recollected the turn-off he referred to, a dirt track slanting towards the hills. Somewhere in that direction lay the road that skirted the western edge of Altapasaeda, one I'd studiously avoided because it passed so close to…

Of course. The barracks of the Altapasaedan City Guard.

So what did Alvantes want at the barracks? I supposed I'd find out soon enough. Then again, given the difficulty the corner was causing those ahead, it might be a while yet. The Altapasaedan guardsmen had swung round easily, but the change of direction was wreaking confusion amongst the undisciplined Castovalian Irregulars. There followed much swearing and squabbling, at least until Alvantes angrily intervened. By the time we got moving again, it was hard to imagine these were the same men who'd been singing their hearts out mere minutes ago.

As if on cue, the darkening clouds above chose that moment to unburden themselves, further dampening everyone's mood and entirely soaking their bodies. The pace picked up immediately.

The westbound road here was confined by banks of dry earth and shale, already glistening and running in the downpour. We were heading somewhat upward, and it was difficult to see much through the cascading water. I knew it couldn't be far to the barracks, but the journey seemed interminable. Then, from the head of the column, came the beginnings of a ragged cheer – that turned rapidly into murmurs of shock and indignation.

We stopped abruptly.

I couldn't see anything for the blockade of bodies. I turned an inquiring glance on Saltlick, whose extra height should have equated to an increase of perspective. His only reply was a shrug of massive shoulders. I realised he had no idea what he expected to see. Left to rely on patience, I made a few unsuccessful attempts to jump on the spot, drawing irritated looks from those in front.

Alvantes waited just long enough for my clothes to become utterly sodden before he called, "Move on. Keep your eyes open. Tread quietly."

We did as instructed, so much as was possible in hammering rain. It was falling so heavily by then that when the barracks came into view, a bleared smudge against the hillside, I couldn't tell what the fuss was about. It took a brief reprieve in the violence of the shower to make me understand.

The building was a heap of blackened timber.

Estrada had dismounted, off to one side of the devastation. I hurried over to her. "What's happened?" I said. "Who did this?"

She shook her head. "I don't know. I don't think Alvantes does either."

It could have been anyone with a grudge against the guard. That didn't exactly narrow the list. However, another more immediate worry had struck me by then. "Could they still be here?"

"I doubt it. Look at the damage."

I did – and I saw what she meant. Even in this downpour, the ruins would still be smoking if the fire were recent.

I nearly jumped out of my skin when Alvantes, behind me, said, "It was set a day ago, at least. Still, I've sent scouts out."

I scowled at him. "So which of your many enemies do you think got there first?"

Speaking to Estrada rather than me, Alvantes said, "It wasn't anyone who knew what they were doing. I suspect there was rain here yesterday as well. The blaze was doused before it completely took hold and they didn't stay to see the job through."

"Does that mean we could get some shelter?" Estrada asked hopefully.

"I've set men to clearing out the most suitable rooms."

"Wait," I said, more irritable for being ignored, "what do you mean? Why sit huddling in your burned-down barracks when we could be safe and warm in Altapasaeda?"

Alvantes finally looked at me. "Where do you think whoever burned it most likely came from?"

"I don't know. Or care. The only thing that's kept me sane these last days is the thought of a warm meal and a soft bed."

Alvantes wheeled his horse away. "Then I'm sure that thought can hold you a while longer."

It wasn't long before the troops had returned a sizeable space to habitability. Even better, the ruined portions had supplied enough dry, relatively uncharred wood for a small fire. With heavy blankets hung over the makeshift doorway – actually a portion of collapsed wall – and the smoke losing itself amidst the cloud-laden sky, not even Alvantes could find anything to complain about.

When his men finally declared the room safe and allowed me inside, I was surprised to see the body of

what appeared to be a goat spitted over the blaze, fill-
ing the room with a mouth-watering odour. Given
Alvantes's oft-stated aversion to stealing, it was anyone's guess where it had come from.

Regardless, dinner proved some compensation for
my extended drenching. Though the portions of goat
meat were on the stingy side, there was plenty of hard
bread and a kind of salty porridge. If none of it was
particularly appetising, it was warm food on an empty
stomach after a wearisome day's walking. Afterwards,
I felt somewhat restored, if barely less soggy or bad-
tempered.

Alvantes's first act after dinner was to call a conference in a small and partially collapsed side room. In
attendance were Estrada, Sub-Captain Gueverro and
two of the guardsmen Alvantes had sent to scout, as
well as two representatives from amongst the Irregulars. Practically everyone who was anyone in our party,
in fact – except for me.

So that was how it stood. No matter that I'd shed
blood in service of the Castoval, no matter that I hadn't
stolen anything in days! I still wasn't good enough to
be part of Alvantes's precious inner circle.

Looking for someone to complain to, I glanced about
for Saltlick. There was no sign of him. I could hear the
rain still hammering upon the tiled roof; though it
never seemed to bother him, I doubted he'd rather be
outside than in. Eager for a task to take my mind off
Alvantes and his superciliousness, I decided to track
him down.

I slipped beneath the blanket that covered the

inner-facing door, drawing my hood up. The barracks, in its unconflagrated state, had consisted of a hollowed square of buildings around a large parade ground. From within that quadrangle, I could see how the north and east wings had been reduced to heaps of collapsed stone and jutting black timbers. On the other two sides, the destruction was more erratic. As Alvantes had suggested, it was clear how the fire and rain had fought over the building.

Apart from the area picked for our lodgings, one other portion had more or less escaped damage. Though its door and windows had also been covered, I could make out the muffled glow of torchlight through the heavy cloth. Even before I drew the curtain, I recognised the musty odours exhaling from within. It was no surprise to see the guard horses housed comfortably in their own stalls.

Four guardsmen were in the process of brushing them down, while half a dozen others laboured in the half-darkness at the far end, where the fire had brought down great portions of roof. They'd already dug free a trapdoor in the cobbled floor and were busy hauling sacks from the depths. Presumably, these underground stores were where the bulk of our evening meal had come from.

As for Saltlick, he'd ensconced himself in the farthest stall, amidst a mound of straw. He was eating grain from a bucket, scooping it in handfuls and emptying it into his maw.

"They're taking care of you, I see."

Saltlick smiled and nodded. "Good."

If his vocabulary had improved over the last weeks, his preferred mode of speech still leaned towards the concise. On those rare occasions I actually wanted to hold a conversation, it was less than helpful.

"Alvantes has called a meeting. Needless to say, we're not invited." I sat down next to him. "Another stop on the way to rescuing your people. I hope it's not raining like this where they are. Either way, I doubt they have a roof over their heads or grain to eat."

Saltlick put down his bucket and looked at me enquiringly.

"I suppose it isn't anyone's fault, really. Of course, the way Alvantes is going on, it could be days before we set out again."

He looked crestfallen. "Days?"

"Weeks, even, if Alvantes has his way. It seems there's some problem in Altapasaeda. Isn't there always? Anyway, no doubt Alvantes will be wading in to try to sort it out. I wouldn't be surprised if he doesn't rope you into his harebrained scheme."

Another feature of conversation with Saltlick was how much of what went through his mind could be gleaned by watching the play of his crude features. "Weeks," he grunted, and his brows crumpled together. "Help Alvantes," he added, and the question twitched from eye to eye. Eventually, his face settled into its usual careless arrangement. "Alvantes friend. Help if need help."

I could hardly contain my shock. Not only had Saltlick taken Alvantes's side, he'd done it in what amounted to an entire sentence! Truly, there was no justice amongst men or giants.

"Well, let's just hope there's enough of your friends left to take home when we finally reach them," I said, and marched back out into the rain.

I returned just in time for Alvantes's speech. I should have guessed he wouldn't let the night pass without one.

He'd stationed himself beside the fire. "Listen, men!" he bellowed. Then, when the hubbub had died down, he continued, "As you all now realise, circumstances in Altapasaeda are not as we left them. Clearly, those of us who are guardsmen have a responsibility to investigate. For the rest of you, your help will be welcomed if you're willing to give it… though I'll blame no one who chooses otherwise."

He paused, let this sink in. "A few of us will travel on to the Suburbs in hope of gathering more information. I'll send back news and further orders when I have them. In the meantime – keep sentries, stay out of sight, avoid wearing guard livery or weapons if you do need to go out. If we have enemies in Altapasaeda, our one advantage is that they don't know we've returned. Good luck to you all."

Estrada, appearing beside me, put voice to the question I was in the process of asking myself. "Are you coming with us, Easie?"

"Am I invited?"

"Of course. Alvantes mentioned you specifically."

I didn't like the sound of that. Nor had I forgiven Alvantes for excluding me from his stupid meeting.

Then again, there was nothing behind me but the occasional two-goat village. I could rent a decent bed in the Altapasaedan Suburbs, and travel on from there to anywhere in the Castoval. "I'll come," I decided. "Better that than a sleepless night in this half-demolished barn."

By the time I went outside, the rain had stopped. But the heavy cloud remained, leaving the moon a dim smear of brightness and shutting out all but a few stray stars. Alvantes had a dozen guardsmen gathered round him, including Sub-Captain Gueverro, and all were now dressed in anonymous grey cloaks.

"What I told the men counts just as much for us," he told Estrada, who'd followed behind me. "Until we know what we're dealing with, we'll keep a low profile."

"What about Saltlick?" I asked. "Low profiles aren't exactly his forte."

Saltlick, who was just then squeezing his way out through the hole in the wall, proved my point by dislodging a sizeable chunk of masonry. Sheepishly, he stood brushing stone-dust from his shoulders.

"We agreed we'd bring him with us," hissed Estrada. I realised the words were aimed at Alvantes rather than myself, and that I'd hit upon an already debated sore point.

"We will," he replied defensively. "I'll think of something."

I couldn't entirely blame Alvantes for not wanting Saltlick along. A dozen disguised guardsmen might pass unnoticed, but a giant striding by tended to draw comment. Sooner or later, Alvantes was bound to decide Saltlick was too much of a liability. Judging from Estrada's reprimand, maybe he already had.

Two of Alvantes's guardsmen went back inside. When they returned, they were leading a column of horses, assisted by the men set to work in the stables. One of them handed me the reins of a drowsy-eyed bay mare. Since it was evident we'd be spending time together and that both of us would rather have been allowed to catch some sleep, I decided we should be friends. I patted her muzzle, and received a weary whinny in reply.

We set out in single file, not back the way we'd come but following the road around to the north-east, which would eventually twist back to make its way along Altapasaeda's western edge. Even in daytime, we'd be unlikely to be seen by anyone, for the only entrance on that side of the city was the small gate reserved for the comings and goings of the guard.

However, as soon as the walls came back into sight, Alvantes motioned a halt. "Off the road," he told us. "Stay in the shadows."

Everyone moved to comply, with varying degrees of success. Even knelt on his haunches, no patch of gloom was big enough to hide Saltlick in his entirety.

"Damasco," said Alvantes, "come with me."

"What? Why me?"

"Because it's time you started pulling your weight. And because your insight into the underbelly of Altapasaeda might prove useful."

I wondered what Alvantes was up to that required knowledge of Altapasaeda's underbelly. "I see. You'll look down on me for being a thief until the day comes when you need a thief."

"When did I say I'd stopped looking down on you?"

"Then maybe you should carry out your little mission on your own."

"Unfortunately," he said, holding up his stump, "it requires assets I currently lack."

Damn him, had he really sunk to that? "Fine. I suppose I can spare you a few minutes." It took all my willpower not to say, *lend you a hand*.

Alvantes climbed down from the saddle, as did I. "The rest of you, stay here," he said. "We won't be long."

Alvantes followed the road for a few paces, before abandoning it in favour of a rough path curling off to his left. I followed at a distance, insulting him steadily beneath my breath. It wasn't long before the path had deteriorated to little more than an animal trail over rocks made slippery by the downpour; only then did I give up my muffled cursing, to concentrate on not twisting an ankle.

Perhaps a quarter of an hour had passed before Alvantes held up his one hand. We were some way up the hillside, with an outcrop of dark rock at our backs and other smaller boulders lined haphazardly in front, interspersed with bedraggled bushes and the occasional lopsided tree. Where there were gaps, I could just make out the walls of Altapasaeda beyond, their highest point now somewhat below us.

"See there?" Alvantes said. His voice was low, though it was impossible anyone could hear us.

I followed his pointing finger. Two figures were just visible upon the parapet of the small northern gate-house, lit by a glimmer of torchlight. "Barely."

Alvantes reached into his saddlebag, drew out a narrow metal tube about the length of his forearm. "Try this."

All my irritation at being dragged up there in the dark and cold vanished immediately. "Is that what I think it is?"

"If you think it's a telescope."

"Where did you ever come across that?"

"From my father. It was a farewell gift."

I took it from him, trying to keep my fingers from trembling. The telescope was worth all the money in my purse and more. To my knowledge, no one in the Castoval or Ans Pasaeda had quite figured out how to make them, and the few floating around had origi-nated in some distant land or other. I'd seen one once in Aspira Nero, much larger than this; but actually to use one was another thing altogether. I gasped as I pressed it to my eye and the distant walls sprang into focus. It took me a few disorientating moments to find the two figures, but once I did, it was as though they were standing just before me.

Whatever they were wearing, it wasn't guard livery. One was smartly dressed, with a cape over a brigan-dine of leather armour, an insignia on the breast. The other wore a full cloak with the hood drawn up. It didn't disguise his bulk. Of the two, he stood at least a hand taller, and was even broader in the shoulder. From the way he slouched against the battlements, he had none of his companion's discipline. In fact, the two had nothing obviously in common except their position, and their postures suggested both were aware of that fact.

Once I was certain I'd seen all there was to see, I turned back to Alvantes. He held out his hand, and I grudgingly placed the telescope in it. If and when we parted ways, it would definitely be coming with me.

"The leftmost is likely a retainer from one of the wealthy families," I said, and described his uniform.

"Likely a house guard for the Orvetta family. The other?"

"Could be anyone. If I had to guess, though... he's big and he likes to keep his face hidden. They don't trust each other one little bit. I'd say he's muscle for one of the city gangs."

Alvantes nodded.

"You don't look surprised," I said.

"I'm not. It's what I expected. I only wish it wasn't."

We hurriedly rejoined the others. "There are sentries on the walls," Alvantes told them. "Our priority is to get past without being identified. We'll travel fast, but don't risk the horses. If you can't keep pace, whistle."

He swung into the saddle and the rest of us followed his example. Hardly glancing to see whether anyone was following, he set off into the blackness ahead.

Under normal circumstances, it was quicker by far to cut through the city than to take this narrow, winding back road around its western side. As such, it was little more than a dirt track in places, pitted and overgrown. Negotiating it at speed in utter blackness was only a little shy of suicide.

Unfortunately, I had no say in the matter. Saltlick, capable of matching any horse with his huge strides, was crashing along close behind me. Watching Estrada, just ahead, gave me my only indication of the road's twists and turns. As every moment threatened to hurl me from the saddle, I struggled against rising panic. The damp wind stung my face; tears blinded me to even the few dim stars. Even if I could have pursed my lips, no one could possibly have heard me whistle. Worst was the feeling of falling. Plunging into blackness, my mind threw up the image of a gaping pit and held it.

All I could do was grip my mount's reins with all my strength and struggle to believe she knew what she was doing. She was a guard horse. Surely, she knew this road. Likely, she remembered every pit and rut.

She didn't let me down. After a while, I even began to relax a fraction – as much as was possible when hurtling through pitch-darkness on a road with no right to the name. I even dared to look up. There were the walls, close on our right. There was the gatehouse. Above, I could just see the sentries' torchlight. It bobbed and weaved, perhaps responding to our passage. Someone called out, the words whipped into nonsense by the wind. Then we were past.

The guards must have seen us. Or – they'd have seen riders. Perhaps only heard our horses. We could have been anyone. Unless, of course, they'd happened to pick out one particular silhouette, fully twice the size of any man.

Even once we were in the clear, it was a long time before Alvantes called, "Rein in! Stop here." Motioning towards a muddy side road, he summoned two of the guardsmen with a snapped, "Panchez, Duero, follow me," and to Gueverro, added, "Be watchful, Sub-Captain."

They weren't gone long. Their return was heralded by ear-racking sounds of squeaking and braying. When they came into view, Panchez was leading Duero's mount and Duero was guiding a mule, which in turn drew a small, ramshackle cart.

The look Estrada gave Alvantes was questioning to the point of accusation.

"Borrowed," he said, not meeting her eye.

I smirked. Interesting how it had a different name when guard-captains did it.

To Saltlick, he added a curt, "Get in, please."

Saltlick eyed the vehicle uncertainly. Alvantes had used this trick to smuggle him out of Altapasaeda, but that had been in a large wagon full of straw, not a donkey-cart covered with a scrappy tarpaulin.

Nevertheless, with considerable effort and obvious discomfort, Saltlick managed to scrunch himself into the back. Once he was settled, Duero drew the tarpaulin over. To my trained eye, the end the result looked much like an extremely cramped giant covered with an extremely small sheet.

"That should fool anyone," I said. "So long as they're blind. Or stupid. Or a very great distance away."

Alvantes glared at me. "All the more reason to hurry."

However, the cart, amongst its many failings, had been designed for neither speed nor the weight of giants. It was a long and miserable hour later before we turned east into the outskirts of the Altapasaedan Suburbs.

The Suburbs was so called because Altapasaedans didn't like to use the word "slum". The choice of nomenclature did nothing to change its nature. It was a dingy and ever-changing shanty town, sprung up long ago in the lee of the north wall and somehow never made permanent. In short, it was everything Altapasaeda wasn't: poor, filthy, tumbledown and given over to degrees of crime that the guard hardly bothered to interfere with.

Or so I'd always thought. We hadn't travelled far through the mazy streets before we came to a building more solidly constructed than those around it – built of sturdy timber, rather than wood that looked as if it had been dragged from the river, and with a door that would resist anything shy of a battering ram.

Alvantes dismounted and rapped three times, followed by two short taps, a pause, and one last knock. After a few moments, the door swung open, a slit at first and then fully. A swarthy, dark-eyed man stood in the gap. As he turned his head, I saw that the whole left side of his otherwise handsome face was puckered by white blotches of scarring. "Guard-Captain," he said. "It's good to see you, sir. With the stories flying around, I wasn't sure I would again."

"Not here, Navare." Alvantes turned to the rest of us. "Quickly… get the giant inside."

To his credit, Navare barely looked shocked when Duero whipped the tarpaulin back and Saltlick began to unfold himself from the cart. He was certainly quick enough to move out of the way, though.

"Gueverro, Estrada, Damasco, go in. Duero, see that the cart's returned – discreetly, please. The rest of you, find stabling for the horses. Not all in the same place if you can avoid it."

Navare greeted each of us with a tilt of his head as we went by, and to Gueverro said, "Good to see you, too, sir."

The interior consisted of a single room. If it was large for the Suburbs, it was small by any other standards, housing only a camp bed, a stove and a table. The low ceiling left Saltlick no option but to squat in the middle of the floor, and his presence left precious little space for the rest of us.

Closing the door, Alvantes said, "I know you'll have questions, Navare, but they'll have to wait. These are my travelling companions. The giant is Saltlick. This is Marina Estrada, mayor of Muena Palaiya. Easie Damasco… well, no doubt you remember the name." To the rest of us, he explained, "Navare acts for the guard's interests in the Suburbs."

Navare offered a lopsided grin. "A suitably ambiguous description of a particularly ill-defined role."

"The guard always had explicit orders from the Prince not to make its presence felt in the Suburbs. I followed those orders, of course – to the letter. Navare is a gatherer of information, and a discreet solver of certain kinds of problem."

Navare's grin widened. "Well put, sir."

"I trust you've been keeping up your duties in our absence?"

Abruptly, all humour vanished from Navare's expression. "Of course, Guard-Captain. But truth be told, I doubt I've found much you haven't already guessed. There are rumours aplenty, but facts are tough to come by."

"Go on."

"Well… four days ago, a contingent of Moaradrid's troops entered the city. Soon after, all the gates were barricaded from the inside. I've seen northern soldiers, family retainers and men I recognise from the gangs, all apparently working together. The place is sealed up tighter than a priestess's…" Remembering Estrada's presence, Navare caught himself and finished weakly, "No one's been in or out, sir, except I heard they destroyed the barracks – and even that they did at night."

"I didn't know about the troops. I'd hoped they'd flee back north," said Alvantes darkly. "That makes it even worse."

"What about the families?" asked Estrada. "Even with Panchetto gone, would they really be desperate enough to side with criminals?"

"They think of themselves as Ans Pasaedans, even after all these years," replied Alvantes. "To them, Altapasaeda is an island surrounded by enemies. The gangs are as Castovalian as anyone else, and more dangerous than most. On their own initiative, it's the last thing they'd do."

I thought I followed his implication. "So if it's not their own idea, it's someone else's," I said.

"I've heard word there's one man pulling the strings," agreed Navare. "If it's true, he's doing a damn fine job of keeping his name quiet."

I was beginning to see why Alvantes was so worried.

Combined, the household retainers of the many wealthy northern families numbered in the hundreds. Working apart, they'd always kept each other in check. Working together, they amounted to a military force perhaps half the size of the one Moaradrid had invaded with, and considerably better trained and equipped.

Add to that Altapasaeda's sizable criminal underground and the dregs of Moaradrid's army. Now have them put aside their differences in favour of some common goal. What did that leave you?

It left an army.

And if that army was guided by a single individual, there was a good chance we'd done nothing but exchange one would-be tyrant for another.

"Whoever he is, he's smart," said Alvantes, breaking in upon my thoughts. "Keeping the city bottled up will make the families even more paranoid, and everyone on the outside too." He glanced behind him, as though he could somehow see the city through the intervening wood. "It seems the only concrete answers lie within those walls."

"Getting inside would be tricky," said Navare. "I'd

try it myself, but if they caught me and traced me back to the guard…"

"Yes. That could prove difficult. Better to keep our presence secret for as long as we can."

"They'll be watching the bridge and the wharfs."

"I think there's a way. It wouldn't be pleasant, but it might work. It would take someone who knew the city, who was familiar with its seamier side. Someone with contacts on the inside, who could pass unnoticed. Someone…"

"Hey," I said. "Stop looking at me like that."

For Alvantes's eyes were firmly fixed on me, and everyone else's had swung to follow. "Why, Damasco?" he said. "You wanted to spend a night in Altapasaeda so badly. Now here's your chance."

CHAPTER TWO

"I get it, I really do. Coalition of dangerous forces, shadowy figure lurking in background pulling strings. I've followed all that. It's quite a problem you have here, Alvantes. Do you know what else I followed? It isn't my problem."

Estrada looked at me in horror. "Damasco… if Altapasaeda's in trouble, it's *everyone's* problem."

"You see, I'd swear I just covered that point. Alvantes's, yes. Mine, not at all. Not yours, either, Estrada, and definitely not Saltlick's. I say, back off, let the dust settle. There's a fair chance the families and the gangs will fall out and kill each other off, probably sooner rather than later. The streets might run red for a day or two, but after that everything will go back to normal. They'll welcome you with open arms, Alvantes. You can be the hero of the hour."

Not one of the faces turned on mine showed any hint of agreement. Saltlick's bemused smile came closest, but I was confident it meant he simply wasn't following the conversation. How could they be so stupid?

Altapasaeda was like an hysterical child; always wailing over something, only to forget it the moment a new threat or annoyance distracted its minuscule attention. This current crisis, whatever its true nature, was bound to pass the same way.

Well, I wasn't about to let weight of numbers convince me to sign on for Alvantes's suicide plan. I'd started off with flat refusal; moved through anger, abuse, self-ridicule; listed the failings that made me so unsuited to the job; returned to stubborn negation; spent half an hour cataloguing the deficiencies in his logic... on and on, until I began to suspect I'd win by simply dying of exhaustion.

No such luck. Now I only had one argument left – the most obvious, the one I'd found myself shying away from again and again. "The fact is, Alvantes, I'm through jeopardising my life to solve other people's problems. I'm leaving."

"I can't stop you," said Alvantes.

"That's right. You can't."

"But I *can* make sure that bag of stolen coins you've been carrying around doesn't go with you."

I winced. "It's mine. I've *earned* it." And I had. Stealing from half a dozen of Panchetto's guests in a single night had been no easy feat.

"A room full of guardsmen says different."

There it was, as inevitable as dying. There was a basic incompatibility in how Alvantes and I viewed the world, and the bag of money in my pocket was a prime example of that. I couldn't leave without it. I couldn't walk away empty-handed. Doing that meant returning to the life I'd been leading – a life that had left me desperate enough to try stealing food from a notoriously homicidal invading warlord.

"This is the last time," I said. "This cleans the slate. You don't throw my past in my face. You forget about the money. If I do this, Alvantes, it gets you off my back until the end of time."

It was all the more frustrating that he didn't even pause to consider. "All right," he said. "A clean slate."

"And the coin stays with me. I might need it in there."

"You keep a quarter. The rest back when you return with answers."

"A third. Anything I spend in bribes, you refund."

"Agreed."

Far too late, I saw it. Alvantes had known how this conversation would end before he'd ever started it. Moreover, whatever the reasons he'd given for choosing me, it was the one he hadn't said that clinched it. Guardsmen's lives mattered. Mine was expendable.

I felt the first fluttering of panic. Here, then, was the price of my future. One last gamble. One final job.

In my line of work, those never went well.

We'd waited through the remainder of the night and the next day. The hours had passed interminably. I'd slept a little, in bursts that always ended with me starting awake, heart vibrating with vague fear. Navare had fed us, but I'd hardly tasted the watery stew he'd served up, or managed to stomach very much of it. Alvantes's men went out in small groups throughout the day, no doubt to listen for news from within the city. No one spoke much. Even Saltlick, sitting hunched in a corner, looked moody and dejected.

I was almost glad when the time came. Risking my neck couldn't be worse than another minute in that cramped and increasingly ill-smelling room. My relief lasted fully as long as it took Alvantes to insist he be the one to accompany me. Anyone else would have had the decency at least to pretend they weren't keeping tabs on me.

Even long after dark, the Suburbs were a riot of activity. Drinking, gambling and whoring were by far the most popular local activities, and none of those suffered from a lack of daylight. I hoped no one noticed the frown of disgust Alvantes wore beneath his hood as we wandered through the narrow, torchlit streets.

As it turned out, however, no one seemed eager to pay us any attention. Everyone we passed was conspicuously keeping to themselves, and looked shiftier than was required even for the Suburbs. Time and again, I noticed how their eyes darted towards the looming city walls.

"They're nervous," I whispered to Alvantes, when no one was close. "Scared of the city."

"Perhaps they're right to be."

It was busier still by the waterside, for that was where the majority of drinking dens were to be found. Away from those havens of local culture, however, the din of shouted conversation died to a murmur. It wasn't too difficult to find a spot where we were out of sight – which made stealing a boat that much easier.

"We're not stealing," muttered Alvantes. "We're borrowing."

"That distinction means a lot to you, doesn't it?"

"More than it ever has to you."

Many of the Suburb-dwellers kept decrepit coracles and rowboats, for communing with passing river barges and fishing useful debris from the Casto Mara. We settled for a mould-blackened skiff that looked as though it might at least last the night. Even then, it floated much as a drunkard would walk, and leaked more than seemed reasonable.

"I mentioned your plan is idiotic."

"Quiet, Damasco. They'll be watching the bridge."

The Sabre, the Castoval's largest river crossing, continued the northward boundary into Altapasaeda begun by the walls. It was the only entrance to the city not gated, which meant barricades and armed men if you wanted to keep unwelcome visitors out. Alvantes was right, of course; as we entered its vast shadow, I thought I could hear voices drifting through the stonework overhead.

Of course, the first, most obviously cretinous flaw in Alvantes's so-called plan was that if they were watching the Sabre, there would certainly be archers guarding the dockside. I'd already decided that if we were spotted I'd take my chances in the river and hope the effort of perforating Alvantes kept them distracted long enough for me to make my escape.

Then again, perhaps Alvantes wasn't quite the idiot I frequently took him for. Beneath the Sabre, he manoeuvred us towards the bank, until we were close enough that our oar blades almost brushed the naked stone. Though we'd slipped from the impenetrable shadow beneath the bridge, we remained hidden by the harbour wall, higher here than where it dipped for the landing stages further on. Unless someone was directly above and looking down, we'd remain invisible.

We were drawing close to the most objectionable part of Alvantes's scheme. Even if I hadn't known what to look for, the smell would have been a sure giveaway. It was a good job in a way, for the closer we drew, the more my eyes watered, until I could barely see at all. Through the tears, I could just make out a large round hole, levelled into a channel at the bottom. Something far too thick and viscous to be water flowed from its mouth into the river below.

Of the virtues that made Altapasaeda unique, its sewers were the least spoken of. I suspected the wealthy brought them up in only the most drunken moments of dinner-party braggadocio. There was no question they were impressive in their way, though. I understood how much skill and thought must have gone into their construction – to harness two underground tributaries of the Casto Mara, to force them into the distasteful function of evacuating waste from the South Bank manors and the palace and temples further west.

But some marvels were better appreciated at a distance – or not at all. Maybe there really were things in life more important than money. "Turn around," I said. "I can't do it."

"Keep your voice down! You can and will."

Whispering made it even harder not to gag. "The smell…"

"You'll get used to it."

"How do you know? When have you ever done this?"

"You'd be surprised."

I tore my eyes from the reeking outlet to look at him. "You're serious."

"There's more to being Guard-Captain of Alta-pasaeda than someone like you could understand."

"There you go again. Someone like me. That's the last one you get, Alvantes."

I crouched, grasped the first of the metal rungs driven into the wall, swung myself over. If Alvantes could crawl through a sewer then Easie Damasco could as well.

In the instant it took me to realise how absurd that logic was, Alvantes had already turned the boat around.

"Hey!"

"Remember… I'll wait under the bridge. Whistle three times."

"Hold on…"

Our muted conversation was interrupted by the rap of footsteps on the cobbles above, distant but drawing nearer. I cursed foully beneath my breath. There was only one place to hide. It was the sewer or handing myself over to whomever was approaching on the harbour wall.

Even then, I had to think hard about it.

Alvantes had given me a cloth to tie around my mouth and nose. It couldn't have helped less. The stink was dizzying. I could taste it, as though it plastered my throat and tongue. I could even feel it, a physical force buffeting me. It was impossible to break it down into component stenches. Yet every few moments a particular odour – rotten cabbage, spoiled meat, week-old slops – would force its way through the general miasma. The only constant was the reek of human waste.

I moved crab-wise, back pressed to the wall. Not that the wall was anything like clean, but it was as far as I could get from the central channel. The stones beneath my feet were wet with slime – or what I chose to consider slime. My worst fear was that I'd lose my balance and plunge into that evil-smelling stream. The very thought made me want to scream. If I could have done it without opening my mouth, I might have.

(Alvantes had refused me a light. "Believe me, Damasco, you don't want a naked flame down there."

"Then how exactly am I supposed to find my way?"

"It isn't far. You can't go wrong.")

After minutes that seemed like hours, I was certain I'd done exactly that. I couldn't see the pale glimmer from the entrance any more. I couldn't see anything. There was only me, the wall, and the stench, wrapped like a living presence around me. Then I took another step, the wall behind me disappeared, and I really did scream. I tripped backwards, as the stink climbed into my throat.

My hands found something cold and hard. I spun round, too close to vomiting to feel relief. I reached up. Sure enough, there was another rung.

I flung myself up the ladder hammered into the wall, discovered the trapdoor at its top by crashing my head against it. For one horrible moment I was sure it wouldn't budge. However, one firm shove, with my hand this time, was all it took. I hauled myself the last distance, slammed the hatch behind me and flopped to the ground, panting blissfully fresh air.

I'd come out in a closed courtyard, hemmed in by three low buildings and a shallow wall on the fourth side. One of those houses must belong to the poor wretch who maintained this stretch of sewer. Though it felt as if ages had passed, I couldn't be far from the river. Likely I was somewhere in the Lower Market District.

Once I had my breath back and the worst of the sewer's aftertaste had passed, I scrambled to the top of the wall to get my bearings. Beyond was a narrow alley, opening onto a wider concourse to my right and another passageway to my left. If neither looked entirely familiar in the darkness, I still had a fair sense of where I must be.

Having satisfied myself no one was nearby, I dropped down the far side of the wall. One advantage of my revoltingly unusual route into the city was that nobody would be eager to ask me questions. Then again, they might just skip the interrogation and move straight to grievous wounding. All told, the main roads were a bad idea.

I opted instead for the passageway. It led roughly northward by my reckoning, in the direction of the walls. Those were something else I'd do well to avoid;

but if my remembered map of the city was correct, I wouldn't be travelling anything like that far. In small recompense for its horrors, the sewer had deposited me almost on the doorstep of the address I sought.

Sure enough, I soon passed through a cramped courtyard I recognised, and from there ducked into a dead-end lane, whose ramshackle houses leaned madly inward as though eager to touch roofs. Everything about those crumbling abodes spoke of poverty and desperation. In most cases, that was undoubtedly what lay behind their crooked portals. The door I opted for, however, was sturdy and – to the trained eye – double-locked and reinforced. Though its occupant wasn't quite rich, the penury of his location was carefully chosen and studiously maintained.

I rapped three times. After a few moments, a narrow hatch slid open, just wide enough for a pair of wrinkle-skewed eyes to peep through the gap.

"Hello, Franco," I said.

Franco had been old when I first came to Alta-pasaeda. He'd been around for so long that there were those who claimed he'd invented the very concept of crime. However, to say his best days were behind him was an understatement. They were so far in the past that probably even he didn't remember them. It didn't stop him from keeping a voracious eye on the city's underworld, though – that being the first and most crucial reason I'd sought him out.

"Easie Damasco," he said. "Not a face I ever expected to see again. Not still attached to your body, at any rate."

"Not dying is becoming my trademark."

"Strange, though." Franco wrinkled his nose. "You *smell* like you've been dead for a week. Dead and rotting in a sewer."

"Partly true, at any rate. Can I come in?"

The disembodied eyes looked me up and down. "I think not."

"I have money."

He considered again; the rectangle of wizened face tilted to one side. Finally, I heard the sound of locks being opened, and a bar being shifted aside. The door opened a crack. "Then you can buy a new cloak and boots before we go any further," he said.

"Fine by me." Franco was one of the better outfitters for criminal endeavours in Altapasaeda. That was the second reason I'd come here. It made sense to combine my mission with a little shopping expedition. Over the last few months, I'd hocked or lost most of the accoutrements of my trade, and I felt oddly naked without them. In any case, it wouldn't hurt to be prepared for whatever trials my enforced mission threw up.

I wasn't convinced Franco was in any position to offer me sartorial advice, though. He wore a stained and faded poncho over a shirt once gaudily pink, now mostly grey, and – although he was indoors and it was night – a wide-brimmed hat, slanted rakishly upon his snow-white hair. It bobbed dangerously as he led me down a narrow passage and through another locked door, and almost tumbled off altogether when, in the tiny room beyond, he ducked to unlock a hatch in the floor. Franco only clasped his hat decorously, unhooked a lantern from the wall and started down into the shadows.

I'd been fortunate enough to witness the wonder that was Franco's Cellar of Crime on a couple of occasions before now. If anything, it was more astonishing and overstocked than ever. Not a single bare brick could be seen, and there was barely floor space enough to manoeuvre through the trove. Franco's stock consisted mostly of clothing, armour and a quite staggering range of weapons. Amidst these more predictable items, however, were countless less obvious accessories of the criminal trades: caltrops, poisons and acids, mantraps and snares, face paints and false beards, paste gemstones... it was enough to make my head spin.

Forcing my attention to the racks of clothing, my eye fell immediately on a full cloak of deepest charcoal grey. There were other, showier outfits, but they were all in black, a shade guaranteed to stand out on even the darkest night and reserved for foppish would-be thieves.

"That one. The grey," I said, and couldn't help feeling a little pleased at the twinkle of approval in Franco's rheumy gaze.

I added a shirt and trousers of similar colour, and a particularly dapper pair of boots. I completed the outfit with a short, narrow-bladed dagger that sheathed neatly against my hip. It wasn't a weapon for fighting, but it had the potental to give someone a nasty surprise.

When I'd finished changing, Franco had me stuff my old clothes into a sack, pointing out that, "It will make them less bothersome to burn."

I looked around the overburdened walls, trying to guess what else I might need. "I'll take that rucksack, as well," I said, "two – no, three – sets of lock picks, needle and thread if you have them, and a length of your finest climbing rope."

Franco plucked a coil down from a hook. "How's this? Hawser-laid single line, a sisal core with cotton overwrap. I made the grapnel myself, you won't find a better."

"Excellent." I took it, crammed it into the pack with my other purchases.

"That'll be three onyxes. I've rounded up, since you've left me the task of exterminating your revolting cast-offs."

He'd rounded up by at least an onyx, but I didn't have time to argue. As I handed over the coins, I said, "There's one more in it for you if you'll share a little information."

Franco eyed me slantwise from beneath his absurd hat. "Go on."

"What's been happening to the city these last few days… do you know who's behind it?"

"Of course I know. I also know what he'd do to me if he found out I'd talked to you."

Encouraged by my new outfit, I struck my most threatening pose. "And what do you think I'll do?"

"Damasco, I've known you since you were barely old enough to pickpocket. You'll talk a lot, eventually realise you're as intimidating as cold soup, and give up."

He had me there. "Look, Franco, I'm in a fix. I need answers. Alvantes is leaning on me and…"

"What?" Franco looked at me with horror. "You're working with the Boar? Have you gone completely mad, boy? We both know people who'd gut you for just saying his name."

"It's a long story. One I'd like to end sooner rather than later. If you could just give me something to go on, point me in the right direction…"

Franco shook his head wearily. "All right, all right," he said. "I heard a rumour… something going down on the South Bank, some kind of a meet. I don't know where and I wouldn't tell you if I did."

"Thanks, Franco." I offered him the fourth coin.

"I haven't done you any favours. The city's under curfew. If anyone sees you, they'll kill you on sight. You want advice worth paying for? Get out of Altapasaeda. Never look back."

"You know Alvantes. He'd track me down if it was the last thing he did. Still. I appreciate you looking out for me, Franco."

"They can cut your throat and dump you in the river for all I care," he said, starting back up the stairs with the noxious sack containing my old clothes slung over one shoulder. "I just don't want you stirring things up, that's all. They're more than bad enough already."

From the edge in his voice, I could tell he meant it. In fact – and this shocked me more than almost anything could have – he sounded scared. What did it take to unnerve Franco? He was the closest anyone could be to untouchable in the world of Altapasaedan crime. He'd been staring down death for as long as I'd been alive.

As he let me out the front door, I said, "I'll be careful, Franco."

"You won't. But try, for all our sakes," he said – and the door slammed shut.

It was some distance to the South Bank, almost the breadth of the city. Worse, I could hardly hurry, or take the main roads. I moved through back alleys wherever I could, jogging from shadow to shadow and each time pausing to listen, straining my eyes against the darkness.

Once I had to duck into an arch as riders thundered by. Twice I had to sneak past groups of armed men lurking in the shadows. Both times, they were clustered at a junction, where they could see in all directions. Had they been paying more attention to their work and less to talking and drinking, I wouldn't have stood a chance.

As it was, I felt my success vindicated my choice of cloak, and of the boots, which made nary a squeak upon the cobbles. Still, it was taxing on my nerves. The guard had never been this fastidious, or the city this well manned. Someone was making a point – keeping Altapasaeda safe, whether Altapasaedans liked it or not.

Only when I came out on the edge of the South Bank did I realise my problems had barely begun. The South Bank was as well lit as anywhere in Altapasaeda, and didn't contain anything even approaching an alley.

In fact, the street I'd reached was a wide, tree-lined boulevard, with no hint of cover except the widely spaced openings of mansion compounds.

I heard footsteps.

The curfew had one advantage. It told me that anyone on the streets must be there for a good reason. A confident step would have been bad news, but this was anything but, a rapid, anxious tip-tap. I darted round the corner of an archway, trampling some noble's prized flowerbeds in the process. The footsteps drew nearer. I caught the briefest flash of a figure: well dressed though graceless, tall but hunched against the night cold.

I gave him a half-dozen more paces before I stepped out. "Off to the meeting?"

He jumped back, made a noise that sounded like "Wuuh?"

"I should walk with you. Safety in numbers." Encouraged by my new outfit, I did an ample job of making it sound like a threat.

"What... ah... do I know you?"

I looked him up and down. My initial impression had been spot on. He was gaunt and fretful, a few years older than me and impeccably dressed. He had the peculiar accent unique to the Altapasaedan wealthy, but with a nervous tremor all his own. I doubted very much if he'd ever done a minute's work in his life, or anything as dangerous as walking the streets alone at night.

One thing more: he hadn't contradicted me when I mentioned the meeting. That meant there was a good chance my guess was correct. "I doubt it," I said. "I don't think we've mixed in the same circles. Not until recently, at any rate."

"I haven't seen you at the other conferences," he replied, struggling for something approaching authority.

"I've been caught up in some business. Only just found time to get in on the act."

My new companion looked nervous. "I can't imagine *he* liked that."

"Oh, he was understanding. We go way back."

He looked at me with mingled horror and respect. Then, catching himself, he said, "Well, no time to waste, eh?"

"No time at all," I agreed.

He hurried on, and I paced nonchalantly beside him, as though it were the most natural thing in the world that we'd be taking a stroll together through the nocturnal streets. Still, I couldn't think of anything in the way of casual conversation that would be in keeping with my tough-guy act. I was glad when we turned into a side road and he exclaimed, with a nervous laugh, "Well, here we are."

I pulled my hood up and dropped back, just out of sight of my companion but close enough that anyone would assume we were together. One hint of trouble and I'd run. That was the length and breadth of my plan – one whisper of suspicion and I'd flee as I'd never fled before.

Ahead, an open gateway led into one of the smaller estates. Three men stood on guard. I tried not to look at them too closely. Nevertheless, it was easy to see what they represented. One was a uniformed family retainer, the second a scimitar-armed northerner with a beaded mane of hair and beard, the third an anonymous thug of the kind the city was so well stocked with. In short, they perfectly embodied the three factions involved in Altapasaeda's sudden change of fortunes.

My companion hurried forward, only to nearly trip over his feet before the guards. "Lord Rufio Eldunzi. Of the family Eldunzi."

"Boss said come alone," grunted the thug, with a tilt of the head in my direction.

"Oh no," stuttered Eldunzi, "he's, ah…"

I was ready to flee – more than ready. Yet at the last moment, words came bubbling unsummoned from my mouth. "Don't mind him, my lord," I said. "He's just a lowlife with ideas above his station."

Suddenly, it was all very simple. The thug would kill me on the spot, or else he'd back down. It all depended on how high the weak-kneed cretin beside me featured in the pecking order. If he was some nobody lordling hanging off the bottom of the invite list, I was as good as dead.

"'Pologies, milord. Go on in."

I don't know who was more relieved, me or Eldunzi – but I'd like to think I hid it better. Eldunzi practically sprinted down the gravelled carriageway, while I did my best to follow at a reasonable pace. He ignored a grandiose coach house and the manor's porticoed main entrance, carried on towards a smaller doorway. As he ducked inside, I was close on his heels.

Within, a long hall was lit by flickering oil lamps set around the walls. Benches had been set up in the main space and were already almost full. Perhaps forty persons occupied those seats, and despite the copious cushions, not one of them looked comfortable.

I was glad when Eldunzi settled for a place near the back. I slipped in beside him, letting my gaze follow his towards the head of the room. A low stage had been erected there, and on it stood a half-dozen men. None of them looked like the sort I'd willingly tangle with, but even amidst that unsavoury crowd, one stood out – a king rat amongst lesser vermin. He was poised before a podium, clearly preparing to speak to the assembly.

I recognised him – though I'd many a reason to wish I didn't.

What I'd told my newfound companion was true. I really *did* know our host from way back. First as a supposedly ex-criminal barkeeper. Then as an unlikely resistance fighter. Most recently, as betrayer of his companions, myself included, to a certain invading warlord.

He was the last person in the world who should have been on that stage. Yet I didn't feel any surprise, just a nauseating sense of inevitability.

How had Castilio Mounteban come to be running Altapasaeda?

CHAPTER THREE

Mounteban was imposing; I had to give him that.

He'd always been a bear of a man, and though I was sure some of that bulk must be fat these days, he wore it exactly like muscle. He was dressed plainly, in black cotton shirt and trousers that looked more impressive on him than any fine silks could have. His beard was tidier than I'd seen it, a neat wedge hiding his bullish neck. Even his eyepatch of polished leather was new, and spat back the firelight more arrestingly than any real eye.

All told, he dominated the stage – and given the men there with him, that was no mean feat. I recognised them from the time we'd once travelled together, fleeing Muena Palaiya with Moaradrid on our heels. They were something approaching a bodyguard, seasoned professionals at inflicting bodily harm, and each exuded an air of violence uniquely his own.

The one my gaze kept being drawn to, however, was the one making least effort to be noticed. If I hadn't expected him, I might easily have missed his presence. Uncommonly short, improbably thin, he was altogether too innocuous. He sank into the gloom as though it was where he belonged, found shadows where they had no right to exist in a brightly lit hall.

If I remembered rightly, Mounteban had called him Synza. When I'd known him, he'd been acting as a scout, but I'd known from the moment I saw him that his true proclivities lay elsewhere. Synza was a killer of a more subtle sort than his companions: the kind you turned to when you didn't want the bodies inconveniently floating up out of the river; the kind you called in when something more refined than horrible bludgeoning was called for.

Frankly, just being in the same room as him scared me silly.

An explosive throat-clearing drew my grateful eyes away from Synza. "Thank you for coming here," Mounteban said. "I see you all followed my suggestion and came without your usual retinues. I trust you each had a safe journey regardless. Because the streets of Altapasaeda have never been safer than they are tonight."

A tense round of applause pattered up and down the room.

"Why are you clapping?" asked Mounteban, his tone abruptly frigid.

The applause died instantly, replaced with a silence that would have turned a pin drop into a thunderclap.

"The credit is your own!" Mounteban cried – and the room heaved such a collective sigh of relief that every light wavered in its cresset. "In less than a week, you've won a peace for yourselves the likes of which Panchetto and the guard could never have delivered.

How did you achieve this marvel, which decades of royal rule and guard brutality failed to achieve? By embracing new allies. By setting aside meaningless differences."

Mounteban paused to survey the gathering. Instinctively, I dipped my head, let the hood fall further over my face. One hand braced on the edge of my seat, I tensed to run.

I only had to reach the door. I was fast on my feet, and fear always made me faster. Only get out the door and I could outrun anyone. Get out, carry what I knew to Alvantes, take my money, and I could walk away from this damned mess.

I felt his eyes. A word, a hint he'd recognised me and I'd be moving. Just a breath out of place. The muscles in my calves were so tense I thought they'd explode.

Was he still looking at me? If he was, it was all over. I dared to roll my eyes up, twitched the hood a fraction back…

Mounteban's attention was fixed at a point two rows ahead and to my left. "Lord Purda," he said, "you inherited a fortune built by clothmaking and wineries. Black-Eyed Rico, you made your money in extortion and burglary. What difference does that make in the end? You're both men of wealth, of power."

Lord Purda looked particularly uncomfortable at this comparison, while the man named Black-Eyed Rico smirked and giggled.

"I mean no disrespect to the memory of Prince Panchetto. Still, his legacy is clear. By imposing a regime based on privilege and outmoded tradition, by insisting upon an obsolete social order, he held every one of you down. He held *this city* down. Why should Altapasaeda be ruled from a palace in the far-distant north? Why should it be ruled at all? Why, in fact, should it not govern the Castoval from end to end?"

There arose another ragged cheer, and this time Mounteban let it run its course.

So there it was. Mounteban's endgame. He wanted to run Altapasaeda, and he wanted Altapasaeda to run the Castoval. Say what you like about his sanity, but you couldn't fault his ambition.

"That time will come," he went on. "For all of us. Altapasaedan independence means Castovalian independence. Castovalian independence means prosperity and influence the likes of which you've only dreamed. The first phase of our plan is complete. The city is secure. The dangers within its borders have been contained."

At this, I noticed a number of the more finely dressed members of the audience wince. Mounteban must be referring to the Altapasaedan Palace Guard, who would have fought tooth and nail against his new order – likely with the tacit support of many of the families. I wondered what "contained" meant. It would have depended on how far Mounteban dared go. Based on the available evidence, my guess would be *pretty damned far*.

"Our next step is to begin the return to normality: to resume trade, to rejoin with the world outside. I re-alise the last few days have been trying and disruptive

for many of you. I'll take it as said that you understand
the necessity of what we've done. With that in mind,
gentlemen… do any of you have questions?"

The offer was phrased in such a tone that only an
idiot would take it literally. *Of course* there were no
questions. Anyone with the least experience of tyrannical madmen knew better than that. Anyone with
the slightest spark of wit would understand to keep
their tongue still and their head down.

Mounteban's gaze honed in on movement. Forty
stricken faces turned to follow.

Suddenly, everyone in the room was looking at me.

No. Not me. At Eldunzi. The simpering moron had
actually raised his hand.

"Ah…"

I earnestly wanted to snap that hand off and shove
it down his throat.

"Lord Eldunzi," said Mounteban. His courtesy was
chilling.

"Well… the thing is…"

Before Eldunzi could say more, a new expression
interrupted Mounteban's studied disdain. For one
brief moment, his features registered purest astonish-
ment. Then he stepped back, placed his mouth to the
assassin Synza's ear.

I didn't need to guess what he'd whispered. The
snake of ice uncoiling in my stomach told me all I
needed to know. I was already on my feet and moving
by the time he looked back.

"Stop that thief!"

Had Mounteban chosen his words more carefully,

I'd never have left that room. If he'd taken into account just who he was addressing, I'd barely have made it out of my seat. To the wealthy patresfamilias, anyone who wasn't one of their own was a thief of some sort or another.

I was at the door by the time it occurred to anyone even to look my way.

That still left the three on the gate.

"Help! Mounteban's in trouble," I cried. "They've turned on him!"

The fear in my voice was genuine enough. It did the trick for the northerner soldier – he had most invested in Mounteban's continued survival. He rushed past me with an inarticulate roar.

The family retainer looked noncommittal. What was it to him if Mounteban was torn apart by his audience?

Last came the thug. He wasn't moving – and now he had a knife out. Maybe he hadn't liked me calling him a lowlife earlier. Maybe settling that slight was more important than anything happening inside. He was big. So was the knife. There was no way I was getting by him in one piece.

I zagged right, towards the retainer. Before he could get his arms up, I struck him with my shoulder and all my weight. It was enough to hurl him back against the thug, who barely had the presence of mind not to gut his companion. The three of us went down together in an eruption of gravel and thrashing limbs.

Cushioned by two bodies, I came off lightest. My momentum carried me free, and I rolled back to my feet. But those seconds of delay had cost me dearly.

Now there were running steps pounding the carriage-way behind me, and a dozen voices shouting over each other.

The shriek of a whistle cut the night air.

"To the stables!" someone bellowed.

Stables? I couldn't outrun horses! I was already half-winded. I needed to get off the streets. But there *was* no way off these wide, open boulevards. To the south lay only the walls. In any other direction, I was two roads or more from anything even approaching an alley.

I ran on. There was nothing else to do. Out of the gate, I chose the direction I'd come from, where at least I'd know my way towards the Market District.

Luck was against me. I'd barely left the carriageway when a crowd came crashing from a wide side street ahead. One or more of the patrols had arrived in answer to the whistle's summons. To their credit, they grasped the situation quickly. In seconds, they were moving to cut me off.

From behind came the clatter of hooves on stone.

I glanced back, caught a dizzying glimpse of a single rider bursting from the arch I'd just left. More eager than his colleagues, he hadn't even waited to saddle his mount. I knew him as one of Mounteban's body-guards, and before that as bouncer for his bar in Muena Palaiya. That and the fact the Red-Eyed Dog was the most dangerous dive in the Castoval told me all I needed to know.

If it hadn't, the cudgel he held, with nails hammered through its head, would have filled in any blanks.

Ahead, the line of bodies was spreading out, pre-empting my next thought. I might have dashed for one of the other mansions, but they were close enough now to see me wherever I went. That first mad sprint was already lashing my ribs with fire. Try as I might, I was losing pace.

What did it matter? I had nowhere to go. I faltered, the pain in my lungs struggling against hopelessness for my attention.

Mounteban was nothing like Moaradrid. He wouldn't try to take me alive. He didn't care about questioning me. If the darker rumours I'd heard in Muena Palaiya were true – and I was confident now that they were – then his method of dealing with problems like me was to make damn sure they never bothered him again.

That was the message the bouncer's cudgel sent, like a clarion into my brain. I couldn't tear my eyes from it. As he galloped nearer, each crack of hooves sent light glinting from those fiendishly spiked points. The thing was fully as long as my leg. Every time it tore the air, I could feel, with clarity beyond imagination, what it would do to flesh and bone.

I'd almost staggered to a halt. He could easily have trampled me where I stood. Instead, he reined in, steadying his mount for a blow. The horse whickered furiously as he forced it through a tight half circle, striving to cut in front of me. I dropped to one knee and flung an arm over my head – as though that would do anything to stop the club from shattering both arm and skull. He gave me an almost friendly grin, perhaps grateful I was making life easier by staying still. Tugging the reins harder, digging with his heels, he controlled the panicked horse. Then he lifted the obscene cudgel, almost casually.

I pulled my new knife from its sheath and jabbed it into his thigh.

I did it more from spite than any hope of saving myself. It was hardly more than a prick; the blade was no longer than my middle finger. Insomuch as I'd thought the attack through, I'd hoped to pull it free for another try.

The bouncer ruined that plan by tumbling down his horse's other side and onto the cobbles, landing with a bone-crunching thud and muffled cry.

Damn it, why could I never hold onto a knife?

Still, a horse was some recompense.

Bolstered by my unexpected victory, I leapt up and clutched the reins. I thought the horse might fight the unexpected change of rider, but apparently he was as eager to be off as I was. He shot to a gallop with the barest encouragement, and didn't flinch when our course took us directly towards the men ahead. For a moment, their heads swung between the figure crumpled on the cobbles and the excited animal bearing down on them. Then the line broke. Two of them dashed one way, three the other, and we sailed between.

I tried to guide us towards the nearest turn-off. I'd had more than enough of this street. However, the horse didn't seem terribly interested in my opinions. Only at the last possible instant did he decide to acquiesce, and we clattered round the corner. I nearly sobbed with relief when no one appeared to block our way.

Then my brain caught up with the sounds behind me.

What I'd thought was one set of hooves, the one beneath me, was actually more like half a dozen. Now that I realised, I could make out their individual tattoos upon the cobblestones. It could only be the rest of Mounteban's bodyguard. They weren't on us yet, but they were close and gaining.

I was no kind of horseman. I'd never have made it this far if my mount didn't have an agenda of his own. Whatever slim advantage I'd gained was about to vanish. Maybe I'd changed the rules of the chase, but they were no less stacked against me.

Nearing the end of our current road and left to its own devices, my horse made a beeline for an alley that cut towards the Market District. I approved in theory – except that this particular alley was chiselled through two buildings, its ceiling so low that a man could barely pass without crouching…

"Not that wa–"

Just in time, I realised ducking would serve better than arguing. I bent double over the horse's neck, as timber beams scuffed my hair. The too-close walls shrieked by. We broke back into open air, and another wider passage. This one ended in a ninety-degree turn – which my horse chose to ignore. He ran straight towards the wall. Only when it seemed far too late did he skid to a halt, neighing manically, as though the obstruction was some completely unpredictable impediment that had appeared to vex him.

I yanked hard on the reins, trying to tilt his head towards the turn. Eventually, he understood. He set off again, barely slower than before.

The next turn deposited us somewhere familiar, the main thoroughfare of the Market District, which ran west from the docks towards the palace. From behind, I could hear the pursuing riders navigating the alleys. Our lead was rapidly diminishing. I couldn't carry on like this. My horse was no less determined to kill me than the men closing upon us.

I *had* to get off the streets.

But where could I go? The gates were barred. Even if I could make it to Franco's, he'd turn me in the first chance he got, and there was no way I was chancing the sewer again. Better death than that. Alvantes should still be waiting beneath the Sabre, but it would be guarded and barricaded, and if they had any sense they'd have upped the guards manning the dockside too. What did that leave?

On any other night, nothing.

Tonight, however, I had a brand-new length of rope.

Maybe the walls would be crawling with men. More likely, they'd have been drawn into the hunt. To any-one without a new rope, the ramparts were too high to offer an escape route, just as the city was too cramped for them to offer any useful vantage in my pursuit. Anyway, what choice did I have? I could ra-tionalise all night – or for the seconds it would take someone to catch and murder me – but there *were* no other options. A slim chance was better than none.

My best hope lay in taking the fastest route, regard-less of where it brought me out. I drew my horse round, spurring him with a sharp dig of my heels, and we shot off westward through the Lower Market District.

From behind came the clamour of our pursuers joining the main road. By then, we were passing beneath the arch that joined Lower and Upper Market districts, into the luxurious stretch of shops reserved for the Altapasaedan rich. Ahead, a patrol of four men burst from a narrow sideway. My horse, with his usual indifference to obstructions, made no effort to avoid them. In the fraction of a second they had to judge the situation, they made the right decision. We left them sprawling in the street. The subsequent cries told me they'd proved more of a hindrance to our pursuers than they had to us.

Another grand arch brought us out at the curved junction where Market and Temple districts met. I edged the horse right, to keep our westerly course. To either side, lights burned with bright chemical blues and greens, casting brief, wild shadows of our passage. In cages above, vividly plumed birds screamed their outrage. I was glad I held no belief in the northerner gods; riding at full pelt through their mundane home was sure to be all kinds of blasphemy.

On we went, into the great square around the palace. I had just time to notice how the ornate palace gates had been caved in before we were past. My single-minded horse was in his element in so open a space. I didn't think our followers had gained at all. Now the walls were in sight – and sure enough, no one was visible upon their crest.

However, nothing lay beyond the walls at this point but the ragged highway we'd travelled the night before. I'd barely be safer out there than I was in here. Fortunately, this road ran almost the entire inner circumference of Altapasaeda. I didn't want to push my luck much further, but I let the horse continue, until I thought we must be near the outskirts of the Suburbs. Only then did I guide him towards one of the intermittent sets of steps that led upward.

I wasn't sure he'd stop when I reined in. He did, though so suddenly I almost tumbled over his head. I swung giddily to the ground. "Good horse," I mumbled. "Fine, brave horse."

He bared his teeth and looked as though he'd like to chew my face off.

"Mad, vicious horse," I amended, and flung myself up the stairs.

At the summit, I glanced back – just as four riders swung into view below. Only four? Mounteban had six bodyguards. Discounting the one I'd left bleeding in the South Bank, that still made five.

Then I realised who was missing, and a shiver danced up my spine.

It was Synza. Synza the assassin.

With an effort, I pushed the thought from my mind. All I had time to worry about was getting off these walls. At the head of the stairs, the walkway was cut short by a squat tower. I tried the door, was a little surprised when it opened. Inside were a tiny desk, a stove and a ladder leading to a trapdoor in the ceiling. I hurried to slam and bolt the door, and darted to secure the opposite entrance as well.

I'd bought myself a little breathing space. But locking myself in a tower was a temporary fix at best. I started up the ladder, shoved through the hatch and dragged myself onto the platform there. I pulled out my rope and looped it round a merlon of the battlement, securing it with the grapnel hook.

I had my escape route. Now I just needed the nerve to use it.

It was pure instinct that drew my eyes left and down to the wall walk – the instinct of the rabbit that realises, too late, how the hawk is plummeting towards it. There stood Synza, his face a mask of perfect calm. One delicate hand was raised to his ear, as though he were straining to hear some subtle note.

Then I saw the glint of metal there. His hand flicked forward, unimaginably fast.

I threw myself sideways. Heat seared a line across the side of my head. I kept moving, flung myself at the battlements, half climbed, half tumbled over. My grasping fingers found the rope, just in time to save me from a helpless fall. I wrapped my free hand round the first, let myself slide.

Immediately, fire blossomed in my palm. Why hadn't I bought gloves? I knew dimly that without them, there was no quick way down a rope. But panic was driving me. At any moment, Synza might lean out to finish me.

The pain in my chafed fingers, suddenly, was more than I could bear.

I couldn't stop. I couldn't hold on.

I let go.

CHAPTER FOUR

Anywhere else, I'd have died a messy death.

As it was, the roof I landed on tore like wet paper. I couldn't say it broke my fall, exactly, but at least it didn't break my spine.

The same couldn't be said for the next stop in my downwards journey. The ground was just as hard in the Suburbs as anywhere else. Agony jolted my body and blasted the air from my lungs. I lay struggling for breath, not daring to move so much as a finger lest I find it hopelessly mangled. I felt like a fleshy sack of sharpened rocks and pain.

Then I remembered Synza. Synza the master-assassin. Synza the solver of problems that needed to stay solved. Synza who hadn't gained his reputation by leaving jobs half-finished.

I sat up. Slivers of cold and heat stabbed into my head. When I touched my hair, my fingers came back tacky and red. At least everything still seemed to be where it should be. At least my skull appeared to be in one piece, rather than dripping its contents down my neck.

Looking round, I realised for the first time that an ancient woman and three small children were staring back at me. Wide-eyed, they crouched on a straw pallet. I tried to smile reassuringly and new waves of hurt radiated through my jaw. The resulting grimace couldn't have done much to set them at ease.

"Sorry… 'bout the roof," I managed.

The woman looked up, as though it hadn't occurred to her until that moment that there might be anything wrong with her roof. When she saw the Damasco-shaped hole my arrival had torn, her line-webbed face drooped.

On impulse, I fumbled in my pouch, drew out an onyx and pressed it into her hand.

She seemed confused at first. Then understanding dawned, bringing a toothless grin of sudden comprehension. "Thank ye," she mumbled. "That'll do nice."

"Are you a god?" piped up the smallest child. His tone implied that if I were it would explain to his satisfaction the events of the last two minutes.

I struggled to my feet, unsure until the very last instant that I could manage so complex an endeavour. Everything hurt, but nothing appeared broken. "I'm just a man," I said. "A man with the worst luck in the world."

The child nodded sagely, as though this were every bit as reasonable.

"Well," I said. "Thanks for your hospitality."

I hurried out through the dirty blanket passing for a door, before any further conversation could develop. In the street, I glanced sharply to left and right. I'd half expected to see Synza out there waiting for me. But I wouldn't, of course – for any number of reasons. Unless he'd somehow broken into the tower and found my rope or else leapt from the walls, his only option would have been to leave by the nearest gate. Even with a fast horse, it would take him a few minutes to work his way round.

Then again, if he *had* somehow found a way down, I still wouldn't see him. Not until it was too late, and probably not even then. What had happened there on the walls, be it luck or instinct, it had saved my life by only the narrowest of margins. Whichever it was, I hoped I'd never have to rely on it again. Because Synza wasn't the type to miss twice.

I had to get moving. But where? There was little hope of covering my tracks when I'd left a gaping hole in some old woman's roof, and limping and bedraggled, I'd struggle to melt into even the most dishevelled of crowds. If Synza was determined to find me, the best I could hope for was to delay him.

I started walking. I'd no particular course in mind, except to move in the opposite direction to the one I assumed Synza would appear from. That led me towards the river. The obvious option was to seek out Alvantes and reclaim my money. Yet every minute could cost me dearly now, and for once, my bag of wealth didn't seem the most important thing in the world. I had a few coins. I had my new clothes and lock picks. Those possessions might not promise much in the way of a new life, but what good was a new life if I wasn't alive to enjoy it?

I ducked into a narrow alley between wood-walled shanties. For all that the Suburbs were a slum, they did have a very few things in common with the city they clung to. In places, they had proper streets, even sometimes lined with planks. They had their landmarks; buildings built up and repaired where others had been torn apart for salvage. If you were lucky, you could even find the occasional signpost.

As such, they weren't quite the navigational horror a casual glance would suggest. After a couple more turns, I realised where my unconscious route was leading. I was nearing Navare's outpost. It was as though my bag of money were a thread that guided me, whether I wanted it to or not.

No. Not just the money. If I let them, my thoughts kept turning to Mounteban's scowling, eye-patched face. It was a face I could happily have buried my fist in. How much ill-treatment could I reasonably suffer at the hands of that bloated crook? Insults were one thing; putting a trained killer on my heels was another entirely. The thought of him basking like a toad over Altapasaeda, over the entire Castoval even, made my blood boil.

I'd go back for the money. But if my information happened to get that despicable gouger spitted on Alvantes's blade, so much the better.

A muddy back way deposited me a short distance from Navare's reinforced door. I darted over, trying to remember the sequence of knocks Alvantes had used earlier – for something told me Navare wasn't the type to ask polite questions of unexpected guests.

I raised my fist to knock – and froze. I couldn't put a name to what I'd felt, but it was exactly what had saved my life up on the tower. Yet when I glanced back the way I'd come, there was no flicker of movement. Were my nerves playing tricks? Could I really have lost Synza? He'd shown himself a more than capable tracker when I'd travelled in his company. Then again, I'd seen almost no one, it was a dark night and I'd taken care to leave no signs of my passage. However good Synza might be, he was only human.

I strained my eyes against the gloom. When Synza once more failed to leap from the shadows, I turned my attention reluctantly back to the door. I mentally repeated Alvantes's complicated knock, and once I was sure I had it right, played it out on the boards: three raps, two short taps, a pause and one final, sharp beat.

I'd barely finished before the door swung inward – and I found myself staring down the groove of a loaded crossbow. By the time I'd registered that development, a hand had darted to drag me inside and the door had slammed behind my back. The crossbow, however, never left the vicinity of my face.

"Nice toy," I told Navare, forcing the tremor out of my voice.

"Quiet." A single candle lit the shack. Alvantes was a brutal silhouette against its glow.

There were others. As my eyes began to adjust, I realised everyone who'd been here when I left was still crammed into the confined space. Saltlick was a hulking outline in one corner; Alvantes's guardsmen were arrayed along one wall. No wonder the air was close and noisome.

"A good job I didn't trust you to wait for me," I told Alvantes. "I'd be swimming the Casto Mara with a dozen arrows in me by now."

"With the commotion you caused, it's a miracle either of us made it back. What the Hells did you do in there?"

Navare lowered the crossbow, grudgingly. "And were you followed?"

Did I tell them about Synza?

I wanted to. The burden of knowing he might be still hunting me weighed heavily. Why should I bear it alone? It might even be that someone could suggest a way out of this mess that didn't involve my sudden death.

Or, far more likely, they'd show not the barest interest in my survival. In fact, Alvantes might even tether me outside as bait. Even if, against all odds and his own character, he sympathised with my plight, what could he do? What could *anyone* do? Either Synza had returned to Mounteban and reported his failure, or my continuing existence was numbered in days at best.

Whatever the case, my best hope of survival lay in company. This room was as safe a haven as I could hope for. Four sturdy, windowless walls, a reinforced door and a dozen guardsmen would be proof against even the finest of killers. Until I had a better idea, it made sense to keep myself and everyone else here for as long as I could. Moreover, I stood a better chance of manoeuvring Alvantes if he was in the dark about my motives.

I realised whole seconds had passed since Navare's question, and that he was now staring at me with obvious suspicion. "I don't think so," I told him, trying to sound as though I'd been musing over the possibility. "I was chased, but I lost them at the walls." As far as I knew, it might even be the truth.

"Let's hope so," he replied, not trying to hide the distrust in his voice.

Alvantes stepped closer to the candlelight. "What did you find? I assume they weren't turning the city upside down looking for you for no reason."

"You won't like it," I said.

"I didn't expect to."

"It's Mounteban. Castilio Mounteban is running Altapasaeda."

There was a gasp from the darkness. It could only have been Estrada. Given their history – Mounteban's puppyish affection, which had almost ended in rape when he realised just how unrequited it was, and his subsequent betrayal of her and her cause to Moaradrid – I could understand that the name might provoke a certain reaction.

Alvantes's face, meanwhile, was blank as uncut stone, and bloodless in the flickering half-light. "You're certain?"

"I saw him," I said. "I heard him speak. He's brought the heads of family together, along with the gang leaders and I'd guess a couple of Moaradrid's generals. He was talking about a coalition, running the city and then the whole of Castoval. Only knowing Mounteban, it's going to be a coalition of one by the time he's done."

"This changes things."

"Damn right it does. So what's the plan? Mounteban was talking about reopening the gates. You lie low for a few days, wait for things to quiet down and then…"

"How many armed men did you see in there, Damasco?"

Taken aback, I struggled to add up the numerous patrols I'd passed with the ones I'd subsequently been chased by. "A lot."

"Let's suppose that's only a fraction of the forces at Mounteban's disposal," Alvantes continued.

"I'd say that's a safe assumption."

"And it isn't only numbers. As much as they might not like him or his methods, Mounteban's telling everyone what they want to hear – in some cases, what they've wanted to hear for years. We can't walk in there to arrest him and expect the city to just fall in behind us."

"Who said anything about arresting? I was thinking something more along the lines of…"

Alvantes shook his head. It seemed more for his benefit than ours. "It would get too messy," he said, "and it would take too long. Moreover, with the resources we have, it would probably go against us. Anyhow, I made a vow and I intend to keep it. The King has to know his son is dead. If he can forgive me that failure, perhaps he'll offer the help we need."

"What?" I stared in disbelief. Similar expressions were upon the dim faces watching from around the room. "Isn't your job to arrest criminals? Mounteban's only gone and stolen an entire city."

"Guard-Captain…" began Navare, and trailed off, leaving the obvious strain in his voice to say what words had failed to.

"Mounteban's juggling fire trying to hold so many factions together. He has to keep up the illusion that his way is better for everyone… at least for the moment." I'd never heard Alvantes sound defensive before. It fit ill with the bass growl of his voice. "Navare, I know you – I know all of you – want to see this done. But it's already gone beyond a simple question of guarding the city. We topple Mounteban and what happens? Who takes his place? No. This is the King's business as much as it is ours."

What was wrong with the man? Where had this sudden rush of caution come from? My only shot at safety was rapidly diminishing. I racked my brains for some argument that might sway him, some memory of Mounteban's speech that would demand urgent action.

Then it struck me. Any attempt I made to convince Alvantes was bound to have precisely the opposite effect. I was the last person in the room he'd listen to. All I could hope now was that Synza had given up the chase – or else, for a quick and relatively painless end.

It seemed the mood of the whole room mirrored my own. With the conversation ground to a halt, quiet hung heavy. It was Estrada who eventually broke the silence, and she made no effort to hide the deliberate change in subject. "You must be exhausted, Easie."

I'd hardly noticed it for the still-ebbing adrenalin of the chase, my many bruises and the rising pain of where Synza's knife had nicked my head, but she was right. The fatigue of the night's travails was creeping up on me fast. If I didn't lie down soon, I'd collapse where I stood. Perhaps the morning would offer an argument to sway Alvantes, some way to duck the noose that seemed to be abruptly closing round my neck.

One matter, however, couldn't wait. "Aren't you forgetting something?" I asked Alvantes.

His expression clouded for a moment. Then he said, "Of course. You want your thievings back."

"Manners, please. Remember the terms of our arrangement."

Alvantes reached into a pocket. "Easie Damasco, it's my honour to return to you this bag containing your hard-earned gains. May they bring you great and unceasing joy."

There was something oddly charming in his woeful attempt at sarcasm. "It's been a pleasure doing business, Guard-Captain."

"Damasco… you did good work in there. I only wish you could have done it of your own free will."

"And I wish every night for a mansion made of gold. But I'll still wake up tomorrow in this reeking shed."

Alvantes shook his head. "Thank you. Whenever I'm fool enough to imagine there might be hope for you, I can rely on you to prove me wrong."

I offered him a weary bow. "Disappointing expectations is what I do best."

• • • •

If I'd expected sleep, it was a vain hope indeed.

For a start, there was Saltlick, who could have comfortably occupied the room by himself. As if that weren't enough, Alvantes insisted on cordoning off another corner to preserve Estrada's modesty, presumably to protect her against those of us with the ability to see through blankets and layers of clothing in pitch darkness. That done, there remained roughly enough floor space for four people to bed down, assuming they didn't value comfort even slightly.

Including the guardsmen and Navare, there were sixteen of us.

I ended up in the square of ground beneath the small table, knees and elbows tucked in to minimize contact with my nearest neighbours. The thought of even trying to rest made me despondent. In desperation, I asked, "Does nobody want to hear the story of how I made it out of Altapasaeda alive?"

"Sleep well, Easie," said Estrada from somewhere in the darkness.

"Says the only person in the room with an actual bed," I told her, and shut my eyes.

I woke from nebulous, alarming dreams to agony that made my earlier discomfort seem like bliss. I wasn't sure I'd ever be able to stretch my arms and legs properly again, and my flesh felt like one colossal bruise reaching into the depths of my bones. These sensations came to me hazily, though, through a murk of half-awakeness – and were all the worse for that. I lay caught between the hope of somehow drifting into a sleep too deep for pain and of the morning arriving to offer some reprieve.

I was actually glad when Alvantes rose and one by one roused the guardsmen. I rubbed the life tentatively back into my legs, stretching them by increments until I was confident they'd hold my weight. That done, getting to my feet was merely excruciating. A hesitant inspection of my calves and forearms revealed compelling evidence that I'd been beaten from head to toe. I supposed that falling through roofs, however flimsy, might give that impression.

I didn't need to see outside to know we were up well before dawn. A dull sense of wrongness told me I was awake at an hour never intended for human activity. Alvantes, however, seemed as impervious as ever to a need for physical rest. Had the King arrived just then and demanded an inspection, I had no doubt he'd have passed with a commendation.

He gave us time enough for a brief breakfast – some flavourless, hard biscuit pitted with flecks of dried olives Navare had a store of – before launching into the morning's speechifying.

"Guardsmen, here are your instructions. Sub-Captain Gueverro will travel back to our barracks to command the men there. You'll remain here under the leadership of Navare, who henceforward also bears the rank of sub-captain. In brief, your orders are these: Learn what you can; keep your presence hidden; *do not* attempt to enter the city or interfere with Mounteban's regime in my absence. I know how you feel. I feel the same. But we are not mercenaries. Our first and foremost duty is to King Panchessa, and it's for him to decide what happens next."

Though the only reply was a chorused "Yes, sir," it was easy to sense the dissatisfaction in the room. These men were Altapasaedans born and bred. The City Guard had a tendency to inherit wayward sons from the wealthier families, whilst amongst the middle classes it was deemed a mostly respectable mode of employment. Every one of them had family inside those walls; every one had more vested in ridding the city of Mounteban than Alvantes did.

So would they obey him? Probably, for a while. Absurd as it was, there was an aura to Alvantes, a palpable air of nobility that made it difficult even to think of crossing him. Words became inarguable simply by leaving his mouth. Still, he wasn't going to be around to keep them in check. How long would auras and fine-sounding words last in his absence?

Whatever the future might hold, Alvantes had more immediate worries. As he was making the last preparations to leave, Estrada touched his shoulder. "You're not going anywhere," she said softly, "until I've cleaned and rebandaged your arm. Ointment to hurry the healing and medicine for the pain would be a good idea as well."

"Marina," Alvantes replied gruffly, "there's more at stake here than my discomfort."

For someone who'd once been romantically entangled with our good lady mayor, I was frequently amazed by how little Alvantes seemed to understand her. I'd recognised her tone, even if he hadn't, and it brooked no argument. "Perhaps," she said, "but there's nothing more important than your ability to lead.

These men and everyone in Altapasaeda are relying on you to make the right decisions. If you carry on like this, you'll be in no state to do that."

"Are you suggesting I *haven't* made the right decision?"

Estrada sighed heavily. "What I'm suggesting is that you've recently suffered an appalling injury, lost copious amounts of blood, been through terrible exertion and stress and are in constant pain, and maybe, just maybe, you should address those facts, lest your judgement be clouded or you simply collapse."

"I've no intention of collapsing," said Alvantes.

In a flash of inspiration, I said, "Estrada, why don't Saltlick and I buy medical supplies while you two collect the horses? We can meet where the north road leaves the Suburbs."

Alvantes looked at me with unveiled suspicion. "You've got your money back, Damasco. If you want to sneak off then there's nothing to stop you."

I did my best to look hurt. "Like I said, I'll meet you on the north road. Weren't you the one who said I ought to be pulling my weight? I can save us time and you'll be a little less likely to pass out on us like an old drunk."

"Thank you, Easie," intervened Estrada, "that sounds like an excellent solution."

This time, there was no talk of hiding Saltlick. Mounteban knew we were here, and the odds of Navare and the guardsmen staying hidden were greatly improved by his believing we'd left.

None of that made Alvantes any more patient as Saltlick struggled to manoeuvre through the too-small opening. One slip and he'd likely have removed the entire front wall; if anyone happened to be passing at such an hour, it was a spectacle they couldn't possibly miss.

That suited me. So did Saltlick's company. If Synza was somehow following me, I couldn't think of any discreet ways to assassinate a giant, or to kill someone they were walking beside without said giant noticing. And if we ran into any other of Mounteban's lackeys, they'd be unlikely to know how harmless Saltlick was, or be inclined to tangle with someone fully twice their size.

I bid Navare and the others a brief goodbye and set out in the pre-sunrise gloom. I didn't see anyone in the darkened street. By then, I hardly expected to. Beneath the first grey light of day, it no longer seemed likely that Synza should have spent the night scouring the Suburbs for my trail. Far more probably, he'd returned to Mounteban with a report of how I'd fallen from the walls with a knife wound to the head. He had no reason to assume I'd survived, or even to waste time investigating.

Caught in the rush of the chase, I'd let paranoia get the better of me. Mounteban had once told me, in what seemed a distant other lifetime, that I was only one detail of a bigger picture. That was even truer now than it had been then, and I doubted very much that he'd want his best killer running round needlessly in such a time of crisis.

That said, it was still comforting to walk beside Saltlick, with all the safety his presence implied. Overwhelming pacifism aside, I couldn't have asked for a better bodyguard. By the time I arrived at the small apothecary I'd settled on, I felt considerably less vulnerable than when I'd set out.

The wizened hag who ran the place was just opening up. She greeted my arrival with an unintelligible mumble and a noisy expectoration into the mud. Whether or not that peculiar greeting related to having a giant appear at her doorstep, she didn't seem put off by Saltlick's presence. I hurriedly bought fresh bandages, a pot of pasty green ointment, and a vial of brown ichor that she claimed – as far as I could translate her grunts and mumbles – would alleviate even the worst extremes of pain. On second thoughts, I bought a second vial for myself. Why should Alvantes be the only one free of suffering?

My purchases deposited in my new pack, we set out towards the north road junction. Saltlick and I arrived just as Alvantes and Estrada trotted up from another side road, Estrada leading the horse I'd borrowed when we left the barracks. We greeted each other with silent nods. Even Saltlick sensed the general mood and kept himself to a timid smile.

I handed my purchases to Alvantes and clambered into the saddle. In single file, we made our way out past the scattered border of the Suburbs. As we passed the last tumbledown shack, I couldn't help noticing how Alvantes glanced back towards the distant walls. His expression was grim beyond measure.

Who could blame him? Altapasaeda, Lady of the South, was fallen – and whatever her fate over the next few days, it lay in Mounteban's hands, not his.

CHAPTER FIVE

Our first stop would be Muena Palaiya, Estrada's erstwhile home and seat of mayoral power. In theory, it was three days' easy ride away. In practise, things were likely to prove a little more complicated.

The Sabre and the highway beyond it offered by far the fastest passage northward. Of the many advantages Mounteban possessed in holding Altapasaeda, that might prove most telling in the long term. With the bridge unavailable and the docks closed to traffic, the rest of southern Castoval would soon grind to a halt. Already the river was almost empty of boats, just as the road was clear of wagons.

Our only alternative was to head north-west on this bank and ford the Casto Mara where we could, then travel on through the forest of Paen Acha. Even that would have been simple enough until recently, but the ferry at Casta Canto had fallen victim to our dramatic flight south, and I couldn't imagine they'd returned it to working order in a mere few days.

I had a feeling no one had pointed this out to

Alvantes. I was looking forward to the look on his face when he found out. Even if anything that thwarted his plans thwarted mine as well, it would still be entertaining.

However, I soon discovered he had more pressing issues on his mind than our travel plans. We were barely an hour out of Altapasaeda when Alvantes drew his horse alongside mine. "You remember the giant stronghold?" he asked.

I tried to hide my surprise at so unexpected a question. "I'm not sure I'd call it a stronghold."

"I was barely conscious. You saw far more of it than I did."

"It's a nice place. Are you considering a holiday?"

He ignored me. "You met other giants there."

"Plenty of them."

Alvantes nodded towards Saltlick, who was lumbering a few paces ahead, his relaxed gait more than sufficient to keep pace with our horses. "Tell me. Are they all like him?"

"Not all. Most of the ones I met were female."

Alvantes frowned. "I mean, are they all so... passive? So submissive?"

"I didn't have to break up any fights while I was there, if that's what you mean. What are you driving at?" But I didn't really need to ask. Alvantes had been thinking about the giants waiting ahead. He'd been tormenting himself over his mistress Altapasaeda, currently trolloping herself with another man. Then he'd brought those thoughts together and realised he had the start of an idea.

It wasn't an idea I much liked. The giants had already been abducted once, already forced into violence by Moaradrid. You didn't need to be an expert in giantish culture to realise it ran against everything in their nature. "Yes," I said, "they were all like Saltlick. More so, if anything. The place was a haven of tranquillity. You'd have hated it."

Alvantes eyed me coldly, as though trying to weigh the truth of what I'd said. "Maybe they've just never found the right cause," he observed finally.

Before I could point out that liberating a bunch of spoilt Altapasaedans was probably the least right cause imaginable for giantkind, he spurred his horse forward in a clatter of hooves.

I glared after him, my already doubtful mood entirely soured by the exchange. Casting about for something that might cheer me up, I remembered the pain medicine I'd bought in the Suburbs. I drew it from my pocket, made a brief attempt to read the spidery writing on the label, then gave up and downed the lot in one sharp gulp.

Its taste brought back vivid memories of my time in the sewers. However, if its flavour was beyond repellent, its effects soon began to make up for it. It slowly dawned on me that the countless agonies that filled me from head to toe were being replaced by a mild but pleasant tingling. Everything around me had acquired a golden tinge, which shimmered whenever I moved my eyes. It was interesting enough that I began to rock my head from side to side, curious as to what speeds and angles would produce the most vivid results.

"You should take your medicine," I called to Alvantes. "It's good stuff."

He didn't even bother to look back. "Some of us need to be alert."

"There's nothing to be alert to. If you can't be alert to something, you might as well enjoy not being alert to nothing." This made perfect sense in my head. Another side effect of the pain medicine was an instinctive feeling that, whatever the evidence to the contrary, all was basically right in the world.

As for Alvantes, he merely shook his head and went on riding.

Though I suspected I might be missing the intricacies of the question, my basic point was sound. The region north of Altapasaeda was scenic, dull, and utterly devoid of danger. At first, we'd passed by the great farm estates that serviced and mostly belonged to the Altapasaedan wealthy. Amidst the scattered workshops of stonemasons and carpenters were aviaries and apiaries, orchards and great, vivid plantations of flowers, all laid out in intricate tapestries that spread between the mountains on one side and the river on the other.

As the morning wore on, the farmlands grew more prosaic. Here was the belt of land where everyday produce was grown, both for Altapasaeda and for much of the land further north. Presently we passed between expanses of sunflowers on the one hand and rye grass on the other. According to my current perceptions, every flower and head wore an aureole of gold that shimmered whenever it shifted in the breeze.

The effect was beginning to grow a little nauseating. By the time we stopped for a brief roadside lunch, I was starting to wonder if the pain had really been so bad after all. When I turned down the share of bread and salt fish Estrada proffered, she looked at me with grave concern.

"Easie… you never say no to food."

"Not feeling so good," I mumbled. "Not sure 'bout that medicine."

"Can I see it?"

I handed her the small bottle.

Estrada plucked out the bung and sniffed it. "You didn't really drink all of this, did you?"

I nodded delicately, conscious of how every small movement made my stomach swirl.

"Oh, Easie. That quantity should have lasted you a week."

"Doesn't hurt," I managed.

"I'm amazed you can feel anything. Can you still ride?"

"Think so."

I could, so long as I kept my head still and my eyes more or less closed. That suited me just fine. It was a lot like being asleep, though I was vaguely conscious of the fields sliding by to either side, of Saltlick clumping just ahead, of mingled farmland smells and the mellow warmth of the midday sun.

Only when we drew within the verge of the western forest did I start to grow aware again. I felt better in the shade, and even dared turn my head to examine the way we'd come. Only Estrada was behind me.

She seemed to have stationed herself as far from Alvantes as possible, though I hadn't noticed any falling out between them. Had she finally realised what an obnoxious lunk he was? More likely, it was some expression of womanly emotion that I stood no hope of fathoming.

When she caught my eye, she gave a brittle smile. I did my best to return it.

Beyond Estrada, the highway stretched as far as I could see. It ran in gentle curves all the way back to Altapasaeda, now no more than a haze on the very edge of vision. Its dusty surface was unspoiled by any hint of life.

Except – was that a figure in the very far distance? For an instant, I was sure a speck of darkness stood out on the road's pale surface. I blinked, just as my horse stepped into a patch of shadow. Suddenly, I couldn't be certain.

Anyway... so what if someone *was* behind us? Even with Altapasaeda shut off from the wider Castoval, there must still be the occasional traveller. I tried to remember my determination not to let paranoia get the better of me.

The day wore on, and steadily I found I was feeling better. My head cleared, returning the world by degrees to its usual range of brightnesses and colours. My stomach began to grumble with hunger rather than the urge to empty itself. Most cheeringly, the pain medicine had actually done its work; I was astonished to find that my bruises had even started to fade.

By mid-afternoon, we'd joined the road that would take us the last distance back towards the Casto Mara. The main highway ran on towards the small town of Muena Delorca. Our course, meanwhile, angled sharply aside and into denser forest. It was still there, very quiet, the greenery broken only by the occasional small hamlet or charcoal burner's hut, their rooftops licking the sky with tongues of smoke.

I felt calmer than I had since this nonsense with Altapasaeda began. Had the company been less dull, the travelling might even have been pleasant. Alvantes was his usual brooding self, and even Estrada, who could normally be relied on for misguided optimism, was unusually subdued. I had no doubt it was Alvantes she was worrying about, not herself – and my suspicion was confirmed when she suggested we stop for a break.

"If we hurry, we can be across the river before sunset," noted Alvantes.

"A few minutes won't make much difference," replied Estrada.

"Why waste time we can't spare?"

"Because… Lunto, your arm…"

My gaze followed hers, as did Alvantes's own. He was quick to dip his injured limb out of view – but not so quick that we didn't all see how bright splotches of red stood out on the bandaged stump.

"Look," she said, "there's a glade. The horses would like a rest even if you wouldn't."

Alvantes's mount, an excitable stallion I'd once nicknamed Killer, whinnied vigorously. It sounded like agreement, but might just as well have been the expression of his latest murderous impulse.

"All right," Alvantes said. "For a short while."

I couldn't but smile. How typical of Alvantes to take the word of his horse over the woman who anyone else could see still held feelings for him!

The clearing was a good choice on Estrada's part, an hourglass of open ground hemmed in by close-packed trees, its sward puddled with patches of foxglove and nettle. It was evidently a popular spot with travellers, for rectangles of blanched grass showed where tents had recently been pitched, and the detritus of many a fire littered a shallow pit towards the centre.

Once we'd dismounted, Estrada insisted on ministering to Alvantes. His initial resistance was met with sharp words, and after that, he bore with it stoically. Saltlick, meanwhile, settled on his haunches at the edge of the woodland and began harvesting leaves for an early supper. Not for the first time, I envied his ability to eat seemingly anything.

Despite what Alvantes had said, it was clear we'd be stopping for a while. Hunting in my pockets for something to amuse myself with, I happened upon the lock picks, needle, and thread I'd bought from Franco.

I remembered immediately what my intention had been. It wasn't something I felt like doing in sight of Alvantes and Estrada, so I wandered to the far end of the glade, where I'd be sheltered from view by the encroaching forest. A tree on the perimeter had been sheared by storms, and the shattered trunk made a convenient seat. I shrugged my cloak off, peeled my shirt over my head, climbed up and perched cross-legged.

I might not be thieving as much as I was accustomed to, but some things I couldn't bear to be without. I'd been given my first lock picks when I was thirteen, and had rarely lacked for a set since. They always came in handy sooner or later, and often when I least expected it.

Buying three sets might seem excessive, but I had my reasons. I started with the shirt, taking the utmost care. Then I drew it back on and moved onto the cloak. It was a shame to unpick so excellently sewed a lining, but I knew my clumsy repairs would make the subterfuge all the more effective.

I was almost done when four things happened, in such close succession that I could hardly separate them. I heard Alvantes call my name. Alarmed, I rocked backwards, lost my balance. As the world began to spin away, I thought I saw a flash of motion in the far tree line. A sound, as of a large insect, whirred past my ear.

The next I knew I was tumbling back, my head barely missing a tree trunk. The grass wasn't as soft as it looked; my drug-benumbed bruises woke with a jolt.

Stumbling to my feet, I snarled, "What's wrong with you? Sneaking up like that."

"What's this, Damasco?"

Alvantes was looking at my cloak. I'd dropped it when I fell, and the carefully secreted picks had tumbled from the half-sewn seam.

Well, there was no law against carrying lock picks,

even if Alvantes were in a position to enforce it. "I thought they might come in handy," I said.

"Already planning your return to a life of petty crime?"

I was in no mood for jibes. My bruises ached and my right ear stung furiously. "It isn't twenty-four hours since you were begging me to break into Altapasaeda. Why don't you stick to your misguided heroics and I'll help in my own way?"

He looked ready to argue. Instead, with an obvious effort of self-control, he said, "Any decent search would turn them up."

"A decent search would turn up the set in the right pocket. A *determined* search would find the second set hidden in the lining. That still leaves the third set I've sewn into the collar of my shirt."

He considered. Then, to my surprise, he asked, "What about something bigger? Could you apply the same principle?"

"I don't see why not. Most people are basically lazy. The trick with misdirection is to give them something they expect. If they expect to find something and do, nine times in ten they'll stop looking."

Alvantes nodded thoughtfully. His next words were even more unexpected. "Can I borrow that needle and thread when you're done?"

"I suppose."

"Thank you. Oh, and Damasco," he said, touching fingers to the side of his own neck, "you're bleeding."

I mirrored the gesture. Sure enough, my fingers came back slick with red.

"You should be more careful falling off logs," said Alvantes, and turned back towards the wider clearing.

But I hadn't cut myself when I fell.

I felt suddenly cold, despite the late afternoon warmth. My gaze darted to the far trees, where I'd thought just for an instant that I'd seen movement. There was nothing now. I turned, drawing a mental line across the clearing. The chill deepened, settled in my spine. Buried finger-deep in a tree trunk, directly behind where I'd sat, a thin-bladed knife jutted.

I stared at it in horror. Though I was certain death hovered invisibly nearby, I couldn't help but reach to yank it free. It was light as a feather, delicately balanced – the weapon of a master.

The spell broke. Panic took over. I vaulted the tree trunk, caught my cloak and picks and dashed after Alvantes.

Estrada looked up. "Are you all right?"

"We need to go," I said. "Right now."

"What?"

I strove to steady my voice. "Alvantes is right. If we hurry, we've a chance of a decent night's rest. One more night sleeping rough will be the death of me."

"We were about to set out anyway," said Alvantes.

I grasped my horse's bridle and swung into the saddle. Common sense told me that if Synza was willing to kill me in sight of the others he'd have done it already – but common sense was a whisper in the back of my mind compared to the fear screeching through the rest of it. It was excruciating to wait for Alvantes, Estrada and Saltlick to fall in. I set a quick pace for the first ten minutes, until their curious glances and the undeniable absence of killers leaping from the forest began to calm me a little.

Only then did the realisation truly sink in… Synza had waited to get me alone. So long as I had company, I was safe.

I dropped back to ride between Alvantes and Estrada, ignoring the looks they gave me. My mind was still awhirl. Now, however, it was less fear, more the simple question of self-preservation that set my thoughts spinning.

It wasn't one I had any easy answers to. Only when we came in sight of the Casto Mara did the inkling of an idea present itself. As I'd suspected, the ferry had yet to be repaired. In its place, though, a crude and presumably temporary replica had been constructed. Ropes were strung taut across the river, a rough platform had been constructed from cut logs with mounted metal wheels at either end, and two burly men were hauling it by hand from bank to bank. It was less than half the size of the old ferry and looked distinctly rickety, but it was a way across.

Ever so slowly, the two ferrymen heaved their makeshift transport over from the far bank. When they arrived, they passed another five minutes in whispered conversation, sparing us only the occasional glance.

Estrada was first to lose her patience. "May I ask what the problem is?"

The nearest ferryman looked at her uneasily. "Thing is," he said, "we've rates for people and rates for horses.

We don't have rates for…" He pointed at Saltlick. "For anything like *that*."

"Saltlick is a giant," she said tartly, "but I don't think he'd been offended if you chose to consider him a horse for the duration of our trip."

Saltlick nodded sagaciously. "Horse good."

The ferryman's expression brightened. "Horse it is then. All aboard!"

As it turned out, the craft was sturdier than it appeared. Casta Canto was a logging town after all, and if the folk knew little else they knew wood. After a few minutes, I let myself ignore our creeping, creaking progress in favour of thinking over my next move.

When, what seemed at least an hour later, we brushed against the rough harbour of Casta Canto, my scheme was ready. As Estrada went to pay the two ferrymen I said, "I'll get this. Why don't you go ahead and find us somewhere for the night?"

"Where can we rent rooms?" Estrada asked the ferrymen.

One pointed to a two-storey building a little way up the main street. "Try the *Bear Trap* first," he said. "Lindi's been cooking up a batch of her famous boar stew."

Estrada nodded and set off, with Alvantes and Saltlick close behind.

"So," I said, "What do we owe?"

The man attempted to calculate on his fingers. "A twelfth-onyx for each of you," he said, "two each for the horses… another two for the man-horse…"

"Let's call it an onyx," I said. "Now, how much more would it take for you to close the ferry for the rest of the day? In fact, to close it and make sure it stays closed until noon tomorrow?"

He squinted in concentration. "We'd have shut up soon enough anyway."

"It has to be now. No more passengers today."

"It'll mean a whole night's drinking," he said, as though this were the only conceivable outcome.

"And the morning too," inserted his companion.

"Ah, right. That's... well, three bottles each, at a pinch..."

I held out two more onyxes. "Will that cover it?"

His eyes widened. "It might."

"No more passengers. I'll be checking."

"No need for that." He sounded faintly offended. "With what this'll pay for, that ferry might be down for a week."

By the time I reached the *Bear Trap*, the others were just leaving. "What's the problem?" I asked.

"They only have two rooms available," Estrada told me.

That sounded like excellent news to me. "Let's not be needlessly extravagant. Why can't Alvantes and I share?"

Estrada eyed me with astonishment bordering on horror. "Weren't you the one who swore another night without a bed would be the death of you?"

It might. But not as quickly as having a room to myself would if Synza found a way across the Casto Mara. The little bastard had managed to keep up so far. He was nothing if not resourceful. "Our money won't last forever," I pointed out. "Who knows what surprises might be waiting? Let's be practical."

Estrada looked at Alvantes. "He has a point."

"I am not sharing a bed with Damasco."

"I'll take the floor," I said. "I'm sure they can rustle up a few spare blankets."

Alvantes shook his head wearily. "I can't but wonder what goes on in your mind, Damasco. Very well then, if coin is so much more important to you than comfort."

"Coin," I said, "is more important to me than anything. You should know that by now."

Once we'd settled in, my first step was to find a quiet corner of the taproom in which to finish sewing the lock picks into my cloak. This time no one paid me any heed, and I was done in minutes. I sought out Alvantes, where he was tending the horses in the stables to the rear. I nodded to Saltlick, comfortably installed in a double stall no doubt intended for carriages rather than giants, and handed Alvantes my needle and thread. "I suppose there's no point asking what it is you want to hide?"

Alvantes opened his cloak, revealing a rip in the lining. "Who said I want to hide anything?"

He had, of course. Not explicitly, maybe, but Alvantes wasn't one to ask idle questions – or for that matter, to concern himself with a torn lining. Still, if this was how he wanted to play it, I was confident I could find other ways to satisfy my curiosity. I left him to it and, having stepped outside to confirm that the ferry operators had indeed quit their work, returned to the taproom and settled to a cup of wine.

The next I saw of Alvantes was well over an hour later, just as dinner was called, when he handed back my needle and a much-diminished spool of thread.

"May I admire your handiwork?" I asked.

He drew back his cloak, revealing a neat line of stitches. Well, neat it might be, but there was no way it had consumed such quantity of thread as was missing. What *was* the man up to?

It was a mystery that would have to wait. I was worn out – from the long day's journeying, from my healing injuries, from the lingering effects of the pain medicine and the shock of my most recent brush with death. Dinner, the promised and surprisingly delicious boar stew, was the straw that broke me. Never mind that my bed was a heap of blankets on the floor; never mind my fears that Synza might have made it across the river. I barely had time to close my eyes before sleep hauled me down into its depths.

I woke feeling almost refreshed.

After a breakfast of stewed plums, Estrada insisted on redressing Alvantes's arm, and I ventured out to check the ferry. It was tied off to the harbour, just as I'd left it. I considered hacking through one of the overhanging ropes, but I doubted Synza would have waited on the far bank, or that the two ferrymen would be in any state to renege on our bargain. No, my best hope now lay in widening whatever start I'd gained.

With that in mind, I insisted on taking the lead when we set out again, and on maintaining the fastest pace I could without drawing comment from Alvantes and Estrada. When we'd passed this way in the opposite direction, Estrada, Saltlick and I had been forced to travel cross-country, led by that despicable shark Mounteban. This time we followed the winding main road out of Casta Canto, which led east and a little north. If it was quicker, the going was still frustratingly slow and dull.

Evening found us out of Paen Acha proper, in the eastern region where the forest broke into scattered woodland and wild meadows. We stopped at a small village I was barely familiar with and paid for lodgings in its dingy, weather-beaten inn. The fact that I'd seen no sign of Synza had done nothing to alleviate my worries, so I was glad to find that in place of rooms the inn had two large dormitories, one for men and women each.

Somehow, despite the fact that most of the beds were occupied by raucously snoring loggers, I managed another sound night's sleep. As we set out the next day, my mood was almost upbeat. We made good speed in the morning, and by lunch we'd joined the north-south highway, the last vestiges of woodland behind us. Far ahead, high above, Muena Palaiya was visible as a spatter of white in the weak sunlight, where its southernmost edge showed above the plateau called the Hunch.

Only then did I start to realise how misjudged my good humour was.

It crept upon me slowly – a subtle sense of wrongness. The few people we passed were sullen and uncommunicative, just as the inn's small staff had been the night before. They looked furtive, on edge, expressions that summoned all-too-ready memories of our time in the Suburbs. One or two I could ignore, but each downturned face, each averted eye, reinforced my doubts. As much as I told myself it didn't mean anything, I couldn't believe it.

We spent the afternoon crawling towards the broadening line of white that was Muena Palaiya. Once we'd passed the crossroads, where the road down from the mountains met the highway, our route began to climb – steadily at first and then more steeply. I found myself watching Estrada. She'd been absent for days. Would it be unreasonable to expect her to look pleased at the sight of her home? Yet as the afternoon wore on, all I could see was tension that set like mortar, drawing her face into harder and harder lines.

When we crested the edge of the plateau late in the afternoon, I realised the gates were closed. Well, there was nothing so strange in that. They were often kept shut. I couldn't even say why the sight unsettled me.

I glanced again at Estrada. Her countenance was rigid.

I knew Muena Palaiya as well as I did anywhere. I couldn't see anything out of place. Had she noticed some detail I was missing? It struck me that there were no guards on the walls either, nor anywhere in sight. Yet even that wasn't entirely unexpected. After all, hadn't most of the local guardsmen died in the fight against Moaradrid?

We were almost at the gates when Estrada called a halt – and said aloud what I was trying so hard not to think.

"Can you feel it?" Her voice was stiff with forced calm. "It's not just Altapasaeda. Something's wrong here too."

CHAPTER SIX

We guided the horses to the side of the road, dismounted at a point where a stand of ragged trees hid us from view. The surest sign of the unease in our small party was that Saltlick didn't immediately start devouring the foliage. Instead, he watched Estrada with a steady, sorrowful gaze, evidently sensing her disquiet but not knowing how to help.

Would that Alvantes were so tactful. "I'm not doubting you, Marina," he said. "But consider the strain you've been under these last days. Probably what you're noticing is just the disturbance of everything that's happened lately. After all, Muena Palaiya's been without a mayor, and without most of its guard."

"Lunto… something's wrong. I know this town better than I know myself. You should understand what I mean as well as anyone. It's just like Altapasaeda. You can almost smell the fear in the air."

"So, say you're right. What do we do?"

"We?" Estrada shook her head, a sharp judder of resolve. "No. This is my problem. If something's happened

101

here, it happened because of my absence. It's my job as mayor to set it right."

"That's absurd. We've come this far together. Let us help you. What if it's more stragglers from Moaradrid's army?"

"Then what can four of us achieve that I can't do alone?"

"All right, perhaps Damasco could…"

"Hey! Not a chance," I cut in. "The last time I broke into somewhere for you, I barely got out with my life."

"It's all right, Easie," Estrada said. "I have friends inside. People I trust. And you three have business you need to attend to, business that's already waited far too long. Not least, making sure Saltlick gets back to his people."

Saltlick looked more abashed than ever. "Help Marina."

"Thank you. Really. But Muena Palaiya's my town, and I have all the help I need right here."

"Marina," Alvantes said, "I won't let you go in there alone."

The look Estrada turned him would have frozen boiling water. "How exactly do you intend to stop me?"

I saw the anger flare in Alvantes's eyes – and quickly dissolve into frustration, with perhaps even an edge of helplessness. "I didn't mean it like that. But you can't seriously expect to tell me you'll be in danger and then think I'll let you ride in there alone."

"That's precisely what I expect. It's how it *has* to be. When we fought Moaradrid, you knew your men needed to see you leading them, that you weren't afraid. It's the same here, with my people. I won't let them down again. But Lunto – it's going to be all right. You really don't need to worry."

Estrada stepped suddenly forward and reached to put her arms around his neck. Alvantes stood rigidly at first; then, forcing himself to relax, he put his own arms round her back and returned the embrace. For a moment, all the clumsy formality went out of the gesture and they pressed each other close.

It was Estrada who drew away first. "Thank you," she said. "For everything. Come find me once your business is settled with the King."

Alvantes only nodded.

She turned to Saltlick and me. "Easie… take care of yourself. Try to be good."

"You too, Mayor Estrada. Don't do anything I wouldn't do."

I held out my hand and she shook it, with the faintest of smiles.

"Saltlick," she said, "will you bring your people to visit on your way home? I promise we'll make you a good welcome."

"Meet friends," beamed Saltlick. Bending almost double, he offered her his hand as well. Though it was fully twice the size of hers, she managed to wrap her five fingers around two of his and they shook.

Then, without another word, Estrada caught up her horse's reins and led it towards the southern entrance of Muena Palaiya. Watching her cross the short distance, I realised my breath was catching in my throat. At the gates, she rapped hard, three times. Seconds passed – enough that I began to think no one would answer. Estrada only waited patiently. Finally, the rightmost gate opened. Whoever was on the other side was masked by the nearer gate. I heard a man's voice, too low for me to pick out words. Estrada responded briefly. The gate opened a little more and she led her horse into the gap. She was barely through before the portal swung shut behind her.

I let out the long breath I'd been holding. "There she goes," I said, more to break the tension than because I thought the comment worth making.

I turned to Alvantes – and was startled to see the fury in his face. "Damn you, Damasco. Do you care so little that you couldn't say one word to talk her out of this?"

He looked as if he'd like to throttle me with his bare hand. I tried to keep my voice steady as I said, "Do you know the woman at all, Alvantes? She became mayor of the most crime-ridden town in the Castoval. She led an army into battle and did more to stand up to Moaradrid than anyone. Whatever's going on in there, if she can't handle it no one can."

I wasn't trying to pacify Alvantes. I was just sick of his arrogant conviction that only he knew best. I might not have always agreed with Estrada, there might in fact have been times when I could have cheerfully pushed her down a well, but I didn't for one moment doubt her ability to look after herself.

Nevertheless, I realised it had been the right thing to say. Alvantes already looked marginally less murderous.

"The sooner we get moving," I added, "the sooner we can come back and check on her."

I could see his indecision. His respect for Estrada didn't sit well with his lug-headed notions of gallantry. I knew there was a part of him itching to mount a one-man assault on that gate and carry her out over his shoulder. Seconds passed. Then Alvantes swung up into the saddle. "We won't get much further today," he said.

I followed his example. "We'll have to make camp somewhere," I said resignedly. Until just now, I'd been expecting to spend the night in a comfortable Muena Palaiyan bed.

"Agreed. But not near here."

With Muena Palaiya cut off to us, the only way onward was the cliff road. Between the high whitewashed walls of Muena Palaiya and the edge of the decline to the valley floor ran a wide strip of ground, dusty red-tinged soil broken by patches of scrub. Where the land became sheer, knotty trees clung desperately to its verge.

The road ran right upon that edge. Beneath the late afternoon light, the view was spectacular. The river wending below, the vast green of Paen Acha to the south, and even the distant far bank were all clearly visible, all filigreed with gold. Muena Delorca was just visible to the west, its white walls stained amber, and very far behind us lay the faintest suggestion of what could only be Altapasaeda.

Mounteban had claimed Moaradrid had no interest in ruling the Castoval, that his only desire was to wrest the crown from Panchessa. Perhaps there'd even been a degree of truth to that. True or not, though, I understood now that he would have come back. The man had been a wolf; sooner or later, he'd have needed something new to sink his teeth into.

The Castoval was a beautiful land, its people mostly peaceable and decent. I was glad I'd played some part in keeping it and them out of a tyrant's hands.

Then I remembered Mounteban, nestled like a fat spider in Altapasaeda. I remembered Estrada's fears for Muena Palaiya. The problem with tyrants, it seemed, was that they just kept on coming.

"We're being watched," Alvantes said softly.

"What?"

"From the walls."

I felt a prickling of my neck hairs, an urgent impulse to look around. Was it only because Alvantes had planted the suggestion in my mind? I couldn't say. "We're within range of bowshot," I pointed out. "If they wanted us dead, we'd be dead."

"It isn't us I'm worried about."

Of course it wasn't. "Could it be you're imagining things, Alvantes? I'm sure Estrada has the situation well in hand."

He didn't reply, but for the rest of our passage past Muena Palaiya, his gaze hardly left the walls. It was almost as though he were challenging whoever lay hidden to come out and confront him.

Eventually the road began to curve inward and we passed the north-west corner of Muena Palaiya, coming out upon the wide patch of ground where visitors – and the occasional passing army – were prone to bivouac. The last time I'd been here, I'd been rescuing Saltlick from the midst of Moaradrid's forces. Now, aside from a few charred patches where fire pits had been made, all trace of their presence was gone.

Well, maybe not *all* trace. Happening to catch Saltlick's eye, I was startled by what I saw there – an unmistakeable glint of horror. He'd been tortured here by Moaradrid's men, probably for hours. Knowing Saltlick, however, I suspected it was more the memory of what he'd done after that, of the violence he'd committed himself, that haunted him so deeply.

"Let's get away from here," I said – and he was quick enough to follow.

We continued north, Muena Palaiya diminishing at our backs until a projection of the mountainside that walled the road to the east lopped it from view. Just before the town vanished, Alvantes stopped to stare behind, shading his eyes with his one hand. I thought he might be about to turn back. But the moment passed, and he rode to rejoin me. Still, the strain of the decision was carved deep in every line of his face.

There were only minutes of daylight left by then. The sun had already dipped beneath the far-distant western mountains, edging their peaks a rich saffron. At the point we'd reached, the road was hardly more than a band clinging between the mountainside and the drop to the valley floor. There was nothing that could be called shelter.

Eventually, by the time a few stray stars were pricking through the purpling sky, Alvantes pointed to a line of stubby trees and said, "That will have to do."

There was a fringe of grass for the horses, and at least we were cut off from the wind. We ate a scanty dinner from our provisions and set a small, sputtering fire. I picked a patch of ground that looked less stony than the rest, did my best to arrange my cloak and a blanket into something approaching a bed and settled down to snatch what rest I could.

I woke, chilled and stiff to the bone, to wan grey light and the sight of Alvantes already packing his bedding away. He had his back to me. Lacking energy or motivation to call out, I chose to watch him struggle instead. One last blanket didn't want to fit, and its resistance was clearly working on Alvantes's nerves.

As the struggle drew to a climax, I became steadily aware of something nagging at my attention. I couldn't say what at first; it was just the vague sense of a detail not right. Then I saw. Every time Alvantes tried to thrust the blanket inside, the contents of the bag shifted, and the sides moved correspondingly – except for the lowest segment, a finger's length in depth. That bottom portion always stayed perfectly rigid.

I mightn't have noticed it if Alvantes hadn't asked his cryptic question and borrowed my needle and thread. Laying there though, barely awake, I nevertheless felt certain beyond doubt: Alvantes had hidden something in the base of his saddlebag.

He cursed, strapped the bag clumsily shut over the offending blanket, and turned around. Seeing me, he started almost guiltily. "You're awake. Let's get moving."

Saltlick was already up too, and had stripped one tree nearly bare for his breakfast. I had time for a brief snack of my own before we were on the road again. Within an hour, we'd left the narrow highway for the Hunch-proper, the great tableland that spread from the east mountains to where the Casto Mara sliced a gully through its western edge, leaving the plateau's end a rocky wedge on the far bank. Though there were a few large farms and many villages scratching out a living, the Hunch was barren compared with the valley floor. It was a region of dry red soil and juts of stone, desiccated brush and the occasional skewed cactus, and it only grew more desolate as we followed the dirt road north-west towards its farther corner.

As usual, Alvantes was marginally less conversational than my horse. I started when out of the blue he said, "We won't reach Saltlick's tribe today."

Numbed by boredom, I'd hardly considered the next stop on our itinerary. I'd only been vaguely aware that all this while I'd been retracing my route, from that fateful day I'd somehow imagined stealing from Moaradrid to be a sane and sensible idea.

That meant we were close to where Saltlick and I had last seen the captive giants – though as Alvantes had said, not so close that we'd arrive today. In the meantime, we'd need somewhere to pass another night. Memories of the last time I'd crossed the Hunch, and the frantic flight from Moaradrid's riders I'd made carried on Saltlick's shoulder, pried their way into my mind. With them came another image I'd sooner have forgotten: the sight of Reb Panza burning on the horizon.

"I know a village," I said. "If it's still here, that is.
I'm not sure how pleased they'll be to see me, but I'd
like to go there."

"If we have to find a village where they're pleased
to see you, we'll be up all night."

"Ha! There's that famous, lightning humour again.
No wonder they call you the Jester of Altapasaeda."

"No one calls me that."

"Not to your face."

Alvantes snorted. "Very well then. We'll go to this
village of yours, and see if they can tolerate your company any more than I can."

After that, I was grateful for his stubborn silence.
We kept a steady pace upon the rough road and the
day wore on by slow degrees, as tedious as the landscape we passed through and Alvantes and Saltlick's
taciturn company.

The sun was setting before we drew near Reb Panza.
The horses were growing weary, and even the usually
indefatigable Saltlick was starting to slow. I could sense
Alvantes was on the verge of suggesting we find somewhere else to stop. I dreaded having to explain the
significance of this one particular village – how
Moaradrid's thugs had set it afire soon after we'd left,
and how in all likelihood it had been my fault.

Then we rounded a corner and Reb Panza came into
view, a tiny cluster of miserable buildings gathered
round a well and a square, its few cracked paving stones
the only sign the village had ever enjoyed a heyday.

At least it was still there. That was more than I'd
feared.

We drew nearer. Reb Panza was still there, all right – but there was no question it had burned. The adobe walls, once pinkish-white, were charred in dirty streaks. The wattle animal stalls were gone altogether. The roofs had been clumsily rethatched, or else left with gaping holes and patches singed to blackness. Even the cobbles of the square were scorched towards the outer edge.

Closer still and I could discern a figure sat upon a bench before one of the houses. I recognised the ancient village patriarch I'd encountered on my previous visit by his absurdly long and well-maintained moustaches, which hung in striking contrast to his general shabbiness.

Unfortunately, it seemed he recognised me too.

His tiny eyes widened. His mouth lolled open. He leaped to his feet, with surprising agility. Just as swiftly, he grabbed a pitchfork from a nearby mound of grass and hurried towards me, the fork levelled before him like a spear.

Alvantes looked at me more with amusement than concern. "And this is where you want to spend the night? Is there anywhere in the Castoval people don't want to kill you on sight?"

"Not lately, it seems," I admitted.

Just then, the Patriarch, who had struggled to keep up his pace and was now huffing badly, lurched to a halt before us. "You," he wheezed. "Thief! Monster!" He took a moment to catch his breath, propping himself with the pitchfork. "Enemy of all that's good! Have you come to laugh at the harm you brought to our door?"

Bad as I felt about what had happened, it was hard to say Reb Panza looked that much worse than when I'd last seen it. Still, I did my best to play along. "I swear I had no idea Moaradrid would do that. Will you tell me what happened?"

The Patriarch's face contorted, while he struggled to judge whether this was some fresh trick or mockery. "All right," he said eventually, "I'll tell you what you wrought upon us." At the memory, though, he seemed to shrink into himself – and his voice was faint as he said, "The northerner warlord was furious. He ranted about a stone. When I handed over that accursed gem you forced on me, it just made him angrier. He told his men to teach us a lesson. A lesson in taking what wasn't ours."

The gem had been part of the trove I'd stolen from Moaradrid. It had been the giant-stone he was really after, of course, but I doubted that detail would make the Patriarch feel any better. "Was anyone inside?" I asked. "Did anyone…"

"He rounded us up in the square. He made us watch." Much of the anger flushed back into the Patriarch's tone as he added, "He said he was being merciful."

"But you saved the village."

"We saved the *buildings*. With water from the well. Likely, Reb Panza won't last the winter, for we've neither money nor goods to replace what's lost." At that, his brows wrinkled. "Lest we forget," he added, "you still owe us three onyxes. They'll hardly compensate for the food you stole, and won't begin to cover the repairs your deception left us with. Nevertheless, pay up, you fiend, or... or..."

I watched as he struggled for an appropriate threat. In the end, he settled on thrusting the pitchfork towards me. The effect was more hopeful than intimidating.

"You're right," I said. "That's only reasonable."

He squinted with fierce suspicion, and gave the pitchfork another hesitant shake.

"We'll also require shelter for the night and an evening meal. Saltlick, as you'll no doubt remember, will be content with a generous portion of hay or grain."

The Patriarch gaped in astonishment. "You?" he asked. "You, who brought disaster... burning of our village... you... shelter?"

"For the night. And food."

Mastering himself with considerable effort, the Patriarch looked me in the eye. "Payment up front," he said. "In full."

"Of course."

It only occurred to me then that this was what I'd come here for. A very small part of me, a part that for want of a better name I called my conscience – negligible, erratic and easily ignored as it generally was – had been nagging since the night I'd seen Reb Panza burn. It wasn't a problem I'd even suffered from before and I didn't like it one bit. Whatever the future might hold, I certainly didn't want a nagging conscience to be part of it.

I drew out my coin bag. At no point had I actually

bothered to calculate exactly how much was in there. The reason was simple: two of the coins, half the size again of the infinitely more common onyxes, were of solid gold, and together they outvalued all the rest.

Moving quickly enough that I couldn't consider what I was about to do, I took one out and pressed it into his palm.

He felt the weight before he looked at it. I could see him about to complain. Then his eyes flickered down and caught the colour. "This is… that's… but…"

"You'll need to send someone to Muena Palaiya or Aspira Nero to get it changed. Once that's done, you should find our debts more than settled."

His eyes crinkled. "Another trick?"

"This man is Guard-Captain Alvantes of the Alta-pasaedan City Guard. I think that, on this occasion if no other, he'll vouch for me."

"We're on guard business," said Alvantes, grudgingly. "We do need lodgings. The coin was… acquired… in the royal palace of Altapasaeda. It's quite genuine."

The Patriarch nodded dreamily. "Well then. Indeed. Lodgings," he said.

At his lead, we trooped the last distance to Reb Panza, the dazed Patriarch leaning heavily on his pitchfork. As we entered the square, as though at some hidden signal, doors began to creak open and wrinkled faces materialised in the gaps. Two dozen sets of eyes latched onto us. A hum of aged voices rose, swelling rapidly towards anger.

The Patriarch held up the coin in his hand. When the last murmurs had subsided, he said, "These gentlemen will be staying the night. Let us show them the unequalled hospitality Reb Panza is so famous for."

In my experience, Reb Panza had had little enough to offer the weary traveller even before it was burned half to the ground, so that prospect seemed doubtful at best. To his credit, however, the Patriarch made every attempt to fulfil it. He insisted on giving up his own house, and though it was hardly less of a hovel than the others, it at least offered four whole walls and an unperforated roof. Once we'd fed and brushed down the horses, his wife – a rickety, good-natured woman who drew obvious amusement from her husband's posturing – served up a meal of thick, aromatic, and unexpectedly delicious bean stew.

Afterwards, we sat outside in the cool evening air and drank cups of watery wine. Just as on our last visit, the children were fascinated by Saltlick. Well fed on dry grass, he sat sleepily as they prodded, climbed on and otherwise tormented him. The Patriarch asked a few vague questions about events further south, and I answered as well as I could, without saying too much about the situation in Altapasaeda – a subject I guessed Alvantes would want kept quiet.

It didn't take us long to run out of conversation. The Patriarch lit his pipe, and the fragrant smoke reminded me of how tiring yet another day on horseback had been. I yawned exaggeratedly. "I think it's time I was turning in."

"We've an early start tomorrow," agreed Alvantes.

The Patriarch's wife ushered us inside and pointed

out where we'd be sleeping. To my amusement, this meant a straw pallet in one corner in Alvantes's case, and in mine, the Patriarch's own bed. If it had suffered damage in the fire, with one end more or less charred away, it still promised by far the more restful night.

"I hope you'll be comfortable," I said. "That thing looks prickly."

"You're unbelievable, Damasco."

"You know, it's normally women who tell me that. But thank you, Guard-Captain."

"After everything you went through to get and keep that gold… yet you hand it away so easily."

"It's for a good cause."

Alvantes looked at me steadily. "Do you really think a clean conscience is so easy to buy? That making up for one misdeed can pay off a lifetime's wrongs?"

I considered. Asides from a little harmless thievery, it was hard to say what other significant wrongs I'd committed. Certainly, nothing had preyed on my mind the way the burning of Reb Panza had. "Yes, I do."

"You mean it, don't you?"

"Absolutely."

Alvantes shook his head, reached to snuff our candle. "Then gods help you, Damasco."

Perhaps I was getting used to the inhuman hours Alvantes kept, because I woke of my own accord before dawn. When we went outside, it was to find the Patriarch waiting on the bench before his house. "Four hours of sleep is more than enough for me," he said, by way of explanation. "My wife prepared you lunches," he added, offering us each a cloth-wrapped bundle.

"Thank you. And thanks for giving up your bed. I haven't slept so well in weeks."

He grinned toothlessly. "A small show of appreciation. Practically the least I could do in the face of such generosity."

"Spend it wisely," I told him.

"Oh, I will," he said. "Be assured of that."

We roused Saltlick, saddled the horses, and set out with the first flush of dawn. It wasn't long before we'd left Reb Panza behind and rejoined the main road. For the first time I could remember, Saltlick took the lead. It was always difficult to judge his mood; now, he seemed both excited and nervous. He travelled at a fast walk bordering on a trot, and picked up speed as the day wore on, until our horses were almost cantering.

By midday, we were staring down towards the valley floor from the northernmost edge of the Hunch. Straining, I could just make out where Moaradrid's army had camped before the battle all those many days ago. If there were giants to be seen, however, my eyes weren't up to the task.

As we descended, a rise far ahead cut off our view. I could sense Saltlick's frustration. Back upon the valley floor, we raced past small farms and rice paddies. Often, farmers looked up or tipped their wide-brimmed hats in our direction; no one seemed surprised or concerned to see a giant rushing by.

Saltlick, oblivious to everything but the road ahead, paid them no attention. It was as though all the emotion he'd kept in check these last days, all his fears and doubts for his people, were finally breaking to the surface, converting into energy that propelled him forward.

For all his speed, it was late in the day when we reached the rise. Saltlick picked up his already considerable pace once more. With so little distance left, I encouraged my horse to match him, though it whickered miserably.

A couple of minutes' hard riding, with Saltlick labouring ahead, and the rise began to level. The last time I'd witnessed the view that opened beyond it, I'd been hanging upon Saltlick's shoulder as we fled for our lives. Their vast encampment had stretched from the farms at the waterside to halfway up the shallow hillside. Beyond, the slope had been busy with Moaradrid's troops, and littered with the fallen dead of the recent conflict – some northern, most Castovalian. Lastly, amidst the carnage, splashed with gore, there had been the giants.

I still shivered to think of the violence they'd wreaked, violence Moaradrid had forced upon them. Under his control they'd been his secret weapon, had irresistibly turned the battle's tide. If I hadn't accidentally intervened, he would have gone on to use them against the King, with undoubtedly similar results.

Now, the tents were gone. The northerner troops had all left. The fallen bodies had vanished, their spilled blood long since washed into the earth.

Nothing remained of either camp or battlefield – nothing except the giants.

And even they were barely recognisable from when last I'd seen them.

CHAPTER SEVEN

There must have been almost a hundred giants scattered upon the hillside. It was as bizarre a sight as I'd ever seen, as though the land had spat out living monoliths by the dozen.

Though they were unmistakeably huge – even sitting, they reached as high as I did on horseback – it was hard to believe they were of a kind with Saltlick. Where he was broad-limbed and barrel-chested, they were hardly more than pale grey skin wrapped round great, jutting bones. Most strange was how their thinness made them seem, somehow, less giant. It was as if they were out of proportion now, all height with no width.

Saltlick bellowed something in giantish and broke into a run.

He covered the distance to the nearest of his brethren in moments. There followed a brief, incomprehensible exchange, with most of the talking on Saltlick's part. Whatever was said, it didn't satisfy him. His eyes skimmed over the assembly and settled on one particular giant near the centre. He was older than those around him, skin wrinkled and mottled with patches of white. He didn't look at all surprised to have been singled out.

It occurred to me that this might be the former chieftain, from whom Moaradrid had wrested the giant-stone. The length of the ensuing conversation seemed to bear out my guess. Even then, however, Saltlick did most of the talking. The former chieftain answered in brief snatches, when he bothered to reply at all.

Whatever was occurring, it obviously wasn't going to be resolved any time soon. I dismounted, stretched saddle-sore muscles and sat down on the grass.

I couldn't say what I'd expected to find. It struck me that until that moment, I hadn't entirely believed the giants would even have waited here. Despite everything I'd learned about them and their society, despite everything I'd witnessed, it was hard to imagine any people could be so bound by tradition. Surely, once a day or two had passed with no sign of Moaradrid and no fresh instructions, they'd have began to question? If not then, surely when the last of Moaradrid's army packed up and left?

Alvantes caught up and watched Saltlick and the former chieftain for a while, with obvious irritation. Then he too dismounted. "What are they doing?" he asked. There was disgust in his voice, as though he found something offensive in the sight of so much apathy.

"They're waiting," I said, "for Moaradrid to come back with the giant-stone and give them new orders." Another thought occurred to me. "I bet it was the last thing that bastard told them."

"Surely they realise he's not coming back?"

"I'm not sure it's that simple." After my experiences with Saltlick, I thought I understood, at least a little. Putting it into words was another thing entirely. "Imagine if someone told you that you didn't need to breathe any more. Even if you knew it was true, even if there was no doubt in your mind, could you bring yourself to do it?"

"That's absurd. Nobody's telling them not to breathe. They simply need to forget their stupid stone and go home."

"When," I said, "the most basic rule of their society says they can't."

"Then they should have sense enough to realise the rules have changed."

"Says the man trooping the length of two countries to deliver bad news to a king he's never met."

Alvantes frowned. "I've met the King."

"Fine. I'm sure that once you arrive it will be straight to the nearest inn to catch up on old times. My point is, you're hardly one to lecture on discarding outmoded social values. In fact, right now I'd say Mounteban's the expert on that front."

"If you're so enamoured with his ideas, perhaps you should join him."

"And perhaps you should be more understanding of the giants. They've been dragged from their home, tormented, forced against their every instinct to fight someone else's war and abandoned – while in the meantime, the system they've relied on for countless generations has been turned inside out and used to

enslave them. That should be enough to confuse anyone."

"Make whatever excuses you like," said Alvantes.
His voice was taut with restrained fury. "The fact is,
they're no use to anyone like this."

Then I understood. I remembered what Alvantes had
asked me on the road from Altapasaeda; I knew why
he'd agreed to accompany Saltlick, and why he was so
angry now. Even after everything, he'd still hoped the
giants might be recruited in his battle for Altapasaeda.
He hadn't heard a word I'd said.

I'd never hated Alvantes more than I did just then.
Yet – on some level, I really *did* understand. Altapasaeda meant everything to him, and it was in
Mounteban's hands. I doubted there was anything he
wouldn't risk, harm, or sacrifice to save it.

It was a good thing Saltlick chose that moment to
break off his conversation with the former chieftain.
As he lumbered towards us, his expression was as despondent as any of his brethren's.

"What's going on?" I asked.

"Old chief won't leave," he said, speaking low
enough not to be overheard. "Wait for new chief."

"Surely you told him what happened?"

Saltlick shook his head, so slowly that the gesture
seemed almost painful. "Stone makes chief," he said.
"Chief makes orders. No stone. No chief. No orders."

"You mean, because Moaradrid can't take back his
command and no one can make a new one they're
just going to sit here and die?" Damn Moaradrid, if
only he'd thought to give back the giant-stone before

plummeting to his death this would all be so much more straightforward. "Can't you talk them round?" I asked.

"Tried to talk." Saltlick sat heavily, cupped his chin in his hands. "Think now. Try more."

Despite what I'd told Alvantes, it was hard to credit that the giants were really willing to sacrifice their lives over some loophole in their social order. Most absurd was the fact that to all intents and purposes, Saltlick was now their chieftain. Perhaps I was missing the subtleties of giant politics, but he'd certainly been ordained when we'd visited their enclave high in the Castoval's southernmost tip. Surely that counted for something? Could they really be so hidebound that only Moaradrid's miraculous return from the grave would release them?

Either way, nothing I could contribute would help. I doubted the majority of the giants would even understand me. This was one Saltlick would have to work out alone.

Looking round for a diversion, my eyes fell on a wagon approaching in the direction we'd come from. A man and woman a few years older than me and dressed in peasant garb sat together on the driver's seat, with two small children running along beside them. A great quantity of yellowed grass was piled in the rear.

I hailed them as they drew close and the man replied with a wave. He drew the wagon up beside the road and walked towards us. Though he was dressed in the traditional plain white shirt and trousers of the local farmers, complete with ragged wide-brimmed hat, something in his manner told me he wasn't accustomed to poverty.

"That's a new one, isn't it?" he called.

It took me a moment to understand. "This is Saltlick," I said. "He's been away… travelling with me."

"Ah. More sense than the rest then. My name's Huero." He offered me his hand.

I shook. "Easie Damasco. And my travelling companion's Alvantes."

Alvantes tipped a noncommittal nod to Huero.

"Good to meet you," Huero said. "Any friend of the giants is a friend of ours. Not that they'd consider us friends, I don't suppose. Half the time they hardly know we're here."

Behind, I could see his wife manoeuvring the wagon off the road, towards the centre of the congregated giants. In a flash of insight, I said, "You've been looking after them. Since the soldiers left."

"We have." Huero pointed to a cluster of buildings near the river. "We owned that farm. We fled when the northerners came. Just in time, I'd suppose. When word had it they'd left, we came back to see. The rumours were true – except for the giants."

"But just now, you came from the south," I pointed out.

Huero nodded solemnly. "They didn't leave much of the farms here. We've been staying with family of my wife's, further down the river."

"You lost your home? And you're still looking after the giants?"

"It's a long story. But yes, we bring food every

morning and evening. All the families try to help a little. Trouble is, we don't have much left for ourselves. If it weren't for the fact that they'll eat almost anything, either they or we would have starved by now. Although, it's as much a problem getting them to eat or drink at all. I think they only do it so as not to offend us."

That sounded about right. In my experience, just as violence seemed anathema to the giants, so consideration and a sort of fundamental politeness came naturally to them. Now, it seemed, politeness was the only thing keeping them alive.

"We'll keep it up so long as we can," added Huero. "They don't much care about the weather, that's something. But they can't last out here forever."

Abruptly, both Huero and I looked up, as a great shadow loomed over us. Saltlick had approached almost silently. One glance at his face told me he'd followed the entire conversation. He squatted on his haunches, bringing himself closer to Huero's height. "Thank you," he said. "Friend to giants."

He spoke with such solemnity that it was almost funny. Yet, for once, I found I couldn't laugh at him.

Neither did Huero. "You're welcome," he said, emotion welling in his voice. "I wish we could do more."

At that, Saltlick destroyed the moment with a grin so wide it threatened to dislocate his jaw. Then I really couldn't help but laugh. After a brief struggle, Huero followed my example. "Listen," he said, "it's going to be dark soon. Do you have anywhere to spend the night?"

I glanced at Alvantes, who acknowledged me with a barely perceptible tilt of the head. "We don't," I said. "We'd be grateful for anything you can offer."

"We'll find you something," he said. "In the meantime, I'd best help my wife with sharing out the food."

Trying to force-feed depressed giants wasn't the most appealing task I could think of, but the opportunity to stretch cramped muscles definitely appealed. "Wait, I'll join you," I said, and walked with Huero up the hillside to where the woman – who he introduced as "My lovely wife, Dura" – was already doling out portions of dried grass. The two children – "Little Ray and Loqueisa" – were following behind with cups of water filled from a cask in the back of the wagon.

I caught up my first bundle of grass, only for Dura to appear at my elbow. "Not so much," she said softly. "If you give that to one, another will go hungry."

I went back to the wagon and replaced a few handfuls. The remaining amount seemed very meagre.

I turned back, just in time for Dura to return from distributing her own portion. "Better," she said. "But still too much."

She reached over, removed a couple more handfuls and returned them to the cart. What remained looked as if it would barely qualify as a giant's midmorning snack.

"You might have to encourage them," she added.

I glanced round to judge who had or hadn't been fed, and singled out a target, a giant somewhat smaller than his neighbours with alarming sprouts of orange hair protruding from his head. I sidled into his line of sight, held out my hands and said, "Here's your meal. It isn't much, I'm afraid. Maybe you should stop sitting on this miserable hillside and go home for a delicious nine-course dinner."

I couldn't tell if he was looking at me or through me, but there was nothing in his expression to suggest he'd understood. I'd grown used to Saltlick and his ability to follow simple conversations. Though Moaradrid's men had presumably taught the other giants enough to follow basic orders, I doubted their education had extended much beyond "Stand there" and "Kill those people." "Food," I tried. "For you."

I pushed my hands closer to his mouth. Another thing about my familiarity with Saltlick was that I'd forgotten how intimidating a giant could be. I didn't feel remotely comfortable with my fingers so near that alarming maw.

Fortunately, he chose that point to catch up with the situation. Holding out his own cupped palms, he offered a shy smile of acknowledgment. I tipped the grass into his hands; he spilled it into his mouth, chewed twice and swallowed. Then he bobbed his head, which I took for a sort of "thank you."

After that, I fed a half-dozen more giants. Every exchange went more or less the same way. Each time, just as Huero had said, I came away with the impression that they'd only accepted their food because it would have been rude not to. When I went back the last time, I found the wagon empty but for a few stray strands.

"That's it," said Dura. "At least they've all had something."

Huero wandered up and put his arm about her shoulders.

"I don't get it," I said. "I'm sure Moaradrid told them to wait until he got back, maybe he even ordered them not to move, but I can't believe he'd have told them not to eat. It's like they really want to starve."

"I think they seem more shocked than anything," replied Dura. "Don't you?"

I thought about what I'd told Alvantes, about what the giants had been through. I recalled how traumatised Saltlick had been after our escape outside Muena Palaiya, the sight of him standing amidst tumbling rocks with the blood of Moaradrid's soldiers smeared across his knuckles – and then what I'd witnessed the giants do to the Castovalian troops at Moaradrid's command.

Perhaps there was something deeper here than the issues of Moaradrid's absence and the loss of the giant-stone. Could it be violence was so repellent to them that they'd sooner die here than go home with the memories of what they'd done? If so, I wondered if anything anyone said could change their minds.

When we rejoined Saltlick, I could see that he'd come to similar conclusions. He looked sad and worn. Clearly, whatever thinking he'd done hadn't provided much in the way of new arguments to confront the old chief with.

"Why don't you join us?" I said. "It's not like they won't still be here tomorrow."

Too late, I realised my lack of tact. But Saltlick merely shook his head. "Stay with people."

I patted his knee. "We'll see you in the morning, all right?"

He offered me a weak smile.

With Huero and his family upon the cart and Alvantes and I riding beside, we headed back up the road. A few minutes later, Huero drew in to one of the tiny, tumbledown riverside villages. Had I thought about it, I might have realised his offer of hospitality had been based more on kindness than practicality. Only when we stopped did I remember that he was practically homeless himself.

The relative of his wife's Huero had mentioned turned out to be a brother – and he too had a wife, not to mention their four children and her elderly parents. If their farmhouse was large by the standards of the village, it was wholly inadequate for two families. Introductions were conducted on the doorstep; anything else would have risked suffocation for all concerned. Huero waited until the others had gone back in and then said sheepishly, "I'm afraid the barn is all we can offer. If we try to sleep any more inside, I fear the walls might collapse."

"We'll be fine," I said. "If it weren't for you, we'd be up on the hillside with the giants."

Huero grinned. "If nothing else they'd keep the wind off, eh? I'll see what I can do about food for you. Make yourselves as comfortable as you can."

At least it was a sturdily built barn, half-filled with hay – much of it probably destined to be eaten by the giants in due time. Part of me marvelled at how low my standards for accommodation had sunk. Another part was simply glad to have somewhere soft to sit. I couldn't recall ever having spent so much time on horseback. I was growing more bow-legged with each passing day; if I kept this up, I feared it might become permanent.

Circumstances seemed considerably better when Huero arrived with two steaming bowls of soup. It was mostly rice and vegetables, but there was a little chicken in there, which I suspected they could ill-afford to spare.

Huero sat with us while we ate, and once we'd scraped our bowls clean, took them back to the house. When he returned, it was with a bottle in one hand and three wooden cups in the other.

"Not for me," said Alvantes. "It's late." Without waiting for anyone to try to persuade him, he paced to the far side of the barn and started setting out his bedding.

It *was* late, but unlike Alvantes I wasn't about to throw Huero's generosity in his face. When he handed me a brimming cup, I recognised it by scent as the notoriously potent local rice liquor. I took a tentative sip. Fire cascaded down my throat, turned my insides molten. I gasped. "That's good."

"The best. I've been saving it for a special occasion. There haven't been so many pleasant ones lately."

While Alvantes snored in the background, Huero and I swapped tales of recent events, and he filled in some of the gaps in my knowledge regarding the time Moaradrid had spent there. He spoke jovially, but I could tell it was mostly for my benefit. He skimmed particularly lightly over the loss of his farm and lands, and carefully avoided the subject of how long they could continue to stay with his wife's brother.

Meanwhile, I finished my first glass of rice liquor, and then a second. By the third, I was used to the burning sensation, and even starting to enjoy it.

"'S'agoodthing…" I took a breath, began again. "It's a good thing for the giants they had people like you nearby."

"Yes." Huero looked meditative. "It might have gone very differently."

An edge to his tone snagged a more sober part of my brain. "Is there something you didn't tell us?"

"Yes," he said. "There's more." He paused – and the pause dragged on. Not knowing if I should prompt him, I chose to wait; and eventually he continued of his own accord. "We had a second son, Dura and I, older than Ray. His name was also Huero."

Thinking back to my own experience, I asked, "Did Moaradrid force him to fight?"

"No, no one forced him. The day of the battle, we got up to find his bed empty. He'd gone in the night to join up with *our* side."

Understanding, I spoke so Huero wouldn't have to. "He never came back."

"Not many did. As soon as the last soldiers left, we went to burn our dead. But we couldn't be sure which one was Huero. The ones the giants had killed… some of them were hard to recognise."

"That doesn't sound like much of a reason to help keep them alive."

Huero coughed into his fist. "I suppose it doesn't. The truth is, we'd planned to kill them – or try to, anyway. Everyone from all the villages went. But when the time came… the giants must have realised what was going on, but they didn't try to defend themselves. They didn't do anything at all."

From what I'd seen of Huero and knowing the giants, I could imagine the scene as clearly as if I'd been there. "You couldn't do it."

"How could we? And once we'd realised that, there seemed to be only one other choice." Huero lowered his head, brushed at his eyes. "Afterwards, we were relieved. We understood… it's much better this way."

I couldn't think of a thing to say. My mind boggled at the kind of decency that could see the giants for what they really were after what they'd been made to do. Yet even through the fog of alcohol, I understood that Huero was right. Any other outcome would have destroyed him and his people forever.

He looked up. "Well. I think I've talked at you enough. You should get some sleep – like your friend there."

I glanced at Alvantes, still snoring sonorously. It didn't seem the time to explain how far he was from being my friend. "Goodnight," I said.

I watched as Huero walked to the barn doors and pushed through them. The space was spinning very gently. The warmth of the rice liquor seemed to have permeated my entire body. I stood – and was surprised. As I crossed to the double doors, I had no conscious idea of what I was about to do. Even as I stepped into the cool night air, my brain was in complete denial of my actions, as though observing from a great distance.

I caught up to Huero halfway between barn and house. He looked at me in surprise.

"You should take this," I said. I clasped his hand.

He looked at his palm and then at me, and there was nothing in his face but bewilderment.

"To feed the giants. When Saltlick talks them into going home, take whatever you need to get your farm back. If there's anything after that, you can give me it back when I'm next through here."

"This is…"

"You'll need to get it changed somewhere."

"But…"

"One more thing. Can you keep an eye on Saltlick? He can talk fairly well now. He could translate if you need him to. He's more sensitive than he lets on – a few compliments go a long way. He's fond of children."

Huero nodded, without his eyes ever leaving the golden disk in his hand. "We'll look after them all," he said. "Far better than we've been able to, with this." Finally, he managed to tear his eyes from the coin. "Thank you," he said.

"It's just money," I told him. "Goodnight."

I woke, bleary-eyed and thick-skulled, to another overcast dawn and a vague sense of horror.

What had I done?

I tried to think about the coin – the coin I'd so impulsively given away, the coin that had been the one remaining hope for my future. I couldn't. It was a cavity in my mind. Whenever my thoughts came close to it, they vanished. It was the same when I tried to ask myself what happened next. Was I really about to go with Alvantes? Alvantes who hated me, who I despised in return? If I didn't, what option did I have? Every question was like a sinkhole. My thoughts fell into it and nothing came back.

If Huero had come out then, I might have told him I'd made a terrible mistake. If Alvantes had asked whether I still planned to go with him, I might have said no. Neither thing happened. We packed our bedding, saddled up and rode into cold morning drizzle.

Saltlick was already about when we reached the hillside, and deep in a one-sided conversation with one of his brethren. I couldn't help noticing that it wasn't the former chieftain this time. He gave up when he saw us and ambled down the hillside.

When he drew near, I said, "I suppose this is goodbye, then. I know you have to stay and talk some sense into your friends."

Saltlick struggled against his limited vocabulary for a suitable reply. After much obvious thought, he settled on a booming, "Easie friend."

I managed a half-hearted grin. "Saltlick friend too."

It was true – and perhaps I hadn't entirely realised it until then. I'd grown used to the clomp of his footsteps beside me, the tectonic grind of his jaw as he ate, his impossible, indefatigable good-naturedness. It struck me with the sudden jolt of an unexpected blow – I would miss him.

"I don't expect we'll see you when we come back

this way," I told him. "You'll have convinced the other giants and you'll all have gone home together. Perhaps, though, some day... I mean, if I happened to have nothing better to do... I could come visit you?"

Saltlick beamed. "Easie visit," he agreed.

I could see Alvantes was getting impatient. Maybe Saltlick noticed too, for he chose that moment to reach down and offer me his hand. I let him clamp it around mine and we shook.

"Take care of yourself," I said. "Good luck."

Riding away, I fought the urge to look back. I managed well enough for a couple of minutes, and then allowed myself a glance over one shoulder. Sure enough, Saltlick was waiting where we'd left him. He grinned and waved.

I returned the wave; I couldn't quite manage the grin.

I would have been hard pressed to think of a single moment I'd enjoyed since I'd stolen the giant-stone from Moaradrid. My escapades with Saltlick and Estrada had seemed an unremitting nightmare at the time. Yet the knowledge that they were over, that we'd never travel together again, left me with a sense of emptiness.

What made it worse was the thought of who I still travelled with – a man who made no secret of loathing me, who until recently had wanted nothing more than to see my head on a chopping block.

Estrada was gone. Saltlick was gone. Now it was just Alvantes and me.

CHAPTER EIGHT

Though the ground to our right rose quickly into over-grown hillside, the road ran straight and uninterrupted and the land beside the Casto Mara remained more or less level. For the entire rest of the day I could see Aspira Nero as a streak of grey crawling shallowly from the wide-flowing river at its base to the outcrop of mountainside that marked its highest extreme.

There was little else to see there at the northern tip of the Castoval. The slopes were too stony and uneven for farming, and settlements were few and far between. Occasionally I'd catch a glimpse of the Casto Vidora, the river that flowed from the western mountains to merge its turbulent waters with the Casto Mara. Mostly, though, I was left with the walls of Aspira Nero and my own deliberations to keep me amused.

Neither was remotely up to the task. The view was tedious, and my thoughts insisted on tormenting me with questions I had no way to answer.

Like, *What happens now?*

What do you think there is here for you?

And last but far from least, *How much of a dung-brained moron would you have to be to give away all your gold?*

I tried to concentrate on Aspira Nero. Not only was it still dull, it served to remind me how desperate my circumstances had become. Minute by minute, I was drawing nearer to the edge of the world I knew.

The northernmost wall of Aspira Nero and the Casto Vidora joining the far bank were the absolute limits of the Castoval. Beyond was Ans Pasaeda and eventually, far to the north, the royal city of Pasaeda itself. But Aspira Nero belonged to neither north nor south. Defined by its location, it was a gateway and a melting pot, wedged between two very different nations.

Its grand walls, however, were mostly for show. They certainly hadn't done much to keep Moaradrid from tramping his armies through here. In fact, all he'd have needed to do was knock – for unlike even the smallest of the other towns, Aspira Nero had no garrison of defenders. Had there been troops here, the Castovalians would have considered them northern, the Ans Pasaedans as Castovalian. There *were* guardsmen, but they served no role in the town's protection, focusing all their energies on policing the streets instead. For all its unpredictable mingling of cultures and despite its labyrinthine streets, crime was practically unheard of in Aspira Nero.

In short, it was a depressing place, and I'd never wasted much time there.

Alvantes, of course, had no way of knowing that. When we were still a short distance away, he asked abruptly, "Are you wanted here?"

"What?" I said. "How would I know? No one sent me an invite if that's what you mean."

"*I mean*, have you committed any significant crimes that are likely to get you arrested on sight?"

"Oh. Not that I remember."

I'd never stolen anything bigger than an apricot in Aspira Nero, but I wasn't giving Alvantes the satisfaction of a straight answer.

He rode forward, dismounted, rapped hard on a smaller door set into the main gate and called, "Two travellers seeking ingress. I'm Guard-Captain Alvantes of Altapasaeda, and my companion is Easie Damasco."

I was a little disappointed when rather than shouts of, "Not Easie Damasco, the notorious thief and outlaw?" we were met with a disgruntled, "Hold your horses, damn it!"

A minute later, the door swung inward. A squat man in plain leather armour and conical helmet stood in the entrance. "Couldn't you have got here before we shut the main gate?" he complained.

"Evidently not," replied Alvantes.

The guard had sense enough to read his tone correctly. "Right. Evidently." He stepped out of the way. "Welcome to Aspira Nero. Portal between north and south and all that."

Dismounting, Alvantes led his horse through the gap, and I followed.

The narrow street beyond ran crookedly, somewhat up hill. The buildings had little of the Castovalian in their design. Like the walls, they were built from stone quarried in the mountainside behind, over two and even three storeys. Each seemed supported by its neighbours, giving the unsettling impression that if any one should collapse, the entire town would come tumbling down. The bare stone was harsh and unwelcoming, just as the few locals to note our arrival did so without a hint of friendliness.

I hoped Alvantes's local knowledge was better than mine was. "So what's the plan?" I asked. "I tell you, another day of riding will be the end of me."

"Damasco," he said, not turning. "It's time we talked. Or rather... it's time I talked and you listened."

"I'm not sure I like the sound of that."

"There's an inn I know nearby," he continued as though I'd never spoken.

There was an edge to his tone that brooked no argument. Instead, I trailed after him, down first one and then another twisting side street. From there, we turned into the yard of an inn named the *Fourth Orphan*. Alvantes called out a stable boy to take our horses, passed him a coin, and led on into the taproom.

It was clean but gloomy, full of purposefully dark corners. The handful of patrons stopped their conversations to watch our entrance with a little too much interest. In general, it struck me as more the kind of establishment I'd frequent than somewhere I'd expect to find Alvantes.

Still, it was clear he knew his way around. Pointing out an isolated table towards the back, he said, "Sit down."

I did as I was told, tucking myself into one of two opposing benches that shared a low table. A minute later, Alvantes eased onto the opposite bench, placed a cup of wine before me. Not much caring that he'd bought nothing for himself, I took an eager sip. It was headier and sweeter than any Castovalian wine I'd tasted, perhaps a vintage from across the border.

"So," I said, "this is pleasant. But perhaps it's time you got out what's on your mind."

"Damasco. I've never made any pretence of liking you."

"You haven't. No one could ever accuse you of pretence."

"However, I did agree to civility. I want you to understand, therefore, that this is not intended as an attack. It's simple fact, and it requires saying."

"I'll keep that in mind."

Alvantes leaned forward, single palm flat on the table. "Some days ago, I made two promises to Marina. The first was to make certain Saltlick was reunited with his people. The second was that I'd allow you to accompany me for so long as you wanted. For reasons I don't begin to understand, Marina thinks my company will do you good."

"She knows how you make me laugh," I tried.

"The fact is, I don't trust you or your motives. Frankly, I'd hoped you'd have taken the hint by now and found some other way in which to occupy yourself. I don't know what the current situation in Ans Pasaeda is, but if anything should happen there, I won't be able to protect you. Nor would I try. I won't break my promise to Marina by forbidding you to continue, but I will say this: you aren't welcome, Damasco."

I was taken aback. No witty rejoinder came to mind. It wasn't that I didn't expect bluntness from Alvantes, but in the past, it had always arrived in small and easily dismissed doses.

The worst of it was, I knew he was right. I could admit a certain fondness for Saltlick, even Estrada I'd grown to tolerate – but they were gone, and who knew if I'd see them again. What could be more pitiful than trying to imitate my time with them by following after Alvantes like some starved puppy?

"Look," he said – and I was appalled to hear a note to his voice not entirely removed from sympathy – "I understand that on some level you may occasionally mean well. Maybe you're even serious in these infrequent, half-hearted attempts at repentance. My advice, for whatever it's worth, is that you take some time to think over your next move. I need to gather information before I cross the border, and I can't do it with you there. Why don't you take the night to consider? If you really feel the need to accompany me, I'll be leaving at dawn."

I felt empty – as though Alvantes's words had hollowed me from head to toe. I could tolerate many things from the man, but pity? "There's nothing to consider," I said. "I didn't want to tell you this, but Estrada asked me to look after you too. 'He's been acting so strangely since Moaradrid made him a cripple,' she told me. 'With that and failing to protect the Prince, I'm not sure he can cope without someone looking over his shoulder.'"

Alvantes jerked towards me. My cup sloshed its

contents over the table, rolled to shatter on the floor.
"You're lying."

"I told her I'd do my best. But I won't go anywhere
I'm not wanted."

Alvantes gave a brief, bitter laugh. "You've spent
your entire life going where you're not wanted."

"Well, no more. Find another nursemaid, Alvantes."

I stood up. My knees felt mushy, my legs were shaking – with both anger and fear, for the look on
Alvantes's face was one of barely held rage. With all the
calm I could muster, I marched towards the door. At
the last moment, I slammed a twelfth-onyx down before the serving girl and said, "That's for the broken cup.
You'll have to excuse my friend, his handicap makes
him clumsy."

I wasn't certain I'd get out the door without Alvantes catching me and beating me into a bloody
puddle. I never doubted he could do it, missing hand
or no. I'd already decided I'd run at the first hint of
pursuit; battles of words were the only kind I could
ever hope to win against him.

No footsteps came. I made it through the door, out
of the courtyard, into the street, around a corner. I
moved mechanically, barely thinking. I still felt empty,
and painfully on edge. I'd put Alvantes in his place,
but there was no satisfaction in it.

Because everything he'd said was true. I'd known
it all along.

My planned trip north might have begun as some
harebrained idea about stealing from the King, but
that particularly fantasy had dissolved in the first cold

light of day. Such schemes belonged to the Damasco of old, the one who'd rob a warlord's tent on hardly more than a whim. The new Damasco was tired of hurling himself into jeopardy; the new Damasco wanted a week to go by with no one trying to kill him.

No, the reason I'd followed Alvantes was simply that it was easier than confronting the question of my future.

Now I was alone – and alone, there was no respite. As much as it sickened me to admit it, Alvantes was right about something else as well. For reasons I couldn't comprehend, I was suffering from fits of do-gooding, which invariably sabotaged my own prospects. This time, I'd really gone too far. I'd given up my wealth for a few raggedy peasants and a herd of giants too stupid not to sit and starve.

It's just money. Could I really have said that?

Those two gold coins might have become a small house, even a business of my own. My remaining onyxes would keep me for a few weeks, but when they were gone, they were gone. What could I do then? The only trade I'd ever known was thieving. If Mounteban's schemes succeeded, that career choice promised to be more hazardous than ever.

I could leave the Castoval, try to start again else-where... perhaps pilfer from deserving northerners instead of my own kinsmen. Then again, the Royal Court was notoriously tough on even the pettiest of crimes. What if I were to steal my coins back? It wouldn't even really be stealing. How could the Patri-arch and Huero reasonably expect me to put the

welfare of dim-witted giants or unwashed villagers before my own?

"Watch where you're going, you slouching lice
herder!"

I sidestepped just in time to avoid the man who'd
so colourfully insulted me. I'd been walking almost
without realising it, not paying attention to where I
was going or who was in my way. There were perhaps
haps a dozen streets in Aspira Nero I might have
recognised from my previous brief visits, and this
wasn't one of them.

Apart from a thin slice of land by the waterside, Aspira Nero clung entirely to the steep hillside, climbing
in waves until it crashed against the sheer mountain
wall. There were hardly any real roads, few routes that
could be travelled except by foot. Most ways through
the town were little more than winding crevasses between high buildings, punctuated by steps in the more
precipitous portions, shadowed by arches where other
walkways crossed overhead.

I'd been ascending one such path. Close on either
side were narrow houses with deep, recessed door-
ways. Curves of the trail cut off any view above or
below; I couldn't even judge how far up the hill I'd
climbed.

Since I had nowhere to go, it didn't seem to matter
a great deal. I carried on uphill, paying just enough
notice this time to avoid collisions. Now that I was actually looking, I was surprised by how many people I
passed. Evening was close enough that the confines of
the thoroughfare were sunk in gloom, with bands and

squares of ruddy amber slatting the higher walls; but the hour had done nothing to quieten the town.

Abruptly, a turn brought me out on a wider avenue, even busier than the alley. Again, despite the approach of evening, there were countless stalls and shops still open. A hundred overlapping conversations assailed my ears. If there was one thing Aspira Nero was famed for, it was that anything could be purchased within its walls, regardless of day or night.

I had no interest in shopping. I might have been tempted to indulge in its close cousin, if a brief glance hadn't identified half a dozen guardsmen in plain view. I was tired of walking, though, and even more tired of thinking. I came to a halt before a shop window. Unlike most of the stores, its goods were displayed behind a clear pane of glass. That was rare stuff, expensive to produce to such a quality; the signs beside the flamboyant hats within confirmed that I'd happened upon a particularly high-class establishment. Even if I hadn't idiotically given away my money, I'd have been hard pressed to afford its wares.

Well, I had no desire for an absurd hat. It wasn't the display that had caught my attention. Something else had stirred me from my mood of half-awareness. I glanced left and right, wondering if I'd glimpsed some detail in the corner of my eye.

There was nothing. The stores to either side were blank-walled, goods hidden behind closed doors.

My sluggish brain woke a little more. If it hadn't been the display, it had been the window itself. The setting sun had left it in shadow, turning its surface into a murky mirror of the street behind. I could make out the outlines of buildings, and of people too. Most were smudged by motion, like fish passing underwater.

One, small and distant-seeming, didn't move at all.

When I turned, it was like moving in a dream. Part of my brain was convinced he wouldn't be there. It was an illusion, made plausible by the distorting reflection. Just some market patron waiting for an assignation. Because there was no way, no way at all he could have followed me.

Synza, across the street in the darkness of a doorway, touched his fingers to his forehead in salute. His smile was like a razor.

I'd known fear before. Lately, it had been a constant companion. Yet nothing could compare to the rush of pure horror that passed through me then. Synza stepped from the doorway, began to walk towards me. There was nothing threatening in the motion. He looked indifferent, at ease. That, more than anything, held me in place. Synza had always clung to secrecy. Now here we were, staring at each other across a busy market street. It made no sense.

He'd covered half the distance before it even occurred to me to run.

A narrow side street branched to my left. I broke towards it. A couple of nearby guardsmen turned their gaze to follow. Seeing no one chasing, hearing no one calling "Thief!" they were quick enough to dismiss me. In turn, I noticed them only vaguely, as through a haze. What did they matter? Only Synza and the fear were real.

I nearly lost my balance at the turn-off, careened hard against a wall. There was no pain. I didn't want to look back, didn't want to do anything except run. The fear left me no choice, though; it reached out, dragged my neck around.

There was Synza, strolling down the market road towards me.

The side street was narrower than it had seemed. I didn't like the look of it. But Synza was drawing closer. Seeing me watching, he gave a small wave. My heart bobbed like a rotten apple into my throat.

I ran.

I managed twenty strides before a sheer flight of stairs came out of nowhere. I made the first half-dozen on foot; the rest I descended in a whirl of limbs. If I was hurt, I didn't feel it. All the tumble did was redouble my fear. I staggered back to my feet.

Synza gazed down at me from the highest step.

I wanted to scream. All that came out was a high-pitched squeak. This was a nightmare. How was he keeping up with me at a saunter? What was wrong with the fabled guardsmen of Aspira Nero that a murderer could stalk his prey unhindered through the streets?

Again, I ran. Now, however, each bound sent shudders through my left leg. I'd injured myself tumbling down the flight of steps, or perhaps crashing into the wall. There was still no pain as yet – but I knew it was on its way.

The passage slanted sharply right. This time I had sense enough not to look back. Beyond the corner, it became a sort of terrace, with just a metal rail to separate it from the town's descending tiers. I was shocked to see how high up the hillside I'd climbed; more than half of Aspira Nero lay below.

Ahead, the path dipped again, into a crevasse of the buildings. Before I could start for it, my leg buckled. Just in time, I caught the railing, and hobbled on. I wanted more than anything to watch as Synza bore down on me, with nonchalance worse than any menace. The urge to glance behind was actually painful. I fought against it. Every movement was energy better spent in trying to stay alive. That was the message my instincts screamed: *Keep moving!*

Except – one tiny part of my mind cried out in dissent. It was faint but it was determined, and what it said was, *This makes no sense!*

Why would Synza abandon discretion now? Why in Aspira Nero, where there were so many witnesses?

Only there weren't.

Not here. Not one.

I was being herded.

He'd gambled on my urge to go to ground. He'd guessed my instinct would choose a narrow alley over a busy market street. Maybe he knew Aspira Nero far better than me. Maybe he'd planned for me to see him; picked his moment, made certain I'd go just where he wanted.

Maybe I was running into a dead end.

I could be wrong. But the next turning was close. Beyond it, my options dwindled to nothing. Here, I had a choice. It wasn't one I dared consider. If I picked wrong, I was done for. Chances were I was done for either way. Maybe all I could hope for was to go out my own way, not Synza's.

I vaulted the railing, wincing as my hurt leg clipped the bar. I landed on damp, steep-angled tiles, barely kept my footing. Now I was facing back the way I'd come. Synza had reached the last turning – and for the first time, his face showed a reaction. For the first time he didn't look like a fox who knew the rabbit had nowhere to go.

I'd dinted his indomitable confidence. This wasn't over.

I hurled myself right. Even as his hand flicked up, even as bright metal glinted, I was falling. Striking the tiles blasted all the air from my lungs.

I didn't care. I could roll without breathing.

I heard the clack of knife on slate. So long as it wasn't the squish of knife in flesh. The rooftop was steep. It didn't take much effort at all to tumble down it. In fact, I doubted very much if I could stop. Well, I didn't intend to try. Instead, I snatched an instant of silent pleading to whatever forces governed the fates of dashing sneak thieves.

Something soft! Something soft! Something…

I fell – onto a second rooftop. It could only have been a short distance; just enough to slam out what little breath I'd managed to recover. This roof was even steeper. I picked up speed. The world was a flurry of tiles and ruddy sky, whipping about my head. I scrunched my eyes. I didn't need to see whatever came next.

I knew when I left the second rooftop that it wasn't another small drop. I knew because I had time enough to realise I was falling. Then I hit something. It wasn't exactly soft. Nor could it take my weight. I'd barely registered the sound of tearing cloth before I struck the ground.

The ground was definitely not soft.

Yet neither had it smashed every bone in my body. Once again, it seemed the universe wanted me alive.

Of course. It couldn't very well torment me if I was dead.

I opened my eyes, took a moment to compensate for my surroundings not spinning. I'd come to rest in another market street, shabbier than the one I'd left. Before me stood the remnants of a small, canopied stand. Half of it was more or less intact, though most of the fruit once exhibited on stacks of crates was now displayed in the road instead. The other half was smashed to rags and firewood.

The stall keeper – who happened, thankfully, to have been inhabiting the undemolished portion – was staring down at me, his eyes huge with shock. With one hand, he made a fluttering gesture that took in the explosion of produce pulped into the cobbles.

My eyes roved up, to the edge of the building I'd plummeted from. I'd covered a respectable distance. But it was more than idle curiosity guiding my gaze; I wouldn't put it past Synza to descend more carefully, hoping for a vantage point and another shot at my life.

No… no assassins. Only a few cracked tiles to mark the point of my departure. I wobbled to my feet. Shakily, I took out an onyx, slipped it into his palm.

"That should cover it," I managed.

This was becoming a habit I could ill afford. If I kept falling through things at this rate, I'd be bankrupt in days, not weeks. He looked at the coin, looked at the damage, performed a few swift mental calculations. "Just about."

"Well then." I teetered, managed with considerable effort to stay on my feet. My mouth felt bloated and tasted of blood. "Could you point me to the *Fourth Orphan*?"

He considered, pointed downhill. "Second left onto White Flag Way, then the first right. Follow Longditch."

"Thanks. Pleasure doing business."

I reeled away, before he could decide he was being entirely too cordial to someone who'd just annihilated his livelihood. Through the fog of pain and disorientation, I tried to make sense of the last few minutes. Might Synza have waited in Aspira Nero on the chance we'd pass through? Then again, I'd hardly been covering my tracks since Casta Canto. It wouldn't have taken a skilled tracker to follow my trail; anyone asking the right questions in the right places could have managed it.

That being the case, I had to assume he knew where I'd be heading now. He might even be moving to cut me off. Perhaps that should have changed my plans, but I was too battered and fuddled to formulate any sort of plan. If I was to survive another night, I could think of only one solution. It was indescribably unappealing – but marginally better than letting Synza bury a knife in my throat.

I'd followed the stall keeper's directions without any conscious attention. Ahead of me was the *Fourth*

Orphan. Though the crowds were thinning with the press of evening, there was still a fair amount of traffic past its entrance. Even if Synza was on my tail, I had to hope that would protect me. I lurched through the throng, across the yard and inside – all without being murdered. Steadying myself against the door frame, I called to the serving girl, "The man I came in with earlier… is he here?"

"He's taken a room upstairs. Third from the stairs." Her eyes stayed on me. Bruised, dripping with the detritus of smashed fruit, I must have made quite a sight. "Do you need me to call a guard?"

"Just an accident," I told her. "More my fault than his. Should have thought about where I was going."

That at least was true.

She didn't look entirely convinced, though. Fortunately, a patron at the far end of the bar chose that moment to call for wine, and I took the opportunity to limp upstairs. I made my way to the door she'd identified, rapped three times.

It took Alvantes a while to open up. When he did, it was with an expression of caution that, recognising me, he changed rapidly to disgust. "I didn't think you'd dare return." Then, registering my appearance, his eyes narrowed. "What in the Hells have you been up to?"

"Alvantes… it's Synza. I know you know the name. Mounteban sent him after me, and he's been on my tail ever since Altapasaeda. I thought I'd lost him…"

Alvantes's blow was so sudden, so unexpected, that it carried me off my feet. It was all I could do to stop myself tumbling over the balcony. Instinct made me tense for another attack. Only when seconds had passed and none came did I dare look up.

Alvantes hadn't moved from his spot. His fist hung tensed at his side.

"You bastard," I mumbled, massaging my jaw, "what was that for?"

"All this time – you put us all in danger. You put *Marina* in danger. You'd have led a killer to the King's very door if he'd let you. Why didn't you tell me this straight away?"

I hoisted myself to my feet, keeping a careful distance from Alvantes's still-clenched hand. "Because you wouldn't have done a thing. In fact, you'd have probably left me somewhere for him to find, with a note thanking him for all his hard work."

"You damned fool," he said. "Is that what you believe?"

It wasn't, of course. However much Alvantes disliked me, I knew he hated a career killer like Synza more. "All right. What could you have done? How exactly would you have protected me?"

Alvantes's expression changed, the anger ebbing abruptly. "Get inside, Damasco."

I did as instructed – though warily. The room was spare, the only furnishings a narrow bed, a small chest and a single chair. I sank into it, almost sobbing as my battered muscles relaxed. "You didn't answer my question," I said.

"You're right. There probably wasn't anything I could have done. Synza's not just some twelfth-onyx thug. There were a dozen murders in Altapasaeda I suspected him of, but I could never find one shred of evidence."

"If you're trying to make me feel better, it's not working."

"I couldn't care less how you feel." Alvantes massaged the bridge of his nose furiously, sank onto the end of the bed. "As if things weren't bad enough."

"Cut a long story short. If you've no intention of helping me, just say it."

"Of course I'll help you. Whatever's between you and me, I keep my promises. I told Marina I'd look after you and I will. Damn it, though," he added, a new note of tension entering his voice, "if only you knew how you've forced my hand."

Before I could even think to ask what he meant, Alvantes was back on his feet and pacing to the door.

"Wait," I cried. "You're not leaving?"

"Unless you want to sit here and wait to die, there are things I need to take care of. Lock yourself in."

"How long are you…"

The door slammed shut behind him.

I scurried to slam the bolt into place. After a moment's thought, I went back for the chair and jammed its back against the door. Then I closed the window shutters and bolted them too. I considered upending the bed across them, but it looked excessively heavy. I sat down in the chair instead.

I realised I was shaking. Despite how I felt about Alvantes, I'd have given every coin I had left to make him come back. But he wasn't about to. Perhaps he never would. All his noble talk could easily have been a lie to rid himself once and for all of the irritation that was Easie Damasco.

Damasco? I can't understand it, Marina. He was perfectly fine when I left him.

No. I couldn't expect any help from Alvantes. And Synza surely knew where I was. What were a bolted door and a shuttered window to a master-assassin? Yet there was nowhere else I could go either, nowhere that would be less dangerous.

I was trapped. I was alone.

All I could do was wait.

CHAPTER NINE

I didn't think I'd sleep. Not then. Not ever again.

Yet as the night wore on, so my thoughts began to muddle and turn in on themselves, the darkened room becoming more of a blur. The next I knew, I was being woken from shapeless nightmares by the sound of hammering on the door. I lurched to my feet – or tried to. My bruised muscles were in no condition for swift movements. The chair spun sideways, and I ended up in a heap on the floor.

I crawled to the door on hands and knees and tried to listen. There was nothing except silence now. I didn't trust silence. In my mind, it shaped itself around a small, gaunt man, and the glistening blade he held in one lean hand.

"What are you doing in there? Open the damned door, Damasco."

It certainly sounded like Alvantes. "How do I know it's you?"

"You'll know in five seconds' time when I kick it down."

Maybe it was possible to imitate Alvantes, but imitating an angry Alvantes was a stretch too far. I dragged back the bolt and opened the door.

Alvantes pushed past me. "Are you ready to leave?"

I could see that the passage outside was doused in gloom, with one lone lamp burning at the head of the stairs. "It's still night," I said.

"An hour before dawn."

I took a moment to digest that fact. "Yes. Of course, I'm ready. I never even had a chance to unpack my saddle bags."

"You won't need them. We're leaving the horses here."

I couldn't help noticing that even as he said it, Alvantes was dragging his own bags from the chest in the corner. If he was aware of the hypocrisy, he gave no sign.

In all that had happened, I'd forgotten the mystery of what Alvantes was hiding. Now, as he hoisted the bags over one shoulder, I could just discern the faint bulge I'd noticed before. Should I be lucky enough to survive the next few minutes, it was something I'd have to investigate. Now that we were apparently stuck together, it wouldn't do for Alvantes to be keeping interesting secrets from me.

As for myself, I had everything I really needed: my rucksack, what little money I had left and the clothes on my back. "All right," I said. "I'm ready."

"Follow me then. And try to keep up. We don't have much time."

I did as I was told, keeping close to Alvantes as he

marched along the balcony, down the stairs, out through the door of the *Fourth Orphan*.

The moment we stepped into the open air, my heart began to hammer. There were no street lights in this portion of Aspira Nero. Beneath a cloudy and moonless sky, the shadows were thickly black. One glance showed me countless places Synza could be hiding.

Perhaps his earlier attack hadn't been as reckless as it had seemed, but it certainly suggested he'd relaxed his standards. There was no reason to think Alvantes's presence would deter him. In this darkness, Synza could kill me a dozen times before Alvantes even noticed I was gone.

I stayed near as we crossed the courtyard and turned into the street, trying to keep in Alvantes's line of sight – a next to impossible goal when I had no idea where we were going. If Aspira Nero was mazelike by day, it was doubly so at night. All I could gather was that we were heading downward, which meant we were travelling roughly west. I struggled to construct a mental map of the town, but it was hopeless. Between pain, tiredness and my basic lack of knowledge, I was helplessly disorientated.

Only when we came out into clear space through a gap in the buildings did I realise our objective should have been obvious. There were only two routes across the border, and only one lay to the west. In fact, I should have guessed the moment Alvantes told me we were leaving the horses. Before us lay the dockside.

The harbours of Aspira Nero were almost as large as those at Altapasaeda, and more impressive in their way. Though the low stone wharfs and occasional wooden jetties were basic enough, they were home to craft far grander than the skiffs and barges that dawdled along the southern portion of the river.

Such was the vessel Alvantes was leading us towards. It might have been the biggest riverboat I'd ever seen. Even if it could somehow have passed under the bridge that rose to our left, it couldn't possibly have navigated the southern Casto Mara without scraping its bottom out on the shallower sections. Only to the north, where the river broadened and deepened, could such a craft be of use.

It bore a single sail amidships and a low, rail-enclosed aftcastle. I could see men moving on board despite the hour, and a small group clustered near the gangplank. As we drew near, Alvantes hissed, "Don't speak of the King. Don't bring up Panchetto or Moaradrid. Definitely don't mention the situation in the far north or the Bastard Prince."

"Who's the...?"

"Shut up. In fact, in general, keep your mouth shut."

One of the men on the dockside broke away to block our path. "Who goes there?" he said.

"It's Alvantes, with the companion I spoke of."

The man moved nearer. I saw he was dressed in uniform, though it wasn't one I recognised. "Just in time, Guard-Captain. Get aboard, please."

Alvantes hesitated. "Damasco, this is Commander Ludovoco of the Crown Guard... also captain of this boat, the *Prayer at Dusk.*"

"There'll be time for introductions later." Ludovoco made no effort to mask the impatience in his voice.

Alvantes nodded, and led the way across the last stretch of dockside and up the narrow ramp. Ludovoco and his men fell in behind, and I couldn't help noticing how the sailors on deck stopped what they were doing to form around us. On that unlit deck, at that predawn hour, our welcome seemed more menacing than gracious.

As the gangplank was hauled up, Ludovoco said, "Come. I'll show you your quarters."

He led us through the leftmost of two doors set either side of the aftcastle, down a narrow flight of stairs and through another door off a claustrophobic passage. The room beyond was tiny, just big enough for the two bunks it contained. There was a hurricane lamp suspended from the ceiling, already lit. In its light, I got my first proper look at Ludovoco.

He was to the younger side of middle age, his dark hair shorn short beneath a skullcap, clean-shaven but for a thin moustache and a jut of beard beneath his sharply angled chin. His uniform was of fabric so starkly black that it seemed to eat the light, relieved only by the flash of silver insignia at his breast. He wore a sword, slightly curved, though not so much as the scimitars favoured by Moaradrid's plainsmen. It didn't look remotely ornamental.

In short, he cut a daunting figure – and his manner did nothing to allay the impression. "Somewhat spare," he said, in a tone that made it clear he wasn't the least concerned with our comfort. "We're a military vessel, not prepared for guests."

"We're glad of whatever you can provide," replied Alvantes, matching our host's tone of bare civility note for note. "If our mission weren't of the utmost importance, we'd never have imposed."

"If it weren't, you'd never have been allowed to. Now, as I'm sure you'll appreciate, I'm needed on deck. May I ask that you confine yourselves to quarters for the time being."

It wasn't a question, and Ludovoco didn't wait for an answer. He stepped out, shut the door behind him. I almost expected the click of a lock, but none came; at least we were trusted to do our own confining, it seemed.

I sat on the lower bunk. "Your friend doesn't seem too pleased to have us along. Are you sure this is a good idea?"

"I doubt it is. But it's the only way to ensure Synza can't reach you."

"So who is this Ludovoco?"

"He's a commander in the Crown Guard. They're something like Altapasaeda's Palace Guard, though with a broader mandate – and of course, far greater territory. Within their jurisdiction they have absolute authority, answering only to the King himself."

I gave a low whistle. "That's a lot of power. No wonder Ludovoco doesn't go in much for manners."

"He's doing us a favour," said Alvantes. But he sounded sceptical. As was so often the case lately, it was obvious there was more here than I was seeing.

I was too tired to riddle it out then, though, and trying to get straight answers from Alvantes was wearisome at the best of times. It could wait until morning. I lay back on my bunk and pulled the single thin blanket over me. "Well," I said, "I suppose it beats another day on horseback."

I slept a broken and murky few hours' sleep, unable to find any portion of the hard bunk that didn't make my damaged flesh hurt more. I was almost glad when Alvantes clambered down and relit the storm lamp.

With no portholes, it was impossible to judge the time of day. However, sounds of activity from the rest of the boat suggested it was well past sunrise. I sat up, kneading swollen eyes, to see Alvantes looking down at me.

"We should show our faces on deck," he said. "Damasco, if you only ever listen to one thing I say, let it be this. Be careful around Ludovoco and his men. Don't engage with them if you can help it. One wrong word could put us both in grave danger."

"I'll be on my best behaviour," I said. "Better still, I'll be on *your* best behaviour." I tried to sound glib, but I couldn't help wondering what exactly we'd swapped Synza for. There'd been definite unease in Alvantes's voice.

On deck, Ludovoco greeted us with a curt nod. "Good morning," he said. "I won't be assigning you work, but please take care to stay out of my men's way."

I glanced at Alvantes, wondering if this suggestion of delegating labour to the guard-captain of Altapasaeda was as much a slight as it seemed. If it had registered, Alvantes hid it well. "Perhaps the upper deck?" he asked.

"That would be suitable. One of my men will bring you food when they eat."

I followed Alvantes up a near-vertical flight of stairs. As he must have observed, there was no one on the small aftcastle deck. He picked a spot upon the horse-shoe of balustrade that ringed its edge and sat with his back against it. I followed his example, choosing a point as far from him as possible.

And that was how we spent the day. Within minutes I'd come to two obvious realisations, which only grew more apparent as the hours wore by. Being on a river-boat was boring. Being on a riverboat with Alvantes and a crew that made no secret of resenting our presence was the most boring thing imaginable.

At first, I found some distraction in watching Ans Pasaeda go by and noting how its sights differed from the scenery back home. Unfortunately, in most ways the answer was barely at all. The fields looked like Castovalian fields, the trees like Castovalian trees, and the dim purple hem of mountains far to the west looked very much like the mountains that bordered the Castoval. Even the farms and small settlements we passed were only a little dissimilar, built mostly of unplastered yellow brick with pale thatched roofs. The only significant differences were a sense of wide-open space the Castoval could never offer and the wheeling white specks in the sky far to the east that marked the presence of the ocean.

After a few hours of having my mind turned steadily to mush, I asked Alvantes, "How long until we reach Pasaeda?"

"Perhaps two more days," he said. "Assuming this wind holds."

I groaned inwardly, cursed my own survival instincts. Would it have been so hard to let Synza kill me? Better that than death by scenery.

I'd realised by the second day that if I didn't find a distraction I'd undoubtedly go mad.

At first, I entertained myself by wondering at all the things Alvantes might have hidden in his saddlebag. Perhaps it was a rare treasure he'd stolen from Panchetto's palace. Perhaps he was a spy, sneaking documents to shadowy conspirators in the Royal Court, or was bolstering his meagre guard salary by smuggling rare contraband. Maybe he was really an assassin like Synza, with some outlandish weapon stashed for the one moment he'd need it.

While the possibilities I came up with offered brief amusement, they were all absurd – which only made me more determined to satisfy my curiosity in a more practical fashion. However, that line of thought led me quickly to the second of the day's insights.

For guests, we were being treated an awful lot like prisoners.

It took a while to sink in. Though Ludovoco and his crew lacked manners, they weren't without discretion. Hour on hour, however, it became more clear that whatever the business on deck, someone always had an eye trained in our direction.

What did it mean? Would Alvantes have been foolish enough to fill Ludovoco in on my career history?

Had my notoriety crossed the border into Ans Pasaeda?
Yet the attention didn't seem aimed specifically in my
direction; quite the opposite in fact. Perhaps it was just
that Ludovoco's service to the King had made him unduly paranoid, even towards his own. After all, being
guard-captain of the Castoval's only city might not
carry much weight to an Ans Pasaedan.

As it turned out, both questions came to a head late
in the afternoon. We'd arrived at a junction in the
river, an almighty confluence of fast-flowing water.
The Casto Mara (called the Mar Corilus here, according to Alvantes), continued east towards the sea,
already twice as wide as it ran anywhere in the Castoval. To the north-west, it was met by another river,
narrower but still impressive, known as the Mar
Paraedra. That was the course that would take us on
to Pasaeda.

On the left bank of the junction was a small harbour
town, and here the *Prayer at Dusk* docked, for reasons
no one felt the need to share with us. A few of the
men immediately hauled the gangplank into place and
descended.

To my surprise, Alvantes left his place against the
stern railing and strode towards the ladder joining
upper and lower decks. It was the first time I'd seen him
move purposefully since we'd come on board – and that
immediately stirred my interest. Whatever he was up
to, it might just help alleviate the day's tedium. I hurried to follow.

Ludovoco had just arrived on deck. Alvantes swung
down the ladder and came to a smart halt in front of his

fellow officer. "I see we've stopped," he said. "Perhaps I could take a few minutes ashore to stretch my legs."

"I'm sorry," said Ludovoco, "I can't spare anyone to accompany you."

"I won't need any assistance."

"Let me speak plainly. You are under the protection of the Crown Guard. As long as that remains the case, you're my responsibility. To have you wandering un-escorted is a risk I'm not willing to take."

"I've no intention of going far, let alone placing my-self in danger."

"Nevertheless…"

"Commander, I must insist."

The silence that followed was heavy as the minutes before a storm, as though the very air was holding still in anticipation. The moment seemed to stretch impos-sibly. Then, as if nothing untoward had been said, Ludovoco waved over one of the sailors. "Labro," he said. "I'm assigning you to Guard-Captain Alvantes. Take him wherever he'd like to go in town." He put particular emphasis on those last two words. To Al-vantes he added, "Might I suggest you take your companion with you."

"Fine by me," I agreed.

"I can give you an hour. After that, Labro will escort you back."

"An hour will be ample," Alvantes agreed.

"Good." With a gesture somewhere between a salute and a wave of dismissal, Ludovoco turned and disap-peared into the lower deck.

I watched his retreating back in fascination. What

I'd just witnessed was a pissing contest, pure and simple, and Alvantes had instigated it. I wondered if the results were what he'd hoped for. Ludovoco had given ground, but in such a fashion as to make clear who was in control – and that we were going nowhere without his say-so. If Alvantes had been feeling out the limits of his status aboard the *Prayer at Dusk*, he had his answer right there.

Now it was time for me to do the same. I'd seen an opportunity that might not come again. "Just a moment," I said, "I've left my coin in my cabin. This is my first time in Ans Pasaeda. Who knows what I might find?"

Labro wavered, obviously unsure how this fit into his orders. In the end, he looked to Alvantes.

"Be quick," Alvantes told me.

"I'm always quick."

And I was – when I was up to something I didn't want to be interrupted.

I scurried down into the aftcastle and on into our room, closing the door quietly behind me. Alvantes's bags were crammed into the slender gap between the bunks and the outer hull. I took a moment to memorise their precise position, then pulled them free.

Now that I knew what to expect, it was easy to see which had the slight bulge at its base. I drew out the bag's contents, a blanket, a change of shirt and other personal effects, taking care to remember how everything was packed and piling them accordingly.

The bags were leather, lined with heavy cloth. I could see immediately that the bottom of the other saddlebag's lining had been cut out and sewn into this one. Feeling around, it wasn't hard to detect a half-dozen shallow bumps beneath the fabric, or to identify them from shape and size as onyxes.

Not bad. Quite clever even. Alvantes's ploy might have fooled anyone who didn't know what to look for – and hadn't been the one to educate him in the art of hiding things. With that in mind, it didn't take a genius to notice there was another thumb's length of space beneath the false bottom. My guess was he'd removed the bottoms of both bags and sandwiched them together, with the coins between and a shallow hiding place beneath.

It would be tricky to investigate further without leaving evidence – and time was running out. I pushed one hand within the bag, placed the other on the outside and teased along the edge of the false bottom. Something solid ran around the circumference. It didn't give at all, but nor was it heavy enough to much affect the bag's weight. Perhaps some reinforcement for the compartment? Then again, the stiff leather outer would suffice for that. More likely, this was the hidden object itself. What could it be? A perfect ring of metal, thin, light, a thumb's length deep…

I realised I wasn't breathing – hadn't been for I couldn't say how long. With a great effort, I forced myself to draw air.

It was a crown.

No. It was *Panchetto's* crown.

To all intents and purposes, Alvantes had been carrying round the princedom of Altapasaeda.

Mounteban would kill without hesitation to have it.

So would many others – maybe even Ludovoco. Who knew what nest of political vipers we might have stumbled into?

Using the tiny portion of my mind still functioning, I heaped Alvantes's belongings into the saddlebag, put both bags back as I'd found them. It was tricky to remember how to walk, but I managed it. I left the cabin, climbed the stairs to the deck. Alvantes gave me a brief glance of suspicion but said nothing.

"Shall we go?" I asked. I felt as if I was trying to talk around a mouth full of treacle, but if either of them noticed, they hid it well.

Panchetto's crown.

He'd been wearing it when I first met him. It had been exceptionally shiny. In bare weight of gold and jewels, it would be worth a fortune. Symbolically, it was worth a city, perhaps the fate of the entire Castoval.

No wonder Alvantes had taken pains to hide it.

The remainder of the day passed in a blur.

Before I knew it, we'd returned to the *Prayer at Dusk*. I couldn't recall a thing I'd seen, or any detail of the town we'd walked through, not even its name. On the rare occasions Alvantes or our "escort" Labro had bothered to speak to me, I thought I'd managed a coherent response. I couldn't remember the conversations any more than I could anything else.

As I lay in my bunk that night, my mind was a whirlpool, broken debris of thoughts whipping about its rim. How had Alvantes come upon the crown? It could only have been during the interval between

Panchetto's murder and our escape from Altapasaeda.
Knowing him, he had some high-minded idea about
keeping it from falling into the wrong hands.

Probably that was all this trip had ever been about.
Alvantes's talk of bearing the news of Panchetto's
death and recruiting the King's help against Mounteban had been little more than a smokescreen. In truth,
he was striving to return the crown to the safety of
royal hands.

What an appalling waste!

By the third day, I felt I was behaving more or less normally again. It helped that normality involved sitting
in silence on the aftcastle deck, watching Ans Pasaeda
drift by.

Here at least the landscape was moderately diverting.
To either side were vast and almost level plains, so
boundless that they made my eyes ache with their
magnitude. Scattered upon them were groves of unfamiliar willowy trees, great grazing herds of cattle, goats
and sheep and endless farms, each in its own rectan-
gular compound. There were villages too, a few larger
towns, and a couple of far-distant places that must
surely have been cities. Perhaps they were as big as or
bigger than Altapasaeda, yet the sense of scale made
even the largest communities seem insignificant.

I had to gaze far westward to see the land rise up,
where it finally gave way to the incline of the mountains. Even farther to the north, it was just possible to
make out the point where a great ridge of mountainside
jutted outward. According to Alvantes, our destination

lay at the lowest tip of that spur. If the wind continued to favour us through the night, we'd be there by early morning.

I slept restlessly. Numbing tedium and then the thrill of Alvantes's secret had served to quieten my other worries for most of the journey. As I lay there, wondering what the morrow would bring, they returned in force. I might have evaded Synza once again, but it was hard to escape the sense that I'd only swapped one threat for another. I was friendless and far from home. In fits of madness, I'd given away most of my money. Even finding one of the greatest treasures imaginable within my reach offered scant comfort, for what hope did I have of separating the crown from Alvantes before he hurled it away upon the King? All told, I could see no grounds for optimism.

When I woke, Alvantes was gone from his bunk. I'd grown accustomed enough to the sounds aboard boat to realise I'd overslept. Perhaps it was my troubled night, but I couldn't resist a creeping sense of anxiety, which worsened when I saw Alvantes had taken his saddlebags with him. That could only mean we were in or very near Pasaeda.

I hurried on deck – just in time. As I'd guessed, we were drawing into harbour. The walls of a colossal city were visible in the near distance, a city far greater than anywhere I'd seen, with the mountain outcrop rising dramatically behind. Alvantes stood against the port rail. Seeing me, he gave a terse nod. Then, as the men tied off against a bollard onshore, he moved to intercept Ludovoco.

"Commander... thank you for allowing us to travel with you. We can make our own way from here. I have a brief visit to make before I speak with the King."

Ludovoco eyed him coldly. "I'm afraid that won't be acceptable."

"It wasn't a suggestion," replied Alvantes, holding his gaze.

"Nor is this. You'll come with us now, to the palace."

"I came here of my own free will, in service to the King, and..."

Ludovoco silenced him with an upturned palm. "Guard-Captain," he said, "I hoped this needn't become difficult, but you leave me no choice. Henceforward, it will be easiest if you consider yourself under arrest."

CHAPTER TEN

I suspected I was taking our detention better than Alvantes.

Arrest, after all, was hardly a novelty. In fact, there was something almost comfortingly familiar about the presence of armed guards. Given the turmoil and uncertainty I'd endured in recent days, there was a lot to be said for knowing exactly where I stood.

In credit to Alvantes, however, for a man who'd just had the fundamentals of his existence turned on their head, he was bearing up as well as could be expected. I'd imagined he'd pick a fight with Ludovoco, or start raving about his honour. Instead, he'd clammed up completely. His mouth was set in a jagged line; his eyes were the barest slits. He followed directions with only the most terse of nods.

Ludovoco had made no attempt to explain our unorthodox treatment. My knowledge of local customs might have been meagre, but it didn't seem to make much sense. As we set out towards the capital, I amused myself with the possibility that this was what passed in Ans Pasaeda for humour; that at any moment Ludovoco and his men would break down in fits of laughter. As they marched us along the grand tree-lined boulevard joining harbour and city, I imagined giggling courtiers behind each tree. Drawing near the walls, I pictured the King himself leaping out, amidst general hilarity.

Needless to say, none of those things happened. Instead, we were forced to wait while the sentries in the gatehouse, who must have recognised Ludovoco, laboured to open the titanic portals via some mechanism inside. That it would have been far easier to let us through the smaller side gate apparently occurred to no one. The impracticality and needless ritual of it seemed a clear indication of the authority Ludovoco wielded.

While the gatekeepers struggled to make way, I craned my neck to gain my first direct impression of Pasaeda. Like Aspira Nero, the capital was built with its back to the mountain. Here, however, the diminishing crags split in a great crook that the city nestled within. From above, Pasaeda would appear as a rough diamond, with the fortifications completing the other two sides and this gate at its lowest tip.

And they were most certainly fortifications. No other word would do. They were higher even than the ramparts of Aspira Nero, receding in a series of shallow indents with a tower at every junction. There was no point on our side that couldn't be observed clearly from left or right. I caught glimpses of men within the towers, and others upon the walls – more than I'd have expected of any peacetime city.

Before I had time to wonder at that, the gap in the gates widened enough to admit us, and Ludovoco waved us on.

It was dark within the gatehouse and the day was bright. I was half-blind as I first stepped into Pasaeda. All I could see was a collage of incandescent shapes. Slowly, my eyes focused. Still I found I was hesitant to trust them. It was easier to believe I was still dazzled than that anything made by the hands of men could be so splendid.

I'd always thought the wealthier portions of Alta-pasaeda were the height of opulence. Now I realised that even at its grandest, Altapasaeda was only a shadow of the place it was named for. Here were no cramped alleys, no shabby markets, no homes that could possibly stoop to accommodate the poor – or if there were, they were well hidden.

Every house within view could have competed with and bested the finest of Altapasaeda's mansions. The reason the city blazed beneath the morning sun was that every single wall and roof was startlingly white. Unlike the buildings south of the border, however, that whiteness wasn't the result of stucco or paint but of luminous stone. Every surface was then carved into friezes, porticoes and columned arcades, which in turn were enriched by subtle designs in silver and gold. Gates and sections of ornate ironwork offered glimpses into meticulously tended grounds, where lush blooms bigger than my head tumbled amongst wide-fronded trees and mammoth, wavering ferns.

I continued to gape as Ludovoco marched us

through the city streets, all thoughts crammed out of my mind by the desire to soak in every detail. Who could have imagined there was so much money in the world? Truly, the thieves of Pasaeda must live like lords.

Then again, maybe thievery in Pasaeda might not be such a lucrative career after all. There were armed guards everywhere, all robed and turbaned in the same smoke grey the gatekeepers had been wearing. On the face of it, they actually seemed to outnumber the populace, for aside from their presence the streets were all but deserted. We saw only a few passing rich folk, travelling without much apparent sense of purpose on foot or horseback. Men and women both were dressed in long pale-shaded robes much like the guards, though in their cases jewellery and the obviously fine material set off any hint of austerity.

For people who lived amidst such magnificence, they didn't look particularly grateful, or even very happy. Certainly, they were quick to look away whenever their eyes chanced on Ludovoco and his men.

Which made it all the more startling when someone nearly rode into our small convoy. The guards snapped to attention and Ludovoco looked furious – at least until he recognised the rider. The man was advanced in years, though well preserved in the fashion only wealth could accomplish, and dressed in robes of crisp crocus yellow. He was flanked by two guards of his own, their outfits a more muted shade of the same.

Something about him put me in mind of a tall water bird, perhaps a crane, and his voice – a little high-pitched and warbling – did nothing to dispel the image. "Commander Ludovoco," he cried gladly.

Ludovoco considered the new arrival with barely stifled distaste. "Senator Gailus."

"And who's this with you? The aspect seems familiar. Do my eyes deceive, or is that Furio Alvantes's boy?"

"We're accompanying Guard-Captain Alvantes to the palace," replied Ludovoco, leaving no doubt in his tone as to whose business he considered the information.

"On royal affairs?"

"Are there any other kind?"

Gailus gave a shrill chuckle, though there'd been no hint of humour in Ludovoco's question. "Not for the likes of us, eh?" He trotted his horse leisurely around our little gathering, as though we were street sellers and he was appraising our goods. "If I didn't know better," he said, "I'd think you had our friend here under armed guard."

"Under escort," said Ludovoco.

Gailus chuckled again. "It so happens we're also riding to the palace. We'll accompany you."

"Of course," said Ludovoco. The look he gave Gailus said, *Since we both know I can't stop you.*

As Gailus fell in beside us, I noticed how his men exchanged hard looks with Ludovoco's. What enmity had we stumbled into now? I saw from Alvantes's face that he recognised this Gailus, but nothing gave me the impression they were friends or allies. This day was worsening by the minute – and it had hardly started well.

That conclusion had barely crossed my mind when Gailus proved it beyond doubt. Turning to Alvantes, he said, "I'm sure you appreciate that Commander Ludovoco is merely doing what he deems necessary."

"I've no doubt," said Alvantes. He even managed to sound like he meant it. Ludovoco, meanwhile, stared straight ahead. The only indication he was following the exchange was a nerve ticking rhythmically in the corner of his eye.

"The fact is," continued Gailus, "these last days have seen a dearth of information from across the border... no news even from our dear Prince Panchetto. Commander Ludovoco has been waiting in Aspira Nero, so I hear, to try and gather information."

"So I understand," Alvantes agreed.

"Until now, he's only been able to send back rumours, all disturbing. If his behaviour seems heavy-handed, I'd ask you to bear that in mind."

Ludovoco had had enough. The nerve in his eye gave one more compulsive shudder and he said, his voice like frosted iron, "If I may, Senator, Guard-Captain Alvantes will be thoroughly debriefed once we reach our destination."

"A polite way of telling an old man to mind his own business."

"I would never tell the senator what is or isn't his business. I'd only ask that he be careful how he speaks of mine."

Gailus chuckled once again. "I'll say no more."

After what I'd seen, I doubted very much that Gailus would be able to keep his word. It seemed I'd underestimated him, however. He trotted alongside us, his men to his left, and his only lapses from silence were to give one of his characteristic gurgles of mirth, as though his mind was still digesting whatever aspects of his conversation with Ludovoco had so amused him.

With the show apparently over, at least for the moment, I turned my attention back to the marvels of Pasaeda.

At the point we'd reached, a barricade of temples cut off the residential districts from the palace, just as in Altapasaeda. Though these were infinitely grander, their decoration was fundamentally the same. Festooned with flowers, perfumed with incense, hung with birdcages and strung together by arches, they formed an immense hive of worship that must have traversed an entire quarter of the city. Statues representing the gods loomed in every recess and burst forth from every prominence. Weird minglings of men and women with animals, birds and fish, which held the most unlikely things: a child's rattle here, a bucket or a three-pronged sword there. Some I recognised from Altapasaeda, many more were new to me; all were bizarre and terrifying.

It was a relief when we eventually broke through to the district of the palace – at least until I got my first proper look at it. Nestled deep in the crook of the mountains, its monolithic grandeur was the final move in Pasaeda's game of architectural one-upmanship.

The palace struck an unlikely compromise between splendour and defence. Somehow, it managed to be half plaster and glass confectionary, half unassailable fortress. In contrast to the rest of the city, it was also a riot of garish colour. Every window was stained glass, every roof a mosaic, every wall illuminated with bright curlicues or murals or clutters of inter-locking geometry.

It should have been chaotic – and it was. Yet it didn't seem to matter that nothing matched when every col-umn and balustrade was a masterpiece in its own right. The palace crept – in layers of roof and archway and balcony, through endless juts of tower and spire and cupola – up the sheer face of the cliffs, like an or-nate beetle clambering to safety.

All told, it made the palace in Altapasaeda look like a dung-collector's cottage. I'd never wanted to steal anything so badly in my life.

As we drew close, however, the fortress aspect of its character grew more apparent, and by the time we en-tered the palace grounds I felt more intimidated than impressed. We were ushered through a gatehouse in the outermost layer of defences, across a courtyard as big as many a Castovalian village, through another gatehouse, down a wide street bordered by tiers of ex-quisite garden, into yet another gatehouse in yet another set of walls into *yet another* courtyard – where Gailus left us, drifting off towards the stables with a jovial "Goodbye!" – and up a flight of marble stairs, through enormous double doors… until I found my-self, at last, within the palace itself.

By then, I'd had my fill of marvels. My head ached to match my feet, and I barely glanced at the colossal hall we'd ended up in. I chose to stare at the floor instead, which was mercifully plain, at least in comparison with everything else.

It seemed too much to ask that someone would offer us lunch, or at least a cup of wine. Minutes passed, punctuated with low-whispered conversations between Ludovoco and the palace staff. Just as I was sure I'd topple over, he ushered us on towards a small, draped archway.

Before we could pass through, however, a voice called, "There you are!"

It was Gailus – and I couldn't escape the feeling that he'd been waiting for this moment, though I hadn't seen him. He trotted over at a leisurely pace, to Ludovoco's obvious frustration.

"Off to the reception hall?" Gailus asked. "Why don't I take over from here?"

Ludovoco tensed. "Take over?"

"I'm a friend of young Alvantes's father, as you're no doubt aware. Since I agreed to hold my tongue on affairs of state, mightn't it be reasonable to ask for a minute to discuss affairs of family?"

"Alvantes is in my custody," said Ludovoco.

"He must pose quite a threat if you daren't leave him alone for even a minute."

"Not so far as I know."

"Or else be determined to escape?"

"There are... protocols."

"One minute, Commander, is all I ask. Your men can stay close to ensure our friend the guard-captain does nothing uncharacteristically treasonous."

Ludovoco froze. It was clear he wasn't used to being

talked to this way. I suspected a part of his brain was already busy plotting harsh reprisals.

The rest of him, however, seemed paralysed by the unfamiliar prospect of conceding defeat. Eventually, he tipped his head. Without a word, he led us through the curtain, down one long corridor and another, and off into a much smaller room, which I took from its sparse furnishings to be some sort of antechamber.

"Wait here," he told Alvantes. Gailus he carefully ignored. He motioned his men to one side of the room and disappeared through the drape that hung across the room's only other exit.

Scowling at Ludovoco's men, Gailus beckoned Alvantes and me towards the farther corner. "With all due respect to the Crown Guard," he intoned loudly, "I'm sure your father would prefer his private affairs to stay that way." When we were as far away from our black-clad escorts as the space allowed, he dropped his voice and added, *We don't have long.*

In that moment, his manner was unrecognisable. Gone was the cheerful, buffoonish figure who'd ridden beside us through Pasaeda.

"How *is* my father?" asked Alvantes. He seemed just as thrown by Gailus's changed tone as I was.

"Anxious for news. He thought you might try to come here. One of our men on the walls was ordered to send signal if there was any sign of you."

"*Our* men?"

"The faction of which your father is a part – as I am also. He thought it would be more discreet if I met you in his place."

"I don't know anything about factions," Alvantes said, sounding unexpectedly defensive. "I've come here in service to the King."

"We're *all* in service to the King. But lately, it grows harder to know how best to serve. His Highness feels himself assailed by enemies... and not without reason. The reports of Moaradrid's death have done nothing but fan the flames in the far north."

"I heard such talk in Aspira Nero."

"No doubt. The Bastard Prince. A joke that has long since ceased to be funny."

There was that name again. What was going on in the far north that had everyone so nervous? As far as I knew, Moaradrid's rebellion had begun with him. I'd assumed until now that it had ended in much the same way.

Any last hint of levity left Gailus's voice as he asked, "Are the rumours true? About Prince Panchetto?"

Alvantes looked uncomfortable. "The news I have should reach the King's ear before any other."

Gailus nodded. "Then they are. Your commitment to duty does you credit, Lunto – but be careful. Enduring so much has made His Highness... unpredictable."

It was obvious he had more to say, but Ludovoco chose that moment to reappear from behind the door hanging. He looked at Gailus and Alvantes with unconcealed suspicion, and to Alvantes said, "Go through. His Highness will arrive shortly."

"Well... your father will be glad to hear you're well," said Gailus. He'd unblinkingly resumed his previous character, with the ease of someone pulling on a favourite overgarment. "Pass on my regards to the King, won't you?"

Alvantes replied to Gailus with a short bow, which he noticeably failed to extend to Ludovoco. Then Alvantes led the way through the narrow doorway Ludovoco had left and returned by, and I followed close on his heels.

The room beyond was large and hexagonal, built around a raised stage at its centre that echoed its shape. Opposite where we'd entered, a throne of elaborately engraved, gold-inlaid wood perched on a stepped dais twice the height of the platform. Along the other five walls, high-backed benches were arrayed. There was ample space for a hundred people, so seating a mere dozen men and a couple of elderly women left them conspicuously empty. All of those present were finely dressed, at least, more than enough so to show up our own travel-stained garb.

Alvantes took a seat on the bench to our left, and I sat beside him. As though our arrival were a signal, discordant pipe music blared immediately from behind another drape in the wall to the left of the throne. I couldn't help noticing how the three men waiting nearby jerked to their feet and edged away.

The music died abruptly. The curtain swept back. In the space beyond was nothing but darkness.

Then two figures danced out with rapid steps and leaped onto the stage. They wore long, open robes over loose shirts and trousers. Alarmingly, their faces were covered with cloth masks, blank apart from narrow slits for eyes and mouth. Masks and clothing both were patterned with interlocking diamonds, black and white endlessly alternating. Any two diamonds appeared identical, yet together the effect was chaotic, seeming to shift whether the pair moved or not. Worse, their costumes were contrastingly chequered, as though each was a distorted reflection of the other. Between their disguises and the bagginess of their clothing, it was impossible even to guess at their sex.

I knew I'd never seen them before, or anyone remotely like them. Yet I couldn't escape a sense of familiarity. The sight as they took up opposite places on the stage, the rippling, ever-shifting black and white, the inhumanly blank masks and a certain too-quick, almost insect quality in their movements all made my skin want to crawl off my bones.

I didn't feel any better when they each pulled fanned handfuls of knives from the recesses of their cloaks.

What followed was indescribable, even as I watched it. It possessed qualities of a juggling act, an acrobatic display and a sadistic fight to the death, all in apparently random combination. Knives flashed through the air, were caught – with hands, feet, occasionally teeth – and ricocheted back, in a blur of blades and limbs that was impossible to follow, let alone make sense of.

I had no idea how long it went on for. It felt like hours. When they stopped – when they *finally* stopped – I let out a long-held, shuddering breath, and realised my forehead was slick with cold sweat. I'd sat paralysed through the performance. Now, every muscle ached with the exertion of stillness.

I didn't think I'd ever been as relieved as I was when they closed with a jagged bow and scuttled off the stage, back into the waiting darkness behind their curtain.

I tried to speak, managed a muffled squeak. With a struggle, I calmed myself enough to form actual words. "What – who – what was that?"

"They call themselves Stick and Stone," murmured Alvantes. "Rumour has it, they're brothers. They're the King's favourite entertainers."

"That's funny. I feel the exact opposite of entertained."

If it was possible, Alvantes's voice sank even lower. "Rumour also has it they've been known to operate in *other* capacities."

Then I understood why they'd seemed familiar. The way they'd moved – it had reminded me of Synza. It was the absolute, incontestable confidence of men who could kill without qualm or effort. I said, "Someone has a funny idea of keeping us amused."

"Perhaps."

"You think it was some sort of warning?"

"I think someone doesn't want me here. Or else wants me here for reasons I wouldn't like."

"Alvantes, why do I get the feeling none of this is going how you intended?"

His mouth turned up slightly, in a smile that went nowhere near his eyes. "You know what they say, Damasco. If you want to make the gods laugh…"

"What? Tickle their feet? Let them win at cards? Given the state of their creation, I'd think the difficulty was getting them to take something seriously once in a while."

"You tell them your plans," he replied.

A fanfare of trumpets sounded from somewhere invisible – and Alvantes's faint smile vanished. Everyone, Alvantes included, slid from his or her seat and onto the floor, where they kneeled with heads hung low. I followed their example – just too late for the King's entrance, so that his first impression of me was my falling face first into the clumsiest grovel imaginable.

For the instant it took my head to smack the tiled floor, I got a clear view of him. He arrived from the right of the throne, flanked by four black-robed guards. I wasn't the least surprised to see Ludovoco amongst their number.

King Panchessa was recognisable as Panchetto's father – but barely. The same features were there, the bulbous nose and broad lips, the piggy, jewel-like eyes. However, the softness that had defined his son was entirely absent; what had been fat in the son was bulk in the father. Panchessa was imposing, despite his age. It was as if those indulgences that had kept Panchetto a plump, extravagant child had turned inward, been focused into something altogether less pleasant. I couldn't guess what was going on behind those gimlet eyes, but it was hard to imagine I'd like it.

In fact, it was someone altogether other than Panchetto he put me in mind of. Someone who shared that impression of violent intensity, of darkness shifting beneath a still façade – someone who'd set my nerves on edge in exactly the same way.

Strange as it was, Panchessa reminded me not of his son but of the man who'd murdered him.

One of the guards stepped forward – though not so far as to place him in front of the King. With a look and a wave, he dismissed everyone else in the room, one by one. They appeared more resigned than annoyed, and I guessed this wasn't the first time they'd waited, only to be unceremoniously banished.

When the chamber had emptied, the guard called to Alvantes, "Step forward."

Alvantes raised his eyes, not enough to meet Panchessa's gaze. "Yes. Altapasaeda is in the hands of enemies. Northern soldiers, many of the families – perhaps under duress – and an alliance of criminals led by a man named Castilio Mounteban."

Panchessa nodded, slowly and deliberately. "Then my son…" he asked, letting the question hang like a sword blade.

"With the greatest sorrow and shame, I must tell Your Highness that Prince Panchetto is dead. He was killed by Moaradrid, in a cowardly and unprovoked attack."

Panchessa's voice remained cold and level as black ice. "And Moaradrid?"

"Dead as well. It was… an accident, of sorts."

Panchessa reached out one hand to the throne, steadied himself just slightly. The four guards edged closer. He warned them away with his free hand.

"My sons…"

Or so I thought I'd heard, and the sentence hung tantalisingly unfinished. Surely he must have meant to say "son's". But his son's what? His son's body? Could he be asking about the crown?

Then he drew himself erect, not looking at Alvantes. Abruptly, he turned to leave, and his entourage fell in around him. At the last moment, Ludovoco – who until then had played no part in proceedings – leaned to whisper something in his ear.

The King stopped. With a gesture, he picked out two of his personal guard. Without turning, he motioned to where Alvantes still stood on the stage.

"Take him to the dungeons," he said, "and cut his damned traitorous head from his body."

CHAPTER ELEVEN

"Easie Damasco. I fear you fail to appreciate the severity of your situation. You are guilty of treason, despised in the eyes of men and gods alike. And tomorrow, your head shall be struck from your shoulders."

"It isn't that I don't appreciate the severity," I said. "It's more that I don't see it as being significantly worse than any other day I've had lately."

The Royal Inquisitor looked at me with struggling annoyance and disdain, as though I were an insect and he was trying to decide whether swatting me would justify the effort involved. "I'll ask one more time. Will you answer my questions sensibly? I can't promise clemency, but perhaps your honesty will be rewarded in another life."

All I could manage was a weary sigh.

If I'd learned one thing that afternoon, it was how underrated boredom was as a tool of interrogation. It was a constant struggle not to confess to something, *anything*, just to enliven the conversation. My questioning was well into its third hour, and it was fair to say that progress had not been quick.

I looked to Alvantes for the hundredth time, desperate for some hint of affirmation. He was sat just as he'd been since our incarceration had begun, knees tucked to his chest, eyes focused on some distant point beyond the barred window. The fingers of his right hand played idly around the grubbily bandaged stump of his left arm. All told, he seemed to be taking imprisonment for treason even worse than I might have hoped.

The Inquisitor tutted to draw back my attention and said, "Let's start from the beginning."

I managed one word, which sounded to my own ears like, "Gfargh." Summoning what mental energy I had left, I tried to rephrase my complaint into something more like language. "We've started again five times now. Why won't you believe I'm telling the truth?"

He rolled his eyes. "Because I strain to find one aspect of your story that's less than preposterous."

"It *is* preposterous. That doesn't mean it didn't happen."

"You really expect me to believe that you kidnapped a giant?"

"Not kidnapped," I said. "Borrowed. Or, at any rate, liberated."

"You kidnapped a giant from the insurgent Moaradrid. You stole the stone he was using to control this giant and others of his kind. Then you escaped..." The Inquisitor paused to make a great show of consulting his own notes. "By *riding upon* said giant."

"Until he got tired. Then I liberated a horse instead."

"And it was your theft of this so-called giant-stone that set about the chain of events which ended in Prince Panchetto's murder."

"No! I mean, how am I supposed to know? Maybe if I hadn't taken the stone… if Moaradrid hadn't been a murderous lunatic…"

Had my brain not caught up with my mouth just in time, I'd have added, *if Panchetto hadn't had all the sense of a wet sponge*. The truth was, every time we went over the events preceding Panchetto's death I found myself feeling a little more guilty; every time I narrated my role in the last hours of his life, I sounded more culpable. I was slowly being condemned by the power of suggestion.

The Inquisitor frowned down his nose, apparently now trying to impress my guilt on me through sheer intensity of expression. "*Maybe?* Why can't you admit your iniquity?"

"I've admitted plenty of iniquity. It just hasn't been for the crime you're planning to execute me for."

He stamped his foot. The gesture should have seemed petulant and ridiculous, but the suddenness of it – in the close confines of the cell – set my nerves jangling. "Admit it. Your visit to Altapasaeda ended with Prince Panchetto's death."

I struggled to keep my voice level. Something told me that losing my temper in a royal prison cell had the potential to end badly. "His death *at the hands of Moaradrid*. Look, I feel as bad about Panchetto's death as anyone…"

"You refer to His Highness, Prince Panchetto," hissed the Inquisitor. "And I sincerely doubt you feel as badly as his father."

I fought back a groan. "I feel as badly about His Highness's death as anyone who barely knew him could. But the fact is, he got on the wrong side of a madman – a madman with a large sword. Of course I'd have tried to help him if only I'd realised what was happening."

"Perhaps that responsibility, at least, can't be laid at your feet."

The Inquisitor turned his hawkish glower on Alvantes. Sensing his gaze, Alvantes glanced up just for an instant – and a faint shudder ran through him.

The sliver of a smile hung on the Inquisitor's lips as he looked back at me. "However, even if your version of events is true, the fact remains that it was your actions that placed Prince Panchetto in jeopardy."

He had me there. As much as I'd have liked to deny it, and even without all this interrogation, I did feel a certain amount of responsibility for Panchetto's death. After all, it was a safe bet he wouldn't have been promenading the dockside in the middle of the night if I hadn't burgled his palace.

Nevertheless, the truth was that Panchetto had practically offered his neck to Moaradrid – and Moaradrid had been only too willing to oblige. That left only two real culprits. Both were dead, and one of them also happened to be the victim.

If there was a tactful way of explaining this to the Royal Inquisitor, however, my brain was missing it. In fact, considered like that, it was easy to see why he might be eager to pin the blame on Alvantes and me. It might not be the truth, but it had virtues the truth lacked – things like neatness, closure, and the satisfying spectacle of lopping the culprits' heads off in a public place.

Maybe I really wouldn't be able to talk my way out of this one.

"I'm not saying my time in Altapasaeda was blameless." Seeing the glint in the Inquisitor's eye, I added hastily, "But I'd like to think I've been punished enough by subsequent events, not to mention this chastening spell of imprisonment. Given all that, and the fact I helped bring the real culprit to justice…"

The Inquisitor raised a hand to silence me. "Here we return to your claim that Moaradrid is dead."

"He *is* dead. Extremely dead."

He spared a glance for his notes. "Your claim that the giant pushed him off a bridge."

"Not pushed," I said. It was an accident. He fell."

"Yet no one saw the body."

"Fell from the top of a mountain."

"Nor did they see the impact."

"*Into the sea*. Assuming he missed the rocks."

"But no one *saw?*"

"He's dead!" If I didn't quite shout it, I definitely came closer than was prudent. Doing my best to sound apologetic, I added, "Believe me, the King can be safe in the knowledge his son's death has been avenged."

The look the Inquisitor gave me was as intent as ever, but uncharacteristically guileless, as if he were searching my face for some clue he'd found missing in my words. I couldn't judge whether he saw what he was looking for, because he quickly caught himself and erased the expression. However, his reply was cryptic enough. "That remains to be seen," he said.

Pausing, he again seemed distracted. Could it be that a glimmer of reality was beginning to penetrate his fabrication of the last few weeks' events?

"Let us agree," he said finally, "that Moaradrid is dead – just as Prince Panchetto is dead. Meanwhile, Altapasaeda has fallen into the hands of a petty crook and his band of miscreants, who are now set on wresting the Castoval from the just grip of its Pasaedan masters."

"I think you'll find Alvantes would be more than glad to go back and deal with that last one. If the King could spare a few men and he wasn't imprisoned for treason, that is."

"No doubt. Were His Highness to allow it, you'd both be valiantly rushing to rescue Altapasaeda at this very moment. You were a hapless witness to Prince Panchetto's murder. Even Moaradrid's death, which robbed the Court of the alleged culprit, was an unfortunate misunderstanding." He sighed heavily. "This is the story you'd ask me to deliver to the King?"

"It's the only one I have."

"I could torture you, Damasco. You realise that, don't you? I'm well versed in torture. More than you could probably imagine."

For all our intimate discussion, it was obvious he still didn't know me very well. Imagining physical pain had always been the thing my brain excelled at over any other. Moreover, alarming as the prospect of torture might be for someone with secrets to hide, it was infinitely worse for me, who'd just spent three hours blabbing his every thought in minute detail.

Holding my voice as steady as I could manage, I said, "You *could* torture me. I'm willing to believe you'd be very good at it. But all you'd get out of me would be the same things I've been telling you all day – only at a higher pitch."

The Inquisitor sighed, too theatrically for my liking. He nodded solemnly, as though through his efforts we'd achieved a milestone in our relations as interrogator and prisoner. He snapped his book shut, with a musty slap that sounded to my ears like a death knell. "You know," he said, "the sad truth is I believe you."

For a moment, I actually felt dizzy with relief. It was like a tidal wave pouring up from my feet to the tips of my hair. "You believe I'm innocent?"

"Of course not. You've been condemned by the King. Your innocence is an impossibility."

"Oh."

"I just don't believe you're clever enough to make up anything so patently absurd."

He took up his book, quill and ink from the low alcove he'd rested them in when writing and placed them in a case of black leather, which he tucked into a pocket of his robe. Then he turned to the door and rapped sharply. It swung inward on well-oiled hinges, revealing a guard stood at attention in the opening.

"Wait," I called. "Haven't you forgotten something?"

He turned back. "Not to my knowledge. If you wish to enlighten me, please be quick. You're not the only one in the royal dungeons in need of interrogation."

I tipped my head towards Alvantes. "My point exactly."

For the first time in our conversation, a touch of genuine interest entered his voice. "You want me to interrogate your friend?"

It didn't seem the time to point out how far opposed to friendship my relationship with Alvantes was. "Absolutely."

The Inquisitor took a step back towards me. "Do you think you can strike a deal?" He actually sounded intrigued now. "Perhaps we'll execute Alvantes twice and let you go?"

"I just don't see why I should go through three hours of interrogation and he gets to sit there sulking."

"Ah. I see." His disappointment seemed every bit as real as his brief curiosity had been. "I won't be examining former Guard-Captain Alvantes because nothing he could tell me would keep his head on his shoulders for another day. Whereas you might conceivably have saved your life if you'd answered a little more wisely."

At that, my heart sank like a stone – a cold, grey stone plummeting into the depths of a frigid, bottomless lake.

The Inquisitor spared me one last look. "Any more questions? Shall we discuss the weather or catch up on local gossip?"

"No," I said, "I think we're done."

• • • •

I couldn't say I wasn't glad of a little peace and quiet.

Yet the Inquisitor's departure had shut off one narrow avenue of hope – perhaps the only one I'd really had. It wasn't as if I'd truly imagined I could convince him to let me go; based on my experiences so far, qualities like reason, justice and even basic sanity had no place in Pasaeda's public affairs. Now that he was gone, though, my approaching fate seemed real for the first time.

Still. I wasn't without my resources. Few they might be and limited, but I wasn't quite done for. All through my interrogation, a minuscule part of my mind had been plotting. While most of my consciousness hung on the cusp of panic, it had calmly analysed my circumstances. Studiously, it had broken my big problem – being locked in a cell awaiting all-too-imminent execution – into smaller, more manageable difficulties.

There was the chain round my ankle.

The locked door.

The guard outside.

All of those might, if against my every experience luck should somehow favour me, be managed.

After that, however, the challenges became uncertain. I had only the vaguest idea of where we were within the palace, of its layout or what routes might take me safely through its boundless grounds.

Now, with the benefit of silence, I did my best to plan the unplannable. I went over and over the scant details I knew, racked my memory for every recollection of my time in Pasaeda, tried to tease out the shape of those many dangers I couldn't foresee. Where might guards congregate? What mistake would be likeliest to raise an alarm? If I should miraculously make it into the city, where could I hide and for how long? In the past I'd found that simply hammering my thoughts against such unsolvable-seeming dilemmas would sometimes offer the hint of a direction.

This wasn't one of those times. The more I considered, the more desperate the possibility of escape seemed. I might get out of my cell; but getting out of the palace, let alone the city, let alone the country were other things entirely. I had to try, of course. The alternative was to wait and die. However, the idea of a getaway attempt without hope of success left me increasingly despondent.

Such was my mood when I was jarred to attention by the sound of the door. As I watched, half-petrified by alarm, it swung open. Had I deliberated too long? Were they here to take us already? I'd been so mired in my thoughts that I had no idea how much time had passed since the Inquisitor left.

My fears appeared to be ungrounded. Asides from the familiar guard, the entrance was occupied by an elderly man. He was smartly dressed in a plain white robe with simple, silver adornment along the hems and a dark green sash about the waist. He had a military bearing; he held himself straight – and despite his age, was broad-shouldered, with a suggestion of enduring fitness. His white hair was shorn close above a lined, square face, with features strong enough to be considered severe.

He barely glanced at me. Instead, his gaze fell on Alvantes. Like me, Alvantes had looked up when the door opened, and his attention held now to the old man's face. I could read nothing from either of them. They were still and expressionless as two opposing statues left to weather eternity.

Then, in a voice without inflection, the old man said, "Hello, Lunto."

Only then did Alvantes let go his stare. His eyes dropped to the floor. "Hello, Father."

"No. You no longer have the right to call me that."

Alvantes's father advanced into the room, the guard following close at his heels. I couldn't tell whether he was there to supervise Alvantes Senior, to protect him from us, or was warding against some improbable escape attempt. His expression suggested no one had bothered to fill him in on such trivial details either; he made do by trying to watch all three of us at once.

Meanwhile, Alvantes's father never took his eyes from his son. I did think I saw them shift to note his missing hand, just for a fraction of a moment; but if the grim sight registered, it brought no hint of sympathy to his voice as he went on, "That's what I'm here to tell you. You have failed the King, the Court, the people of Altapasaeda. You've failed me – more than I ever could have conceived. For these reasons, I've begged the King to let me see you one final time… just to convey my shame. These will be my last words to you, Lunto, do you understand? My last words."

Alvantes's father stepped closer, as though concerned that one syllable of his vitriol might be missed. Yet when he spoke, it was with inhuman calm. "I won't be there to witness your execution. I shall treat tomorrow as I have today and as I will the day after tomorrow. I'll set out to the Court at seven. Unlike you, my duties are something I would never try to escape. As always, I'll return home at five. I will spend the evening as I do every other, and have not a single doubt against which to guard. By nine, as every night, I'll be soundly asleep."

Could Alvantes's father really have such an outrageous sense of his importance that he felt the need to share his itinerary in the last hours of his son's life? It wasn't even as if his heart was in it. His expression showed more concentration than anger. It was obvious his first concern was in keeping to the bizarre script he'd prepared.

"Let me tell you one more thing before I walk out that door. In my service to His Highness, I've always strived to be honest and open. Would that you'd done the same when it came to be your turn. Now, in your last hours, I urge you to do what's right. Think of those who are left. Think of those you've let down. What happens now is on your own head. It isn't something you have a right to blame His Highness for. He knows as well as anyone that justice must be vigorous if it's to keep a kingdom stable."

Alvantes Senior intoned this maxim with clear finality. As though nothing of any significance had been said, he turned away.

Alvantes opened his mouth to speak. No sound came.

Then, apparently as an afterthought, Alvantes's father turned back and struck his son with all his strength across the face. It was a ringing open-handed blow, and it left a glowing welt in its wake. Yet Alvantes's head moved not one iota. He hardly seemed to feel it.

Alvantes Senior turned away once more. This time he marched from the room without another word – just as he'd promised. The confused guard hurried after, still trying to divide his attention equally between all three of us. Once they were both across the threshold, the door slammed shut.

For once, I couldn't but feel genuine pity for Alvantes. His thanks for loyalty was to be called a traitor and condemned to die; now his father visited solely to rub his nose in those facts. As if that weren't all bad enough, it was clear the old man was playing with a severely depleted deck of cards. Bad enough to endure so cruel an invective from a parent. For it to be hardly more than gibberish seemed to me that much worse.

I thought about making some attempt to express my sympathy. But nothing came to mind that did the situation justice – and based on what I saw in Alvantes's face, I doubted he'd even hear it. Moreover, I was quick to remind myself that my own circumstances were hardly any better, and identical in the long run. Anyway, wasn't it Alvantes's blind faith in his vindictive King that had landed us in this mess?

At least I understood now how he could have been so calm before. Alvantes had expected his father, evidently high up in the Court, to pull whatever strings it would take to secure his son's freedom. I was actually disappointed. Waiting for someone else to pick up the pieces didn't fit well with the Alvantes I knew –

especially when the father he'd been so naively relying on was an unfeeling lunatic.

Alvantes's scheme, such as it had been, was a dead
loss. No last-minute reprieves or eleventh-hour res-
cues would be forthcoming. There were only two
ways I was leaving that cell, and one of them would
end on the headsman's block.

It might be hopeless, it was almost certainly suicidal,
but my options had narrowed to just one.

It was time I put my plan into action.

CHAPTER TWELVE

Getting the shackle off my ankle was easy enough.

The lock was ancient and showy, constructed to look sturdy rather than be difficult to overcome. In fact, the harder part had been unpicking my shirt collar for the lock picks concealed there. I was almost disappointed no one had bothered to search me more thoroughly. They'd confiscated my cloak and found the loose picks in its pocket, they'd patted me down from head to toe, but that was all.

If I'd been relieved at the time, I now found it worrying. Either the Royal Guard were incompetent or they were profoundly confident in their wider security. In that case, the shackle was little more than ornamentation. It was the layers of locked doors and armed men they relied on to keep me in place.

Then again, there was another explanation, perhaps even more likely. With our execution so imminent, they'd assumed we'd have no possible time for escape.

I felt duty-bound at least to try to prove them wrong.

I spent a minute massaging circulation back into my ankle. Across from me, Alvantes sat with his eyes closed, as he had since his father left. I doubted he could be sleeping, but he was so perfectly still that it was hard to judge. I'd have expected my sympathy for him to have dried up by now; it surprised me to realise it hadn't. There'd been something peculiarly affecting in hearing him be torn apart so thoroughly and yet so nonsensically. If Alvantes's father had been determined to convey how little his son's death meant to him, there were pithier and less senile ways he could have gone about it.

Which led me to the question I'd be agonising over. Did I try to take Alvantes with me? Of course we despised each other, but there was a definite divide between that and leaving him to die. Anyway, there was no denying he'd make a useful ally. However little he knew of the palace, it would beat my plan of blundering at random until I stumbled upon a way out.

All well and good. But something told me Alvantes was unlikely to approve of my interventionist approach to incarceration. He might be just obstinate enough to have his head chopped off out of some misplaced sense of duty – and if he wasn't usually, his father's speech could have tipped the balance. *Shut up and die with dignity* was exactly the kind of message a man like Alvantes didn't need to hear.

The truth, though, was that I couldn't very well leave him. If I should ever meet Estrada again, even I'd have trouble explaining that one. *Alvantes? The last time I saw him, he was in a cell waiting to be beheaded. I'd have asked if he wanted to escape with me, but it seemed rude to wake him.*

I crept over, all ready to wake him with a tap to the shoulder. At the last moment, his eyes snapped open. They glided quickly over me, absorbing my unfettered ankle, the empty shackle loose upon the flags behind.

"Damasco," Alvantes said softly. "Whatever you're doing, stop it now."

"Don't make this more difficult than it has to be," I hissed back. "I'm escaping. If you don't like it, fine, stay here and give my regards to the executioner. But nothing you say is keeping me in this cell."

"Gods damn it! If you try and leave now, you'll ruin everything."

"Much as I hate to put out the noble folk of Pasaeda, I'm sure I'll learn to live with myself somehow."

"Things aren't how you think. You need to trust me. Just listen…"

"Wait… you lost me at *trust*. Whenever I do that it never ends well."

Alvantes obviously wasn't going to be convinced, and there was no way I'd risk letting him persuade me. Maybe he had some grand scheme in mind; maybe he was just suicidal. Either way, I was through chancing my life on the whims of others. Waiting for death in the royal dungeons of a foreign land, *that* was where trust had led me.

Still crouched, I scampered to the door. Now that I'd begun, now that my plan was in motion, I was twitching with barely contained fear and tension. If I didn't keep moving, I knew I'd lose my nerve altogether.

Of course, there was a small yet significant flaw in that logic. My plan was more or less a plan in name alone.

The chain bolted to my shackle was unusually generous. Whoever had determined its length had either been a humanitarian devoted to the consolation of prisoners or had only had an exceptionally long chain to hand. Even shackled, I could have crossed our cell from corner to corner.

It was long enough that with the door open, it would reach outside. It might even be long enough for the shackle to be snapped closed around a certain guard's ankle. If it was, I might have a fighting chance of getting past him.

"*Damasco*."

Then again, it was a hundred times more likely that he'd hear me picking the lock, opening the door, sneaking up on him or all three, and jab a sword into some part of me that didn't function well with metal stuck through it.

Still, it was that or try to fight him with a lock pick.

"*Damasco!*"

Was it even possible to turn the lock without the guard hearing? Slipping my picks into the keyhole, closing my eyes, I focused all sensation into my fingers. There was no way this would be as easy as the shackle. No one made cell doors easy; fiendishly complicated was more the fashion. It was going to take every ounce of my skill and ingenuity…

Unless the lock was already open.

Well, that was undeniably strange. Poorly made

shackles were one thing. Open cell doors were quite another. That went beyond the pale of careless security.

"It's unlocked, isn't it? Will you listen to me, damn it!"

My mind was awhirl. Something was bafflingly wrong here. Alvantes clearly knew at least a little of what was going on; logic demanded I stay and listen. But an insistent voice told me that whatever it was I wouldn't like it, and the shriek of my instincts drowned out everything else. I'd been caged. Now I was almost free. Who cared about hows and whys? Fate had thrown me a bone and only a fool would ask what it had come out of.

There was no handle on this side, of course. However, the lock casing was a broad iron sheet that slightly overlapped the wall. When I teased my fingers round the plate and pulled, it came easily, revealing a chink of wavering light. I tensed, fear drawing tingling fingers down my spine. I gripped the open shackle in my right hand, the edge of the door in the other. Striving for an impossible compromise between silence and speed, I drew the door towards me.

A choked, dry wheezing met my ears. Even as I registered it, it turned into a derisive grunt. Another wheeze, another grunt...

The guard was snoring.

He was dressed differently to those I'd seen upstairs, in baggy trousers and a jacket of leather covered with brightly glistening studs. His helmet, knocked off-kilter where his head rested against the bare stone wall, had tilted over one eye. A spear rested beside him, and a curved short sword hung at his hip. His expression of unassailable peace contrasted oddly with the cacophony of rasps and snorts coming from out of his mouth.

Perhaps the sensible precaution would have been to draw his sword and slit his throat. But whatever else I might be, I was no killer. Anyway, I was sure enough of my light-footedness that I knew I could get past without him waking. From the sound of those snores, I could probably have herded cattle past him.

I darted a last glance back at Alvantes. Having given up trying to persuade me, he was now fumbling with his own shackled ankle. Perhaps he thought he could get it off by sheer, brute strength.

He looked up when he felt my eyes on him. *"Damn it, Damasco!"*

I had no doubt he was privy to facts I lacked. Why else the open door, the sleeping guard? Yet nothing about that fact made me want to stay and listen. Alvantes, after all, had gotten me into this fix. His no-good king was the one who'd thrown me in prison for no good reason.

Well, no more. It was time Easie Damasco started trusting his instincts again.

Or so I tried to tell myself. As I shuffled out and drew the door closed behind me – I couldn't put it past Alvantes to shout out to the guard – it was all I could do to keep my hands from shaking. Because the truth I didn't dare admit was that the odds of my even getting out of the dungeons, let alone making it to the Castovalian border intact, were just below non-existent.

I couldn't afford to think like that. One step at a time.

The first step was clear, at any rate. To my left, the passage ended in unbroken wall. That meant I was going right – which, inevitably, took me past the sleeping guard.

The knack to sneaking has little to do with trying to be quiet. Trying to be quiet makes noise, however slight, and of exactly the irregular kind that draws unconscious attention. I'd do better to move smoothly and swiftly, making sounds that would be easy for a barely aware mind to dismiss, forgotten even before they were acknowledged.

Knowing the theory didn't make the practise less intimidating. I sucked in a deep breath and started walking.

Thirty or so light, easy strides took me to the end of the corridor. If the guard heard me on any level, it didn't register enough to break the rhythm of his snores. I'd made it – that far, at least.

I paused to take the measure of the adjoining corridor. It ran both ways for a considerable distance, ending in each direction at further junctions. Every so often, cell doors punctuated the stone-blocked walls. I'd no way to tell which, if any, were occupied.

Though bronze cressets hung at regular intervals from the ceiling, only one in three was lit, leaving the intervening spaces swathed in thick shadow. That suited me. It wasn't enough to hide in if anyone should pass by, but it would suffice to make them doubt their eyes if they caught a fleeting glimpse at a distance.

From the point of finding a way out, however, the corridors were less promising. There might only be two choices, but I had nothing to base my direction on. Our journey down here had been long and meandering, and my thoughts had hardly been on memorising the route. Perhaps either way was as good as the other, yet the risk of heading deeper into the prison's depths was enough to give me pause.

Once more, I reminded myself I couldn't afford to think like that. To the right, the passage looked fractionally gloomier. With nothing else to go on, that would have to decide it.

I ducked out and scurried that way, taking care to crouch whenever I passed a window grille – in case there were other prisoners like Alvantes who frowned on escape attempts. I was nearly at the end of the corridor when I heard a sound. It was vague and muffled, impossible to identity – but it was still more than enough to chill my blood. It had come from somewhere ahead of me. More than that, I couldn't say.

I thought about turning back, but uncertainty had me in its grip. I froze instead, and strained my ears. I dreaded a further noise, yet at the same time almost craved it, just to break the tension building like a drumbeat in my mind.

When it came, it was so soft that anyone else would certainly have missed it. Another advantage of knowing how to move quietly – once you were familiar with the tricks, it was a thousand times easier to notice those hardly existent sounds that marked a stealthy approach.

This was only the faintest swish, as of light cloth brushing skin. Once I'd identified it, however, I could follow it – impossibly quiet, but steady, rhythmic.

Someone else was sneaking through these passage-ways; someone with a tread so close to silent that if I hadn't been concentrating with all my attention, if I hadn't known exactly what to listen for, I could never have heard them. And now that I'd caught the minus-cule noises giving them away, I was sure of something else as well. They were heading my way.

I thought about retreating towards the cell. But my advantage cut both ways. Odds were that anyone so proficiently furtive would identify my tread just as I had theirs. Whoever they were, the fact that they were sneaking at all made me doubt I'd want to make their acquaintance. Who knew what went on in the dungeons of a mad king? Who could say what types might stalk its mazy depths?

I glanced around for an alternative. To my astonish-ment, luck was on my side. I'd passed the last cell door, but between me and the next junction was an-other entrance, a wooden gate with no grille or lock. I guessed it was a storage cupboard or some such, since no light showed from the wide gap at its base.

Sure enough, when I opened the gate it revealed a small alcove. The walls were lined with wide shelves, empty but for a few bags and loose bric-a-brac; the remaining space looked just big enough to contain me. I slipped inside, drew the gate closed. Sure enough, there was ample room. So long as no one happened to glance at the gap beneath the door, I'd be perfectly safe.

Unless this cupboard was exactly where the ap-proaching steps were headed.

Trapped in that close darkness, I felt sure of it. Poised perfectly still, listening to that negligible rasp of cloth on flesh drawing nearer, I convinced myself beyond question that I'd concealed myself in the most dangerous place imaginable. Only the tiniest voice of doubt kept me from running as the near-inaudible steps drew closer, closer...

And passed.

They continued down the passage. They began to fade. Soon I doubted whether I could hear them at all.

Still, I waited. I stayed motionless – determined to catch even the minutest sound. Even when I was sure beyond doubt there was nothing to hear I continued to listen, until the very silence itself began to roar like distant surf.

It took all the strength of will I had to force myself back into life. Maybe the steps had passed and maybe they hadn't. Either way I didn't intend to starve to death in a closet.

At the last moment, it struck me that the alcove might contain something useful to my escape attempt. By the dim light from beneath the door, I appraised the contents of the shelves. Mostly, they were almost empty, but high on the shelf behind me three bags were piled together. They looked oddly familiar – and taking one down, I realised why. It was my own.

Once I got over my initial surprise, I realised it made sense. The alcove could only be a temporary store for prisoners' goods. Everything was as I'd last seen it; my pack didn't appear to have been so much as opened. Even my coin bag was there, and judging from its heft as I slipped it into a pocket, undiminished. Whatever the royal guards might lack in competence, they were at least honest. I reclaimed my cloak and boots and drew them on. I slung my pack over one shoulder. I was about to slip back into the corridor when my brain caught up with what had been staring me in the face the whole time.

Two saddlebags.

Alvantes's saddlebags.

Alvantes's apparently undisturbed saddlebags.

Which meant...

Instinct took over, the force of a lifetime's habit, so powerful that I couldn't have resisted even had I wanted to. In the darkness it was hard to judge which bag was the one I wanted, so I dragged a couple of shirts from one, spread them over the stone floor to mask the sound and emptied both out. That done, I found the false bottom easily by touch. It had been carefully stitched in place, but I wasn't in any mood for niceties. I prised my fingers through the seam and pulled with all my strength. It held for just a moment and then began to tear, with the ping of individual stitches reaching crescendo with one steady, brutal rip.

Too excited by then even to heed the noise I was making, I tossed the scrap of fabric onto the clutter of Alvantes's belongings and reached into the freshly re-vealed portion. My fingers closed around metal – perfectly smooth, not at all cold to the touch. I drew it out. It was splendid, so refined and elegant in design that it was hard to believe it had ever sat on fat, fop-pish Panchetto's head. Yet I hardly glanced at it.

Instead, I shrugged off my cloak, wrapped the crown in it, crammed both together into my pack and slung the pack back across my shoulders.

Just as I was about to leave once more, I noticed something amidst the heap of Alvantes's turned out possessions. It was a tube of metal, catching the scant light from beneath the door. I recognised it as the telescope – the one I'd used outside Altapasaeda, the one I'd coveted until its existence had been crammed from my mind by the events that followed.

I reached down. Now it was mine, after all.

As I stepped back into the passage, my heart was hammering. Rationally I knew I'd been condemned to death anyway; but somehow, having indulged my light fingers in so grand a fashion seemed to make it all the worse. Now, not only was I condemned, I was actually guilty of something. I glanced left and right, disorientated by my time in the darkness of the closet.

I heard footsteps.

I knew straight away that it wasn't the same tread as before. This person was striving for quiet as well, but they weren't half as capable. They were moving too quickly for a start, as though they weren't quite decided which they cared more about, stealth or speed. What was going on? Just how many people were wandering around these dungeons? I'd been in less lively market streets. This time, I was sure the steps were behind me, approaching from the direction I'd arrived by. It was tricky to judge distance, though; the naked stone seemed to distort and re-echo sound.

I wasn't about to take any chances. Nor was I trapping

myself back in the storeroom. Instead, I scuttled around the next bend, keeping low, ready to drop into the shadows at the slightest provocation. Once I'd passed the corner, I paused again to listen. Had the steps drawn closer? It was impossible to judge. Those dim passages were disorientating. One moment the sound seemed to be behind me, the next in front. Or could it be that there were two people approaching? I didn't think so, but my nerve was slipping. It was easy to imagine a teeming horde of guards closing from every direction.

The corridor beyond the junction was much the same as the one I'd left, but bare this time of cell doors. Again, it ran to left and right. This time I chose left. The passage seemed to go on forever. I was sure I wouldn't reach the end before whoever possessed those phantom steps came into view. The more I lost my nerve, the surer I felt it wasn't one set of feet but many – that I was hurrying into danger, fleeing from one threat towards another.

However, the next junction revealed not guards, nor even another passage. It opened onto a short landing between flights of stairs.

I managed to calm myself a fraction. This was progress. Every instinct told me I was underground – weren't prisons always underground? – and so the logical choice was to ascend. Yet something made me doubt. Maybe it was only my natural sense of direction awakening, or maybe the sudden realisation that perhaps the reason those distant footsteps seemed all around was that they were reverberating from the floor above.

Yes, that must be it. Now that I concentrated, with the worst edge of my fear receding, it made perfect sense. It was easier to judge here, too, with the uninterrupted access of the stairwell. These stone walls were like the coil of a seashell, siphoning noise down into their depths. I was confident that what I'd actually been hearing was activity from the higher level, a constant, barely audible rapping of feet against flags.

Or maybe not. With a shiver, I realised one set was different. One set was definitely behind me. And it was definitely getting nearer.

That settled my decision.

I plummeted down the stairs, taking them three at a time. At the bottom was a small antechamber, with one low door to the right and another, larger and heavier, in front of me. There was a narrow, barred window set high in the door ahead. Through those bars, I could see darkness and the vague impression of distant walls. Close up, I could feel the faint breath of cool night air.

I'd found a way out.

There was only one problem. I knew there'd be a guard waiting on the other side.

There had to be. I'd been far too lucky getting this far. Luck always ran out eventually, and when it did, it generally went with a bang. I might have the element of surprise, but he'd be armed and armoured and infinitely better at fighting – not to mention capable of calling his many colleagues to his aid.

Above and behind me, the footsteps were drawing nearer. They must be in the second corridor by now. My bid for freedom was rapidly coming down to a choice of who got to catch me first. If I was quick, perhaps I could overpower the guard outside. I could put him down long enough to make a run for it at least. I might even get as far as the first gates. And then… and then…

One step. One step at a time.

Gently, hoping beyond hope that it wasn't locked, that its hinges were well oiled, I gripped the great ring that served as a door handle, twisted, pulled.

The hinges hardly complained; a whisper of metal on metal, like a breeze through dry grass. The door drew inward. A rectangle of purple velvet sky unfurled in the opening. I pressed against the wall, craned my neck to see through the slim gap.

There was no guard.

What there was, however, propped against the wall at the top of the short flight of stairs leading down to the courtyard, was a halberd that must surely belong to one. For reasons I couldn't quite explain, the sight of it sent a shudder through me. Perhaps he'd just gone to empty his bladder and would be back at any instant? No, it wasn't that. Something about the incongruity of it there, something about the angle… I didn't know why, but it felt wrong.

I knew I should run, take the opportunity while I had it, but I couldn't. I ducked back inside.

The footsteps were close now – still soft, but near. Unless I was very much mistaken, they'd almost reached the landing above. That only left the smaller door. Hardly even thinking, hardly trying to be quiet, I wrenched it open and darted through.

My heart stopped dead. My breath turned to ice in my throat.

I'd found the missing guard. The guard who should have been outside. The guard who'd so carelessly left his halberd.

I wouldn't need to worry about him.

Whoever had killed him, though – they were another matter.

CHAPTER THIRTEEN

My first instinct was to forget the guard's spread-eagled body and make a run for it, before the approaching footsteps could catch up.

I was already too late. They were on the stairs. I wondered, absurdly, if it would go more badly for me to be found over a dead guard's body with the crown of Altapasaeda in my rucksack. Or *was* it so absurd? There were more terrible fates in the world than a swift beheading.

I pressed myself against the wall, as though that would somehow hide me. The steps were quiet, cautious, but rapid nevertheless. None of those characteristics suggested their owner was meant to be here, any more than I was. Yet the fear sliding cold fingers around my throat told me they could just as well be an over-cautious guard – or someone worse.

After all, there was a corpse at my feet. Whoever had killed him might still be nearby. Whoever had killed him might be killing *me* next if I wasn't careful.

The muffled patter reached the last steps. My

lungs clenched in my chest. The footsteps paused in the alcove. I could hear breathing – muted but laboured. I very much wanted to run, I didn't care where... but fear had nailed me in place. I could only stand and listen – to the whisper of a door beginning to ease open...

Fortunately, it wasn't the door in front of me. There came another brief tapping of footsteps. Then the noise was swallowed in silence, and presumably by the night outside.

The wash of relief made my head swim. I almost let out the breath I'd been holding.

Lucky for me I didn't.

Had I been breathing, had I not been mute with fear, I might never have heard the second tread. As it was, I recognised it immediately; the first set of feet I'd noticed upstairs. Just as before, their possessor moved with consummate skill. He – or she, or it – was close upon the heels of whoever had just passed by. They didn't hesitate at the door. Almost before I registered their presence, they too were gone.

I waited. I couldn't guess for how long, except that it seemed like an age. I had no idea what could be going on, or if it was over. What kind of prison was this, where disembodied steps roved the halls all through the night? I felt as if my nerves had been grated. Even by the standard of escape attempts, this was proving extraordinarily stressful.

When I could stand it no more, when I was certain as I could be that neither set of feet was returning and that my heart had stopped trying to wrestle its way out of my chest, I turned my attention back to the corpse at my feet.

It was impossibly convenient that this particular guard should have chosen this particular moment to get himself murdered. Could it be another part in the mystery Alvantes had hinted at? Yet that made no sense. I couldn't believe Alvantes would have gone along with the killing of a royal guardsman, not even to secure his own freedom. Anyway, unless he was capable of plotting and effecting a brutal prison escape whilst chained in a cell, there had to be another explanation.

If so, whatever it was it eluded me. Moreover, given my immediate circumstances, it hardly mattered. For careful inspection had revealed one useful fact. The corpse I stood over was about my height and build.

Not having a clue as to why he was dead needn't stop me from exploiting that fact. Whoever had taken his life had at least been good enough to do so in a fashion that left his uniform – loose trousers and shirt with a knee-length jacket and helmet of studded leather – unmarked by blood. His uniform wasn't so much as crumpled. It couldn't have been more convenient if he'd been left there for my benefit.

Following that logic, I tried to assure myself that stripping his clothes was the only sensible thing to do. Necessity and barely subdued terror helped, making me less squeamish than I might otherwise have been. Nevertheless, I couldn't help cringing every time my fingers brushed his cooling, lifeless flesh.

Left with only a loincloth, however, his corpse

looked more pitiful than alarming. I comforted myself with the thought that my own remains would have looked even less dignified if he and his colleagues had had their way. Dead and practically naked he might be, but at least he still had his head.

I hurriedly undressed. My pack was just big enough to hold my clothing; bundled with my cloak, I wrapped it carefully around the crown and telescope. Then I pulled on the guard's trousers, shirt and long studded jacket. I strapped his sword at my waist and drew on the helmet, a cone of leather with flaps across the ears and a vicious spike protruding from the top, presumably for those exigencies when all that remained was to charge an enemy headfirst. After brief consideration, I decided to keep my own boots. If anyone was inspecting that closely, chances were I was already done for.

I looked down at myself. What I saw looked more like a skinny thief in stolen armour than a burly sentry out on his rounds.

I considered procrastinating a little longer; mightn't hiding the dead guard's body delay the discovery of his absence? But it had gone unnoticed so far, and once his desertion *was* noticed, I doubted anyone would wait for proof of foul play before sounding the alarm. No, I was ready as I was going to get, and every further delay was only stretching my already slim chances.

I hurried back through the door. In the antechamber, the outer door had been left ajar. I could smell the warm nocturnal air, faint odours of old straw from out in the courtyards and even the pungent perfume of night-blooming flowers drifting from the gardens below.

I opened the door fully and darted through. Skipping down the short flight of steps that linked door and courtyard, I barely managed to keep my footing. My intention was a dignified speed for a guard in a hurry, but the swell of panic was close on my heels. Once I reached level ground, it was all I could do not to run.

For all that, the night air felt good, like soothing breath on my skin. I was profoundly glad to be outside. If it turned out that I really had to die, better it be like this.

Still, the courtyard was vast. That alone was enough to keep my nerves jangling. I couldn't see anyone, but that didn't mean a thing. Besides the tremendous edifice of the palace and its countless windows and balconies, there were the walls, rolling in serpentine folds, innumerable shadowed nooks formed by their passing. Anybody could be watching from anywhere and I'd be the last to know.

I hurried on. The yard was flagged with white stone, glimmering in the dim starlight. The more my eyes adjusted, the more I felt like a bullseye on a target board. I strove to remember the layout of the grounds from what I'd observed on our arrival, but all I could say for sure was that the opening ahead must be the gatehouse joining this tier to the one below.

It was certain to be manned. There were bound to be questions. They were sure to be the kinds of questions I had no answers to.

I slowed. I needed time to think. Was there another way out? Perhaps across the walls, but there were bound to be patrols. My presence would be even more conspicuous and unexplainable.

I slowed further. The darkness of the gatehouse looked ready to swallow me whole. I was certain I could feel eyes staring. Wasn't I walking straight into the hands of my enemies?

I stopped. I might be the master of bad planning tonight, but even I had my limits. If this was the only route out, then what I needed was some detail to complete my disguise, perhaps the halberd I'd foolishly left propped outside the door, or else…

I finally remembered what I'd seen on the journey in, and cursed myself beneath my breath. *The stables*. If one thing was guaranteed to complete my disguise, it was a horse. What escapee would have the nerve to steal their own transport on the way out? Only one as terrifically daring and foolhardy as Easie Damasco.

Or so I tried to tell myself. Now that I looked, far to my right where the stables were, I saw lights burning in the stalls at the upper end. Lights meant people. People meant trouble. Yet the only alternative remained trying to walk my way out. All else aside, it might take me the rest of the night to make it to that distant final gate.

Trying to retain a dignified and guard-like pace, I hurried towards the stables. I knew I'd be most convincing if I kept my gaze fixed steadfastly ahead, but I couldn't resist the occasional glance around. Though I knew there must be patrols on the walls, I could still see no one.

As I drew close, I found I could hear the hushed drone of conversation from within the lighted portion of the stables. Nearby was an open side door; the area beyond was sunk in shadow. I weighed the risk of being seen against the potential value of overhearing whatever was being discussed inside – not to mention the fact that my horse-theft scheme was the only one I had left.

That dearth of better ideas was the clincher. I slunk inside. The door led into a region of empty stalls, apart from the wide central corridor where the lantern hung. Ahead, through a gap in slats, I could see two silhou-etted figures with their backs to me. One was speaking, steadily and softly, to the other.

I was astonished to realise it was a voice I recognised, though it took me a moment to place it. *Gailus*... the senator we'd run into on our journey through Pasaeda, who'd warned Alvantes outside the King's audience chamber. His voice was unmistakable – and as I focused my attention, his mumbled tones became intelligible: "...if he acts on two fronts at once. Yet day by day it seems inevitable."

"Can the boy really be so much worse than his father?"

That voice I *definitely* knew – incredible as it was that its owner should be here. I nearly burst in there and then, but something made me hesitate for Gailus's reply.

"Not the boy, his grandmother. Or so we hear. Still, the situation might yet be contained... if circumstances were different. The King is sick with rage and grief. To lose them both, after everything that had happened. For it to happen how it did. And the rage is stronger in him, now, than his sadness. Well, you saw first-hand." Gailus's voice took on a weight of added weariness as he finished, "Then again, perhaps it was always that way."

Intoned with grim seriousness it might be, but Gailus's speech was just as unintelligible as the ranting of Alvantes's senile father had been. Time was too short to be wasted on indulging lunatics. I stepped from the shadows.

"Guard-Captain. Senator. Always a pleasure."

Alvantes wheeled. "*Damasco!*" He recovered himself quickly. "So you made it."

"Of course." I noticed then that he'd changed his clothing, for a uniform much like mine. "You've been busy, I see."

"What are you doing here?"

"Well, I'd say escaping the same distasteful fate as you, except it seems you'd rather catch up with old friends."

"This is none of your affair."

"He has a point, Lunto," Gailus interrupted. "Sunrise isn't so far off. Your father told me he'll be waiting in your grandfather's shadow. Anything more you need to know he can tell you. You should join him, while you still can."

Two horses were already out of their stalls and saddled, their reins wrapped loosely round a post. Gailus freed the nearer set and passed it to Alvantes, who led his new mount out into the courtyard. The second Gailus handed to me.

Did that mean I'd been included in Alvantes's escape plan? That however he'd secured his freedom, he'd intended to take me along with him? If so, I wasn't about to get sentimental. It wasn't as if I'd needed any help. Well, not except for the locked door, anyway… and maybe the guard… and…

My steed was good enough to divert me with a shrill snort. He was eyeing me nervously. No doubt it was a novel and unwelcome experience to be dragged from his stall in the middle of the night. I stroked his nose and whispered a few soothing words in his ear while I led him outside.

Alvantes swung into the saddle and I did likewise. My horse took a couple of quick sidesteps and then settled.

"Thank you, Gailus," Alvantes said. "Take care."

The senator smiled, an expression more sinister than mirthful in the lamplight. "I'm a politician. I'm *always* careful."

We set out at a trot, heading back towards the gate-house. I tried to assure myself that being on horseback made my disguise more convincing. Perhaps it did – but only fractionally. I was still wearing an ill-fitting uniform, I doubted my riding style would have passed muster, and speaking more than a couple of words would reveal my Castovalian accent. All told, if the urge to panic had retreated for the moment, it hadn't gone far.

Trying to distract myself, I hissed at Alvantes the most pressing of the many questions I had. "I take it you had nothing to do with the dead guard then?"

Alvantes started. "What? Where?"

"At the bottom of the staircase." My brain filled in another gap in the events of the last few minutes. "If you'd turned right instead of going straight on, you might have tripped over him."

"That spells trouble."

"A dead body spells trouble? With those deductive skills, I can see how you flew up the ranks to guard-captain."

Alvantes dropped his voice to a tremor. *"Quiet. Slow down."*

He reined his mount to a steady walk. I followed suit, though the reduced speed only heightened my unease. The darkness in the mouth of the gatehouse was all-consuming. As we broke the threshold, my breath snagged. Thanks to the decline, all I could see amidst the thick gloom was a half circle of dim light far ahead – as though I were staring out the throat of some great monster.

"Late business?" The words came from nowhere and hung like phantoms. I couldn't say for sure if they were meant as challenge or polite inquiry. To me they seemed an accusation coughed up by the dark itself.

Fortunately, Alvantes's nerve was stronger than mine. "So it appears," he said. "And us supposed to be on day watch."

To stay in character, I yawned exaggeratedly. That, at least, I could do without giving away my accent.

"Could be a worse night for it," pointed out the dis-embodied voice.

"There's that," Alvantes agreed.

When no further inanities materialised from the gloom, I heard Alvantes urge his horse to a walk. Once more, I followed his lead.

Seconds later, we were in the open air once more.

Here were the gardens, clambering in elegant tiers to either side of the wide concourse, split in turn by islands of tilting palms and ornate fountains that still chuckled to themselves despite the hour. If anything, the countless stepped beds of flowerbeds smelled more fragrantly than they had in the day. The way the night muted their colours into endless shades of blue gave them a simple elegance they'd lacked in sunlight.

Less pleasant were the silhouettes of guards patrolling the parapets. Of course, it made sense that the defences would grow more vigorous as we neared the exit. On the other hand, it made equal sense that the further we got, the more likely anyone seeing us would assume we were meant to be there.

"Keep slow," hissed Alvantes.

This time, I didn't need to be told. A little of my courage had come back. We'd gotten farther than I'd have imagined possible. If I could keep my head, I might have a chance – well, to keep my head, for a while longer anyway.

It didn't take us long to reach the second gatehouse. My eyes had grown better adjusted by then. I could just make out the dim forms of two guards waiting within the entrance. One greeted us with a disinterested "Evening," which Alvantes returned in the same tone.

Two more guards waited at the far end. They acknowledged us with a nod.

We were through.

The final courtyard was, if possible, even bigger than those we'd already passed through. Various buildings clustered round its edges, and a few even had plots of cultivated ground attached, as though someone had caught up a village and scattered it like dice against the walls. I guessed these must be homes of craftsmen and farmers whose goods were in constant demand at the palace.

The guards upon the walls were even more numerous than those above the gardens. Yet they barely deigned to notice us. I felt almost courageous. I'd been right. The fact that we'd made it this far and were heading out rather than in was enough to shield us from suspicion. One more courtyard, one more gate, and we were free.

"Keep steady," muttered Alvantes. "Follow my lead."

"I get it."

"But if I say go…"

"*I get it.*"

Growing more and more accustomed to our assumed identities, we walked our horses across the vast expanse of paved ground as though it were natural as breathing for us to be there. Only as we drew near the last gatehouse did my nerves begin to trouble me again. For unlike the previous sets of gates, these were closed. There was no way we were getting past without a confrontation.

This time, Alvantes initiated it. With impressive feigned confidence, he called, "Gates open, ho."

There was a small room built into the walls next to the gate. It had its own door, and even a narrow window. A tall guard stepped out and asked, "Late errand?"

"For the stablemaster. Says if he doesn't get some liniment for his back he'll have to close up and take the whole day off. Where we'll find it at this hour is anyone's guess."

"Sounds about right for old Pieto." The guard motioned through the small window. An instant later, a hidden mechanism began to rattle and grind. The gates parted, and split by slow degrees. A sliver of city grew in their absence.

Strange to think I'd been awed by the wonders of the palace only a few hours ago. Now, that growing shard of nocturnal street seemed a thousand times more beautiful. Watching it, my heart swelled with joy.

"You two new here then?"

Exuberance turned leaden in my chest.

"He is," said Alvantes. "I just don't have a memorable face."

It sounded convincing. But I couldn't see the guard's expression. He still had his hand raised. He could halt the opening gates at any moment.

"What did you say your names were again?"

"Go!" cried Alvantes. At the same time, he spurred his mount forward.

I didn't need to be told twice.

Alvantes made it through the opening with the barest clearance. The noise of the gate mechanism had changed, assumed a deeper, more grinding pitch. Even as my horse surged forward, I realised with horror that the gap was no longer widening. In fact, it was contracting.

Time warped. Somehow, the gates were closing with

unfeasible speed, whereas my horse was plunging through treacle. I tried to scream something motivating, but no sound came. I could feel the animal wanting to shy, lest he dash his brains out on the reinforced wood. I lashed his side with my heels. He gained speed – but we were still too slow. Alvantes, ahead, seemed an impossible distance away. The street might have belonged to another world.

My mount's head entered the waning breach. Forced to commit, he surged again. A flash of fire washed my thighs as they scraped the wood to either side. I gritted my teeth, crushed myself flat and narrow.

He gave a brief, high shriek. It could only mean we were trapped, about to be crushed by the inexorable apparatus of the gates…

No. Still moving. Cobbles flickered by beneath his feet. I glanced back.

The gates were shut. The tip of the poor beast's tail had stayed with them.

But we were through.

Alvantes was still riding hard ahead, though there was no way we could be followed immediately. Closing the gates had backfired, and bought us a breathing space from any pursuers. I encouraged my horse to forget his foreshortened tail with another tap of my heels, and did my best to close the distance.

We were in the crescent of temples that curved around the palace, on a wide thoroughfare that appeared to stretch the entire length of Pasaeda. By the time I caught up with Alvantes, he'd slowed slightly, and was turning his mount into a side road.

He rode hard for the next few minutes, leading us by twists and turns through the starlit streets until I'd altogether lost my sense of direction or any notion of where we were. Eventually, he slowed to let me draw alongside. We were approaching a small square. At its centre was a circle of cultivated woodland, and in the midst of that a squat building of white marble. From its roof rose a statue, also of marble, representing some ancient warrior brandishing his sword towards the heavens.

"Thanks for the tour," I said, "but was this really the time?"

"It won't have taken them long to follow," Alvantes replied. "At least that route should keep them chasing their tails awhile."

If Alvantes had really bought us time, I felt I was overdue an answer to some crucial questions. "So what's going on here? If you and your father have cooked up some conspiracy, I've a right to know."

"Conspiracy? It's nothing like that."

"Yet one minute you're locked in a prison cell and the next you're catching up with old friends."

Alvantes shrugged resignedly. "All right. As you must have realised, my father's a senator in the Court. Back in the cell, he passed me a message. A simple code."

"A code?"

"Something we settled on years ago. A message hidden in the final words of each sentence."

How had I missed it? I'd been so quick to write Alvantes Senior off as senile that I'd hardly bothered to consider what he was saying. From what I could remember of his diatribe, I could even piece together a little of what he'd told his son. There had been directions in there – and hadn't he mentioned something about the stable? All those strange allusions to times made a lot more sense now.

Thinking back brought another realisation – one I'd have made at the time if only I'd been paying attention. "He gave you the key to your shackle, didn't he? When he hit you."

"Yes."

"Then he arranged for the door to be left open and the guard to be drugged."

"Something like that. If the details are so important to you, ask him yourself."

We'd almost reached the wooded glen and the small columned building with its militant passenger. It struck me almost in the same moment that it must be a tomb, and that a figure on horseback was just visible in the thick arboreal shadows.

"Good morning, Father," said Alvantes.

Alvantes's father walked his horse out to meet us. "Gailus passed you my message, then?" he said. "I half-expected him to forget."

Alvantes tipped his head towards the statue. "He remembered. Grandfather, at least, looks well."

"Sometimes I envy him. He fought his battles in simpler times."

"Probably they didn't seem that way to him."

"Perhaps. Perhaps the fights never seem straightforward when you're in the midst of them." Alvantes's father sounded weary – more so even than a man of his age would normally be for staying up all night. "It's good to see you free. But you should never have come to Pasaeda, Lunto."

"I did what I had to do," said Alvantes.

"Maybe. Either way, you're ahead of schedule. I take it they know you've escaped?"

Alvantes nodded.

"No time for pleasantries then. We'll talk as we ride." Alvantes Senior turned his horse's nose toward a road other than the one we'd arrived by, and set off at a trot. He waited for us to match his speed before he continued, "Panchetto's loss was a terrible blow. For the King and the kingdom. For all of us."

Alvantes hung his head, much as he'd done when they last spoke. "I know. Believe me."

"I'm willing to accept that you'd have saved Panchetto if you possibly could. I think the King would be too, were he in his right mind. Moaradrid's rebellion and the uproar in the far north have been poisoning his thoughts for a long time now; and there are always elements in the Court ready to inject fresh bile."

"Is there any way I can help?" asked Alvantes.

"Absolutely not." His father's voice had acquired a note of iron forcefulness. "Lunto, listen to me now, if it's the only time you ever do. The best and only thing you can do is to go home. Help Altapasaeda however you can. We'll send aid if we're able, but don't rely on it. In fact, for the time being, anticipate the worst."

"What will you do?"

Alvantes Senior shook his head. It struck me more as a response to circumstances in general than to Alvantes's question. "His Highness must not be allowed to become a tyrant. There are many of us in the Court who strive to keep him on the higher path."

By then we were halfway down a long street, quite narrow by the standards of Pasaeda, hemmed on either side by two-storey buildings fronting directly to the road. They were still impressive, but considerably less so than the manors I'd seen on the way in. Perhaps here was the answer to my wonderings as to where Pasaeda's not-quite-so-wealthy citizens resided. Ahead, the walls were clearly visible about the rooftops, no more than a couple of minutes' ride away. Our freedom was truly within reach.

Pulling just ahead, Alvantes Senior wheeled his horse. "We're near the gates," he said. He motioned skyward, where the first light of sunrise was gilding the rooftops. "Unless someone's had the foresight to pass on the alert, they'll be opening the gates at any minute. Go, while you still can."

"The King's bound to realise you helped us," said Alvantes.

"He'll see reason eventually. He'll understand my motives."

"And if he doesn't?"

"Then he's still the King," said Alvantes Senior. "Go, Lunto."

There was strain in his voice that hadn't been there an instant ago – controlled but unmistakeable. I glanced at Alvantes, saw I wasn't the only one to have noticed it.

"Come with us," he said. "For a while, at least. Give the King time to calm down."

"It isn't for you or me to predict the moods of a King."

"Father…"

"Don't insult me by asking me to further dishonour our family. I told you to go." If the words were angry, his father's tone betrayed them. The strain had become something more. Could it be fear?

Whatever it was, it sent shivers through me. "Come on," I told Alvantes.

I could see the conflict in his face. But his father's was an inscrutable mask, offering no room for argument.

"Goodbye," Alvantes said.

"Go!" Alvantes Senior stirred his horse into motion and rode swiftly past us, back in the direction we'd come.

After a moment's pause, Alvantes encouraged his own mount forward. Relieved that the family drama was done with, I followed.

We were almost at the end of the road before we heard Alvantes Senior's voice again. It was faint, but there was a clear note of remonstrance in it, as though he were arguing with someone.

I didn't want to stop. I didn't want to look. There was no good reason he'd be arguing with anyone in the street at this hour. Alvantes had already jerked to a halt – as though the sound were a shock of thunder that his gaze had sought out. His expression showed something worse than my own mounting alarm.

It was grief. It was the grief of loss.

There was no way I could have known what to expect. Yet when I looked round and saw them, I felt only a sick sense of inevitability. Stick and Stone, the King's chequered jester-assassins, had come to a halt just ahead of Alvantes's father. They looked absurd, dressed up like that in the middle of the street, all the more so because their horses were piebald – one black but splashed with white and the other white with stains of black. That absurdity did nothing to make them less terrifying. If anything, the opposite was true.

Though they were too distant for me to catch individual words, it was clear Alvantes Senior was protesting. It was hard to imagine any complaint penetrating that grim, clownish exterior, and yet they seemed to be waiting patiently enough.

Or so I thought.

As far as I saw, neither one moved. When Alvantes's father jerked backward, it seemed purely of his own accord. He kept his balance a moment, reaching with one hand to his chest. He might have been struck by indigestion. Then he slid backwards, sideways.

The crunch as he struck the cobbles was loud even where we were.

CHAPTER FOURTEEN

"Alvantes…"

I meant to say *Let's go*. I meant to say *There's nothing you can do*. But the sounds just wouldn't come.

It hardly mattered. Even if I'd managed to get the words out, I might as well have pleaded with a wall. Alvantes held himself so utterly still that it was hard to believe he'd ever move again.

The jester-assassins waltzed their steeds delicately round his father's body, as though its presence on the cobbles was in questionable taste. They showed no sense of urgency. They were hardly even looking in our direction. Every nerve in my body ached to flee, yet I couldn't. Not alone. Because the prospect of being alone and hunted through Pasaeda by those freaks was more than I dared imagine.

I racked my brain for words that might rouse Alvantes. All the while, the distance narrowed. It certainly wasn't fear that had frozen him, I knew that much. He was waiting. He was *letting* them come. My tongue felt thick and infinitely heavy in my mouth.

My thoughts swirled uselessly, like water down a drain. When they flung up something half-coherent, I grasped it without question.

"You can't ignore the last order he gave you," I hissed.

Alvantes tore his gaze from his father's killers, looked in my direction. There was confusion in the depths behind his eyes, and fathomless hatred. I didn't know if the latter was meant for them or me. Nor did I care – because I could see something else there too. What I'd told him had done the trick.

Alvantes wheeled his horse and kicked it savagely. The steed shot forth like a stone from a sling, as though it had been waiting for such a signal. With the slightest encouragement, my own followed its lead. Clearly, they both had sense enough to realise what was bearing down on us.

I caught one glimpse of Stick and Stone as we shot off. They were bent low, coaxing their horses to match our speed. As far as I could judge from body language alone, they didn't look at all upset that we'd run.

All I could think was, I bet they don't get off the leash too often.

I shuddered, turned my attention to the road. We were coming up hard on an avenue running beneath the walls. Alvantes swerved in a tight arc that took him within touching distance of the brickwork. I did my best to emulate him – but I wasn't half so good a horseman. White stone crashed by, seemingly flush against my nose.

Then we were clattering up the road, already far

behind Alvantes, who'd cleared half the distance to the vast gatehouse ahead.

Despite what Alvantes's father had claimed, I hadn't believed the gate would be open. That it was definitely had to count as good news. Nor had I expected it to be busy at this hour. Yet an endless-seeming caravan of wagons was streaming through the entrance and on up the road ahead. And there was the bad news. Because there was no way past. We were trapped.

If Alvantes had noticed, it wasn't slowing him. If anything, he was accelerating. His only concession had been to guide his mount to the farther side of the road. Assuming he must have some plan, I followed his lead. Only when it was too late did it occur to me that maybe he had no plan at all. He'd just watched his father die. What kind of planning could I really expect?

Not much, it seemed. Now that he was close, he'd adjusted his angle once more, was drifting back across the road towards the gatehouse opening. If his course didn't smash him through a wagon, he'd mash himself to jelly across the walls.

Then I saw what he'd seen. It was the slightest of gaps. One wagon had paused in the gatehouse while a guard interrogated its driver, the next was pressing on into the city. Conceivably, there was just room for Alvantes to squeeze through, and then – if his riding was exemplary beyond measure – to turn at speed within the gatehouse and slip through.

As quick as I spotted it, the guard waved the first driver on. The driver, not having seen Alvantes bearing down on him, yanked the reins. His cart trundled forward. The already negligible gap began to close.

It was far too late for Alvantes to turn aside. Something told me he wouldn't have anyway. Recklessness might be a new approach for him, but he was certainly making it his own.

The driver, surely stressed by his interrogation, managed to ignore what was happening until the last moment. Had he glanced up a second later, Alvantes's horse and his would have grown violently acquainted. As it was, he reined in so hard he nearly tumbled backward into his cart's load. Alvantes flew through the breach, slammed his poor horse into a turn so sharp it must have nearly snapped its spine, and was swallowed by the dark of the gatehouse.

Meanwhile, shocked by its master's sudden violence and another animal whipping past its nostrils, the wagoner's great carthorse reared. Jerked sideways by the abrupt movement, the vehicle began to list. At first, the driver clung to the reins. It took one wheel shivering into chunks for realisation to dawn.

Left with no choice, the driver half leaped, half fell to one side – just as the second wheel cracked behind him, tipping the wagon further. The wagon tipped completely, heaving its cargo of long-necked amphorae into the street. Amidst shards of exploding pottery, a wave of oil flooded the debris round the petrified wagoner.

While he strove to crawl away, his horse – still caught in its twisted harness – somehow managed to maintain its balance. Mad with fear and in defiance of gravity, it reared, its forelegs pawing the air.

All of that had occurred in moments. I'd had no time to adjust my course, even had there been anywhere to go. With Stick and Stone gaining behind me, it hadn't even crossed my mind to slow down. Which meant I was still charging towards the wagon – or more precisely, the panicking animal at its front.

My choice was simple. I could turn, hit a wagon and die. I could keep going, probably have my head knocked clean off by a hoof and die.

It was a choice that made itself before I'd had the barest instant to consider. Straight on or nothing. That didn't mean I had to see it coming. Terrible horseman that I was, we were no more likely to make it through for my involvement. I slid down, flattened across my horse, crushed my face into his mane.

For a moment, there was only darkness, scent of sweat and spilled oil, a cacophony of sound cut through with equine terror.

Then came the pain.

It was so piercing, so abrupt, that I almost let go. All my held breath was torn clean away. Slipping down my horse's withers, I just barely clung on.

That agony could only have been a hoof dashing against my shoulder. It felt as if my right arm was shattered like glass.

It was only the beginning. This new pain was a flood cascading through all parts of my body at once – though no less excruciating for that. On some level, I understood that we'd passed the ruined cart and careened into the inner wall of the gatehouse. The knowledge was no help. Even if I could have persuaded a part of

me to work, I doubted my horse had the faintest interest in anything I wanted.

He proved me right the moment he set off again.
Travelling straight ahead surely made perfect sense to
a horse brain. That doing so meant scraping his pum-
melled rider against the stone wall likely didn't much
concern him. In fact, under the circumstances, he
probably saw it as an advantage.

I found the strength to haul myself upright, sending
huge jolts of anguish through my hoof-imprinted right
arm. As I opened my eyes, the pale sunlight seemed
blinding.

On some unfathomable level, I was aware I'd escaped Pasaeda. But any relief was buried under pain
and shock. I pressed on past the tail of the wagon convoy, hardly registering the bewildered looks the drivers
turned my way.

Alvantes was waiting some distance down the road.
I managed to guide my horse towards him, though I
couldn't have said how. As I drew close, he motioned
towards the carnage we'd left in our wake. "That
should hold them awhile."

Neither the sentiment nor the voice that spoke it
sounded anything like the Alvantes I knew. He didn't
seem remotely worried by the chaos he'd caused, or the
innocent wagoner – and his horse – who'd been
harmed at our expense.

Still, if the shock of sudden grief had done bad things
to Alvantes's moral compass, he remained a better bet
than the harlequin assassins behind us. He was right,
his recklessness had bought us time – but that didn't

mean much in the scheme of things. Our horses weren't cut out for a prolonged chase. Given the obscene patience Stick and Stone had shown, it was safe to guess theirs would be.

Therefore, when he encouraged his mount to a gallop, I didn't let my doubts about his current sanity keep me from following. Before us, the tree-lined highway we'd arrived by descended steadily towards the harbour. If I'd had any say, that would have been our destination, for commandeering a boat would do much to consolidate our lead. Alvantes, however, ignored the harbour, veering from the road. In that direction was only rugged grassland, stretching down to broken strips of forest in the distance.

If it didn't seem to offer anything very promising as an escape route, I still wasn't ready to argue. Not that Alvantes gave me much opportunity. He was riding hard, showing no interest in whether I could keep up – and I was starting to doubt I could. Realistically, I probably hadn't sustained any terminal damage. I could just about twitch my fingers, despite my injured right arm. But between that and the red-raw flesh of my left side, it was hard to pay much attention to riding. Nor had having my head slammed against a wall at high speed helped. Whenever my concentration began to slip, the scene grew foggy and unreal.

Thankfully, Alvantes reined in again when we broke through the first copse of trees. He stared out from the deep shade, back towards the gates. Drawing alongside, I looked where he looked.

Though it made me shudder, I wasn't surprised to see that Stick and Stone had made their way through the carnage inside the gatehouse. I could easily imagine how quickly the carters would have moved to clear the way.

The two assassins were making good time in our direction. More unexpected was that Stick and Stone had gained a tail of their own. I couldn't judge details, except that he or she was small-built and plainly dressed, with a hood drawn over the face. They'd only just slipped from the gloom of the gate and were hanging well back. Stick and Stone, focused on us, seemed oblivious to their presence.

Might this new party be an ally? Some agent of Alvantes's father? It seemed unlikely. Yet I felt sure that this unknown was following the two assassins, whilst studiously keeping in their blind spot.

I glanced at Alvantes. If I was expecting enlightenment, it was a vain hope indeed. His expression was murderous. "I'll lead them away," he said. "Keep south." Then, as an afterthought, "Avoid the cliffs."

Before I could tell him to stop playing hero, or decide if I even wanted to, he was off again. He broke from the copse, turned sharply to pursue its edge. His intention was clear. So long as I kept the bank of trees between us, I'd be invisible to Stick and Stone. His motives were more doubtful. I was sure Alvantes didn't intend to run far. He planned to find somewhere to make his stand; any saving of my life would be a purely incidental benefit.

He was overwrought, blind with anguish. They

were killers fit for a king. I doubted very much I'd ever see Alvantes again.

As for me, I was scared sick and in pain. If Alvantes's self-sacrifice bought me a few more minutes of life, then I was about ready to accept it. I plunged my mount into the bank of woodland with hardly a second thought.

On the farther side, the land dipped in a shallow bank and continued much as before. Far to my left was a crude hint of the river's course, far to my right the western mountains. Between stretched a vast tract of grassland. More tufts of woodland like the one I'd passed through were scattered about, and far ahead, a denser wall of forest severed the view altogether.

There was no sign of any cliffs. Had Alvantes meant the mountains to the west? If so, his last words had been wasted. There was no cover at all in that direction. Even if Stick and Stone had taken Alvantes's bait, they'd have ample time to murder him, pick up my trail and track me down before I could make it halfway to those remote peaks.

No, the dense blockade of foliage ahead was my only option. I could make good time on the shallowly descending sward, and once I was through the tree line, perhaps hunt out a hiding place.

My horse seemed happier now that we were out of the city. Perhaps he'd rationalised the whole affair as a grand escape he'd orchestrated himself. If he kept a decent pace and didn't dash me against any more walls, I was willing to leave him to his illusions. The miasma in my head had cleared just slightly, too. The general pain had dulled to a teeming ache. Only my arm remained an immediate concern. I could just about flex my fingertips, but doing so sent such jolts through the distressed muscles that I almost fainted. For any serious purpose – say, fending off assassins – it was useless.

Still, with the horse more or less cooperating, I could ride at least. The land was firm and even, and we were making good speed. As the forest drew closer, I tried to count that short list of blessings, and not think unduly about what might be happening behind me. Alvantes was surely dead by now. However fast my mount and I were, Stick and Stone were faster.

I made it two-thirds of the distance before my fears got the better of me. Doing my best to balance without jeopardising my damaged arm, I risked a glimpse over my shoulder.

There were still two riders. They'd both come after me. And they were already far too close.

I encouraged the horse to speed up. To my surprise, he did. It probably wasn't enough to stop them gaining, but I appreciated the effort. By the time we came to the edge of the forest, however, he was growing fretful. Worse, what had looked like airy and pleasant weald from a distance revealed a tangle of thick foliage carpeted with vines and nettle.

There was no way we were galloping through there. I let the horse slow to a walk – though it felt like baring my throat for those rapidly nearing killers. Even that indulgence made no difference. He could barely manage two steps before a branch lashed his side or a snare of thorns tried to trip him. He began to huff and fret again. Freedom was obviously proving a disappointment.

There was nothing for it. I dismounted and crashed on foot into the brush. I was leaving a trail a corpse could follow. Worse, I was tiring myself uselessly. Time and again, I crashed my arm against a trunk and wanted to weep for the raw shock that dashed through it. But I couldn't bring myself to stop. If I was moving, I had a chance. If I was in pain, I was alive. It was when the pain and moving stopped that I had to worry.

I was more right than I knew.

Head down, arms up to protect my face, I had the barest moment to realise I'd broken through the edge of the forest. It was just time enough to see the cliffs at my feet, not nearly enough to halt myself.

By way of small mercies, the view was outstanding. As I toppled into it, I saw clearly how the broken ground declined in narrow steps, all the way to where the grasslands continued far below. It was a very small mercy, however, because I only received its benefit for the briefest of instants before I was tumbling head over heels.

If the slope promised to be gradual enough that it might conceivably not kill me, there was still no way to pause my plummeting descent. Nor did it lack for jutting rocks and bushes. They didn't slow my plunge either, just made it more eventful. The only thing guaranteed to stop me was hitting somewhere horizontal – and that happened quickly enough.

I still managed to roll a couple more times before I came to a rest. I flopped onto my back and gulped air as jagged as ground glass. There was no way I was getting up. It was impossible. My arm, in particular, felt as though the bones had been removed, heated to melting point and clumsily reinserted. I'd seen enough of the cliffs to know that the slope back to the edge of the forest was infinitely beyond my current abilities. The only way on was down – and the only way I'd be continuing in that direction was if I didn't mind being in pieces at the bottom.

Instead, I lay still. Consciousness slipped and slid. The sky seemed to darken and flush with brightness, as though days were spinning by. In the dark, I almost accepted my impending fate. Under the brilliance, I was helpless and terrified. Neither could quite give me the will to move. I doubted anything could. Better to lie still and wait – for death would arrive soon enough, whether I liked it or not.

And there he was. Perhaps I'd been unconscious, because one moment I was staring at the grass-tufted edge of the decline, the next he was standing above me, gazing down. The distorted patterning of his costume made my eyes cross. There was a knife in his hand.

I wanted to say something. It didn't seem right to die without some suitably Damascoesque last words.

He raised his hand, tipping the knife hilt skywards.

If nothing else, I wanted to ask him who the mysterious stranger was. The one who'd pursued us from Pasaeda, the one I'd mistaken for his partner when I'd looked back earlier – the one standing behind him now. I raised my good arm, tried my best to point. He ignored me in favour of sighting carefully along the flat of his blade.

When he flicked his hand, it was quick as any adder striking.

The blade spun away – turned a perfect half-circle, neatly impaled a clot of grass. Stick, Stone, whichever he might be, took a drunken step forward. He tumbled, flipped three times, landed with a crisp crack like breaking ice that could only have been his neck. He came to rest just to my right, laying along the very edge of the outcrop.

Finally, I persuaded my throat to produce sounds. Surely, it could manage two brief words, at least. I addressed them to the second figure, now staring down in place of the one he'd just so casually killed.

"Hello, Synza," I mumbled.

CHAPTER FIFTEEN

Even for a master-assassin like Synza, descending to my level took some time.

While he worked his way down, I concentrated on sitting up. All the while, I tried to ignore the body beside me. I didn't doubt he was dead; no one could fall like that, make a sound like that, and not be. But while having a dead killer next to me might be better than having a live one there, his presence still made my skin creep.

Sitting proved as difficult as anything I'd ever tried to do. My injured right arm was worse than useless. The faintest tremor became a seismic shock of pain. Since all of me was hurting already, that just made me want to pass out or to vomit. Passing out was actually a promising option, but vomiting certainly wasn't. The possibility of doing both together was enough to keep me grasping to consciousness.

By the time Synza reached me I was half sitting, half laying, propped on my one good arm. If I kept still, the pain was bearable. I couldn't possibly defend myself –

but then, I was facing a professional murderer, unarmed, with one arm likely broken, on a ledge above a sheer cliff face. Under the circumstances, dying with a shred of dignity would be a laudable achievement.

Given how powerfully I wanted to soil my trousers, I suspected even that might prove beyond me.

Synza dusted himself casually with one hand, as though climbing down cliffs was the kind of petty inconvenience he encountered on a daily basis. He covered the distance between us in two neat strides, stopping before the body that until recently had been either Stick or Stone. Synza observed the still form at his feet carefully for a few seconds, before nudging it gently with his foot. When it didn't stir, he gave a slight nod, as a teacher might respond to a bright student. He looked at me.

"You're an impossibly lucky man, Easie Damasco," Synza said.

"You obviously don't know me very well." I hadn't been sure I could stretch to an entire sentence. That small success made me unreasonably proud.

"But then, no man ever considers himself lucky, does he?"

Synza drew a short, thin-bladed knife. I knew without doubt it was the one he'd just killed with, yet there was no spot of blood on it now. It returned the morning sunlight in a flash of shimmering silver. Synza looked at it with something resembling curiosity. With his free hand, he flicked the tip of the blade, sending a shudder down it like a breeze over water.

"No one has ever survived my attentions before," he said. "To do so not once but three times is beyond absurd. If I hadn't been going to kill you anyway, I'd have to do so simply to make a point."

"Which would be?" I managed.

"That some things are inescapable. And that I'm one of them."

Synza didn't sheathe the knife. Nor did he look as though he was about to use it. In fact, it was as if he'd momentarily forgotten he was holding it. His eyes were flitting between the body at his feet and me. A small, convulsive smile played over his lips. "I shouldn't have done that, you know," he said. "There will definitely be consequences. But oh, what a pleasure! The great Stone, finest killer in all the lands. Not so, it seems."

Well, that cleared up whom the body at my feet belonged to, at least. Slowly, delicately, Synza tipped the prone figure over with the tip of one boot. On its back, splayed limbs cocooned in complex motley, it looked more grotesque and less human than ever. Synza knelt down, put his knife to Stone's throat, and with his other hand began to peel back the chequered mask. He wasn't looking at me, yet I had no doubt he could register my slightest movement. I tried hard not to make any, though my good arm was starting to shudder under my weight.

The mask seemed to resist a little before coming off. It revealed a thin, sharp-contoured face, more yellow than the bronzed brown typical of Ans Pasaedans. The eyes were so narrow that even open they'd have been little more than slots in that sallow flesh. Those facts aside, it was a visage that made no great impression. In death, unmasked, the royal assassin looked more pathetic than terrifying.

"Not that I'd ever brag," Synza said. "Only you and I will know. Which means, of course, that very soon only I will know."

He stood and, with gentle pressure from his foot, tipped Stone's corpse towards the edge. It didn't take much effort before the body gained its own momentum. I heard small stones skitter, heralds of the larger object in their wake. The body sagged, and then fell from view with sudden, alarming speed. Dirt burst from the edge like a cloud of angry wasps.

Synza looked at me once more. There was amusement in his eyes.

"I suppose you'll have some questions."

In fact, at that precise moment, my mind had been frantically calculating the possibilities for survival if I were to throw *myself* off the cliff. If Synza wanted questions, however, it seemed wise to come up with some. Every moment he was talking was a moment he wasn't killing me. Yet my mind was blank. My natural verbosity had vanished like dew under a midday sun.

I'd never imagined there'd come a time when *not* talking would place my life in jeopardy.

I hunted frenziedly through my memories of our previous encounters, desperate for anything that might have piqued my curiosity. There was only one thing I could remember wondering over, and it was so obvious and mundane that I couldn't imagine it being what Synza was after. I could find nothing better though, and moment by moment, the humour in Synza's eyes was shifting towards impatience.

I picked my words carefully. "What order did Mounteban give you, back in Altapasaeda?" I tried to sound genuinely curious rather than merely petrified. "You could have killed me a thousand times over between there and here. You could have done it easily in Aspira Nero or at the ferry port."

"Yes, there it is. The crux of our unfortunate relationship. There are venues no good assassin would ever consider, of course; knifings in bars or busy streets are the province of cutpurses and petty thugs. However, in this instance, it's fair to say the instruction was unfortunate, not to mention counterproductive. My master's dictum was: *Kill him. But make sure no one sees you do it.*"

An order that would have made perfect sense in a room crowded with people Mounteban didn't want to alarm, none at all once I'd made a run for it. "Easier said than done," I ventured. Actually, it didn't sound hard at all. It sounded like something that would only be difficult if you were the kind of person who purposefully made their career difficult – if, for example, you took satisfaction from seeing your victim's face in their very last moments. But if ever humouring someone had seemed like a sensible idea it was then.

"I was incautious, I admit. Had I not revealed my presence to you on the walls of Altapasaeda, we wouldn't be where we are now. You'd have died a swift and painless death and I'd be elsewhere, pursuing some no doubt infinitely more productive goal."

"I'm sure we'd both have been much happier," I hazarded.

"I hope that wasn't sarcasm. You can sit up, you know."

As Synza had evidently noticed, my good arm was quivering like a reed under my weight. Gratefully, I levered myself forward and shifted into a crouch.

"You look as though you're in considerable pain. Let me know when it becomes unduly bothersome." Synza gave the dagger another experimental tap. This time I thought I could hear the faintest chime, like a finger dragged round the rim of a glass. "For once, I have no particularly timescale in mind. Within realistic bounds, I see no reason why you shouldn't have a say."

"Thanks," I said, "I think I'm managing for the moment. I still have a few questions I'd like answers to."

Truth be told, I didn't have even one. However, I'd never lacked for imagination. Surely my fertile subconscious wouldn't fail me now? Except that it felt as though a hundred scurrying rats were ringing bells in my head, and that wasn't a sensation conducive to making up questions, even to keep insane assassins from slitting my throat.

It occurred to me that the details of our journey through the Castoval and then Ans Pasaeda were of importance to Synza. Perhaps the only way he'd been able to justify his repeated failure was to reimagine it as a cat and mouse chase of dramatic and unlikely twists and turns. To me, it had rarely been more than a nuisance. How could I explain that in recent weeks, people trying to kill me had practically become an accepted frustration of life? How could I say that these days I was generally terrified of something, and he'd just happened to be the most frequently recurring source of alarm?

I couldn't. If it was important to Synza that our runins gain the proportions of some mythic duel of wits, then all I could do was play along.

"You were unlucky in Paen Acha," I said, striving for a tone of professional indifference.

"There's no such thing as luck," snarled Synza. "As I said, I was careless. Please don't imagine you can pander to my ego."

I strove to keep my voice steady – and not to point out how he'd just contradicted himself. "I'm just offering my opinion. It was a chance in a thousand that Alvantes startled me at that precise moment."

"A chance I should have accounted for. Do you really imagine such factors can't be predicted, with sufficient care? How did you ever manage as a thief?"

"Not so well," I admitted.

"Hmm. At least you admit your failings." Synza mastered his irritation with a visible effort. "Anyway. Before we go further, don't you think you ought to thank me?"

I'd just started to get to grips with inventing questions, and now here was a fresh conundrum. What could Synza possibly believe I had to thank him for? He'd been trying to kill me for days, and he certainly hadn't failed through a lack of effort. He'd killed Stone, but that had hardly been for my benefit. Even letting me live while he rambled psychotically didn't seem enough to warrant gratitude.

I dredged my mind to think what else had happened recently that might hint at a professional killer interfering in my affairs.

Yet the instant I realised, it seemed obvious. "You killed the guard in the palace," I said.

"Of course I did."

"Thank you," I added, remembering how we'd arrived at the subject. "That can't have been easy."

"Penetrating the most protected building in the land? Disposing of a guard unseen whilst inside its environs? It certainly wasn't."

It was clear he was itching to tell me the details. Was this really the same composed and silent killer I'd once found so unnerving? He was no longer composed, and he certainly wasn't silent. Nor did he seem to be on anything approaching the right side of sane.

"I'm curious," I said. "What were you doing there?"

As I'd predicted, Synza began to reply almost before the question was out of my mouth. "Rumour in the city was that the guard-captain of Altapasaeda and a companion had been imprisoned, pending their execution. What a maddening twist! Getting into the palace was a chore, even for me. Fortunately, the guard was good enough to let me know where they were keeping you before I relieved him of his duties. I waited in a nearby passage to calculate my next move... and before I knew it, your friend Alvantes was blundering past. After I'd checked your cell and found that you'd also vanished, what could I do but follow and hope he'd lead me to you?"

If I'd had any thoughts of trying to keep him talking,

I was wondering now if I'd ever get him to shut up. It was as though a dam that had been in place for years, perhaps his entire life, had suddenly and irrevocably ruptured.

I decided it might be better if he didn't know he'd crept past me not once but twice in the prison corridors. I went for ambiguity instead. "You must have been close."

"If I hadn't had to work my way round the outside of the courtyard, I'd have had you at the stables. By the time I realised you'd blundered within my reach, you'd blundered out of it again. It took me time to pick up your trail once you'd fled the palace. Again, I was near. But who could have imagined Alvantes's fool of a father had been careless enough that the King would send out Stick and Stone? Saved from the attentions of one assassin by the intervention of two others!" Synza chuckled hideously. "As I suggested at the opening of our conversation, you are an impossibly lucky man. And as I further intimated, your luck has finally run out."

So that was it? He was happy to keep me breathing so long as I was listening to his rambling exploits, but now he had them off his chest, my services were no longer required? "Wait," I said. "Are you really telling me you broke into the dungeon to kill me so nobody else could kill me first?"

"Of course. How else could I possibly fulfil my orders?"

"I think Mounteban might have let that one slide, under the circumstances."

"*This isn't about Mounteban!*" Synza roared.

I tumbled back. My rucksack ground hard against my spine, but I barely noticed. Suddenly my heart was thumping in my ears. The rage in his face, normally so expressionless, made me want to crawl off the cliff just to avoid him. He was trembling with fury, head to toe. I couldn't tear my eyes from the slender-bladed knife in his hand, shaking now like a ship's mast in a storm.

Synza took a step towards me.

Then, more slowly, he dragged the knife down to his side, as though he were only partly in control of his own body. He exhaled, scrunched his eyes and clenched his fists, held like that for a long moment.

Synza opened his eyes. "This isn't about Mounteban," he repeated, softly. "This is about professionalism. Something I pride myself on, and in which I've inexcusably failed. What is there to do but put right what I can?"

"I can appreciate that," I said distractedly. Now that I wasn't in immediate fear for my life, I was fully aware of how excruciating was the pain in my back. Something was digging there, a sharp-edged circle pressed into my flesh. And I'd remembered what it was. That knowledge sent a flush of heat through my whole body, a sensation precariously balanced between hope and panic. All this time, I'd been thinking I was helpless…

"Frankly," said Synza, "you exhausted my patience. Who knew such a thing was possible? I grew indiscreet. Though I take some comfort from the fact that Alvantes and yourself will certainly be blamed for my more careless deeds, the fact remains that I've failed my master – failed for the first time in thirty years." He smiled – and the knife in his clenched fist came up once more. "But I tell you this… it will be worth it all to hear you scream."

"Well, that's something, I suppose."

I could see that my cheerfulness threw him. "Shall we to business then?" he said.

"I agree. Absolutely."

This time, Synza eyed me with undisguised curiosity. "I confess I wasn't expecting such enthusiasm."

"To business. And our first order of business should be the extremely good reason you have not to kill me."

"Oh, Damasco. I hope you don't intend to spoil the moment by begging." Synza looked genuinely dejected. "Hasn't this exchange been amicable so far? What a pity to shame yourself now. You can't outbid Castilio Mounteban. Even if you could, you *couldn't*. You have nothing that could interest me. You never have had and you never will."

"I don't doubt it," I said. But I do have something I think will interest Castilio quite a lot. Far more than my head. Something, in fact, that he'd find so intensely interesting he might even overlook just how long it's taken you to follow his order."

"You run the risk of wounding my feelings. I've made no secret that my performance in this matter has been unsatisfactory. But that is a concern for me and my master only."

"Still, a little added incentive couldn't hurt. Say, if you were to take me back alive, with the one thing he wants most in the world. The thing I'd been planning to take him anyway, to bargain for his protection. Since we're here, I don't see why the negotiations shouldn't start a little early."

"I struggle to know whether you're entertaining or annoying me," said Synza. "Very well. For the sake of ending our unduly long acquaintance on an agreeable note, why don't you explain?"

I began to shrug my pack from my shoulders.

"I don't need to tell you that you shouldn't make any sudden moves," he added. "Or that no move you make could possibly be sudden enough."

The average tortoise would have been unlikely to describe my movements as sudden; but I slowed even further, inching the straps off by degrees. Once they were free, I laid the pack on the strip of tousled grass between me and the edge. If I still wasn't sure how I could turn my one hole card into a genuine bargaining tool, common sense suggested that placing it in jeopardy was a good start.

I unbuckled the pack's straps, folded back the flap, loosened the drawstring within. I reached inside, drew out my bundled cloak and placed it delicately beside the bag. I didn't need to look to know I had Synza's interest. Making my movements all the more deliberate, I peeled back the layers of cloak and clothing as though they were the skin of some impossibly delicate fruit.

I only looked up when the first glint of gold was revealed. Now I had his attention, all right.

"Is that what I think it is, Damasco?"

"If you think it's the royal crown of Altapasaeda," I

said, "the one object that could consolidate Castilio Mounteban's authority over the city beyond doubt or question, then yes, it's what you think it is."

"How did you… no, that's a redundant question. You're a thief and, as I've observed more than once now, improbably lucky. Let that be explanation enough. Give it to me now."

I picked up the crown with my good left hand – but instead of passing it to Synza, I held my arm straight out behind me. "I could do that," I said. "Or I could just let go."

"Not before I got to you."

"Maybe."

"And not without abandoning your only hope of bargaining for your life."

"Is that what we're doing, then?" I asked. "Bargaining?"

"Perhaps we are." His tone was grudging.

I shifted closer to the edge. "I think I'm going to need something a little more definite than 'perhaps'."

"It's all you'll get with such transparent bluffing."

"You're really willing to chance it?"

"Perfectly so."

This wasn't going well. Then again, what had I expected? Synza was right. I was bluffing, it was obvious, and it was getting me nowhere. I was tempted to hurl the crown off the cliff, just to reclaim a shred of dignity before my inevitable demise.

The thought must have shown in my face – because unexpectedly, Synza said, "Since the advantage is in every way mine, however, why take chances? Bring it to me, and we'll discuss the possibility of your continuing existence."

"What guarantee do I have?"

Synza sighed with mock weariness. "None at all. I could make you a promise you'd have no reason to believe, if it would make you feel better. You have my word that we'll discuss the matter. It's all you'll get."

Fair enough. I had no intention of giving him the crown anyway. I just wanted to get closer, while anger and frustration were blunting his killer instincts. The crown might not be heavy, exactly, but it had some heft. Anyway, this was my one and only option. Synza would certainly spot an attack, probably faster than I could conceive it. His knife would be acquainting itself with my guts in a flash. It was a chance, though. If nothing else, it was a chance.

"With your right hand, please."

There went my chance.

"I hurt my arm," I said, sounding even more pathetic than I'd intended. "It's useless."

"Nonsense. You've suffered a slight fracture. If you should survive the next few minutes, and if you're careful, it will heal within a week. If you weren't such a coward in the face of pain, you could use it perfectly well."

I almost asked how he could possibly know such a thing. Then it struck me that if anyone would understand the intricacies of the human body, it was a man who'd spent a lifetime studying how to damage it in imaginative ways.

I tried to flex my fingers. Pain thundered up from them, nailing itself in my shoulder. But my fingers moved, if slightly. I tried again. The pain redoubled. So did the degree of movement. Synza was right, damn him. If I could only endure the excruciation, the arm was useable.

Gritting my teeth, I transferred the crown from my left hand to my right. That meant clasping my fingers all the way, and *that* meant a rush of liquid fire, as though every drop of blood from the tips of my fingers upwards had spontaneously combusted. I was determined not to give Synza the satisfaction of hearing me scream. However, the whimper I made instead was far from manly.

I kept my arm as outstretched as I could stand. Now the crown was suspended over thin air – and my threat was suddenly far less empty. In fact, it was all I could do *not* to drop it.

I took a short step forward. Synza put his free hand out. The knife was in his right, forcing him to use his left. One pace would bridge the gap between us.

"I give you the crown and we'll talk?" I asked.

"We'll talk."

"About you letting me live?"

"Absolutely." He made no effort to hide his impatience.

I edged forward. "You promise?"

Synza reached for the crown, still just barely out of his reach. "I *promise.*"

I shuffled another short step. "On Mounteban's life?"

"On Mounteban's…? For the love of…"

I hit him in the face with the crown.

It might have been the weakest blow ever struck by one grown man upon another. It definitely hurt me a thousand times more than it did him. Still, Synza looked inordinately shocked. He licked a trickle of blood from his lower lip. "Did you really just…?"

I hit him with all my strength. This time, I used my good hand and aimed specifically for his jaw. I felt it crunch like a bag of grit.

"You *did*."

He lurched towards me, knife first – or rather, towards where I'd been the barest instant before. Synza wasn't the only one who could move fast when circumstances called for it. Now there was no Easie Damasco where he expected me to be. Now there was only my outstretched leg.

If he'd been even remotely calm, I'd never have got away with it. That made the bewildered anger contorting his face all the more satisfying.

I only got to enjoy it for a moment.

Synza spun into a crouch, in one long-practised defensive movement. It was graceful, elegant – and performed on the verge of a sheer drop. Further, it was a sheer drop that a body had been kicked off not so long ago. The ground was already loose and broken.

Synza realised it just before I did. But not in time to stop himself. A hunk of dirt and stone shuddered and sank. It happened to be the only thing supporting his left foot. The chunk of cliff edge tore free in an explosion of dirt, and disappeared.

Synza's foot followed. Then his leg. Then the rest of him.

The last I saw was his face. There was no fear in it, no anger even – just a look of the most profound frustration.

CHAPTER SIXTEEN

I couldn't pretend I'd felt the slightest affection for Synza. I certainly hadn't wanted him to kill me. Yet, as the last skittering of falling pebbles subsided, I couldn't but feel a little horrified by his abrupt vanishment from the world.

I fell back against the trampled grass. My struggle with Synza had drained what little strength I'd managed to recover. The possibility of staying conscious was as remote as the likelihood of my climbing one-handed back up to the forest edge above.

One thought, however, rattled in my brain, even as it sank into welcoming darkness. Synza had defeated Stone, reputedly one of the greatest killers in the land. I in turn had played a part, more by luck than intent, in Synza's demise. Perhaps I'd never been much of a thief, but my ranking as an assassin had just gone through the roof.

I almost wanted to laugh. Knowing how much it would hurt, I passed out instead.

• • • •

I dreamed someone was shouting my name. Every time they called, they kicked my head – *inside* my head, somehow, with a boot covered in hot pins.

It didn't take much of that to make me open my eyes. The light had changed; it was softer, yellowed like new butter. The kicking, however, continued unabated.

"Damasco!"

I was curled over, feet towards the brim of the ledge. Alvantes's voice came from behind me and above.

Where was the crown?

If he saw it, it would mean more explaining than I could even begin to contemplate. My eyes flitted desperately across the narrow outcrop. There – a clump of tall grass close to the edge, and stripes of gold amidst the green. It must have rolled from my fingers when I blacked out. I made it to all fours, though the rush of pain through my hurt arm made me want to weep. Now I could see Alvantes, peering down. He, too, was hurt. A gash in his forehead was bleeding liberally, staining the left side of his face a rich, moist crimson. Another cut on his arm had clotted but looked, if anything, deeper and more unpleasant.

"What are you doing down there?" he called.

I crawled forward, placing myself between Alvantes and the crown. "I used to be a thief. Now I mostly seem to fall off things. It's not a change I much planned."

Alvantes's gaze wandered further down the cliff face. His face showed faint surprise. "Is that Stone?"

"Yes."

"And...?"

"Next to him? That's Synza."

I might have expected admiration or at least approval, but Alvantes's tone was lifeless as his expression. "How?"

"Long story. I've lived through it, and you don't want to. Any chance of a rescue?"

His only response was to disappear from view.

Alvantes was gone for almost an hour – ample time for me to recover the crown, wrap it once more in my cloak and cram both into my pack. That done, I propped myself against the rock wall to try and recuperate a little. When he returned, it was with a bundle of knotted creepers, presumably gathered from the strip of forest. Tied together, they made a length of rope just long enough to reach me.

It was a sound enough plan in theory, utterly hopeless in practise. Between Alvantes's single-handedness and my recent injury, it wasn't long before his rescue attempt had come to seem like a particularly bad joke.

How did the one-armed man help the other one-armed man climb the cliff?

Very, very slowly.

Eventually, after colossal discomfort and much cursing, I caught hold of a tree perched on the ragged rim of the cliff and hauled myself up, to lie panting in the long grass before the woodland.

Once my head had stopped swimming and my eyes had uncrossed, I took a moment to consider Alvantes's latest injuries. The blood on his face had dried now, a grotesque half-mask of gore. He'd made no attempt to clean himself, which probably made the wounds appear worse than they were – but they certainly looked bad enough.

"You got him?"

Alvantes didn't answer. For a moment, I considered pressing the question, pushing to discover how he'd single-handedly dispatched one of the most notorious killers in the land. It took me that moment to realise I really didn't want to know. There was something behind his eyes that told me all I needed and more.

Instead, I asked, "Do you think it was him? I mean, was he the one who..." Even that sentence wasn't worth finishing. "Either way," I finished lamely, "they're both dead now."

I almost added something like, *Your father's death is avenged*. However, I could read Alvantes's face even through its half coat of red – and for all my occasional tactlessness, even I could see that the grief ingrained there could never be cleansed by anything as simplistic as revenge.

If I'd ever felt real sympathy for him, it was then. Yet it wasn't quite enough to make me forget my own misfortunes. After all, I'd just tumbled down a cliff, nearly been assassinated, nearly been assassinated *again* and then been dragged back up that self-same cliff – all with an arm that, medical opinions of recently deceased assassins aside, certainly felt broken. Nothing I said was going to make things better for Alvantes. Platitudes would only waste the strength I needed to endure the next few hours.

We were, after all, still fugitives. Sooner or later – likely sooner – Stick and Stone's absence and therefore the possibility of their failure would come to the royal attention. Given the King's penchant for lunatic overreaction, it was hard to imagine what forces he'd marshal against us next. If we had the faintest hope of survival, our only hope lay in not waiting to find out.

We had one thing in our favour, at least. Alvantes had managed to hang onto his mount, and to recover mine as well. They were tied to a spindly aspen near the verge of the forest, watching us steadily.

I walked to my horse and patted his nose. "So what's our plan?" I asked.

"Plan?"

"How do we get out of here? Back to the Castoval?"

"What does the Castoval matter?" said Alvantes, without interest.

I could have argued, could have mentioned Estrada or the Altapasaedan guardsmen he'd left in jeopardy. But I knew enough to recognise a man who was beyond the point of being reasoned with, not even by himself. If I was going to get through, I'd need to keep it simple.

"Have you forgotten what your father told you?"

Alvantes's dark eyes flashed like embers in his half-bloodied face. "I haven't forgotten."

"Then what's the plan?"

"An acquaintance I met in Aspira Nero mentioned he'd be stopping near here," he said. "If we ride fast, we might catch him."

I wasn't convinced either of us could ride at all, let alone fast. I wasn't about to tell Alvantes that. "You'd better pick our route," I said. "I haven't had much luck in that department so far today."

We travelled westward at first, towards the distant mountains, following the line of the cliffs below and the edge of the forest to our right.

Eventually, the dense trees petered out, revealing plains much like those we'd crossed outside Pasaeda. Soon after, a way downward presented itself; the cliffs to our left became broken ground, then steep slope, and finally a steady decline to another vast swathe of grassland.

The ground was still uneven, though, littered with blunt protrusions of rock as though the sward was flimsy fabric tearing around the contours of the Earth. It was sheer in places, and slow to navigate. To our left I could still see the cliffs, descending in jagged tiers. On one of those lay Synza. I had no reason to feel guilty for my part in the momentary carelessness that had cost him his life. I should have been glad to be rid of him, glad our interminable chase was finally over. I *was*. But the memory of watching him plummet from sight still plucked at my mind. If nothing else, it was a reminder that I hardly needed of how tenuous life could be.

After a while, the ground levelled once more. Ahead, it was bracketed only by the mountains to our right and a shimmer of heat haze in the direction of the river. We made sure to keep our distance from the only signs of life – herdsmen marshalling great squadrons of cattle and of horses, which drifted across the land like cloud shadows.

We camped that night near a thread of stream, in a clearing neatly fenced by trees. It was my suggestion; Alvantes would probably have ridden all night if I'd left him. We had no food, and neither of us was in any state to catch any. However, I did struggle through my languor to carefully unpack my cloak without revealing its precious cargo.

Had I given the matter a little thought, I could have saved myself the effort.

"Your pack." Alvantes's voice was ethereal in the darkness.

I started. "What about it?"

"They took it. When we were arrested."

"Oh." My heart was in my mouth. I wanted urgently to gulp it back down. Instead, I said, "That's right. I found it."

"Found it?"

"Your bags were there too. But empty." I strained my ears, trying to catch a reaction. All I could hear was the sigh of wind in leaves. "There must have been something in them they wanted."

I sat tensed, not even quite sure what to fear. More questions, which would penetrate my obvious lie? Alvantes to tear the pack from my shoulder?

When I eventually dared look, long minutes later, he was curled with his back to me, obviously sound asleep.

In the morning we used the stream to wash. For the first time, Alvantes made some effort to bathe his wounds. The gash on his forehead was messy, though shallow. The cut on his arm was deep, as I'd expected, but cleaner than I'd have guessed. I counted it a small mercy that neither showed sign of infection.

For my part, my arm hurt abysmally. I reluctantly asked Alvantes to help me strap it, and was surprised when he did an excellent job. If the splint he improvised rendered it even more useless, it at least dulled the pain to a level I could about tolerate.

"How much further?" I asked. "Can we still reach this friend of yours?"

"Who knows?" was Alvantes's only reply.

We set out riding once again, through terrain much like that we'd crossed the day before. Though I could sometimes see towns and cities in the distance, we never came close to one, just as we continued to keep our distance from the roaming herdsmen and their charges. As the day wore on, it began to seem that Ans Pasaeda consisted of one colossal, more or less empty field.

Then, around noon, the glistening stripe of a river came into view ahead. It cut down from the western mountains to carve a ragged line that frayed into nothingness far to our left.

"The Mar Fex." It was so long since Alvantes had spoken that I jumped at the sound of his voice. "It runs to meet the Mar Corilus," he said. "We need to follow it."

A highway kept close to the water in the shallow river valley below, its grey thread stringing together wide-spaced beads of villages, villas and farms. It was well travelled – the closest we'd come to civilisation since we'd left Pasaeda. By unvoiced agreement, we chose to avoid it. The higher ground was easy enough to ride, and our view of the river was clear.

Late in the afternoon, Alvantes pointed out a dirty smudge of grey against the riverside green. From a distance it looked like a long-abandoned quarry. "That's Ux Durada."

My impression didn't improve as we grew nearer. I came to realise that what I'd mistaken for ugly slabs of uncut stone were in fact the ugly slabs of buildings; but even then they looked as if they could only have been made by something else falling down. Closer up, there was at least an air of faded glory to Ux Durada's sagging edifices. A few, like a large temple with cracked windows of stained glass, had clearly once been grand. Yet whenever its heyday had been, I couldn't imagine any of the town's inhabitants were old enough to remember it. All else aside, the atmosphere was so noisome and the streets so foul that it was hard to believe anyone lasted long in Ux Durada.

In the end, we had no choice but to abandon our solitude for the road. Even then, no one showed us much interest. Those who did glance in our direction looked away just as quickly once they registered our palace guardsmen's uniforms. It apparently didn't matter that they were torn and bloody, that one of us had a splinted arm, that the other was missing a hand and had a clumsily bandaged head and shoulder. Uniforms told them all they needed to know.

It took us barely ten minutes to reach the strip of dockside I assumed to be the justification for Ux Durada's pitiful existence. It was located at a point where the Mar Fex broadened to a navigable width, and once it had probably been a valued link in Ans Pasaeda's net of transportation. Perhaps a larger port had sprung up downriver or the requirement for whatever goods were moved this way had dried up. Whatever the reason, only a few shabby craft were moored here now, and the air was thick with lethargy.

I realised Alvantes's interest was focused on one particular boat, moored to a decaying wharf at the farther end. At a distance, the vessel looked curiously familiar. I'd only been in Ans Pasaeda for a few days, and to the best of my recollection I hadn't spent any of that time in studying boats. Yet the nearer we drew, the more that sense of recognition nagged in the back of my mind.

At the last moment, I realised it wasn't just the craft's wretched appearance that was ringing bells. A peculiar stench rose off it, so virulent that I could taste it too, so richly foul that it staked its own space amidst the general miasma of Ux Durada.

A figure, previously hidden by the heaped cargo on deck, stepped into view.

"Oh no," I said. "Not you. *Anyone* but you."

The man upon deck was of clearly significant but otherwise indeterminable age. He wore a dress coat, once red, now faded to roughly the same shade of coppery brown as his deep-lined face. His shovel of beard would have been impressive had it not been trimmed so unconventionally. Just then, his mouth was hanging open and his eyes were bright with horror.

"I won't have that... ruffian... near my boat," he said.

Alvantes held up his hand. "Anterio..."

"I thought he'd be dead by now. Didn't I help you

arrest him? Did he somehow escape? Have you travelled all this way to bring him back to custody? Far
better to lop his head off right here and leave his body
for the fish."

"Anterio."

"He's even posing as a guardsman again. Has he no
shame? Guard-Captain Alvantes, with the greatest
respect…"

"*Anterio!*" Alvantes's roar did the trick – but not
without attracting the notice of half the dockside. At
a more subdued volume, he added, "Perhaps we can
discuss this more privately?"

"Of course," agreed Anterio sheepishly. "Come
aboard, Guard-Captain." Even his nervousness, however, wasn't enough to stop him throwing a last glance
of disgust in my direction.

"Wait here," Alvantes told me as he set foot on
the gangplank. "Do nothing. Touch nothing. Speak
to no one."

Anywhere else, I might have struggled with such
exhaustive restrictions. In Ux Durada, I was more
than happy to keep my head down. There was no one
on the dilapidated dockside I had the faintest desire
to talk to, nothing I'd feel safe touching. The people
were every bit as filthy as the boats, as the heaps of
cargo, as the water lapping thickly round the wooden
harbour.

At least it made sense that we should run into Anterio here. In our previous encounters, his riverboat
had seemed uniquely fetid, just as he himself had been
a paragon of uncleanliness. In Ux Durada, however,

Anterio and his boat hardly stood out. In Ux Durada, they *belonged*.

The first time I'd met Anterio was when Estrada, Saltlick and I had been fleeing towards Altapasaeda. The last time I'd been trying to escape that fair city. On both occasions, he'd betrayed me; on both I'd ended up losing my freedom. As Anterio had just made clear, our relationship could fairly be described as antagonistic.

However, the man had a boat. As much as I didn't like it, he offered a way out.

Alvantes and Anterio conducted their discussion out of view, behind the tarpaulin-covered mounds of whatever unpleasant cargo Anterio was currently hauling. Their conversation seemed to go on for an unreasonably long time. All the while, I was increasingly aware that my presence was drawing attention. Likely, it was only the local underclass's trained response to anyone in uniform, but it was hard not to feel conspicuous. Ragged uniforms were the kind of thing that stuck in the memory when people came asking questions.

Just as I was starting to give up hope, Alvantes and Anterio materialised on my side of the boat.

Anterio cleared his throat and glowered at me. "The guard-captain assures me you'll receive due and thorough punishment once he's returned you to the Castoval," he said. "That being the case, you may come aboard. Still, you're a vile reprobate, and I won't trust you one jot."

"You have a point there," I agreed. "I doubt there's

a viler reprobate between here and Altapasaeda. Very good of you, Captain, to help make sure I get my just desserts."

Anterio looked me up and down, trying and failing to judge if I was mocking him. "Quite right," he said. "Best hurry then."

I trotted up the gangplank. As soon as I was on deck, Alvantes pressed past me. "I'm going to get rid of the horses," he said. I assumed he meant sell them, though his manner left some doubt.

What composure Anterio had managed to recover vanished once more. "You're leaving him here?" he asked. "Unguarded?"

"You'll be safe enough," said Alvantes.

"It's not myself I'm worried for," replied Anterio darkly. "More that I mightn't be able to keep from shoving him overboard."

"I'm sure you'll restrain yourself."

Alvantes's tone offered no room for argument. Anterio nodded dumbly.

Still, I felt I should do something to alleviate his concerns – especially if the alternative was a swim in the filthy water lapping the boat's flank. Talking was unlikely to improve matters, so I sat down instead, and swung my feet above the scummy surface of the river.

It didn't help. Whenever I looked up, Anterio was staring fretfully. Each time he caught my eye, he tried to turn his expression to one of menace, which only served to make him look unbearably constipated. On the third occasion, he noticed that the two boys who shared the boat with him – sons, I'd assumed, though it was hard to see any resemblance – were spying from the stern. Anterio waved them away and fell to pacing, with such energy that the vessel shuddered bow to stern.

I willed Alvantes to hurry. If Anterio wound himself up any further, one or both of us was bound to get a dunking.

When Alvantes did finally return, it was from the opposite direction, and the first I knew was the sound of his footsteps on the gangplank. My nerves were so frayed by then that it was all I could do to keep my perch on the boat's side.

"Those were royal horses," I said, trying to sound jovial. "I hope you got a handsome price."

Alvantes scowled and said nothing.

"Best be casting off," called Anterio to the two boys. It was evident Alvantes's black mood was only adding to his jitteriness.

One boy hopped ashore to free the rope that held us moored, then dashed back up the gangplank and hauled it in behind him, a feat of agility obviously perfected through long practise. The other, meanwhile, having shoved us clear of the docks with a wide-bladed oar, hurried to take the tiller. He swung us in a wide arc, until we'd matched the direction of the river's lazy flow.

"We need to get out of view," Alvantes told Anterio. "They may be watching the river junction."

I hadn't thought to wonder where we'd be passing our time during the journey. Only now did it strike me that the possibilities were distinctly limited.

Apart from its inimitable odour, Anterio's craft was much like any other that plied the broad inland waters of the Castoval and Ans Pasaeda. They were wide and shallow-bottomed, propelled by the currents where possible, by sail when the elements chose to play along, or in desperate circumstances, by oar. The result was a method of transport that had long ago become a byword for inefficiency.

The only shelter on Anterio's boat was a tiny structure, too low to stand up in, rising from the tip of the stern. That must be where Anterio and the two boys slept on colder nights, presumably piled atop each another. Excepting a band across its middle where the mast stood, all the remaining space was filled with Anterio's rank cargo. In short, there was no room for us except the narrow perimeter of deck, and certainly nowhere we'd be hidden from sight.

"This way," said Anterio, beckoning towards the back of the boat. Catching his eye, I saw a twinkle I definitely didn't like. He paused just before the tiny shelter and with a few vigorous kicks, forced back the edge of the tarpaulin. His efforts revealed a narrow trapdoor; he reached to pluck up a ring laid in its surface and drew it open.

There was only darkness in the cavity beneath – wet, cramped, impossibly foul-smelling darkness.

Now I understood how he'd managed to restrain himself from trying to kick me into the river. Compared to what he'd had in mind, it would have been an act of mercy.

• • • •

What followed were the worst three days of my oft-miserable life.

Three days in blackness, nostrils and throat and lungs filled to bursting with the stink of rotting vegetables. Three days in silence, alleviated only by the ancient craft's creaking threats of disintegration, the stifled noises from on deck and brief periods at dawn and dusk when Anterio let us out to eat. Three days wishing that repulsive boat would finally sink, wishing we'd be found by the King's troops, wishing I'd go mad – longing for anything that would alleviate that interminable torment.

The King's interrogator would have been in awe of Anterio's efforts. The most imaginative sadist couldn't have invented a more hideous torture. The pain in my arm, which had been steadily diminishing since Alvantes splinted it, grew to epic proportions in the boat's cramped hold. The immobilised appendage throbbed and itched abominably – and if reason told me that meant it was healing, reason wasn't enough to stop me wanting to chew it off to end my suffering.

Worse even than the pain, however, was the boredom. Or rather, the boredom made everything else a hundred times more intolerable. Without relief or distraction, all that was left was to dwell on every minuscule detail of my discomfort. In comparison with the inside of Anterio's boat, the sewers of Altapasaeda had been a paradise; the King's dungeon had been the height of luxury. I mentally replayed every hardship I'd ever endured, wondering how I'd ever let myself be discomposed by such harmless provocations.

In short, it was almost a relief when the soldiers came.

I was vexing myself with thoughts of the many things I might have done with my two gold coins when the shouting started. I didn't know how far downriver we were. Even during our limited deck time, conversation had been scant. Neither Alvantes nor Anterio had volunteered any information, and I'd been too busy trying to eat without gagging to ask. If we'd been unlucky with the wind, we might only be halfway to the border. However, I had a feeling, perhaps based on some remembered shoreside detail I'd glimpsed, that we were closer than that.

Mouldering wood and foul produce muffled the raised voices. One I recognised as Anterio's. The other, more distant but nearly as loud, I assumed to be coming from the bank or a neighbouring vessel. The two exchanged half a dozen abrupt sentences. Then the timbers groaned with a new note; the noise of the water roundabout changed from a swish to a dull slap.

We were turning against the current – heading towards the bank.

The sounds from outside seemed to grow clearer. I thought I could differentiate Anterio's slow tread from the quick tap-tap his sons made as they scurried back and forth. I recognised the whoosh of the boat's mooring rope being hurled into wet grass. There was more shouting, not quite so loud this time, and the distinctive creak of the gangplank.

Then came the thud of booted feet.

I counted. The gangplank gave a particular groan

whenever anyone crossed its midpoint. A dozen feet.
Six men.

Even Alvantes couldn't handle six men. Not single-
handedly – and especially not now that he *was*
single-handed. Our only hope lay in not being discovered.

It was a small hope indeed.

Because Anterio would betray us. I had no doubt.
His loathing for me would inevitably outweigh whatever loyalty he felt for Alvantes. He had cast me into
the arms of the authorities twice before. Likely, he'd
only taken me on board in the hope that this moment
would arrive.

Sure enough, six booted pairs of feet, led by Anterio's
lighter step, marched in our direction. When the voices
returned, they were quieter – furtive. Still, I thought I
could make out the occasional word. The steps were so
close that it sounded as though they were inside the
boat rather than on it. When they stopped, they
stopped together.

I tried to tense. I'd already decided to fling myself
overboard if I could. Better that than what the King
would have in store for me. But my muscles, turned
to jelly by days of stillness and cramp, refused to comply. I was helpless. All I could do was wait for the creak
of the hatch.

There was no creak. In its place came another round
of conversation. I caught snatches of queries, and of
Anterio's answers. I couldn't piece sentences together
but I followed the gist. Had he seen anything suspicious? Heard any rumours? Spoken to anyone out of
the ordinary? If they'd seen the hatch, they wouldn't

be asking vague questions. If they'd seen the hatch, they'd have opened it now. Which meant...

Which meant Anterio wasn't entirely a fool. He'd been keeping the trapdoor covered during the days with his repellent cargo. No one would ever go digging through that unless they were damn sure what they wanted lay beneath.

A few last words were spoken. The footsteps trooped away. Again, I heard the gangplank's complaint. Moments later, the timbers round me shuddered and I knew we were heading back out into the current.

We'd made it.

Or had we?

Every charged nerve in my body told me not to trust Anterio. Twice I'd done that. Twice he'd tricked me. Probably they'd left to gather reinforcements – a sensible precaution when it came to Alvantes. Probably they were just making sure that the trap, when sprung, was inescapable.

Seconds turned into minutes. Minutes dragged by. Then, sure enough, I felt us heave back against the current. The boat protested as it scudded against something solid. Again, there were footsteps above us – and this time, the wet slither of mouldering produce being cleared.

Abruptly, the hatch sprang open.

I heard it more than saw it. At first I thought I might have gone blind in the pitchy hold. As my eyes adjusted, I realised I could just make out the dimples of pale stars. Half blocking that glimmer-studded sky, a shadowy figure hovered over the opening.

"Out you come," grunted Anterio.

I clambered up, flopped limply onto the deck gasping for air. I gazed about me, blinking.

There were no soldiers.

Yet it wasn't for that reason I almost sobbed with relief. I knew now that even capture and the promise of violent death would have been a relief after those three horrible days of stinking, claustrophobic horror.

By the standards of the hold, the air on deck was sweet as a fine lady's perfume. Compared with its lightless depths, the night-time black was the caress of softest velvet. Set against its muffled creaks and groans, the faint echoes of life from the shore were the choiring of songbirds.

There before me, scattered in gleams of gold upon the silhouetted mountainside, was Aspira Nero, entrance to the Castoval.

CHAPTER SEVENTEEN

Given the late hour, Anterio offered to let us spend one last night aboard. Though Alvantes declined politely, the edge in his voice told me he was nearly as horrified by the prospect as I was. "I'm sorry I can't pay you," he said, perhaps by way of a diversion.

"Don't mention it," replied Anterio, sounding faintly hurt by the suggestion. "Just make certain that reprobate receives a dose of honest Castovalian justice this time."

"I'll be glad to be receiving honest Castovalian justice, rather than that weaselly Ans Pasaedan kind," I agreed.

I wondered what tale Alvantes had spun the old captain that could explain why arresting me involved fleeing from the King's guardsmen. Perhaps it was better if I never knew, for I doubted it cast me in a very favourable light. It was enough that his subterfuge had worked. We were back in the Castoval – or as near as damn it.

We said our goodbyes to Anterio. Alvantes did, anyway; the captain's glower was enough to still my tongue. I'd expected Alvantes to return to the *Fourth Orphan*, but instead he picked a dingy place near the harbour called the *Drowned Sparrow*. I didn't debate the choice, for he knew better than I did where we'd risk running into agents of the Crown. They might not be able to arrest us openly in Aspira Nero, but everyone knew they could find ways around that rule when it suited. In any case, the *Drowned Sparrow* might be squalid by any normal standards, but compared with Anterio's boat it was little short of a pleasure palace. Just the sight of an open fire and of wine bottles stacked behind the bar made my heart leap.

I never heard what arrangement Alvantes made to pay for our stay. As far as he knew, we had no funds between us, and I wasn't about to disillusion him. Whatever the case, the night passed without incident. Alvantes knocked on my door before dawn, and we set out to reclaim the horses we'd left stabled at the *Fourth Orphan*.

Our exit from town was uneventful. So was the day's ride south. Alvantes's dejection had become a storm cloud that gathered him in its depths, and I'd long since given up on trying to make conversation. I concentrated instead on enjoying the simple pleasures I'd missed in Anterio's hold: fresh air, crisp sunshine, the smells of grass and horse and a hundred other things that weren't rotten vegetables or bilge water.

At no point had we discussed a route, or even a destination. I assumed Alvantes would want to check in on Estrada. For my part, I had only the most half-formed of plans. I'd been lying, of course, when I'd told Synza I was taking the crown to Mounteban. However it should go down, there was no way I'd walk away from that one alive. If I could find the right broker, however, perhaps a deal could be struck with one of the more powerful Altapasaedan lords. It might even be that I held it in my power to overturn Mounteban's rule with a minimum of bloodshed, for the lords would be quick to rally behind one of their own against that fat crook.

It was a heart-warming plan in theory. In practise, it had more flaws than virtues, and a host of practical difficulties besides. Far less risky a strategy would be to go far away, maybe to Goya Pinenta, and find someone who could strip the crown down to sell as gold and jewels. Perhaps it wasn't quite so noble, but if Alvantes had proved one thing it was what a terrible career choice nobility made these days.

I'd thought only a little of Saltlick and his people. Though only a few days had passed since I'd last seen them, it seemed an age. Even after everything Saltlick had told me and everything I'd witnessed for myself, it was hard to believe they wouldn't have packed up for home by now.

It was the sight of dark shapes on the horizon, late in the day, which brought them back to the forefront of my mind. Whatever those shapes were, they weren't giants. My first impression was that a village had sprung up, but as we drew nearer and the dim forms resolved out of the afternoon haze, I realised it wasn't quite that. It was more like a shanty town – but a shanty town scaled for huge inhabitants. Out of poles driven into the ground, heavy sheets of oilcloth and windbreaks of twined twigs and reeds, a score of large structures had been built across the hillside, each just about sufficient to shelter a half-dozen giants.

Now I knew where at least some of my gold coin had gone.

Saltlick saw me before I saw him. He appeared from beneath one of the canopies and broke into a run. Careening to a halt just in time, he rumbled, "Alvantes, Damasco. Friends to giants."

I grinned – partly to hide a lump that had swum unexpectedly into my throat. "Saltlick. Friend to Damasco."

Saltlick returned a hesitant smile.

"You're still here," I said.

I wasn't sure if it was a statement or a question, or whether I said it for any good reason at all. Whatever the case, Saltlick didn't try to respond. He was clearly overjoyed to see us – but behind that temporary elation, I saw a depth of misery in his eyes I'd never have thought him capable of. He'd managed to stay cheerful through inconceivable hardship and suffering; more, he'd always remained hopeful. Now, it was as though all that optimism had deserted him.

"Damasco hurt?" he asked, tilting his head towards my splinted arm. It was a clear attempt to change the subject – something else I'd never have expected.

"Not so much," I said, wiggling my fingers to demonstrate. The truth was, Synza's diagnosis had been correct. With rest, however bewilderingly horrible that rest had been, my arm had healed better than I'd dared hope.

"Friends make," Saltlick continued, taking in the hillside and its makeshift constructions with an expansive gesture. "Treat well."

"I'm glad," I said. "Why don't you show us around?"

Saltlick led the way across the hillside. As we drew closer, a few giants glanced up to acknowledge our approach. Were they less skinny than when I'd last seen them? They hardly looked healthy, but at least they weren't quite so wasted. However, they were quick enough to forget us, to return to staring at nothing. However well they'd been taken care of, it obviously hadn't been enough to shake them from their stupor.

Meanwhile, Saltlick made a show of touring the encampment – though the shelters were all much the same and all equally unimpressive. Close up, it was evident they'd been thrown together in haste, with whatever materials lay to hand and no pretence of being more than a temporary measure. Our tour ended with a smaller dwelling on the outskirts of the camp. Where most of the others were ample for five or six giants, this was just big enough for one.

As Saltlick came to a halt, I realised it could only belong to him. The hopeful thought flashed across my mind that such solitary status might be an honour, recognition of his courage in escaping only to return to rescue his brethren. But that was absurd. If Saltlick had been recognised as a hero, the giants would be long gone. His isolation was no privilege. More likely, it was a stark reflection of his new status amongst his people. He'd left without explanation. He'd returned with strange talk, strange ideas, strange claims they couldn't – or wouldn't – believe.

So that was what he'd endured these last few days. Bad enough that his attempt to liberate his people had been a crushing failure. How much worse that he should be made an exile for his efforts? I dismounted and sat beside him, wondering if there was anything I could say that might possibly make him feel better.

"I'm going to water the horses," said Alvantes. He caught my mount's reins and led it away downhill, not waiting for an answer.

I was more than usually glad to see him go. I still had no idea what I was going to say, but I was sure of one thing: it was time me and Saltlick had a talk, man to giant.

"Saltlick," I said, "you need to tell me what's been going on. We've been away for well over a week. Why haven't they left?"

I could see he didn't want to answer. "Some might. Old chief says no. Old chief says wait."

What a coincidence! The old chief, who'd lost the giant-stone to Moaradrid in the first place, happened to be the one arguing for perseverance when any fool could see that hope was long past lost. I'd seen the strange things guilt could do to men, the tangles it knotted them into. It seemed giants weren't so different. "But you're chief now," I said. "Haven't you told them that?"

"Not chief. No stone."

"You're just as much chief as the old chief. Neither of you has the stone. So why can't they listen to the one who's talking sense?"

Saltlick didn't reply at all this time, just swayed his head with weary misery.

I had to try to keep in mind how little sense factored into giantish politics. "All right. I get it. As far as they know, Moaradrid was the last one to have it, and the last one to give them an order. They'll follow that order if it kills them – which it will, once the winter comes. You giants may be tough, but you're not indestructible. So the whole chief, stone, tradition argument, that hasn't worked out so well. What *else* have you tried?"

Silence again. Saltlick might not be the idiot I'd once taken him for, but there was no denying his mind ran in certain clear-cut channels. Ask his thoughts to flow outside those courses and they tended to get helplessly bogged down.

"Don't you realise you can't always play fair? What about threats? Blackmail? Bribery? What if the old chief were to vanish for a day or two? What if we found another stone and someone who looked a bit like Moaradrid? How about if…"

I couldn't continue. He looked too appalled.

"Fine. But you have to do something – and soon. You understand that, don't you?"

Saltlick nodded. Of *course* he understood. Whether the giants accepted him as their chief, he'd taken every iota of that responsibility on his shoulders – and it had been crushing him, that much was clear.

Perhaps he'd passed the point where he was even capable of helping his people. Perhaps it was time someone with a little more flexibility in their ideas of right and wrong had a try. "We'll figure something out, Saltlick. I'm not leaving here again without you."

It sounded very much like an empty promise to make him feel better – and it shocked me to realise I actually meant it. Yet didn't it make a certain amount of sense? Long weeks ago, I'd vowed to ensure Saltlick made it home, and the thought of having succeeded against absurd odds had been a thrill unlike anything I'd experienced. However, I could see now that it had been a job half done at best. Without his people, Saltlick could never truly go home.

Anyway, what else was I going to do? I'd given away most of my money. My heart just wasn't in a return to my old life. And even if I gave half a fig about the fate of Altapasaeda, it was a lost cause with Alvantes drowning in his despair. I was tired of running around, of being pushed about, of doing what others thought I should be doing. I needed a direction, and I couldn't think of anything better than this.

There was only one problem. I didn't have the faintest idea how to help Saltlick. My suggestions had been ridiculous. What could anyone threaten, blackmail, or bribe the giants with? They'd already lost everything, and even the promise of regaining it wasn't enough to get them moving. Now that I thought about it, I couldn't even speak a word of giantish.

Maybe it *was* an empty promise after all.

Later, as the sun was beginning to set, a man and woman arrived to feed to the giants. I was disappointed to see it wasn't Huero and Dura. This couple were elderly in comparison, and looked at me curiously. We shared a brief greeting when they came to feed Saltlick, but I wasn't in the mood for conversation with strangers. I did notice that the portions had become a little more generous though, even stretching to a handful of what I took for chopped turnips – one more sign that my coin hadn't gone to waste.

A small comfort. The money would run out. When it did, the food would follow soon after. The shelters wouldn't survive a single hard storm, never mind an entire winter. Gold had put off the problem, but it hadn't changed it. If the giants couldn't be persuaded to move, they'd die, and Saltlick with them.

Yet later, as night began to draw down, Alvantes returned with the horses in tow and a small bundle of deadwood crooked in his abbreviated arm. He made a fire and produced three fish from inside his cloak, which he proceeded to spit over the blaze. I didn't want to wonder about how he'd caught fish with one hand and no weapons, but I was glad enough to take the share he offered.

We ate in leaden silence, with Saltlick close by in the darkness. The air of hopelessness hanging over the three of us was thick enough that I could feel it on my skin, a stifling blanket wrapped close and barely out of sight.

As we finished eating, Saltlick pointed to his shelter. "Sleep," he said.

"We can't take your house, Saltlick."

He lay back in the grass where he'd been sitting. "Sleep."

I had no rejoinder to so concise an argument. "Thank you, Saltlick," I said. "Sleep well."

Alvantes set himself up against one wall of the shelter, which – having been designed with one giant in mind – was more than ample for the two of us. I curled up at the other side and tried to make myself comfortable.

I resisted the temptation to take my cloak from my pack. The risk of Alvantes seeing the crown was too great. Reasoning that it was a mild night and that the shelter did a surprisingly good job of keeping the wind out, even for someone not giant-scaled, I tucked the pack beneath my head instead and hoped it would make an adequate pillow.

It worked well enough at first. I even flirted with sleep. But the cold, little by little, crept into my flesh, finding its way through every slight gap in my clothing. It teased around my collar and sleeves, sneaked up round my ankles. My makeshift pillow was no better. Just as I was sure I'd found a comfortable position, an edge of crown found a way to press against my ear. Fidgeting to rearrange it exposed some new part of me to the cold. Tucking my shirt to cover that chilled spot of skin somehow rearranged my pack by the fractional degree needed for the crown to push against my cheek.

I tried to assure myself I could take my cloak out now, when Alvantes must undoubtedly be asleep. Except what if he woke? What if he was feigning? Given his recent state of mind, maybe he no longer slept at all. Then I thought about simply shoving my pack aside, doing my best with the thick grass. But I couldn't escape the fear that in the morning Alvantes would see it, observe a peculiar bulge, decide to investigate and happen upon my treasure.

Would losing the crown be so terrible? As the night wore on, as the cold settled into the ruts of my spine, I wondered what good it had done me. What good, in fact, had it done anyone? It hadn't helped Panchetto keep his head. It hadn't done Alvantes any favours. All right, it had allowed me to distract Synza, not to mention its brief success as an improvised weapon, but I doubted a similar situation would arise any time soon.

The truth was, I'd stolen the crown from my magpie instinct towards anything shiny and valuable-looking. There was little real hope of anyone giving me money for it, not with the state of affairs in Altapasaeda. The only ones who might take it off my hands would be more likely to do it with horrendous violence than the exchange of coin.

The crown was a useless hunk of metal and stone. Panchetto's ridiculous ornament was every bit as worthless as the giant-stone had been. Once again, I'd managed to steal something without the slightest practical value. Once again, I'd made off with an empty, worthless symbol.

A symbol. Empty, worthless.

Like the giant-stone.

My heart missed a beat. Another. A shudder ran through me that had nothing to do with the cold.

I had an idea. I had my answer.

The rest of the night passed with mocking slowness. I knew I'd have only the briefest window in which to put my plan into action. I drifted through brief fits of sleep, waking each time convinced I'd missed my opportunity. On the fourth occasion, I was startled into wide-awakeness by the realisation that I almost had. The hillside round about had lightened to a deep, formless grey. At any moment, the first flush of morning would break above the eastern mountains.

Quiet as I could manage, I goaded icy muscles into life, stifled a groan, and crept from the shelter. I kept one eye fixed on Alvantes, but he didn't stir. Neither did Saltlick as I tiptoed by.

Careful not to miss my footing in the near blackness, I found a space away from either of them where I could prepare.

Between uncomfortable bouts of half sleep, I'd been grappling with the practicalities of my idea. Of the components I needed, one was readily at hand. I'd agonised over a way to produce the other. With a knife, it would have been easy. Without one, it seemed more or less impossible.

In the end, with much effort and the aid of a sharp stone, I managed to hack three strips from the lining of my cloak. Tied together and rolled twice over, they made a long, thin pad of cloth that would just about fit my purposes.

I crept over to Saltlick. I knew he slept soundly, and despite his exposure to the raw elements, it appeared this morning was no different; he lay on his side, head lying upon one arm, his snores sending trembles through the grass. If he woke, the plan would be up. Never in a million lifetimes would he agree to what I had in mind. Which was why I had to make the decision for him – for his own good.

I manoeuvred into position behind Saltlick's head. In the pre-morning stillness, his shuddering snorts were deafening. Nevertheless, now that I'd come to it, I doubted how I could possibly succeed without him stirring.

I was right to worry. Surely no philosopher was ever perplexed by a greater test of ingenuity, no swindler faced with such a trial of legerdemain. The minutes wore upon each other, and most of them I spent frozen in place, as some slight stirring or subtle change in the rhythm of his snores convinced me Saltlick would wake at any instant. When I dared risk motion, it was so slow that even I couldn't be certain I was really moving. It was as though time had ceased to beat and left me paralysed in the middle of my absurd task, doomed for all eternity.

There came an end at last. I'd tied and double-tied the last knot, sufficiently tight that Saltlick would struggle to remove it but loose enough that he hadn't woken from strangulation. I shuffled back, until I judged the distance adequate for me to let go the vast sigh of tension I'd been holding.

Ironically, I now found myself waiting for Saltlick to stir. Already moths of doubt were starting to flit around my stomach. It didn't help that hunger combined with a sleepless night was beginning to make me feel light-headed. My scheme was stupid, doomed to failure – and perhaps worse. The best thing I could do would be to undo my handiwork while I still had time.

Saltlick stretched, gave a humongous yawn and rolled over. He shook himself, smacked his lips, half opened his eyes. Not quite awake, he groped with one huge hand, slapped at the thing about his throat. His fingers found the rolled strip of cloth, continued to the metal circlet knotted at its front.

His eyes opened wide.

With both hands now, he tugged at his throat. I could hardly blame him; my gift looked uncomfortable, not to mention ridiculous. But I was sure he wouldn't get it off without a struggle. I'd taken care on those knots, and his sausage fingers weren't made for delicate work.

Still, there was no use in taking chances.

"Time to get up!" I roared in the direction of the giant encampment. "Don't you know it's morning? The day's a-wasting! Is this how giants behave, sleeping until lunchtime?"

I didn't care if I was barely making sense. They couldn't understand me anyway. I just wanted them awake and attentive – and that much, at least, seemed to be working. Everywhere giants were sitting up, rubbing eyes with knuckles big as chestnuts, turning watery stares in my direction and in Saltlick's.

I scampered into position, placing myself directly between him and the other giants. On the off-chance that any of them hadn't noticed his new ornament, I gestured dramatically, hoping that would serve to bridge the language barrier between us.

Eventually I was confident I had the attention of everyone within hearing distance – and that they'd all seen Saltlick's ridiculous medallion. However subtle and elegant the royal crown of Altapasaeda might have been under other circumstances, it looked pretty damn stupid when turned into a choker for a giant.

But this wasn't the time for questions of fashion. Bigger issues were at stake.

"All hail!" I bellowed, at the very top of my lungs. "All hail Saltlick, King of the Castoval!"

CHAPTER EIGHTEEN

I never saw Alvantes coming.

Only as his fist carried me off my feet did I catch the briefest glimpse of his face, twisted almost beyond recognition by rage. Dazed, I tried to shuffle backwards on my rump. His second blow was more a slap, but more than enough to make my head ring. I threw up my arms – an instinct that proved misjudged when Alvantes's third punch hammered needles through the recently injured one.

"Get off me, you lunatic!" I cried.

I rolled aside. Tough Alvantes might be, but he could only hit so quickly with one hand. His next blow went wide. I made it to my feet and skipped backwards. My head was still tolling like a bell – but behind that racket, my blood was boiling. Only a tiny core of sense reminded me that even one-handed, Alvantes was ten times the fighter I was.

"Back off, damn you!"

"Back off? I should tear your spine out for this!" Alvantes pointed a trembling finger at the ornament around Saltlick's neck. "That's the royal crown of Al-tapasaeda, you rat's prick."

"All right. So what?"

"*So what?* You stole it from me, you disgusting little sneak thief."

I wiped a smear of blood from my suddenly bloated lower lip. "I'd say I stole it from the King. But let's not argue semantics. How is that a reason to break my jaw?"

"What? Because..." I could see Alvantes straining to think through his fury. He didn't try too hard. "You're a damned fool. What will this achieve? You can't make someone king by hanging a crown round their neck. Even if you could, it's just a hunk of metal to them."

"Like their stone was just a stone to us? Like I said, back off. Maybe you've given up, but that doesn't mean the rest of us have to. At least I'm trying something."

"*Given up?*" He paused then – or I thought he'd meant to, anyway. Faint shudders like the ruffling of wind on water were coursing down his body, but he didn't seem aware. "Fine. Do whatever the Hells you want. Play your games with these poor bastards. Maybe you'll piss them off enough that they'll give you the thrashing you deserve."

Alvantes spun on his heel, stormed away.

My relief lasted just as long as it took me to turn my head and wonder just how prescient his last words might be. A vast shadow closed round me, as though the early daylight had been snuffed like a candle flame. "*What have you done?*"

I was almost too shocked to hear Saltlick string together four words in grammatical order to be alarmed. "You're going to have to trust me," I told him.

"Not trust! Not king!"

"Just for a little while. Please, Saltlick."

He wanted to believe me. For all his obvious anger, that much was obvious. Given my past performance, I couldn't be surprised that he was finding it a struggle.

Just for once, though, luck was on my side.

"Just give me a chance," I told him. "This is for your own good, I swear it."

Before Saltlick could answer, I was sprinting towards the wagon crawling towards us on the road below. I'd realised straight away it must be the locals coming with the morning's meal – and when I saw Huero driving, with Dura beside him, I couldn't help but whoop a laugh. It was all I could do not to leap onto the driver's board and hug them both.

Huero reined the horses in. "Damasco." There was concern in his eyes. "Do you need help?"

Only then did I realise I'd just charged at him, with a bloody lip, whilst laughing manically. "I do. But not for me. Huero, I have a plan. To get the giants moving... to get them home once and for all. Only, it's going to take everyone. Everyone you know, everyone you can gather. Can you bring them here? The more people, the sooner you do it, the more likely it is to work."

"But... what about the food?"

"The food can wait. Will you do it? The faster, the more people, the better."

Huero nodded. "Of course. I'll try. Give me an hour, all right?"

"As quick as you can."

I caught my breath and watched him turn the wagon, before starting back towards the giant camp. This time, I didn't hurry. There was every chance Alvantes had come up with new reasons to hammer my face by now. Even if he hadn't, every moment weighed in my favour. Whatever slim trust Saltlick had in me, I could only keep it kindled for so long.

Sure enough, he watched me questioningly as I crossed the last distance. I didn't have any answers for him – or none that he'd like. "One hour," I said, "just wait one hour. Give me that much... then you'll see."

Alvantes was gone, at least. I could see him by the riverbank, feeding and watering the horses. Rather than give Saltlick time to answer, I followed his example, heading in the opposite direction. I singled out a patch of hillside far from any of the giants and sat down. With one eye on Saltlick, the other on Alvantes in case of further hostilities, I settled to wait.

For all my good intentions, I was drowsing by the time Huero returned. His voice calling my name shocked me into wakefulness. For a moment, I was bewildered to see an entire village worth of people gathered upon the lower slope. Then I remembered.

Huero had outdone himself. Judging by numbers, he must have brought everyone between here and the Hunch. I hurried down to meet them.

"Thank you, everyone," I said. "For all your kindness

towards the giants, and for coming here now. I'll need just a few minutes of your time."

I rapidly outlined what I wanted them to do. There were a great many gasps, a few appalled looks, and a general rumble of discontent. Somewhere towards the back, a woman exclaimed, "Well, I never. Not in all my days."

Huero chose that moment to step in. "It's a strange request, all right, friend Damasco." He was speaking in my direction, but it was obvious his words were intended for the crowd. "Still, but for you, these giants might have starved by now. It's obvious you want what's best for them."

"Don't we all?" I asked. "And what's best for them is what's best for all of you – to get them back home where they belong. With a little harmless play-acting, that's exactly what we'll do." There was a subdued muttering and much clearing of throats, but I knew Huero had shifted the mood a little in my favour. I could only hope it would be enough. "Excellent. The sooner we start, the sooner it's done."

Helpless before that inarguable logic, the mob of villagers fell in behind me, and I marched them towards where Saltlick stood waiting. If he'd looked perplexed before, his reaction to the peasant army bearing down on him now was one of sheer bewilderment. The other giants, too, were watching with curious fascination.

That, at least, was a good sign.

"All right," I said, as softly as I dared, "On the count of three. One… two… three…"

I knelt before Saltlick, hoping against hope that now that the time had come, the villagers would follow my lead. I gave it a moment, in case of stragglers – and I began to shout.

"All hail! All hail Saltlick, King of the Castoval!"

Huero matched me in both word and volume. For the rest, a few thin voices came to my aid, sounding more apologetic than forceful. Was I the only one kneeling? I dared a glance. Dura and Huero had joined me, of course, their brows all but scraping the dew-dampened grass. Of the others, some were halfway to their knees, others barely tilting their heads.

Nothing for it. I had to press on.

"All hail! All hail King Saltlick!"

This time, it was more of a concerted effort. More people lent their voices than didn't, even if few sounded sure about what they were yelling.

I drew a deep breath, poured it all into my next shout. "All hail! Hail King Saltlick, King of the Castoval!"

Better, far better. Finally, they were beginning to sound as though their hearts were in it.

"All hail! All hail Saltlick, King of the Castoval!"

This time, the sound cascaded over me, a wave that tingled through my every muscle, made the hairs on my neck stand straight. I barely heard my own voice amidst the roar. It was a good job too, because my throat was starting to feel scraped raw. I lowered my volume a fraction, grateful to let others carry the weight.

I gave it half a dozen more rounds and then bowed low as I could manage, forehead to the ground. A rustle of clothing from all around told me the villagers had remembered this final, crucial detail. I regained my feet. Around me, the crowd was already beginning to break up. There was an air of confusion, as if no one was quite certain what had just happened.

I looked towards the giants. Well, we'd certainly kept their attention – and probably that was the best I could hope for at this stage. I turned to Saltlick. He was staring fixedly at the point where we'd been kneeling, with an expression of distant horror.

Huero appeared beside me. "I thought that went well. Didn't you?"

"Honestly?" I said. "I have no idea."

"Should we feed them now?"

"Not yet. There's one more thing I need to do."

"All right. We'll wait. Good luck, Damasco."

For all our sakes, I thought.

I paced over to Saltlick. His gaze didn't move to follow me. Stopping before him, I called his name.

He didn't so much as twitch. If he were a man, I would have stood some chance of guessing what was going through his mind. With Saltlick, it was hopeless even to try.

"Saltlick?"

He could probably ignore me forever if he'd set his mind on it. It was one of his more unique talents. I flailed for words that might draw him out.

"Remember how you agreed to trust me?" I asked.

Saltlick's head twisted, as though dragged. "*Not king!*"

As he spoke, he hooked one finger inside the crown, preparing to tear it loose.

"Saltlick, *stop!*"

He paused – but the finger stayed snagged.

"Do you want to go home?" I hissed. "Do you want to lead your people home?"

Saltlick didn't remove the finger. Nor did he keep pulling.

"Answer me. Tell me honestly that there's anything in this world you want more than that. Is there anything more important? Anything you wouldn't go through to make it happen?"

He released the crown. His hand dropped to his side, as though all the life had gone from it. "Go home," he said – almost pleadingly.

"Then *trust me*."

A barely perceptible nod. Enough.

"I need you to tell the other giants what I tell you. Regardless of what I say – every word, do you hear me? Now, call them over. Explain that I've a message for them and you're going to translate."

For all the unmistakable doubt in his eyes, Saltlick's voice was more than loud enough as he rattled off a couple of brusque sentences in giantish.

"Now… exactly as I say, you understand? No improvising. No cutting the bits you don't approve of. Word for word, Saltlick."

Another hesitant nod. I supposed I had no choice but to trust him too. I took a deep breath, as though I really were about to orate for the extraordinary assembly before me. "Before your stone was lost, Saltlick was made chief of the giants. I saw it happen. He was made chief in front of your elders, your womenfolk and young."

Saltlick was incapable of anything close to self-aggrandisement. If there were to be a sticking point, this would be it. Sure enough, I could see he was hesitating. I took a step closer and hissed, "*They need you. Say it for them.*"

Still, he hesitated.

That was it then. Damn Saltlick and damn his stupid modesty, he had destroyed my plan, and I had no other. He had doomed himself and his people and...

Words burst from his mouth – harsh consonants and stunted vowels rolling out in the thick giantish tongue. It made no hint of sense to me. I could only hope he was repeating something close to what I'd said.

I began again the moment he'd finished, not daring to give him pause to think. "Now, thanks to his noble efforts in the service of all Castovalians, we have asked him to wear our mark of leadership too – making him our king, the king of everyone in this land."

I'd thought nothing could bother him more than revealing his brief, disastrous turn as chief. Yet if anything, he looked more dismayed this time – and not only dismayed but dazed. It hadn't occurred to me until then, but given his ignorance of Castovalian custom, he might really believe I'd just appointed him king of the entire land.

Whatever mental tribulations he was enduring, however, he hardly hesitated – and the way his expression shifted quickly to one of intense concentration told me he was doing his best to interpret the words I'd given him. More than once he stumbled, perhaps tripped by notions ill-suited to his mother tongue.

"Saltlick is our chief now," I went on, "just as he's yours. Before he assumes his royal duties, he would like to take you all home. You must obey him. If you don't, you will gravely insult my people."

Saltlick didn't pause at all this time. As he spoke the last words, in fact, I was certain I noticed a subtle change in his tone. He looked less confused, less intent on simply translating. He even held himself straighter.

Was that hope in his eyes once more?

Either way, we were almost there. All that was needed now was to come to the point. "Go now," I said. "Go where you're wanted, where you're needed. Forget the trials that brought you here. Forget the words of Moaradrid. Step forward. Be led back where you belong."

It was the longest – indeed, the only speech I'd ever given. Like a loud and distorted echo, Saltlick rumbled on in my wake, until he too finished speaking. I turned my gaze from him to our mutual audience, hardly daring to see what effect our words had had.

No one had moved.

Not one giant twitched so much as an eyelash.

They sat as they had since we'd first seen them, immobile as the land itself.

I'd failed. I'd won Saltlick's trust for nothing. And no wonder! It had been a ludicrous idea from the beginning. If Saltlick hadn't been able to move his people in all this time, how could I think anything I said would make a difference? It was horrible to admit, but Alvantes had been right. What was the crown to the giants? What did they care about Castovalian traditions? As if a king meant anything to them!

One giant stood, stepped forward.

He was young; younger, I thought, than Saltlick, and smaller than most of the others. He looked sheepish, and perhaps a little defiant too.

There was the longest pause. Just as I was wondering what possible use a single convert could be, two more giants stepped forward to join him.

The next pause was shorter. Half a dozen giants clambered to their feet, wincing at muscles stiffened by disuse, and moved to join their companions.

After that, it was a steady stream. Once more than half the giants had declared their allegiance, the rest fairly bounded up, as though released from under a weight that had pinned them all this time.

The old chief was the last to step forward. But he did.

It was as if a spell had been broken. Perhaps in a way it had. Moaradrid had subdued the giants with chains more sturdy than any iron – bonds of ritual, loyalty and guilt. Now, it was as though they were waking from an ages-long sleep, or transforming from stone back into living things. I turned my attention to Saltlick. He was staring, jaw slack, eyes glazed, as if mesmerised by the crowd before him.

There was no time for niceties. I punched him on the thigh.

He glanced at me with vague surprise. A single fat tear was working its way down his cheek, apparently unnoticed.

"Get them moving," I said. "Now. Before they change their minds. We'll head for Altapasaeda and work from there."

The tear lost its purchase, splashed into the grass between us. Saltlick, too, seemed to waken. "Damasco," he said, softly. "Friend to giants."

I slapped him on the knee. "Damn right. The best friend you've got, and don't ever forget it. Now get going! I'll follow in a minute."

Saltlick nodded. Then he called three words in giantish and started towards the road. My heart lurched when the other giants fell in behind him, one by one. Watching them go, I couldn't but note how painfully thin they still were, how they laboured against limbs rigid from neglect. They had a long way to go yet. Nevertheless, in that moment, watching that stream of monstrous figures wade across the landscape, I felt happier than I could ever remember feeling.

Eventually, I had to turn away. There was one more loose end to tie before I could leave this tragedy-stained hillside behind.

I started towards Alvantes, where he was still minding the horses near the riverbank. I was halfway there when Huero caught up with me. He was flushed with excitement, and his voice fairly bubbled as he said, "We have a new king, eh?"

"I'm not sure it's entirely constitutional," I said. "Still, it couldn't hurt if you all keep playing along a little longer."

"I think we can manage that."

"Good. Do you think you could feed them on the march? I think it's better if they put this place behind them as soon as possible."

"Absolutely. You're coming with us though?"

"I'll catch you up."

I bid Huero farewell and covered the last distance to where Alvantes stood. Glancing up, he waved his hand dismissively, as though dashing away an insect. "Come to gloat? So keep the crown, Damasco. It's no business of mine if you want to make a mockery of everything it stands for."

"If it gets the giants home, that's more good than it's done anyone lately. But that's not what I wanted to talk about."

"Oh?"

Steeling myself, I reached into my pack, drew forth the thing I'd been keeping there for so long now, almost forgotten alongside its other more precious cargo, and proffered it to him. "I seem to remember you saying your father gave you this. He probably wouldn't have wanted you to lose it."

It was a moment before Alvantes recognised the telescope for what it was. "How did you...? No, of course. You stole it when you stole the crown. Am I supposed to thank you?"

Given how difficult I'd found giving it up, given how rare and correspondingly valuable it was, I had to bite my tongue to keep down the obvious, honest answer. Because there was something else I needed to say, or that I thought Alvantes had to hear, or perhaps both. "Look, I know we're not friends. We never will be, and I wouldn't have it any other way. But how your father died... that was a terrible thing, Alvantes. I'm sorry it happened."

He focused on me properly then, for the first time. "A terrible thing? You talk as if it was an accident."

"No. It was a vicious murder."

"It was a *punishment*. And it was my fault."

Only then did I realise that, on some level, I'd known all along that was how he felt. Of course he would blame himself. He was Alvantes. "It really wasn't," I told him. "It was the King's fault, and it was the fault of those bastards Stick and Stone. But it wasn't yours. You did what you thought was right – just like your father did. And even if he'd known what was coming, I expect he'd have done the same. From what I saw of him, you two were a lot alike."

"He probably would have, at that. Stubborn old man."

Despite the words, and for the first time since we'd left Pasaeda, there was no harshness in Alvantes's voice. I could only hope that meant he was ready to hear what else I had to say.

"Here's the thing, though, Alvantes. Terrible as it was, that doesn't mean you're allowed to quit."

His head jarred up, as though I'd slapped him. "Is that really what you think I've done?"

What surprised me wasn't the response but the note of genuine questioning in his voice. "I'm not sure," I said. "Is it?"

Alvantes looked away. "Honestly? I'm not sure either."

"Well, maybe you should give it some thought. Come with us to Muena Palaiya; see how Estrada's getting on. Then maybe we can see if there's anything we can do about that slug Mounteban."

"I'm done pretending to be a hero," he declared, with sudden vehemence.

"Is that what you've been doing? You certainly fooled enough people."

"I'll come with you to Altapasaeda," Alvantes said. "I have to know Marina's safe."

"Fine. Let's saddle up then. There's a flock of giants near here that could do with a couple more shepherds."

We must have made a truly astonishing sight.

From where I rode at the centre of the convoy, the parade of giants seemed to stretch from horizon to horizon. Like an honour guard, the villagers trooped to either side. A few rode in pony and ox carts, some on horses or donkeys; most had no choice but to keep the pace on foot.

As the day drew towards its midpoint, the villagers trailed off in clumps, heading back to their homes and fields. Their reactions to the giants' departure seemed to range between relief and mild sadness. A few of the women were even mopping at their eyes as they waved goodbye. It cheered me to see that a few of the giants waved shyly back.

A little later, Huero drew his wagon up beside me. "We've been thinking," he said, without preamble. "They've got a long way to go. They'll need to eat." He glanced over at his wife.

"So," Dura took over. "We've been discussing. What would you say to us travelling with you for a few days? We'd feel better for knowing they're safe."

"I'd be glad to have you," I told them, trying to

control the grin that seemed determined to stretch across my face. "They might not say much about it, but I'm sure the giants will be too."

Huero peeled off at a turning to stock his cart for the journey, promising to catch us as soon as he could. By then, the last of the villagers were calling their good-byes and straggling away. I found it strange to think that tomorrow, the giants and the bizarre events of this day would be nothing more than a memory for them, an anecdote to bring out on cold evenings.

Soon after, we met the incline of the Hunch. We were making good time; even emaciated and out of shape, the giants were more than a match for our horses. I'd already decided it would make sense to spend the night in Reb Panza. They were used to the sight of giants, and given the terms of our parting, they might be more tolerant of our presence than other villages in our path.

That was how I rationalised it, anyway. If pressed, I'd have been forced to admit I was curious to see the fruits of my absurd generosity. Given the basic condition of Reb Panza, it wouldn't have taken an entire gold piece to make it as good and better as it had been before Moaradrid's arson. Surely there'd have been a little left over for some token of their appreciation? I was hoping for a statue, but given how difficult my roguish good looks might be to capture, I'd settle for a tastefully done plaque.

As we drew closer, my anticipation grew. Huero had achieved great things with my gold, and it seemed only fair to expect the same from the villagers of Reb

Panza. After all, you could only buy so much thatch and plaster with a gold piece.

I hurried to the front of the convoy, eager for my first sight of the village. Finally, we came upon a point between slopes of baked orange mud that I recognised as the last turn before Reb Panza. I felt a little giddy as I entered the bend, like a child about to receive a special prize. Except the only prizes I'd ever received as a child were the ones I took for myself, whereas this would be a genuinely hard-earned reward. As anticipation tingled my spine, I closed my eyes, the better to open them at the last moment and see…

Reb Panza exactly as I'd left it.

No sign, no hint, of repair. Not one cracked paving tile replaced, not a single wall replastered. I had to fight the uncanny sense that I'd never been away. Or perhaps I'd never given the old Patriarch that coin, had only dreamed it to assuage my irksome conscience?

Saltlick, at the head of the giants' convoy, was close behind me. I held up a hand. "Wait here. Keep everyone together."

My voice was strangled, but there was nothing I could do about that. I rode on, into the square. More than ever, the village was thick with an air of desolation. Could they have decided it would be more economical simply to leave and start again elsewhere? "Hello?" I called. "Anyone here?"

A pregnant silence – then one door opened the narrowest crack. The woman who looked out at me was haggard-eyed; lank hair hung in streaks across her face.

My first thought was that she was in middle age, but I realised quickly that a wash and a good night's rest would reveal her to be hardly older than I was. "Who are you?" she said. "We've nothing for vagabonds."

"Where's the Patriarch?" I snapped, irked by her tone. It occurred to me that I'd never thought to ask his name.

"That scoundrel? Gone. Run off, and taken all of our old folks with him. I'm his daughter, for my sins, so anything you want with him you might as well say to me."

"Run off? Run off where?"

"To Muena Palaiya. Senile old fool!" Despite her initial hostility, it appeared I'd found a subject she was eager to discourse on. "Why else would I be wasting my time here and not working where there's a living to be earned?"

I'd noticed on my previous visits that Reb Panza's population seemed to be restricted to the young and old, with no apparent middle ground. "You work away?" I asked.

"What else? Try to farm this dust?" She waved irritably at the surrounding country. "We hire with our men up in the fields near Pan Marco. It's easiest to pass our nights there and come back when we have a day or two off. Now, thanks to my pig-headed father and whatever fool gave him money, the women of Reb Panza are stuck here caring for our spoiled children!"

"Oh." If it wasn't an adequate response, it was all I had in me right then. My heart had been sinking with each word, as I realised the extent to which my good intentions had foundered.

"Oh indeed! How can we live now? This village was already on the verge of collapse, even before that foreign beast burned it half to the ground. If our parents don't come back soon, we'll have to leave this place to the rats."

"I'm sorry."

I must have sounded sincere, because her tone was a touch softer as she replied, "Well, it's hardly your fault." She stepped out from the doorway. "Anyway, those are my problems. How about you? What brings you to a cesspool like Reb Panza?" She looked me up and down. Then her gaze travelled further – and she froze, mouth open. An incomprehensible sound gurgled free. She tried again. "Those are... those are..."

"Yes. Giants."

She recovered just slightly. "I was going to say monsters."

"Oh."

"They said something about a giant – our parents, and the children. We thought it was a game they'd been playing."

"That was Saltlick," I told her. "My friend."

She looked at me. "You're friends with a monster?"

"A giant," I reminded her. "Now what would be the chances of lodgings for the night?"

Having calmed down a little, the woman introduced herself as Alba. In the end, all I could think to do was give her one of my remaining handful of onyxes to rent two shacks, one for Alvantes and me, the other for Huero and Dura, who had caught up with the convoy while I'd been negotiating.

From their doorsteps, the other women of Reb Panza eyed the giants with horror. However, after countless assurances from myself, Huero and Dura, they did agree to let their children out. Given how they'd taken to Saltlick on our previous visits, they were overjoyed to discover his brethren camped on their doorstep – and the giants, in turn, were every one as patient as Saltlick had been in the face of their zealous attentions.

While they kept each other busy, Huero and I pondered the giants' sleeping arrangements. It promised to be another mild night, and I was confident they'd be all right outside. Even if they weren't, there was nothing we could do. Few of the shanties in Reb Panza were big enough to hold even one of them.

Still, I felt a little guilty to leave them for a warm bed. When I finally slept, I did so fitfully, troubled by the unreasonable burdens suddenly piling upon me. I tried to trace what twists of fate had left the responsibility of a hundred giants on my shoulders, to rationalise how my attempt to set things right could have left Reb Panza more destitute than I'd first found it. It was all too much for a simple thief to be expected to bear.

However, I was pleased in the morning to find the giants no worse for wear, and even in good spirits. It didn't take much effort to get them moving; now that their journey had begun, they were obviously eager to reach its end. While they set out under Huero's administration, I took a moment to say my goodbyes to Alba.

"It so happens we're headed to Muena Palaiya," I said. "Maybe I can find your errant old folks and convince them to return." In truth, there was no "maybe" about it. I'd drag that thieving Patriarch back by the scruff of his wrinkled neck if I had to. Still, there seemed no point getting her hopes up.

"If you do," she replied, "only make sure to give him a good hiding first. And make sure to mention my name as you do it."

It would have been dull to cross the barrens of the Hunch once more but for one thing. To the giants, every sight was fresh and strange, and their enthralment was infectious. Now that they'd begun to accept their freedom, they chattered softly amongst themselves, pointed out new discoveries, and generally behaved much as the children of Reb Panza would have if they'd been suddenly transported to the giants' enclave.

We maintained a good pace, and passed no one – perhaps because any travellers scurried to hide when they saw us approaching. By late evening, we'd drawn close to Muena Palaiya. Educated by previous experience, Alvantes and I left Huero and the giants out of sight and rode on alone to the northern gates.

It was no surprise to find them closed at so late an hour. That the walls were still bare of guards, though, was certainly strange. Estrada would never have let the town's security slip to such a degree, now less than ever.

Alvantes dismounted before the gates and rapped violently. Yet for a long while, no response came. Just as I was sure there was no one beyond to hear, a nasal voice called from the walls, "Who's there?"

Alvantes paced back to see, and I followed. A man

with grimy, grizzled black hair and a hatchet face stared down at us from a platform atop the gates. He was dressed in the livery of a Muena Palaiyan guard, but even I could tell he was no guard. The livid crescent scar inscribed around his neck, the sneer, the short curved knife he wore slung across his chest and the way his fingers stayed near it, all spoke of someone used to killing first and skipping questions altogether. In fact, now that I looked carefully, wasn't he one of the interchangeable cut-throats who'd thronged around Castilio Mounteban's bar?

It was obvious Alvantes had come to similar conclusions, for his voice was sharp-edged as he called back, "We're here to see the mayor."

The guard sniggered, an unpleasant sputtering sound. "Not from around here, are you? Not very up on current affairs?"

"We've been away," Alvantes conceded.

"Right. Of course. I could have told you that." The guard grinned from ear to ear. "Because if you hadn't, you'd know better than to go asking for the mayor – when what you meant to say was *mayors*."

CHAPTER NINETEEN

If Alvantes's fingers twitched near his waist, compulsively reaching for a sword hilt that wasn't there, every other part of him was rigid with self-control. "We would like to see the mayors," he said.

"Now we're getting somewhere," the guard replied jovially. Then his tone changed. All the scornful glee vanished in an instant. "Only, the mayors don't bother with just anyone."

I had a mental image of Alvantes somehow climbing the sheer wall one-handed to tear the man's throat out with his teeth. However, though his voice was rich with menace, he merely said, "My name is Alvantes, former Guard-Captain of Altapasaeda. My companion is Easie Damasco. I think they'll bother with us."

The guard froze. "Maybe," he said. "Maybe they will at that." He ducked behind the walls – then bobbed back to order us, "Wait there," before vanishing again.

Long seconds later, the heavy gates began to shudder open. When the gap was sufficient, the counterfeit guard appeared in the opening with a companion, similarly garbed and just as ill-suited to his uniform. "Get off the horses," said the first guard. "Follow us."

We did as we were told. I sensed Alvantes would have been happier killing them both on the spot and for once I had trouble faulting his logic – except that there were clearly things we needed to know here. Fortunately, it appeared Alvantes had controlled himself enough to recognise that fact. If the violence in his eyes was anything to go by, our guides had better hope he didn't forget it.

They led us up Dancer's Way, the main and indeed only proper street of Muena Palaiya. As on any day, it was thronged with people even at so late an hour: beggars, market sellers and their overflowing stalls, men leading animals for sale or slaughter, and many simply making their way across town by this swiftest of routes. However, if the scene was familiar, the atmosphere was changed entirely. The hawkers and stall owners mumbled more than shouted; the usual hubbub of angry shouts, raucous laughter and bellowed greetings was stilled altogether. Wherever we passed, men turned their eyes away. I knew it wasn't Alvantes and me they were afraid of.

Alvantes leaned close to me. "We should never have left her here."

There was no denying it now. I'd thought there was nothing Estrada couldn't handle – but whatever was going on in Muena Palaiya, whatever had cast this pall over the place, it felt too big for any one person to handle.

Well past the centre of town, our guides veered into

the narrow side streets. I followed hesitantly, nervous that this wasn't an area I knew. As far as I could judge, we were close to the southern gate, in the region reserved for trades that serviced Muena Palaiya behind the scenes. Here were slaughterhouses, warehouses, tanning and drying sheds – and if memory served, somewhere in one of its less noxious portions, the mayoral offices.

We came eventually to a narrow courtyard. In it stood a large building, considerably higher than the single-storey constructions round about and built of white-daubed stone, like almost everything in Muena Palaiya. It had evidently once been a grain barn, for there were still traces of ancient seed ground into the mud round its large double doors. Two men, dressed like our guides, stood guard upon those doors.

There was a brief, hushed conference. The guard who'd spoken from the gates ducked inside, leaving the other three to watch us hawkishly. A minute later, he returned and said, "Go in. Your horses will be safe with these fine gentlemen."

One of the door guards sniggered into his fist, as though this was the funniest thing he'd heard all day. His colleague scowled at him, marched forward and snatched the reins from us. I patted my horse's neck as he was led away, and fell in behind Alvantes. The two who'd brought us entered first, and we kept close behind them.

Since the outside was to all intents and purposes a barn, my expectations hadn't been high for the interior. Therefore, it was a shock to discover something more akin to a mansion house than a dilapidated seed store. Then again, the more I looked, the more the analogy that fit best was to a high-class brothel. Rugs and lush carpets were scattered everywhere, tapestried hangings hid most of the walls, lamps of iron and brightly coloured glass hung from the rafters, and tables had been scattered through the space apparently at random, many burdened with statuettes and varied ornaments.

Yet, while everything was obviously expensive, the arrangement had been done without a hint of taste or logic. All the evidence pointed to a desire to create the impression of wealth, without any actual understanding of its benefits.

Once I'd recovered from the decor, the first thing I noticed was the presence of more thugs at intervals round the room, lounging on chairs or lolling against walls. Each was dressed in guardsman's livery and every one was looking in our direction.

My gaze roved on. A platform had been erected at the end of the room, the hasty carpentry disguised by yet more rugs. Two chairs had been set on the raised tier, one large and ornate enough almost to qualify as a throne, the other plain and more discreet.

Upon the larger chair sat a man I dimly recognised. He had a gargantuan head and body, from which hung disproportionately small arms and legs that dangled over the edges as a child's would. His jowly moon of a face was rimmed with beard and slicked hair that failed to hide either his grotesqueness or his considerable bald patch.

Beside him, on the smaller chair, sat Marina Estrada.

Alvantes saw her as I did. He jerked forward three abrupt steps – to the obvious alarm of our handlers and their cronies around the room. I caught up quickly and grasped his elbow, trying by movements of my head to indicate how hopelessly outnumbered we were.

Whether or not he understood, Alvantes covered the remaining distance at a steadier pace. "Marina. Are you all right?"

Estrada smiled wanly. "Better for seeing you," she said.

"Has this creature harmed you? Is he holding you here against your will?"

The fat man cleared his throat – a greasy, molten sound. The way he occupied the overlarge chair had already made me think of a basking toad, and the impression was made a hundred times worse when I heard the flat croak that was his voice. "I assure you," he said, "that my co-mayor has not been molested in any fashion."

Alvantes ignored him. "We're getting out of here," he told Estrada.

"Guard-Captain Alvantes, I assure you that whatever you imagine this situation to be, the truth is quite otherwise."

Only then did Alvantes acknowledge the fat man's presence. "Guiso Lupa. Nothing you've done since the day your mother spat you out was innocent. Will you try to stop me taking this woman from here?"

Of course. *That* was why I knew him. Lupa had run one of the larger gangs in Altapasaeda, with an

emphasis on extortion and prostitution. Before Alvantes had clamped down on the city's thriving crime
scene, he'd operated quite openly. In the years since,
he'd kept hidden, and his name had dropped from
common parlance.

In many ways, he was Altapasaeda's version of
Castilio Mounteban. Both had been notorious criminals supposedly cowed into retirement by law and
order. From what I'd heard of Lupa, though, he was
in many ways worse, with no time for refinements
like diplomacy or restraint. He was also famously stupid, with none of Mounteban's guile.

However limited his gifts of character might be,
though, Lupa was keeping his patience well in the face
of Alvantes's radiating contempt. "Please, Guard-Captain. While we're certainly glad of your visit, I ask that
you mind your tone. Not for my benefit of course, but
for that of my men. They can be sometimes overen-
thusiastic in their desire to serve me."

"Lunto," said Estrada, her voice taut, "I'm not some
horse, to be led out by the nose. Please calm down."

Alvantes looked wounded. "What is this?"

"As he's tried to explain, Guiso has been… assisting…
with the reconstruction of Muena Palaiya." Estrada's
voice was a numbed monotone, as convincing as a
bored huckster's. "He kindly offered the service of
his employees to fill the diminished ranks of our
guardsmen."

Translation: Guiso Lupa had seen an opportunity and
exploited it, just as Mounteban had. It was no coincidence. An image flashed through my mind; Mounteban

as a bulbous spider spinning his web through every crack and corner of the Castoval.

"So you see," inserted Lupa, "we're all friends here. And as it so happens, your arrival is fortuitous. Since I left Altapasaeda to offer my assistance here, I've received instruction from Governor Mounteban."

"*Governor?*" Alvantes fairly spat the word.

"Indeed. Amongst other matters, he asked that I convey his greetings should we ever meet, and that I pass on how interested he'd be in speaking with you."

"And what does *Governor* Mounteban imagine we have to talk about?"

Lupa gave a gelatinous cough. "He believes your presence would be a – shall we say, calming influence in the current affairs of Altapasaeda. Further, he feels the city would benefit if you were to resume your vacant position. Perhaps not in quite so unrestricted a fashion, but otherwise much as you're accustomed to." Lupa turned hooded eyes in my direction. "In return, he would guarantee that neither you nor your... associates... should fall afoul of any unfortunate misunderstandings that might arise from recent events."

Alvantes's face left no doubt of what his reply was about to be. If I could see it, the dangerous men lurking in the shadows, fingers already resting on blade hilts, could too. I caught his arm once again, dug my fingers deep, and did my best to hang on under the look of fury he turned on me.

"Alvantes has endured a lot of late," I said, "and is more than usually quick-tempered. Lest he should answer rashly, perhaps we could take a little time to confer?"

"Absolutely," agreed Lupa, sounding more relieved than anything. "Take as long as you need."

"Also, we left some friends waiting outside town. We should let them know we're safe and that all's well."

"Friends?" It was startling how suddenly Lupa's solicitousness turned to open suspicion.

"Peasants we met on the road," I said quickly. "You know how it is."

"I can't say I do."

"If we're going to deal," inserted Alvantes with unexpected calm, "you'd do better not to doubt our word."

"Not yours," replied Lupa, his pinprick eyes darting between us. "No, not yours, Guard-Captain. Of course... who am I to keep you from these peasant acquaintances of yours? And in return, I'm sure you wouldn't mind one of my men accompanying you?"

"Not so long as he doesn't mind having his throat cut."

For a moment, Lupa looked as though Alvantes had spat in his face. He recovered quickly. "No, no. Quite right. You should go. Talk with these new friends about what we've discussed." Something dangerous rose in the morass of Lupa's voice then, like a snake darting through swamp water. "In the meantime... we'll be sure to take good care of Mayor Estrada."

Alvantes and I were out of Muena Palaiya, with our escorts left behind closed gates, before either of us opened our mouths again. Even then, it was only for Alvantes to make a long low sound of pure anger, an incoherent growl that made me wonder if I hadn't been safer with Lupa.

"We'll help her," I said.

"Shut up. Damn you, shut up, Damasco."

I shut up.

"We left her there alone."

Unsure if this was an invitation to stop shutting up, I decided not to risk it.

"Damn it all," Alvantes snarled – and there ended our brief, one-sided conversation.

Minutes later, we passed the outcrop shielding the northern cliff road from Muena Palaiya. The giants waited in columns to either side of the highway, like sentinel statues guarding the way. It was clear now why the road had been so quiet; who would want to go near Muena Palaiya with Lupa and his thugs in control? In that one small way, his presence had done us a favour, for many a traveller would have died of alarm to see this monstrous assembly lurking in the gloom.

Huero's cart was pulled up to the verge, while Dura and the children distributed food. Saltlick and Huero were waiting at the head of the column, obviously anticipating our return. They looked anxious when they saw us, no doubt reading the tone of our experience in Muena Palaiya from our expressions.

While Alvantes stood nearby on the edge of the roadside decline, glaring down into the valley below, I briefly explained the situation. It was dismaying to see the strain and worry, so recently removed, flood back into Saltlick's eyes. "Help Marina."

"We will," I said. "I don't know how, but we will."

"You won't." Alvantes turned abruptly. "You can't."

"You don't know that."

"Of course I do! I'll go back. I'll do what he asks, make whatever deal Mounteban wants. There's no other way."

"That's it? Just forget about saving Altapasaeda? Do you really think that's what she'd want?"

A dozen rapid steps carried Alvantes to a point where his face was hardly a finger's length from mine. "I don't *care* what she wants. I care about what keeps her safe." He spun to round on Saltlick, who actually cowered back. "Lupa will have scouts out by now, looking to see who these supposed friends of ours are. If he sees a crowd of giants camped on his doorstep he'll panic. If he panics, he might harm her. Get them out of here."

"Wait," I said. "Just wait."

"Back down the road. Go now."

There was a buzzing building in my head, a fragile note just beneath hearing. I couldn't put it into words or even thoughts, but it was there. Looking at the hulking figures crowded along the roadside, I said, "They're giants, damn it."

"Exactly. Difficult to hide. We need to move quickly."

"No, I mean… they're giants. We have *giants* on our side."

"Be quiet, Damasco."

"Just like Moaradrid did. Only, all Moaradrid wanted was big, dumb soldiers that didn't answer back. He never understood what he had. An army of giants."

"No fight," put in Saltlick plaintively. I hadn't even realised he was following the conversation.

"I know that," I said. "But what if there was no need to fight?"

"Damasco, whatever you're thinking, let it go. They're not an army. They're half starved, exhausted and..."

"Lupa doesn't know that."

"What?"

"Look at them, Alvantes. Look at them! They're terrifying. You and I know they won't squash us like insects just because they feel like it, but Lupa? They're giants, they're on our side, and you want to hide them? You know you can't trust Lupa and Mounteban. You know handing yourself over won't solve anything. We have one chance to fix this and it has to be now."

Alvantes ground the heel of his one hand against his temple, as though trying to bring his thoughts under control by sheer pressure. "I will not let you place Marina's life in danger."

"She's *already* in danger," I said. "Now that Mounteban has her safe and under control, do you think he'll just let her go? The woman he's obsessed with, who just happens to make a useful hostage to keep you and anyone like you from meddling in his business? We have to stop him. And that means stopping Lupa – now, while he's off his guard. But you can't do it alone, Alvantes. You can't talk her out of there. You can't even fight her out."

Alvantes kept the hand in place, gripping his forehead as if it might fly into pieces. "Hells! Damasco..."

"You know I'm right."

He clutched his brow one last time, and the hand dropped to his side. "Yes," he said.

"What?" I really thought I must have misheard.

"This time. You're right. But if you get her hurt…"

"I know, I know. You'll kill me. I'd expect nothing less. But if this has a chance, I'm going to need your help. So you'll have to kill yourself straight afterwards."

"Believe me," Alvantes said, "if our actions bring harm to that woman, my life will last exactly as long as it takes me to rid this world of Lupa and every last one of his vermin."

"I get it. *That woman* happens to be my friend, you know."

I turned to Saltlick. However many times I saw him, there was always a part of my brain that was staggered by just how big he was. Nothing could quite prepare you for seeing the giants together. Even days spent in their company didn't quite remove the instinct to fear them.

For that reason if no other, this might work.

My mind was already speculating on how I could persuade him. But as I gazed up at Saltlick's face, I realised there was no need. I was astonished to find that for once, I could read his expression perfectly – and even more astonished by what that expression was.

It was trust. Trust in me.

"All right," I said. "Here's what we're going to do…"

We gave it an hour.

Alvantes and I stationed ourselves near the bend that closed off the cliff road, and Huero insisted on joining us. "You told Lupa you were going to talk with peasants, didn't you?" he said. "Well, I'm a peasant. Always better not to be caught in a lie."

Meanwhile, Saltlick had taken his people further back towards the Hunch-proper, where they'd be well out of sight. If Lupa had spies out, as no one doubted he would, there would be no way for them to see the giants without passing us. I could only hope they'd give up when they saw us leave, not thinking to wait in case anyone should follow. The possibility that they would was the first great risk in a plan that seemed to consist of little else *but* risks.

Everything rested on the element of surprise. Without it, we were all dead.

The hour passed, Alvantes and I set out by starlight for the town gates, while Huero headed in the other direction, a final corroboration of our story for anyone who might be watching. At the entrance to town, the two thugs who'd escorted us were waiting, slouched against the arch of the already open portal. They didn't acknowledge our return, except to draw the gates shut after we'd ridden past. Then they led us once again up Dancer's Way, back towards Lupa's gaudy mayoral mansion.

Alvantes and I rode as slowly as we dared. In the unlit streets, it wasn't difficult to encourage a leisurely pace. Almost as much as surprise, we needed time on our side. Every moment of delay was a moment in our favour.

Still, our arrival at the mansion-barn seemed to come all too quickly. This time, there were nearly a dozen of Lupa's fake guards waiting outside. Security had obviously risen in Lupa's priorities since our last visit.

We dismounted, let ourselves be led inside.

Everything was practically as we'd left it. Lupa and Estrada still sat in their respective places on the platform. Here as outside, the only difference was in the increased number of armed men spaced around the walls. Whether or not Lupa was really expecting some move on Alvantes's part, he certainly wasn't worried about giving the impression of distrust.

Yet his tone was hearty as he called, "Guard-Captain, good to have you back. You've had ample time to consider, I trust?"

"I have," replied Alvantes.

"And you've concluded, no doubt, that what is right for Mayor Estrada here, what's right for Mounteban and the people of Altapasaeda, is right for you too. You can return to your post – and so long as you keep yourself within the bounds of the new regime, your life can more or less return to what it was before all this... *unpleasantness*."

Alvantes's face gave nothing away. "Yes. A nice idea – in theory. What I'd like to know is what I can expect in practise. Do you have leave to talk terms on Mounteban's behalf?"

Lupa looked uncomfortable. "Terms? Well... to a degree, of course."

"*A degree?* Lupa, can you negotiate or not?"

"Certainly, if a little negotiation is called for, then..."

"If it's *called for?* If you're offering me a job, surely I've a right to discuss details?"

Despite my fears, despite all my doubts, it was hard not to enjoy the show Alvantes was putting on. Even he seemed to be warming to his part. I'd told him to keep the conversation going for as long as possible, but I was beginning to suspect he had far more in mind than that.

Lupa flicked sweat from his brow with a rubbery palm. "Guard-Captain. The situation is one where compromise on your part is both expected and required. You must see that…"

"*You* must see that this arrangement of Mounteban's is one possibility amongst many. I have other options, Lupa."

"But would those options be so beneficial to all involved?" Lupa made no effort to hide the sudden edge of danger in his voice. "To the good folk of Altapasaeda, say, or to my lovely co-mayor?"

"I hope that wasn't a threat."

"A threat? Aren't we simply discussing possibilities and their repercussions, as civilised men will?"

"Because," continued Alvantes, "the only good threat is one you can back up."

As though on cue, a booming crash assailed the room. It came from the direction of the western walls, and resounded for a very long time. Even if I hadn't been expecting it, I'd have recognised the crunch of falling masonry.

Lupa almost jumped from his great seat. I watched his expression vacillate between horror and denial. "Perhaps," he said, "you haven't noticed how many of my men surround you?"

Alvantes smiled – and if that smile chilled my blood, I could only imagine what effect it had on Lupa. "It might take more than a few men."

From outside came a beat like a hundred great drums pounding with no guiding rhythm. It was steady, and it was rapidly drawing nearer.

Lupa cocked his head towards it, his eyes round. "Whatever it is you're doing, make it stop!"

Alvantes held his one hand up, palm out. "I'm doing nothing."

"Whatever *that* is…"

Outside, someone shouted. Another voice joined the first, and another. Then they were drowned out by the hammering swell of noise.

Just as it seemed about to overwhelm us, the cacophony abated. It was the briefest reprieve – barely enough for Lupa to begin a sigh of relief. A moment later, impacts resounded from all four walls, each deafeningly loud. A shiver ran through the floor, setting every man, every piece of furniture, quivering like a tuning fork.

"Damn you!" Lupa had to bellow to make himself heard. "Stop this!"

"Stop what?" Alvantes looked perfectly, terrifyingly at ease amidst the chaos. Dust rained from the ceiling. Chunks of brick rolled in cascades from its edges, as if a great fist were closing around the building. Lupa's lackeys stumbled towards the centre, arms raised to shield their heads.

Then everyone looked skyward, all together.

Everyone except Alvantes and me. I didn't need to look. I knew the roof had begun to heave aside, buoyed upon a sea of massive hands. Instead, I pictured the scene outside in my mind's eye. Saltlick had brought only a quarter of the giants, the youngest and strongest. That still meant more than twenty, each twice the height of a man – and each more than capable of reaching the top of the walls.

Maybe some of Lupa's lackeys would attack them. I hoped against hope they'd be too afraid, but fear was as likely to make them dangerous and stupid. Perhaps swords would be unsheathed. Perhaps arrows would be loosed.

The giants were tough. I'd seen Saltlick shrug off wounds that would have felled a man on the spot. Every one of them had endured Moaradrid's battle against the Castovalians, and all the hardships that had followed. They would keep going. And if a mob of giants tearing the roof from a building was a chilling sight, how much worse if those giants seemed impervious to pain, oblivious to injury? Cowards – and the kind of men who followed a creature like Lupa were always cowards – would not fight an unwinnable fight for long.

At least, that was what I kept fervently telling myself.

"Make it stop! Agree to Mounteban's proposal!" screamed Lupa.

"I have an alternative proposal," shouted Alvantes over the din of tumbling masonry. "You and your men leave Muena Palaiya tonight."

As he spoke, Alvantes began walking unhurriedly across the space between them. With each step, Lupa cowered deeper into his makeshift throne.

"You'll go back to Castilio Mounteban," Alvantes continued, "like the lapdog you are, and you'll carry him this message. Muena Palaiya is off limits. Soon,

Altapasaeda will be too. Then there'll be no rock anywhere big enough to hide him."

Alvantes stepped onto the low platform.

"Or, if that's all too much to remember, simply tell
him this."

One last step brought his face a hand's breadth from
Lupa's.

"Tell him we're coming for *him* next."

Abruptly, Lupa tumbled from his throne. It looked
as though he'd tipped over in his panic – but in another moment, he'd dragged Estrada from her seat,
and had a knife pressed to her neck. It was a short
blade, hardly more than a stiletto. That didn't change
the possibilities of what it would do to Estrada's throat.

"I'll kill her!" Lupa's voice was a squeak now, quite
unlike his usual croak. The expression on his face was
one of sheerest terror.

Alvantes made no move towards him. "You won't,"
he said. "I know you, Lupa. You're gutless through
and through."

"Tell them to stop!"

"I couldn't if I wanted to."

"I'll kill her."

"No, you won't."

Lupa twitched massively, as though lightning had
jolted his rubbery body. Suddenly, the noise of the giants' impromptu demolition was gone, leaving
weighty silence in its wake. Lupa's eyes swung up, acknowledged the naked rectangle of night sky above.

He dropped the knife. It clattered off the platform,
spun, lay still. "No," he said. "I won't."

"Leave," Alvantes told him. "Take your men. If you're not gone in an hour…" Alvantes also turned his gaze upward, studied the cavity that until recently had been the roof. "Well. That could just as easily have been your head."

Lupa nodded ponderously, eyes not leaving the star-specked blackness overhead. For all his swollen bulk, he looked small before Alvantes. He climbed from the platform, with a grunt of exertion. When he stumbled towards the doors, his men fell in behind him. Every one looked petrified at the prospect of what awaited them outside – but no less scared at the prospect of staying to face this man who commanded monsters.

Perhaps they'd have been less afraid if they'd stayed to see the tenderness with which Alvantes held out his hand to Estrada. "Marina. Are you all right?"

She managed a tentative smile. Even from a distance, I could see she was shaking. "Yes. No. Not really." She reached with slim fingers to touch Alvantes's arm.

Then suddenly, with no intervening movement that I could make out, they were holding each other – hanging on to each other fiercely.

Even I could recognise two people in need of privacy. I turned away.

CHAPTER TWENTY

I was happy to give Alvantes and Estrada a little privacy. The sight of so many costly and easily pocketed knick-knacks arrayed around the room had awakened an instinct recently dormant. For the first time in days, I felt an almost uncontrollable need to steal something.

I turned back at the sound of Alvantes's yelped "Ow!" in time to witness the last of the ringing slap Estrada had struck him across the face.

"But damn you, what made you think I needed saving?" she demanded, her voice wavering at some indefinable point between anger and tears. "And how dare you behave as if I'm some damsel in distress?"

"It was Damasco's idea," Alvantes replied, not without a note of petulance.

"That's right," I told him, "blame it on me. Of course, left to your own devices you'd have either surrendered to Mounteban or charged in here single-handed." Realising what I'd just said, I added hastily, "We just wanted to help, Estrada."

"Both of you," she said, "what were you thinking? I had everything under control. I have friends here. We'd have dealt with Lupa, sooner or later. Now he's going to run back to Mounteban and likely return with three times as many of his thugs."

"No," said Alvantes, "he isn't."

"You can't be sure of that."

"Yes, I can. I meant what I told Lupa. Mounteban's time in Altapasaeda is over."

"So you'll charge in there like you did here? Probably get yourself killed?"

"If that's what it takes." There was a note of baffled anger rising in Alvantes's voice.

"No, you won't, damn it! I won't let you."

"Let me? Marina, it isn't your decision. Just as I, apparently, had no say in you staying here alone to be molested by Mounteban's lackey."

"I can assure you," said Estrada icily, "that Lupa never came anywhere near molesting me."

What was wrong with these two? Even watching them shout, it was impossible to miss the attraction between them. "Will you both be quiet!" I cried. "Estrada, you're safe and Lupa's gone. Alvantes, you've just rescued the woman you love. So maybe the recriminations can wait until tomorrow – or at least until we've had some dinner."

I was surprised by Alvantes's failure to come over and strangle me, even more so by the flush of crimson in his cheeks. It never failed to amuse me how helpless the man was in the face of his own emotions. Fortunately for them both, Estrada was a little more capable.

With a small step forward, rising on her toes, she re-placed her arms around Alvantes's neck – more gently this time, less urgently. "I'm sorry," she said, "and thank you, Lunto. I *would* have dealt with him. But I'm glad I didn't have to."

Then, before I could realise what was happening, she'd released Alvantes, darted from the stage and wrapped me in a suffocating embrace. "Thank you too, Easie. It was brave of you to come here."

I levered her far enough away that I could draw air. "It was this or another night sleeping in a ditch," I said. "Now can we please get out of here?"

Outside, the giants were already gone. We'd agreed that they'd spend as little time within Muena Palaiya as possible, lest the entire town be reduced to panic. The roof of the barn-*cum*-mansion was propped carefully against its flank. To the west, I could see the crescent scar in the town wall where they'd made their entrance. It was an unsettling sight – strangely, less because of the extent of the damage than its orderliness. Men could have achieved such destruction, but only giants could have made it look so neat and easy.

There was no sign of Lupa or his henchmen. I couldn't believe he'd dare try to stay. Whether Alvantes had made the right call in letting him run back to Mounteban was another question – but that was a problem for tomorrow and for someone other than me. With Saltlick and Estrada safe, my part was played.

Speaking of which... "Estrada," I said, "there's someone waiting outside town who I think would be glad to see you safe."

Her face lit at the realisation of whom I meant. We found our horses tied in a stable abutting the building and, Estrada mounted behind Alvantes, we headed for the fourth time that night down Dancer's Way. With no one standing guard upon the gates, we had to open them ourselves; still, it was worth a little effort for so clear a sign that Muena Palaiya was free of Lupa's thugs.

We rode in silence across the scantily wooded ground outside the town. Turning onto the northern cliff road, I thought at first that the giants must still be hiding further along – until they edged in ones and twos from the shade of the cliffs.

The sight sent a shudder down my spine. I understood then that nothing Lupa did, no amount of cajolery or bribing, would make his men return to Muena Palaiya. If I'd witnessed these colossi tear the roof from a building, no reward or threat would make me cross their path again.

They all looked more or less identical to me in the gloom. Saltlick's eyes were evidently better than mine, for he rushed forward with a bellow of "Marina!"

"Saltlick! Oh, it's so good to see you." Estrada looked as though she'd have liked to fling her arms around him too. She settled for clasping her two hands round one of his. "And your people are here. Thank you so much for what you did."

"Glad to help," Saltlick replied, framing the unfamiliar syllables carefully.

Estrada stepped back to appraise him. "Around your neck... is that...?"

He nodded bashfully.

"It... ah... it suits you."

"There's a story there," I inserted.

"I don't doubt," said Estrada, an invisible smile clear in her voice. To Saltlick she said, "We need to get you and your people out of this cold."

"Not cold," he replied.

"Nonsense. Give me an hour and we'll see what Muena Palaiya's hospitality can produce."

All of a sudden, Estrada was full of energy and good cheer. I wondered if I was the only one to notice the fragility behind it. It was as if, Lupa gone, she felt the need to prove herself once more as the woman who could lead a town as well as or better than any man. I wasn't at all surprised when despite the late hour she managed to not only rouse a party of volunteers but to have them construct a giant-scaled shanty town on the waste ground outside Muena Palaiya that put the one we'd left two days ago to shame.

I was so entertained by watching the workmen labour frantically to meet Estrada's near-impossible deadline – whilst keeping as far away as possible from the giants – that I hardly realised how exhausted I was. Only as the show drew towards a close did I properly notice the yawns threatening to dislocate my jaw. I was relieved when Estrada materialised from the darkness, Alvantes in tow, and said, "I've arranged tavern rooms for you."

We found Huero and his family and said goodnight to Saltlick, who was busily organising dining and lodging arrangements for his people. If he was still troubled by the fact that he'd been savagely tortured by Moaradrid a mere few paces away, he gave no sign; perhaps seeing the land turned to such an opposite purpose was enough to salve that particular memory. Either way, he waved us an energetic goodbye.

The tavern was an elegant two-storey affair on the more reputable edge of the notorious Red Quarter. It was vertiginously above my usual price range, and I wondered what strings Estrada had pulled to arrange us rooms there. Then again, perhaps its owner had been moved to generosity by the news of Lupa's retirement – for on the way there, Estrada had told us of half a dozen eyewitnesses reporting his hasty departure.

Any fool could have seen that there was much still unsaid between Alvantes and Estrada. However, neither of them was in any state to say it, and they settled for a weary "goodnight."

One thing, however, couldn't be left for morning. Mumbling an improbable excuse about enjoying the night air, I waited for Alvantes to go inside and hurried after Estrada. I told her briefly what had happened in Ans Pasaeda, of the fate that had befallen Alvantes's father and the way it had eaten at him since.

"Frankly," I finished, "it's made him even crabbier than usual. I thought it would be a shame if you took it personally."

"Oh, Lunto," she said, her voice thick with held-back tears. Then, "Thank you, Easie... I mean, for telling me. I'm not sure he would have."

"Give him time," I said – more to end the conversation before I fell asleep on my feet, than because I thought time would ever help penetrate Alvantes's stoicism. I bade her goodnight, hurried inside and let the landlord show me to my room.

He'd hardly left when a knock on my door revealed Alvantes standing in the hallway. I took a nervous step back. The only explanation my fatigued brain could produce was that Estrada had incurred some minor harm during our rescue, a stubbed toe or chipped nail, and he was here to make good on his promise of murderous revenge.

"Damasco."

"It wasn't my fault."

"What? I'm not here to accuse you. I just thought I should... that is, I wanted to... or rather..." Alvantes took a deep breath. "*Thank you*. For not letting me give in. Whatever my father would have wanted, it wasn't that."

"That's true," I agreed, striving to hide my relief.

"I understand now what I have to do."

The zealous note in his voice renewed my unease. "Oh?"

"Something else my father would have pointed out is that protecting the people of Altapasaeda has nothing to do with the dictates of a king."

"He might also have mentioned that he wouldn't want you rushing headlong to certain death."

Alvantes considered. "He might have, at that."

"So... a plan, maybe?"

"Indeed." Alvantes looked embarrassed then, an

expression I'd never have expected his severe face capable of. "Which is the other reason I'm here. The
giants, Marina's rescue... it was quick thinking on your
part. I'll need that, when the time comes. So, if you
were willing..."

It was impossible he meant what I thought he
meant, but I had to at least check. "You're asking for
my *help?*"

"If you've nothing better to do."

That was it? This man who'd insulted and imprisoned
me, who'd struck me more than once, who'd forced me
into danger more times than I cared to count, really believed I'd help him save a city I couldn't care three figs
for? Did he think one apology – or not even that, a
mere half-hearted thank you! – could turn our relationship on its head?

Then again, of the two, there was no denying I disliked Castilio Mounteban considerably more. I'd give
a lot to wipe the smug condescension from his face.

"Fine. I'm in. Now, can I please get a little sleep?"

Having expected my brain to wheedle its way out of
my promise to Alvantes overnight, it was a shock to
wake the next morning with a sense of urgency coursing through my muscles. I'd never felt anything like
it. It had qualities in common with the sensation before a particularly risky job; but where that had been
all raw, jangling nerves, this ran deeper and slower,
like the ache from an old hurt.

For the first time in what seemed an age, we didn't
set out with the dawn. Estrada arrived early in the

morning with clean shirts for Alvantes and me, mine picked out in a suitably dark shade, and forcibly suggested we wash before changing. While I was at it, I stripped off Alvantes's makeshift splint, satisfied that my arm was well on the way to healing.

Once we'd ventured outside in our new clothes, Estrada insisted we eat a proper breakfast together, giants and all. There was fruit and vegetables for them, eggs, corn bread and fresh fish for us. We had an audience almost from the beginning, as early rising townsfolk were drawn by the commotion. Word spread fast, and the crowd grew rapidly. All except the children looked both fascinated and nervous, as though half-suspecting they might soon end up on the giants' menu themselves.

Perhaps Saltlick recognised their distrust – for while the others ate, he insisted on taking a small party to repair the section of wall damaged in last night's hostilities. That news travelled quickly too. Even from the other side of town, I heard the raucous cheer that went up once the last stone was replaced, and the ebb of tension it brought in our own spectators was obvious.

Intentionally or not, Saltlick had achieved his first act of politicking as temporary chief of the giants, not to mention monarch of all the Castoval. If I couldn't help but feel a little proud, it was also a reminder that I still had my own loose end to tie up.

With Estrada's help, it wasn't hard to find the place I was looking for. The inn, once the home of a wealthy local trader and nowadays known as the *Red Cockerel*, was even more imposing than the one I'd passed the night in. Its distinguishing feature was an excess of red-framed glass on its ground floor; three entire walls were interrupted by window after window, and must have cost a not-inconsiderable fortune.

Within, the foyer of the *Red Cockerel* was high-ceilinged, enlivened by dark wood and gilt, and distinctly pleasant. As I pushed through the entrance, a sour, well-dressed man who could only be the proprietor gave me an odd look, and said, "Haven't you heard? We're full."

"Not for much longer," I told him, shoving my way past.

The main room was long and deep, bright with the daylight from outside. Despite the mildness of the day, a fire was lit in the huge fireplace at the far end, making the space stickily hot. The air was heavy with sweet, stale odours of wine and tobacco. The only furnishings were low divans and tables, the latter untidy with half-emptied cups and plates bearing scraps of food.

It could have been many a high-class dive in the Red Quarter, except for one major difference: on every divan, alone or in pairs, were slumped the elderly populace of Reb Panza. A few of them I recognised; where they recalled me in turn, they looked less than elated. That was nothing, however, to the alarm draining every drop of colour from the old Patriarch's face.

"Get up!" I snapped. "Get your things. You've five minutes to be out of here and on your way home."

"What? How dare you?" he replied – but his voice was quavering.

"Thanks to you, Reb Panza is on the verge of collapse. This holiday is over."

"What? We've been away only a day or two. Why shouldn't we indulge ourselves a little? How many times have our ungrateful children stayed out drinking while we remained to watch over their offspring? Shouldn't there come a point in life where a man can finally tend to his own needs?"

"You've been away for a fortnight," I told him. "And in answer to your questions – shut up, and be glad I'm not kicking you around this room for stealing my money."

"Stole? At worst, misappropriated." Bluster was starting to restore his confidence. "We're here now, and we've paid for our presence with good coin. Now you come and tell us we have to leave? I hope you have an army to back you up, you contemptible reprobate!"

Mentally I thanked him for playing so neatly into my hands. "An army? That's a tall order. I'm not sure I could rustle up one of those for a corrupt old ass and his cronies. There must be something I can manage instead, though."

On cue, the doors behind me swung open, to clatter against the walls. I'd thought the Patriarch's face had already grown as pale as human features could, so I was pleasantly surprised when he managed to blanch another shade.

I probably had the cudgel Alvantes carried to thank for that. I was pleased he hadn't lost the last night's unexpected gift for theatre.

"Would an irate guard-captain serve instead?" I asked.

I didn't give the Patriarch a moment to even consider replying.

"Not good enough? In that case, I'm sure you know the lady beside him. Marina Estrada. *Mayor* Estrada, to you. As in, mayor of this particular town."

It must have been her expression that made him tremble so. Given her reaction when I'd explained how he'd come to be throwing money around in Muena Palaiya, I was sure it wasn't all feigned.

"No? *Really?* All right then. If we're talking actual armies, if it's really going to take an army to get you to face up to your responsibilities… well, maybe you should take a glance through that window behind you."

I could see how badly he didn't want to look. It was as if invisible hands were winding his head.

"Remember Saltlick? Of course you do."

Saltlick had actually volunteered for this one. Given how seriously his people took the binds of duty, I hadn't been altogether surprised.

Neither, apparently, was the Patriarch. Petrified certainly, about to make an unpleasant mess of an expensive couch possibly, but not actually surprised. He barely had time to register the huge and hugely ugly countenance scowling in at him before his eyes strayed on, to the next pane of glass and the next – as I'd known they must.

"Well, Saltlick has a few friends."

He was on his feet before the last syllable left my mouth. His eyes were huge with terror. His long moustaches quivered with the wordless twitching of his lips. He lurched past me, almost tripped over Alvantes and staggered onward. I doubted even he knew where he was going.

He wouldn't get far; not with Huero and a half-dozen more giants waiting in the street outside.

"When I next pass through Reb Panza," I called after him, "I expect to be able to see my face in it."

I suspected Huero was secretly glad of the responsibility for getting Reb Panza's wayward elders home. Now that the giants were recovering from their funk, they no longer needed to be looked after, and journeying on to Altapasaeda with us would take him and his family very far from home.

"I'm not sure what Estrada said," I told him, "but the inn's proprietor has agreed to pay back most of what they spent. Do you think you could check in on them from time to time? Make sure the money goes where it's supposed to?"

"It would be a pleasure," he said – and his expression told me it genuinely would. I'd noticed something in Huero since my return from Ans Pasaeda, a quality I suspected he was only just starting to recognise in himself. He really did enjoy making things better. Maybe my coin alone hadn't done much for Reb Panza, but coin and a man like Huero should make a real difference.

I pointed to the Patriarch. "Just make sure he walks every step of the way."

Huero grinned. "It's going to be a long journey."

"Make sure of it."

He offered his hand and I clasped it. "Thank you. For everything. Really, Huero."

"No, thank you, Damasco." He glanced to Dura, busy marshalling Reb Panza's dazed, hung-over runaways. "After everything that happened... well, I think we needed a little diversion in our lives."

I watched them leave, Huero driving their own wagon and Dura another loaned by Estrada, with the old folks of Reb Panza sat sulkily in the back or trailing after like a depressed dog's tail. Last of all went the Patriarch, an expression of sheerest terror hovering above his grand moustaches. How was he to know the giants were out in force to see off the family who'd cared for them for so long, and not to devour him if he should miss a step?

With the secret of the giants' presence out, Estrada had chosen to abandon subterfuge altogether. We travelled in single file from the north gate towards the south, and it was hard to believe that one man, woman or child in the entire town hadn't turned out to watch. Since morning, the general mood had turned to one of amicable curiosity. A few people even clapped and cheered, as though it were all a pageant put on for their entertainment.

Halfway down Dancer's Way, Estrada drew her mount up abruptly. The column of giants shuffled to a halt behind us.

As soon as the riot of pounding feet had died, Estrada cried at the top of her voice, "People of Muena Palaiya!" She waited again, this time for her audience to quieten itself. "You'll all know by now that our town has been under the forced rule of a man named Guiso Lupa. Most of you will know too that Lupa was an agent of the criminal Castilio Mounteban, who has set himself up in tyranny over Altapasaeda. With the aid of my friends here, Lupa has been driven out, and Muena Palaiya belongs to its people once more."

Those who'd been celebrating the giants' parade took this as an excuse for another round of applause.

"However, for Muena Palaiya to stay free, Altapasaeda must be free also. Or else sooner or later Mounteban will make our town, and eventually all of the Castoval, his own. Therefore, I find myself with no choice but to leave you in the hands of your town council, along with the task of repairing the damage Lupa has wrought. I hope you'll pull together, now more than ever, and that I'll see you again soon – safe in the knowledge that we have no more to fear from the ambitions of evil men."

This time, the reaction was more widespread, though perhaps not quite so enthusiastic. After so much unrest, no doubt the people of Muena Palaiya had been hoping for a return to something like normality. Nevertheless, the cheering went on for what seemed an age.

When Estrada rejoined Alvantes and me, her face was set with fierce resolve.

It was matched by the determination in Alvantes's voice as he said, "Marina, absolutely not."

"You'd have me go back on my word?"

"You'll be safe here."

"Only if you win – in which case, I'll be just as safe with you. If you don't…" A little of the bravado went out of Estrada as she finished, "You know fear of you was the only thing that kept him away from me, Lunto."

"Marina…"

"Anyway, Castilio might listen to me. There could be a chance of avoiding bloodshed."

"There'll be no avoiding bloodshed."

"In which case, you *know* I can handle myself. You came here to protect me and you helped free my home. Now I'll do the same for you. Damn it, I'm not waiting like some hand-wringing soldier's wife. If it all goes wrong, if you're hurt…" Estrada clutched his one hand in hers, gripped it tight. "I want to be there."

Alvantes stared at their locked hands for the longest time, as though he were the only witness to some unimaginable prodigy. Then, as if shaking himself from a dream, he said, "Once we're inside, you do what I tell you. That's my condition."

"Agreed."

"You take no chances."

"Absolutely not, Guard-Captain."

He sighed, a sound of utter, wearied defeat. "Then thank you, Marina. It will be a pleasure to travel with you again."

Maybe the man was learning after all.

Over the next four days, we retraced the route through the Castoval we'd taken so recently – and what seemed a lifetime ago. In one great, snaking column, we trekked down the mountainside road to the valley floor, swung west into Paen Acha, forded the river at Casta Canto – a slow and immensely tiresome process with a hundred giants in tow – and continued through the further depths of the forest towards the main southward highway.

All the while, Alvantes, Estrada and I discussed our strategy, with occasional, brief contributions from Saltlick.

In private, I'd already raised with him the possibility of the giants aiding us one last time. "Saltlick, what they did back there. Do you think you could persuade your people to help Altapasaeda the same way?"

"No fight," he said. "No hurt."

"Let's take that as a given. But if there was some way you could help without causing any harm... without putting yourselves in real risk?"

I was being disingenuous, and surely we both knew it. The giants had *already* been in real risk. The morning after the decapitation of Lupa's headquarters, I'd discovered that half a dozen of them had suffered wounds enough to fell a man twice over. They'd all shown Saltlick's remarkable capacity for healing, and a couple of days later the signs of damage were more or less gone. However, Altapasaeda wasn't Muena Palaiya. Where Lupa had had a few ignorant toughs, Mounteban had an army.

So what I was really asking was, *Will you lead the giants into a battle where they can't fight back, but where their enemies will kill you all given the slightest chance?*

Saltlick had understood without me needing to spell it out, though; I knew him well enough to realise that much. He'd taken so long to answer that I'd even thought he might say no.

He hadn't, of course.

That only left the question of what possible help a battalion of pacifist giants could be against the most secure and heavily defended city this side of Pasaeda – another flaw in a plan that, even as we drew close to Altapasaeda, seemed to consist of little else. What hope did we have, when our greatest weapon was no weapon at all?

On the fourth day, we broke free of Paen Acha, stepping from tree-lined gloom into bright sunlight reflected through endless-seeming seas of golden corn. There, barely visible in the distance, were the walls of Altapasaeda. They looked small at such a distance, fragile even, especially compared to the monolithic creatures marching behind me.

Nevertheless, those fortifications were ten times sturdier than those of Muena Palaiya. They'd been built by paranoid northerners to withstand siege from an entire revolting population. Alvantes had stated with absolute certainty that not even the giants could smash those defences, nor were they tall enough to climb over. Even if we could somehow lay our hands on a job lot of giant-sized hammers, the giants would be cut down from the walls before they could make a breach. Perhaps they could shrug off a few arrows, but not the volleys that would be laid down by the forces under Mounteban's command.

Yet seeing the walls like that – so distant, so frail – none of it seemed to matter. I couldn't bring myself to believe that any one of the giants couldn't snap that faraway thread of stone in two.

"That's it," I muttered, more to myself than Alvantes riding beside me.

He started. "What is?"

"We've been tying ourselves in knots about what the giants can or can't do. But it doesn't matter. All that matters is what Mounteban *thinks* they can do."

"They can't bluff their way into Altapasaeda, Damasco."

"Maybe they don't need to."

"I don't understand."

"Neither do I, just yet. Give me time, though."

We rode on – and deep in the workings of my brain, pieces began to click into place. The giants. Alvantes's guardsmen. Mounteban. Wasn't it just like a burglary? I'd never been much of a thief, but I'd gotten by, because nine times in ten it wasn't *about* being a good thief. If you could find weaknesses, work out how to exploit them, then the rest took care of itself. Everyone, everything had a weakness – and I thought I was beginning to see Mounteban's.

By the time we drew close to the Suburbs, only one problem still eluded me. But it was the problem that all else hung upon.

We'd already agreed we wouldn't try to disguise the giants. Thanks to Lupa, Mounteban knew they were coming. In the short term at least, the fear their presence would generate in his ranks outweighed the risk of his trying to move against us. Still, marching them into the filthy streets of the Suburbs would have been a melodramatic, not to mention muddy, business. Instead, we left them camped on the outskirts while we continued on to seek out Navare.

We made no attempt to hide our own presence either. In fact, at Alvantes's suggestion, we rode by the most conspicuous route, even going so far as to risk the main road that ran against the edge of the city. Let Mounteban know we were here. Let him waste energy worrying over what to do about us, even as we plotted our move against him.

At least, that was the theory. In fact, my eyes stayed nervously locked upon the battlements above. Every slight noise threatened to send me tumbling from my horse. I started every time a helmeted head peeked through the crenulations.

Yet if I hadn't been staring at that impenetrable sheet of stone, I'd never have seen it. Not believing, I blinked hard, looked again, even rubbed a knuckle against my eyes.

It was still there. My missing piece.

Now I knew how a handful of guardsmen and an army of peace-loving giants could force their way into a fortified city, and how they might stand the tiniest of chances against its legion of defenders and its tyrant of a ruler.

There was only one drawback.

It meant I was breaking into Altapasaeda again.

CHAPTER TWENTY·ONE

Before we hurled ourselves into untold danger, it was vital we knew what had been happening in Alta-pasaeda these last few days.

That meant a visit to Navare, and *that* meant giving away Alvantes's one and only agent in the Suburbs. I could almost feel the resistance radiating off him as he hammered the reinforced door of Navare's shack.

The resulting pause gave us ample time to imagine the worst. Then the door opened the barest crack – just enough to reveal Navare's crossbow, and the man himself just visible in the gloom behind.

"*Alvantes?*"

"Sub-Captain Navare."

"I'd thought… there were rumours, and…" Abruptly, Navare's face split into a grin. "Well, what are you standing outside for, Guard-Captain?" In a hiss, he added, "*You know they're watching, right?*"

"*Of course,*" Alvantes whispered back as we brushed past.

Inside, Alvantes briefly summarised the events of the last few days, avoiding most of our time in Ans

Pasaeda and touching only lightly on our run-in with Guiso Lupa. His impatience for news was palpable, and I could see Navare recognised it too.

"Our men haven't been discovered," Navare said, "though there've been a couple of close calls, all right. Three times now, Mounteban's sent men to check the barracks. Fortunately, they had scouts out, and got hidden in time. He's also had his thugs hunting through the Suburbs. He calls them 'inspections'."

"But they haven't found anyone," Alvantes said – more to himself than as a question.

"No. Well, not until now, anyway."

Alvantes let the implied criticism slide. "What about the situation inside the city? No one's tried to move against Mounteban?"

"He has things locked down tight," Navare replied. "He's lost ground in a few areas – some of the families, the ones who rely most on trade, are furious the gates are still closed. I think it's thrown his nerve, knowing we're out here, but not knowing where. On everything else, though, word is the families are toeing his line. Mounteban's been making all the right promises… and he's kept a fair few of them too."

"How can he, with the city still shut off?" inserted Estrada.

"Well, there's the thing," said Navare. "Lupa wasn't alone. Mounteban's been sending agents out to all the towns and the larger villages. Most times it's one of his lackeys, but a couple of the families have gone over wholeheartedly to his cause now. I heard a rumour Lord Eldunzi's set himself up in Muena Delorca."

"Eldunzi?" I laughed. "He couldn't run a free water stand in a drought."

Alvantes looked at me with surprise. "You know Eldunzi?"

I realised I never had told the full story of my adventures in Altapasaeda. "We passed a little time together," I said. "It didn't end well. The man has a big mouth."

"That's one of the kinder things the Muena Delorcans have been saying," agreed Navare.

"Whatever Mounteban might have set up elsewhere," put in Alvantes, "the problem stays the same. Chop off the head and kill the body. None of this will hold together with him gone."

"You have an idea?" The hope in Navare's voice betrayed the strain he'd waited under these last days.

"Not me," Alvantes said. "Damasco thinks he can get us inside."

I flushed – partly with modesty, more with a thrill of horror at the thought of what I'd somehow got myself into. "Getting in will be the easy part," I said.

I realised Navare was staring at me expectantly. The heat in my cheeks deepened. Planning was one thing, taking part another, but being pushed into the role of leader was more than I'd ever bargained for.

Then again… it *was* my plan.

"All right," I said, "here's how we begin."

Time was crucial. Darkness was one of the few things on our side, and we'd likely only have a single night before Mounteban concocted a scheme against the giants or shored up his defences.

Navare set out minutes later to summon our forces waiting at the barracks. We would need them in the morning, and a little extra manpower wouldn't hurt in the meantime. Soon after he'd left, Estrada announced her intention to speak with Saltlick and the giants.

"You should get some rest, Easie," she told me.

The idea seemed preposterous. Then again, there was nothing I could do for the next few hours. I sat at the end of Navare's narrow cot bed and closed my eyes.

The next I knew, I was waking to the sound of pounding upon the door. I watched Alvantes cross to it, listen carefully and then draw it wide. Outside, Navare stood flanked by half a dozen figures in hooded travel cloaks. I vaguely recognised them from amongst the Altapasaedan guardsmen; as they strode inside, I caught flashes of the uniforms they wore beneath their cloaks. Tonight they'd be acting in their official capacity for the first time in weeks, and I suspected that fact meant a lot to them.

A few minutes later, the door nearly shivered off its hinges, with a crack like muffled thunder. My first thought was a battering ram; when the blow wasn't repeated, I realised the truth. Someone else was knocking, and only one person I knew could knock like that.

Alvantes opened the door to reveal Saltlick squatted on his haunches, with Estrada stood beside him.

"Ready," Saltlick rumbled, as if concluding a conversation started long since.

Alvantes's only reply was a nod to his men. Together, they trooped into the night, Saltlick falling in behind.

Estrada slipped inside and drew a chair from the room's small table. We sat in tense silence – until the first sounds of banging and clattering began a few minutes later.

"It's started," she said.

I nodded. "No going back now," I added – and wondered how true that was.

For my plan to work, it was vital Mounteban know the giants were coming. For all that there were similarities, invading Altapasaeda wasn't a sly housebreaking in the depths of the night. The last thing it required was discretion. Only when I'd fully accepted those facts had the last details swum into focus.

To anyone watching, the events taking place in the streets of the Suburbs over those next few hours would have looked much like the preparations for a war – a war of giant proportions. Estrada and I sat listening, far past the hope of sleep. I had a fair conception of what was going on outside. It had been my idea, after all. Still, just listening to the jarring shocks of noise from all around gouged at my nerves.

I remembered my first sight of Saltlick, hunched in shadow, a monstrous living sculpture carved from the fire-lit darkness. I remembered how I'd watched the giants fight at Moaradrid's behest, their colossal forms indistinct amidst the rain and the half-light of sunrise. Unless his agents were blind and deaf, Mounteban knew the giants were coming. I thought about how on edge he must be by now, desperately struggling to keep control over frightened minions – and I couldn't but smile.

My smile sagged. The night was almost done. It would be my turn soon enough.

Estrada must have caught my expression. "You really don't have to do this, you know," she said. "Any one of Alvantes's men could go in your place."

"I don't, do I?" Somewhere in the excitement of the last few hours, I'd managed to forget that simple fact.

A knock on the door nearly separated me from my skin. When Estrada opened it to reveal Alvantes and Navare, I wasn't sure if I should feel relieved. Was their arrival a reprieve or the last stick for my funeral pyre?

"The giants are ready," Alvantes said. "The remainder of the guard and the Irregulars have their orders. We're going to get into place now. Then it's up to you, Damasco."

I barely suppressed a shudder. "About that…"

I'd seen scorn for me so many times in Alvantes's eyes that I was astonished to realise it bothered me now. I'd certainly never felt the need to defend myself to him. Yet this time, I was actually frustrated when Estrada put in on my behalf, "I was just telling Damasco that he doesn't *have* to do this."

As Alvantes considered, he pointedly looked at Estrada rather than me. "No. I suppose he doesn't."

"If we're risking our lives," she added, "we should be sure we're doing it for the right reasons."

Now it was Alvantes's turn to be defensive. "This is the right thing to do."

"We're all agreed on that. Still, it shouldn't be for revenge. Not anger either. And definitely not for some king who let his family squabbles get out of control."

Well, I thought, that's all of Alvantes's motives out then. Then I registered those closing words. "Family squabble?" I said.

"You know what I mean," she replied. "If it hadn't been for Moaradrid..."

"I understand how this is *Moaradrid's* fault. The invasion, turning the Castoval upside down, kidnapping the giants, I know all about that. And I'm hardly the King's greatest supporter; but I don't see how..."

Estrada's eyes widened. "Wait. Damasco, are you really saying... you *don't* know, do you?"

"Unless you tell me what you're talking about," I said, exasperated, "how can I tell you what I do or don't know?"

"But what did you think it's all been about?"

"What *what* was about?"

The disbelief in Estrada's face came close to awe, as though she'd stumbled across a level of ignorance she could never have imagined. "He was Panchessa's son, Easie."

Alvantes's face clouded. "It was never proved."

"He was Panchessa's son," she said. "Everyone knew it."

"Who was..."

"Panchessa was stupid and irresponsible. Instead of owning up to what he'd done, he let his mistake fester into a civil war. Damn it, Lunto, don't you dare defend a king who ordered your father's death!"

"How did you know..."

"Wait," I bellowed. "Wait, wait, wait! Are you saying Moaradrid... that the King... are you saying *Moaradrid* was Panchessa's son?"

Finally, both Estrada and Alvantes paid me a little of the attention they'd been reserving for each other. "There were rumours," said Alvantes, almost apologetically. Catching Estrada's eye, he added, "And they were most likely true. In his youth, before he assumed the throne, Panchessa spent some time in the far north – and with a certain chieftain's daughter. He denied it later, of course, and the Court backed him to the hilt. But it turned out Moaradrid was one indiscretion that wouldn't be ignored."

"Hold on... this is ridiculous! It makes no sense."

Yet even as I said it, a part of my mind was busily cataloguing the ways in which it made perfect sense. Stray moments came back to me, cast in an entirely new light. I thought of Moaradrid calling Prince Panchetto brother when I first saw them together, how I'd mistaken it for irony – just as I'd misinterpreted Panchessa's careless mention of his sons. I thought of Moaradrid's barely pent-up rage at the King, which I'd taken for mere tyrannical craziness.

Well, he had been tyrannical and he'd certainly been crazy, but as the disowned bastard of a horse's testicle like Panchessa, I could see why he might have been a little righteously indignant. It was as if a distorted mirror had been held up to my image of the past few weeks, throwing it in strange new shapes, demanding I reconsider every small aspect to see what might have changed. Would I have made the same decisions?

Would I have struggled so hard against Moaradrid if I'd known his true motives?

I couldn't think about it. Not now. Not when there were other questions a hundred times more immediate. Like… "What about Mounteban?" I asked.

Caught off guard, Estrada asked, "What do you mean?"

"I mean, is he related to the King? A distant cousin, maybe? An uncle on the mother's side?"

"Of course not."

"Is he related to *anyone?* Alvantes, tell me he's not secretly your disowned half-brother."

The look Alvantes turned on me would have curdled new milk.

"Well then," I said, "I can't speak for anyone else – and maybe it's not so right or proper – but my motive is wanting to make sure that bloated snake gets his due."

After so much heated discussion, the hush following my proclamation lay heavy. Had I gone too far? Was the truth too unheroic for the likes of Estrada and Alvantes? It was Navare who eventually broke the silence. "He has a point," he said.

Alvantes gave a tentative half nod. "Mounteban's had it coming for far too long."

Estrada sighed. "You men."

"You have to admit…"

"Yes," she said, with a wry smile, "I'd like to see that arrogant bully lose a few teeth before the day's out."

I couldn't say if Alvantes looked more shocked or impressed.

"But it's *also* the right thing to do," she added.

"Agreed."

Navare turned back to me. "So, Damasco – you still haven't told us how you plan to get back into the city."

"Oh. Right," I said. "Getting into Altapasaeda."

Damn it. Amidst the unexpected history lessons and the talk of Mounteban's well-earned kicking, I'd just about managed to forget that part. Now that I thought, there was another crucial detail I'd neglected too.

"The thing is… I'm going to need to borrow some knives."

Scrambling onto the roof of the shanty was hard enough. Since my brief and rapidly descending last visit, it had been crudely patched with boards that wouldn't have supported a starved cat. I kept close to the edge, clung to the wall, and wished I didn't have to perform so hazardous a task in near-absolute darkness.

Reaching the rope, I shifted my weight onto it. I still couldn't quite believe it was still here. Granted, it was invisible from above, and hardly noticeable from below, but still it was hard to accept that so many days had passed without one of Mounteban's lackeys paying sufficient notice to have it cut down. One thing was for sure, it would never have happened on Alvantes's watch.

I looked up at what I had to climb – and up, and up. For a moment, my head and knees turned to jelly and swapped places.

I'd done this sort of thing once or twice in my criminal heyday. That didn't mean I'd ever been much good at it. I'd known men who claimed climbing a rope was no great endeavour, that there were techniques to make it easy as walking. I'd called those men liars, though rarely to their faces. In my experience, its ease could be roughly compared with nailing a rabid dog to a live bear.

At least experience told me the shack would probably break my fall.

Beginning to climb, I found it every bit as hard as I'd expected. I'd barely covered any distance before the strength in my arms had ebbed to nothing and my shoulders felt ready to tear from their sockets. All I had in my favour was that the wall was uneven enough for me to swing close, dig my toes into a gap and rest a little that way. Franco had done right by me, at least. It was a fine rope, and without the weight of my body dragging, my fingers almost clung to it of their own accord.

I found I could progress by rationing my strength and climbing in short bursts. Slowly, my confidence and what little technique I'd ever learned began to return. If nothing else, I knew better than to look down. Down meant hideous dizziness and the sure potential for broken bones. Down was the past; up was my future.

I climbed. I rested. I climbed. Rested. Climbed.

I was concentrating so intently on the top of the tower, where the grapnel was lodged, that the wall walk came on me unexpectedly. I hadn't dared imagine I was so close to my goal. Yet a little higher, a little slower on the uptake, and I'd have been visible to anyone patrolling.

I hugged the wall once more and strained to listen. As far as I could judge, there was no one directly above. There was no point waiting for a better opportunity. Gripping with my right hand and all my might, I let go with my left and drew out the first of the short, flat-bladed knives I had stashed in my belt. I hunted for a suitable patch of mortar, eyes struggling against the darkness. Eventually I thought I'd found a point where the blocks fit badly, creating a wider gap of weather-scoured mortar. I jammed the knife's tip in as far as it would go, wincing at the ring of metal on stone. Not pausing to check if anyone had heard, I laboured to drive the blade further in.

Satisfied, I returned my free hand to the rope. I climbed an arm's length higher, enough that I could angle a leg up and rest my foot on the protruding knife hilt. I reached for another knife, hunted another gap, jabbed this one at shoulder height. Switching hands, I added a third on my opposite side. Finally, using the lowest knife as a foothold and the leftmost as a handhold, I reached over to hammer in a fourth, low as I could reach.

The result was an off-kilter square, just below the summit of the wall.

Of everything my misconceived plan involved, I'd dreaded this part most. Yet what else could I do? It *had* to be just after dawn, I was sure of that much – Moaradrid might have been a madman with chronic paternal issues, but he'd understood what made the giants terrifying. Then, once it started, I'd have a few minutes at most. I couldn't possibly have climbed the entire wall and done everything else that lay ahead in so short a time.

Meanwhile, trying to ascend the last distance would mean passing directly into the view of anyone watching from the wall. Even in my dark garb, it was too great a chance to take. At least, thanks to the knives, I had holds. I only had to hang on for a short while. How hard could that be?

My hands were first to lose their feeling.

Terrifying as that was, I found I could brace against the wall with my feet and calves. Though they felt like clods of meat, my numbed hands still kept me in place, aided by the rope, which I'd managed to loop round my wrists. If I could only stay like that, I'd be all right.

Only, the numbness was spreading. It seemed so much colder up there on the wall than it had been on the ground. The wind flailed across me, dipping icy fingers inside my cloak. Slowly but certainly, it found the flesh of my wrists, my forearms. In its wake came the prickle of pins and needles – and then, far worse, no feeling at all.

I pressed against the stone, concentrating every speck of strength I had left into holding myself in place. Even as I did it, I knew it wouldn't be enough. It was too cold. I was too worn out by my climb. With nothing to distract me, time was passing at the barest crawl. How could I hang on when every minute seemed an hour?

Sooner or later – and I knew it would be sooner – some vital muscle would succumb to the creeping chill. Then the only question would be whether I had feeling left in whichever part of me hit the ground first.

At first, I thought the sound was my own heartbeat shuddering in my ears.

Only, why would my heartbeat be coming from behind me? With utmost care, I shifted my weight to the rope, sending shivers of painful life back into my hands. Once I was fairly sure I wouldn't just plummet, I began to twist around, manoeuvring until my back was to the wall. There ahead lay the Suburbs, sketched in deep shades of grey beneath me.

I'd hardly dared hope. But I'd been right. The giants were coming.

From my vantage point, I could make them out easily. They were approaching through a particularly derelict region of the Suburbs, and they towered head and shoulders above the crumpled shacks. I found my numb face could manage a thin smile. That was a nice touch on Saltlick's part.

A choked shout sounded from close above me. Others followed close behind, from all along the northern wall. I wasn't surprised to make out the word "giants" over and over, along with an impressive amount of cursing.

I could see the giants clearly by then, as I was sure those watching above me could. They'd certainly been busy in the Suburbs. In broad daylight, I'd have easily recognised their helmets as cooking pans and cauldrons, their clubs as broken timbers, their armour as a patchwork of cloth and loose-tied boards scrounged from deserted shacks. In that tricky dawn gloom, though? It made the illusion real. The giants looked nothing like friendly behemoths clad in carnival gear of looted junk. They were armoured monsters, fearsome and implacable.

What made the effect all the more believable was that I could hear the giants clearly too. For every one of Mounteban's men who cried out above me, a giant bellowed incoherently below. On my instruction, they were keeping to meaningless roars or shouting in their own clipped language. It was hard to say which was more alarming.

They were putting on quite a show; if I hadn't been nine-tenths numb and suspended from a wall, I might have laughed. For Mounteban's lackeys, the effect was anything but humorous. I could hear the rising terror in their exclamations – and increasingly, the shouts were joined by the clatter of running footsteps. Just as I'd hoped, they were running away from me.

I gave it another few seconds, as long as my rapidly failing grip would stand. There was always the chance someone would have sense enough to remain on lookout, but it was a risk I had to take. Steeling myself, I began to climb once more. Though I was sure my cold limbs would fail me, that my numbed fingers would lose their hold, somehow they didn't. It took me less than a minute to reach the height of the battlements to my left.

Treading sideways against the stone, I managed to swing a little, to hook a foot into a gap. I used that foot to drag myself over and then lashed out a hand for the edge of the tower. With foot and hand together, I pulled myself further, until, with a leg and arm anchored, I could haul myself the last way. I flopped onto the walkway.

Had there been anyone between the next tower and me, they couldn't have failed to see me. There wasn't. Sure enough, all their attention was absorbed with repelling the imminent assault. How were they to know it was a sham? I didn't doubt Mounteban would have put out word that the giants wouldn't hurt a fly, but who would believe Mounteban's word over their own eyes? Nobody who didn't know them could look at those vast figures, lurching through the shadowed streets, and see anything but monsters set to tear the city down brick by brick.

They'd know differently soon enough. Once the fighting began, even the most fear-blinded defenders would realise it was entirely one-sided. Time was already running out. I had to move.

I pitched to my feet, slumped hard against the parapet, managed to steady myself and keep going. Halfway to the next tower, stairs led down. I took them three at a time. All the while, I strove to prepare myself. Just because this section of wall had been abandoned that didn't mean the gate would be unguarded. If it was, I was defenceless, the only weapons I'd thought to bring still embedded in the wall behind me. Why could I never hang onto a knife for more than ten minutes?

I reached the base of the stairs without slowing. The gatehouse was beyond the next tower, hidden from view. The racket behind me was increasing second by second, the confusion of yelled warnings and barked orders becoming louder and more hysterical, mixing with a building tremor of feet and hooves. Over it all, the roars of the giants massed like a great black cloud, ominous of the storm to come.

As the pitch of the chaos behind me heightened to ear-splitting levels, the tower loomed in my view. A stitch was flaring in my not-quite-thawed side. How could this ever have seemed a good idea? I was on the verge of collapse, sprinting straight into a trap – one of my own design.

I ran on. It was a trap I'd already sprung, for I had nowhere else to go. Anyway, I still had a tongue in my head, didn't I? Even if I couldn't fight, perhaps I could still bluff.

I slowed, struggling to gather my thoughts, to re-cover a little breath. I was barely trotting by the time I passed the corner of the tower, my mouth already working with the beginnings of a speech that would surely end in my pleading for my life.

The gate was undefended.

I was almost disappointed – but that passed quickly enough. Ignoring the main gate, I stumbled to the small side door set in one side. It was secured by a bar, which I dragged off, and a heavy metal latch that I heaved open. The door swung inward on well-oiled hinges.

I could only see a darkened street at first, barely il-luminated by the mealy morning light. Then, from one particularly lightless alleyway, a cluster of figures hurried forward. I recognised Alvantes, Navare and Estrada; the other half-dozen, hoods drawn up, would be Alvantes's hand-picked guardsmen.

"You made it," whispered Navare.

He sounded more surprised than I'd have liked. "Of course," I hissed, at a less judicious volume that drew a scowl from Alvantes.

All of them were dressed in heavy cloaks of various dark shades. We'd look suspicious, but given what else was going on, it might take more than suspicion for anyone to stop us. However, the giants' distraction could only be drawn out for so long. Alvantes had talked of their battering the gates down, but I'd strictly vetoed that – for once the giants were inside, confronted by Mounteban's teeming forces, casualties would be inevitable. The moment our bluff was exposed, they'd be defenceless.

In fact, was it my imagination, or was the tone of the shouting already beginning to change?

"This way," I hissed.

I dashed a little way down the main road that ran within the walls, feeling horribly exposed, ducked gratefully into a covered alley. With a little of my breath back, I managed a pace just shy of a run, the others keeping close behind me. I zigged and zagged through one lane and passage after another, heading roughly towards the Market District, all the while listening for clues to how the giants were faring.

I was certain cheers of exultation were beginning to replace the defenders' frantic cries. Saltlick's instructions were to withdraw the instant they were in real jeopardy. If our diversion wasn't already done for, it would be soon.

At least our first destination was close. Hurrying past familiar landmarks, I saw the particular dead-end street I was looking for, with its tumbledown houses and one door sturdier than those around it. I paced the last distance, wheezing like an old hound, palming sweat from my forehead. I paused just long enough to be sure I could speak actual words and hammered four weak blows upon the wood.

Part of me doubted he'd even open up. But that wasn't Franco's way. If assassins ever came for him, he'd be selling them better knives before they were halfway across the threshold.

Sure enough, the hatch in the door slid open, to reveal familiar, wrinkle-set eyes. "Oh, gods," came a voice from the other side, "not you. Not here. Not *now*."

"A minute of your time, Franco," I said.

The hatch thumped shut.

Long moments passed. Then, its very motion speaking of reluctance, the door edged open. Franco stood in the gap, gaze moving from face to shadowed face. "Guard-Captain?" he asked, squinting at Alvantes. "You're back? I assure you, whatever that wretch has said, this is a reputable abode."

"That's not my concern," replied Alvantes. "Nor will it ever be… if you help us now. We're here for Mounteban. Tell us where he's hiding."

"Hiding? He's hardly hiding!" Franco paused to consider. "Still, I doubt you're the sort of guests he's hoping for. Sorry, Guard-Captain, you'll have to find him by yourself."

"Franco," I said, "help us and you won't have anything to fear from Mounteban. He's not going to be a threat in Altapasaeda for much longer."

"Do you really expect me to believe this little band of yours can roust that fat old wolf?" Franco glanced past my shoulder to add, "No offence, Guard-Captain."

"None taken," replied Alvantes, unexpected amusement in his voice. "However, I'd be neglecting my duty if I didn't point out that once we're done with Mounteban, I'll be coming straight back here to arrest you for complicity."

"With all the respect in the world, that's only a threat if I thought you had a chance."

Alvantes's granite face gave nothing away. "That's true."

"Which I *don't*."

"So you've made clear."

"That's right, I have. So why don't you go find someone else to intimidate?"

"Oh, this isn't intimidation." Alvantes tapped his forehead in mock salute. "I'm saving that for next time. Be seeing you, Franco."

He turned away. Wanting to point out that there were a hundred and one things we could try to loosen Franco's tongue, I had to remind myself Alvantes had been in this game a lot longer than I had. I hurried after.

We'd hardly made a dozen paces when Franco called after, his voice low and somewhat squeaky, "And they'll tell you the same thing in the Dancing Cat." Then his door slammed closed.

Alvantes stopped and turned back to us. "We're in luck. That's barely ten minutes from here. Everyone ready?"

Navare and the guardsmen nodded without hesitation. So did Estrada. That left only me. Was I ready? Of course I wasn't. Maybe my attitude to placing myself in unfeasible danger had been modified a little in recent weeks, but fighting was another matter altogether. And fighting the very cream of Mounteban's thugs, no doubt armed with all the sharpest and most generally lethal weapons in the city?

I wasn't ready. I'd never be ready for something like this.

"Let's just get it over with," I said.

Alvantes caught my eye – and did I see the faintest flash of something that might conceivably have been respect? Then his gaze darted once more across the gathered faces, weighing each of his men, lingering lastly on Estrada.

"All right. Like the man said… let's finish this."

CHAPTER TWENTY/TWO

The city had grown quiet, at least compared with its earlier uproar. As we skulked through the alleys, the fact of the giants' withdrawal became more evident with each passing moment.

Saltlick's instruction had been to disguise their retreat until the very last instant. With Mounteban's ragtag defenders already panicking, any movement on the giants' part was bound to look like a ruse at first, and to send them into further fits of alarm. Increasingly, though, the shouts that drifted to us over the rooftops of Altapasaeda had one note in common: exultation. By the time we drew close to the Dancing Cat, there was no question of it. The distant clamour had settled to the gleeful celebration of men who believed they'd somehow managed to drive monsters back from their walls.

Soon enough it must occur to them that so half-hearted an attack looked a lot like a diversion. How long after that before someone thought to wonder what they were being diverted from? And if anyone were too quick to draw those obvious conclusions, it would go very badly for us.

Lucky then that we had one last card up our sleeve.

Another uproar arose to the west. Though fainter this time, drawn thin by distance, in all other respects it sounded much like the last uproar. Its base rhythm was of hoof beats, a great many. Its high notes were two screams in close succession, followed by distant thuds. If I'd had to guess, I'd have identified those as the last moments of two men falling from on high, probably with arrows stuck in them for good measure.

To anyone curious as to what they'd just been encouraged not to see, here was an appropriate answer: Altapasaedan guardsmen mounted on any horse they could beg or borrow, and Castovalian Irregulars with crude battering rams, all charging hard upon the western gate.

What had I told Alvantes, back in Paen Acha? *The trick with misdirection is to give them something they expect. If they expect to find something and do, nine times in ten they'll stop looking.* Who would have guessed thievery and military strategy had so much in common?

The timing was perfect. Across the street from the alley mouth we'd reached stood the Dancing Cat, a high-class tavern of considerable repute tucked in the band of well-off streets between the upper Market District and the mansions of the South Bank.

It was a long way from Mounteban's previous haunt, the Red-Eyed Dog, in every sense. Yet I found something amusing in the fact that even with an entire city at his fingertips, Mounteban couldn't shake free of old habits. He could have set himself up in any mansion he fancied, perhaps even the palace itself. Nevertheless, here he was, skulking in the back rooms of an inn like the gangster he would always remain at heart.

There were thugs on the door, of course. It wouldn't have been Mounteban without thugs. While their presence was undoubtedly off-putting, at least they provided reassurance that we were in the right place. In addition, they both looked more than a little nervous. If Mounteban's best men were close to soiling their undergarments, there was hope yet.

One, I realised, was the former bouncer of the Red-Eyed Dog, who I'd stabbed in the leg on my last visit. He obviously hadn't taken that reversal of fortunes as a sign he was in the wrong career.

Perhaps there was time to educate him yet.

I sauntered into the street. "Good evening. I'm looking for a washed-up crime boss posing as a politician. Could either of you gentlemen point me in the right direction?"

The former bouncer reacted before his colleague. He looked surprised at first, then relieved. Whatever terrors he'd been expecting, one lone and skinny thief wasn't amongst them. By the time he was halfway to me his expression had made its way round to anger, of a very personal sort. He'd finally recognised this particular skinny thief.

"You'd know if you saw him," I said. "He gets uglier and fatter by the day. Though he's still not quite so fat or ugly as your..."

The sentence choked in my throat, as the cudgel he'd wielded all those days ago materialised from the folds of his cloak. Its length about halved the distance between us. I tried for a step backward and found my feet more interested in pitching me onto my backside. I hurled my arms up instinctively.

That was a shame, because I almost missed Alvantes cold-cocking the one-time bouncer. It was a perfectly neat blow, the hilt of Alvantes's sword connecting cleanly with the side of his head, and it sent the large man crashing sideways like a bag of grit.

His companion, lagging a little way behind, reacted with astonishing speed. Quicker than I could follow, he had his sword in hand and much of the space to Alvantes already covered. I might have been worried, were it not for Navare keeping silent pace behind him. Still, Navare left it a little longer than I'd have liked before he too struck down his mark, with a sharp tap to the nape of his neck. The second thug went plummeting, to land neatly beside his partner.

"You took your time," I pointed out.

"Into the alley with them," hissed Alvantes, ignoring me in favour of the guardsmen lurking in the shadowed thoroughfare behind us. They swarmed round, hoisted the two prone bodies and were gone like a moon shadow.

"When you said distract them," I added, "I didn't realise you meant by letting them cave my head in."

"You're not dead. We were quick enough."

I had to concede that point. In truth, I knew it was only nerves making me argumentative. Alvantes and

Navare had worked their way round through the side streets as quickly as I could have hoped. Everything had gone smoothly. But this had been the easy part. Even getting into the city had been the easy part, compared with what came next.

Behind the grim, black-panelled door of the Dancing Cat? *That* was the hard part.

"Marina," said Alvantes, "you'll stay here. You too, Godares," he added, signalling one of the guardsmen. "Stay out of sight. Watch for anyone leaving and mark their direction, but don't follow. No arguments."

Even by Alvantes's standards, his tone was rigid. Estrada had the sense merely to nod her agreement.

"So do we have a plan?" I asked him.

"Absolutely," he said.

Alvantes set out at a march towards the door, beckoning his men to fall in around him. By the time I realised this wasn't a prelude to the plan but the plan itself, he was running straight at it. His shoulder struck with a colossal, teeth-rattling thud that rebounded him into the street. Unfazed, he charged again, and again. The door quivered like jelly. On the fourth blow, it sprang inward.

I'd seen Alvantes fight often enough. The Boar of Altapasaeda was strong as his namesake. It wasn't his strength that had done the trick this time, however. A thickset man in a leather jerkin had torn the door open, and held a great club at the ready. It was meant as an ambush – and it might have worked had Alvantes hesitated for even an instant. By the time the door opened he was already halfway through it, and by the time the thickset man realised, Alvantes was through him too. The impact hurled him halfway across the room within, and Alvantes didn't even slow.

His guardsmen were at his heels – and for all I didn't want to be, I was at theirs. I felt like flotsam caught in their wake. Turning back now was impossible.

Close as I was, I couldn't believe how rapidly events had developed inside the Dancing Cat. I was looking at a war boiled to its essence, crammed into a single room. The air was thick with shouts and the clang of blade on blade. Alvantes's handpicked guardsmen had thrown themselves without pause into the combat. Mounteban's handpicked protectors had been ready and waiting. Our side was outnumbered; but in the confines of the densely furnished taproom, they were close-matched.

The result was a crescent of violence spreading from the doorway. At its farthest point, I watched Alvantes smash his hilt into the nose of a bald heavy, kick him aside as the other crumpled to his knees – and then roar, "Where's Mounteban?"

The man was a whirlwind. I was entranced. So much so that I didn't notice the thug to my right until it was almost too late. Improbably, his weapon of choice for the cramped space was a double-headed axe. I barely ducked aside. If there hadn't been a table to roll beneath, even that wouldn't have saved me. As it was, the axe blade plunged deep into the wood and through its underside, ending a finger's breadth from my nose.

Crawling on my back, I came up hard against an unseen chair – until someone tumbled into it, driving both table and me halfway across the room. I pushed on through the wreckage of the now-demolished chair, catching a broken-off leg as I passed. Staggering upright, I swung it around me, not caring who or what I hit so long as I cleared a little space.

There was another table ahead, so I hopped up onto it. From that vantage, I had just time to absorb the carnage about me. Already, half the combatants were out of the fight, curled on the floor nursing wounds or not moving at all. That still left more than a dozen men locked in flailing violence – not least Alvantes, fencing at absurdly close quarters with an ugly brute near the base of the staircase ahead.

The sea of combat closed in. The only way out was those stairs. Abandoning my chair leg, I gathered myself and leapt, catching the steep-angled banister with both hands – not a moment too soon, as one of Mounteban's thugs tumbled, thrashing, across the table where I'd been, demolishing it to matchwood.

I swung over the banister. At the sound of my clumsy landing, Alvantes's assailant couldn't help but pivot to look at me. Alvantes took the opportunity to rake his blade across the brute's legs. The man's face contorted, though no noise came. He reeled down the stairs towards Alvantes, who deftly sidestepped, back against the wall.

His gaze passed over me; his eyes flashed a warning. I crouched instinctively, threw my weight left and upward, and crashed into the shins of my unseen foe. He tumbled past – but not without carrying me with him. Together, we rolled in a knot of grunts and curses that ended in the sharp crack of his head against the floor tiles.

I looked up to see Alvantes stepping over me. Shrugging through the hanging that led into the inn's back rooms, he bellowed, "Mounteban! Face me!"

I dragged myself to my feet. Given the choice between taking my chances amidst the still-raging combat and following Alvantes, who seemed deadly and invulnerable as a landslide, I hurriedly chose the latter. I dashed through the curtain to find a long, low kitchen with a vast hearth at one end. Alvantes was already pushing through another door, and I hurried to catch up. Beyond was a sizeable coach yard, closed by the L-shaped wings of the inn and two opposing walls, with wide gates standing open on its farthest side. The yard's most notable features were the brewer's cart - drawn up against the building and recently unloaded, if the hastily stacked barrels beside it were anything to go by - and the small crowd gathered in and round the vehicle.

In the back of the cart stood Castilio Mounteban.

He hadn't yet noticed our arrival. His attention was all on the wing of the inn behind him. The stables there extended further into the yard than the rest of the building and bore their own shallow roof. Upon that roof, Guiso Lupa was shuffling towards the edge with a look of deepest terror on his face. Behind him, I could see where a double window had been smashed entirely out of its frame, along with much of the accompanying masonry.

It was clear what must have happened. Cornered on the higher floor, the only stairs cut off, Mounteban had been forced to improvise an escape route. Had he chosen a more agile lieutenant or been quicker to abandon the one he had, he'd be gone by now.

Instead, we'd caught up with him. Which was all well and good, except that "we" meant Alvantes and me, and Mounteban still had half a dozen bodyguards around him. We were hopelessly outnumbered.

If Alvantes had noticed that fact, he was hiding it well. "No more running, Mounteban!" he bellowed.

Mounteban, in turn, showed no hint of surprise at our appearance. "Who's running?" he cried back – and before anyone could point out the obvious answer, he'd leapt from the cart and dragged his sword free of its scabbard. "Come on then, Boar. We've put this off for long enough."

Both men strode to close the gap between them, mutual hatred in their every movement. Only a half-dozen paces separated them when a cataclysmic crash resounded in the distance. Everyone froze in place; all eyes turned at the massive noise. No one failed to flinch, not even Mounteban or Alvantes, when it was followed by another, another and another – ten detonations in all, ending in a crack like a sky-load of thunder, which rolled and rolled and rolled.

Then Mounteban struck.

It was a wild, inelegant blow, and no less dangerous for that. He'd evidently hoped to catch Alvantes off guard – and it seemed he had. Alvantes's posture was clumsy, his stance half-formed.

Only at the last instant did I recognise his feint for what it was. Alvantes slid Mounteban's blade expertly across his own, before twisting his own sword up towards Mounteban's throat. Mounteban only saved himself by a leap backwards, with athleticism that should have been impossible for a man of his dimensions.

"Did you hope it would be easy?" Alvantes curled his sword point in a complex gesture halfway between threat and salute. If one-handedness had ever impeded his skill, that time had passed.

Mounteban, for his part, finally looked shaken. Perhaps he'd been counting on Alvantes's disability to even the odds. When a couple of his men drew nearer, however, he raised a hand. "This is between us."

The question of whether they'd have obeyed became irrelevant just then, as Navare appeared in the doorway behind us, four guardsmen close on his heels. Blood was dripping down Navare's face from above the hairline, ghastly against the puckered whiteness of the scarring there, and all the guardsmen sported equally apparent injuries – but no one could have doubted they were ready to fight on.

Mounteban's one advantage was gone. His expression shifted to something like acceptance, as he gripped the hilt of his long scimitar with both hands. Three steps bridged the distance between them, and Mounteban swung with all his considerable strength.

Alvantes blocked, with less flourish this time. The blow rang like a bell breaking. Maybe Mounteban still had an edge after all; one-handed, Alvantes couldn't absorb the force of such attacks.

Then again, maybe he didn't need to. When Mounteban tried the same move again, Alvantes slipped smoothly aside. He was a large man, but positively waiflike in comparison with Mounteban. When Alvantes countered with a raking slash, Mounteban just barely edged the blade aside with his own.

I'd been thinking it would come down to strength against speed. But Alvantes was the infinitely better swordsman – and he was no longer defending. This time, he struck first, and with precision. He aimed high, for Mounteban's head. Mounteban caught it with ease, but another blow followed straight away, and another. Faster and faster, Alvantes's blade coiled – high and then low, to left and right, and then in no pattern at all. Each time, Mounteban deflected by a slighter margin. He was losing ground – and there was only wall behind him.

Alvantes drew blood for the first time. It was only a nick, and Mounteban didn't cry out, only gritted his teeth. But Alvantes inflicted it with such casual ease that it was clear he could have done worse had he wanted to. He was sure of himself now. He didn't need to rush.

Mounteban must have reached a similar conclusion. When the next blow came, he blocked in the clumsiest fashion imaginable, throwing his blade across his body like a shield. Rather than retreat or dodge, he shoved forward instead. Taking the full shock of the impact, snarling against it, he pushed on, not giving Alvantes a moment to recover. Then, with a howl of fury, Mounteban threw all his momentum into a great swing. Still he refused to slow, nor to pull back when Alvantes blocked. Rather, he hurled his weight behind his leading arm, turning the clumsy assault into a barge.

On and on he pressed, until Alvantes couldn't help but stagger. I'd been right after all; one-handed, he couldn't defend against sheer brute force. It was hard to see how he was even keeping to his feet. One slip and Mounteban's sword would crush his skull like a blown egg.

Alvantes wavered, struggled to steady himself, all the while back-treading before Mounteban's ceaseless advance. It was hopeless. His balance was gone, and all his fighting poise. Only stubbornness had held him up this long.

Then, even as he began to fall, Alvantes did the one thing I hadn't seen coming. He smashed the stump of his handless arm into Mounteban's jaw.

Pain scorched across Alvantes's face like fire – but it did the trick. Mounteban staggered aside, fingers flying to his bloodied lip. Almost within striking distance of each other, the two stood gasping.

"Stop this!"

All eyes were drawn inexorably to the courtyard's gateway – and to Estrada, who stood in the gap there. Beside her, the guardsman Godares glanced apologetically towards Alvantes.

Again, calm but adamantine, Estrada shouted, "Stop it, the pair of you."

"Keep out of this, Marina." There was urgency in Alvantes's voice.

Ignoring him, Estrada addressed herself to Mounteban instead. "You must realise you can't win, Castilio."

Mounteban took a step back from Alvantes, his sword levelled. "Can't win? I can't possibly lose, Marina. You're bluffing and you know it."

"Put your sword down," Estrada told him. "You won't be harmed."

"Ha! The streets of Altapasaeda are thick with my men. They'll be here at any moment. If you kill me, you'll never make it out alive. If you capture me, you can't hold me."

"Give it up… this whole mad plot of yours. Come back to Muena Palaiya. Go back to your bar. Help me repair the damage that creature of yours did to our town." She flashed a glance of utter hate at Lupa, who almost lost his grip on the rooftop as his face flushed with fear.

"Is that your proposal?" asked Mounteban. "Then here's mine. Alvantes, the offer I passed you through Lupa was meant in earnest. Altapasaeda needs a city guard, and no one will ever trust me to provide it."

"My first act as Guard-Captain would be to have your head for treason."

"Then you're a damn fool. What about you, Marina? I'll give you Muena Palaiya back, and no Lupa this time. That was always my intention anyway, once you'd had time to adjust to our new Castoval. Why can't the pair of you listen to sense? Everything can return to the way it was – but better this time, and in *our* hands."

Estrada made no attempt to hide her disgust. "You've made yourself into a tyrant. How could you ever imagine I'd work with you?"

"Oh, Marina. *I'm* a tyrant? Not that brat Panchetto, who bled this city dry to overload his tables? Not his parasite father, the King who's never cared one whit for his subjects? All I've done is make the Castoval into what you wanted it to be."

"What?" Now Estrada looked genuinely taken aback. "That's absurd."

"Is it really? I know you'll never care for me, Marina. I accepted that long ago. Still, I'd hope you could see the gift I've been preparing for you. A city run by and for its people. A Castoval led by Castovalians. A republic where once there was only oppression."

"Will you really stand there pretending you did this for me?"

"Think about what I've said," Mounteban told her. "Perhaps one day you'll understand. And if you change your mind, you'll know where to find me. In the meantime – leave my city now and I'll make sure you do so safely."

As though that were the matter settled, Mounteban began to back towards the gate. His bodyguard edged to block the space between him and Alvantes, and then they swung to follow, the cart clattering in their wake, leaving Estrada and Godares no choice but to move hurriedly aside.

"Damn you!" cried Alvantes, "don't you walk away from me."

"What about me?" wailed Lupa from his rooftop.

Mounteban ignored them both. He disappeared, as the half-opened gates hid him from view. A moment later and even the bulk of the cart had vanished.

Alvantes hurried after, his face a snarl of rage. Navare and the remaining guardsmen came close on his heels. Watching them rush by, fear caught in my throat and refused to budge. It might have been the fact that they were charging into a fight they were sure to lose. Yet my feet were moving – because along with that suffocating fear came almost irresistible curiosity. I had to know what came next. It was as though we'd arrived at a precipice, and there was nothing left to do but fall. I was practically sprinting by the time I cleared the gates.

There were Mounteban and his men, crowded into and around their cart.

There were Alvantes and his small troop, already almost caught up.

There, ahead of them all, was Mounteban's army.

It was just as he'd promised. The street was thronged with his men. The courtyard backed onto White Corn Road, which joined with the main street running from the north-west gate, and I'd no doubt that the approaching throng were the defenders who'd been gathered there. Now, realising the giant attack for the sham it had been, hearing that the guardsmen's assault on the west gate had ended almost before it had begun, they'd come hunting for a real threat.

Some were evidently lowlifes from the city gangs, some retainers from the families; a few were leftovers of Moaradrid's invasion. But those signs of old allegiances were fading now, and these men were no longer a rabble. In a mere few days, Mounteban had turned them into a real city guard. All wore armour be-

neath their matching crimson cloaks; all bore weapons
appropriate to their function.

Moreover, they outnumbered our tiny band fifty to
one – and Alvantes's men were already dead on their
feet. If it came to a fight... but then, it wouldn't. Because many of them had bows, and we hadn't a shield
between us. The best I could hope for was that Alvantes and Estrada hadn't completely blown our slim
hopes of surrender – or failing that, for a quick and
unexpected death.

All of which begged the question: why did this approaching army look so scared?

Only then did it occur to me that what I'd taken for
the tumult of marching feet must be something more.
Even so many men couldn't have made the noise I
was hearing, the roar of storm-tossed waves pounding
a granite shore. As it grew closer, the very stones beneath my feet began to quiver. In nearby buildings,
shutters rattled in their frames.

The mob didn't slow as they drew near. They hardly
seemed aware of us, or even of Mounteban. These
men weren't attacking us. They weren't rushing to
Mounteban's aid. They were fleeing for their lives.

They broke around us like white water round rocks,
flew past as if we were invisible. I did my best to shield
my face and plant my feet against the cobbles, terrified
I'd be swept away and trampled. All I could hear besides
the thrash of feet and clatter of armour was Mounteban
screaming, "Stop, you fools! Stop! How many times did
I tell you? They won't fight! They can't hurt you!"

On and on he bellowed, his voice somehow rising

above the cacophony. I didn't see one man even pause to listen. Only when the giants tumbled into view did he finally quieten – and for all he'd said, the fear was clear in his eyes.

Saltlick, of course, stood at their head. His mock armour, sheets of cheap painted board strung together with frayed rope, was ragged and studded with arrows. The first drab rays of morning sun struck glints from the crown around his neck, lighting his broad face from below.

"This wasn't the plan," I told him.

Saltlick smiled toothily, picked a splinter of what could only have been the north-western gate from his shoulder. "New plan."

"That isn't how these things work!" I said. "You can't just…"

Can't just…?

Just spot a chance to turn a double bluff into an outright victory? I'd hoped the defenders would recognise the giant assault for the ruse it was; I'd gambled they'd assume the guardsmen's assault on the west gate was the real threat, when in truth it was every bit as much a diversion. What I hadn't considered was how that would leave the north-west gate undefended – or that, while the giants might not fight, nothing in their moral code forbade them to smash a defenceless barrier to smithereens.

I hadn't. Saltlick had.

"You couldn't have timed it better," I said.

Saltlick's grin threatened to split his head in two. But all he said was, "Help friends."

"You have. You really have."

If proof were needed, Mounteban provided it amply. He stood alone now. Even his entourage of bodyguards were gone. Even the cart had been carried away in the rush of fleeing bodies. However much loyalty he'd bought, bullied or cajoled, it didn't extend to facing down a hundred giants.

Alvantes's battered guardsmen had already moved to surround him. Now, Alvantes himself stepped forward. "Here's one last deal for you, Mounteban," he said. "Help repair the damage you've done, help weed out the vermin you've set up in unearned positions of power – and maybe, just maybe, you'll live out your life."

Mounteban's sword slipped from his fingers, to ring upon the cobbles. He looked inexpressibly weary. "I did what I thought was right."

"Is that your answer?"

"I'll do what you ask. Whatever you want." His eyes drifted to Estrada, almost hesitantly. "But I won't do it for you."

And he meant it. I couldn't say how, but I knew; perhaps it was just that I'd never seen anyone look so beaten. Whatever he'd been trying to achieve, whatever twisted motives he'd had, it had all burned to the ground today – and in his gaze was nothing except the ashes of that mad dream.

Estrada and Alvantes recognised it too. I caught a fraction of the glance they shared, saw the sure knowledge that somehow, against impossible odds, they'd pulled this city back from the precipice Mounteban had almost led it over. Soon Altapasaeda would be free again. Soon the Castoval could return to normal, putting Moaradrid's brief, terrible intrusion behind it once and for all.

But there were other things in that brief current of intimacy that made me look away as quickly as I could. It was the look of two people realising that now, perhaps, with duties done, responsibilities played out, the time might be close when they could embrace their own needs for a change.

They weren't the only ones. Now, finally, I could disentangle myself from their wars, their politics, their frantic life-and-death struggles for the fate of the Castoval. I could take the time to figure out a way of life that didn't involve routinely falling off cliffs and buildings, where no one chased me or tried to kill me, or made me break into anywhere I didn't want to break into.

Meanwhile, in the short term – and just like Estrada and Alvantes, like Saltlick and his fellow giants – I could indulge the wants I'd been neglecting for far too long. I could eat a proper meal; wash it down with decent wine. I could find a real bed and sleep a sound night's sleep… sleep for a week if I wanted! If I was appalled by how small my aspirations had become, I was nearly delirious to think how close within my grasp they were.

Moreover, if word spread as quickly as I hoped, it wouldn't be long before every man, child and, more to the point, every woman in Altapasaeda knew that the name Damasco was synonymous with their deliverance. Perhaps I'd find that heroes didn't need to pay for food and wine; perhaps saving the entire land would buy enough goodwill that the bed could be put to more use than mere sleeping.

The thought had barely had time to leave my mind when I saw him.

He was riding from the north-west, the same direction that so recently had produced Mounteban's routed forces and the giants. Though I recognised him, he was someone I'd never expected to see again – outside of the occasional nightmare, at any rate. All eyes widened at the sight of his uniform, matched for sheer blackness by his travel cloak and even the horse he rode. I heard Alvantes's breath catch, even as mine did. For the last time we'd seen this man, he'd been herding us into a prison cell.

Commander Ludovoco of the Crown Guard made no attempt to pick his way round the clustered giants. He seemed to assume they'd move aside of their own accord, and he was right; though he did nothing, said nothing, they shifted hurriedly to clear a path. It was as though he travelled in a bubble that nothing could touch, a bubble of his own indomitable will.

He ignored the guardsmen, Estrada and me. When his gaze settled on Alvantes, the corner of his mouth twitched, just slightly.

"Alvantes," Ludovoco said. He managed somehow to pronounce a silence where the words "Guard-Captain" should have been. "I hadn't expected to find you here."

"Nor I you."

That was apparently all the small talk we could expect. What Ludovoco said next was even more unexpected than his incomprehensible appearance. "I'm seeking Castilio Mounteban."

Unhindered by the guardsmen around him, who – recognising Ludovoco's uniform, if not the man himself – looked more bewildered than anyone by this latest turn of events, Mounteban stepped forward. "I'm he."

Ludovoco reached inside his travelling cloak, drew forth a tight scroll of parchment and handed it down. "Then this is for you."

Mounteban removed the silver ring that bound the material and unfurled it with a flick of the wrist. His eyes danced over its surface. His expression remained inscrutable.

When it was clear he'd finished, Ludovoco asked, "Will you confirm receipt?"

"Yes." Mounteban's tone was no more readable than his face. "I confirm receipt."

"You have seven days. Be ready." Ludovoco wheeled his horse, clipped his heels against its sides and rode back the way he'd come.

He was almost out of sight before anyone reacted. Then it was only Alvantes, reaching to pluck the scroll from Mounteban's hands. Mounteban made no attempt to stop him. In fact, in the instant the manuscript vanished from his view, I thought he actually looked relieved.

Alvantes too read over the document, and then again, more slowly. Even when it was obvious he'd finished, he continued to stare at the yellowed parchment.

In the end, it was Estrada who asked the question –

the one, perhaps, that we all sensed might be better unasked. "What is it?"

Slowly, cautiously, as if the words were something dangerous he was letting loose, Alvantes replied, "The King is coming."

"He decided to send help after all?" She laughed, a little nervously. "Trust Panchessa to join the fight the minute it's all over."

"Help? No. Not help."

He looked up then – and as he turned the scroll to face us, I saw with utter disbelief that Alvantes was afraid.

"This... *this* is a declaration of war."

ABOUT THE AUTHOR

David Tallerman was born and raised in the northeast of England. A long and confused period of education ended with a Masters dissertation on the literary history of seventeenth century witchcraft that somehow incorporated references to both Kate Bush and HP Lovecraft.

David currently roams the UK as an itinerant IT Technician-for-hire, applying theories of animism and sympathetic magic to computer repair and taking devoted care of his bonsai tree familiar.

Over the last few years, David has been steadily building a reputation for his genre short fiction and increasingly his writing has tended to push and merge genres, and to incorporate influences from his other great loves – comic books and cinema.

davidtallerman.net

ACKNOWLEDGMENTS

Extra special thanks to my mum, to Tom and to Anne, for reading *Crown Thief* more times and more carefully than anyone should ever have to read anything. I'm not sure this book could have happened without you, so it's only fair that you should take some of the blame.

Normal, run-of-the-mill (but still very grateful!) thanks to Jobeda, Rafe, Lavie, Rob, Grant, Rachel, Alison Littlewood, John B and John P, Adrian Tchaikovsky, Juliet McKenna, the guys at Angry Robot and my team at work, for your support, help and advice.

Lastly, thanks to everyone who bought and enjoyed *Giant Thief,* and especially to those bloggers and reviewers who helped spread the word. Here's hoping you like this one just as much, if not a little more.

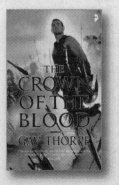

TOO LATE TO STOP NOW

Grab the complete Angry Robot catalog